THE ROSE MARK

```
0 2
2 ?
- 5
```

C000078330

Suffolk Libraries

Please return/renew this item
by the last date shown.

Suffolk Libraries
01473 263838

www.suffolklibraries.co.uk

Published by: SubtleDemon Publishing, LLC
PO Box 95696
Oklahoma City, OK 73143

Cover art by Renee Barratt @ The Cover Counts

To Walter, Joe, Larry, Lee, Dianne, Sarah and Mark.
Thank you.

Acknowledgements

As always, this book is the result of collaboration. If it weren't for the support of my editor, my cover artist and my beta readers, it would be less than it is. All mistakes, as usual, are mine and no other's.

About the Author:

Connie Suttle lives in Oklahoma with her husband and a conglomerate of cats. They have finally banded together to make their demands, which has proven disconcerting to all humans involved.

You may find Connie in the following ways:
Facebook: Connie Suttle Author
Twitter: @subtledemon
Website and Blog: subtledemon.com

Other books by Connie Suttle:

Blood Destiny Series:
Blood Wager
Blood Passage
Blood Sense
Blood Domination
Blood Royal
Blood Queen
Blood Rebellion
Blood War
Blood Redemption

Blood Reunion
* * *

Legend of the Ir'Indicti Series:
Bumble
Shadowed
Target
Vendetta
Destroyer
* * *

High Demon Series:
Demon Lost
Demon Revealed
Demon's King
Demon's Quest
Demon's Revenge
Demon's Dream
* * *

God Wars Series:
Blood Double
Blood Trouble
Blood Revolution
Blood Love
Blood Finale
* * *

Saa Thalarr Series:
Hope and Vengeance
Wyvern and Company
Observe and Protect*
* * *

First Ordinance Series:

Finder
Keeper
BlackWing
SpellBreaker
WhiteWing
* * *

R-D Series:
Cloud Dust
Cloud Invasion
Cloud Rebel
* * *

Latter Day Demons Series:
Hot Demon in the City
A Demon's Work is Never Done
A Demon's Due
* * *

Seattle Elementals Series:
Your Money's Worth
Worth Your While*
* * *

BlackWing Pirates Series
MindSighted
MindMage
MindRogue*
* * *

Black Rose Sorceress Series
The Rose Mark
Rose and Thorn*

Other Titles from SubtleDemon Publishing:

Malefactor
Transgressor*
by Joe Scholes

*Forthcoming

Chapter 1

*P*ast
Kerok

I recall very little about that day, other than the massive explosions that killed many around me, including my beloved escort.

They tell me I *stepped* away from the battlefield with her lifeless body in my arms and deep wounds cleaving my face, chest and legs. A friend tells me he has no idea how I was still standing, and that I walked deliberately until I was clear of other bodies before *stepping* to my father's garden.

There, I lay my burden down for the last time, while others shouted somewhere in the background. The healer came, but I don't remember his presence—I was lost in grief and pain—enough that he swore I should have died from it.

The Rose Mark

Even now, I cannot say whether it is a blessing that I lived, or the curse I believe it to be. My love died with my black rose that terrible morning, and it may take my entire life, as long or short as that may be, to deal with her loss.

* * *

Present

Sherra

We belong to the King—those of us with the black roses tattooed on our left wrist, directly over our pulse. As if every beat of our hearts reminds us that we are not our own. Those around us know it, too, and are reluctant to come close.

Ten gold coins were paid to my father when I was tested young and then tattooed. Another ten will be paid when the vehicle arrives to take me away. That is the full worth of our lives, as short as they will become.

In the King's library, *The Book of the Rose* says to honor the tattooed women.

More than anything, I want to spit upon its pages.

Any girl who wears the tattoo is never befriended, as our deaths are already assured.

Yes, there are tales of some who survive, but I'd never seen any of them. That led me to believe that tales were all they were—with no real survivors.

All those women who were found with talent—the fire burning within them—were culled and taken to the warriors, to provide more energy. Energy that the warriors would then use to defeat the barbarians across the ocean of sand.

Women with black roses on their wrists are emptied of their power by those warriors, who care not that they die a shrunken husk.

Chapter 1

The King also has no care for these—his subjects who give their lives to repel the vicious hordes in their destructive machines of war.

"We fight with what we have," he always says.

What we have are the warriors with the fire within them, who draw more fire from the women who serve them.

Until they die.

The thought of running away is foolish.

The thought of taking a lover before they come for us—also foolish.

We must be untouched when they arrive to collect us; else it is a quicker death when they test us again.

As for running—there is one thing worse than having a black rose on your wrist. That is for the enemy to find you and see the black rose on your wrist. Your death will be slow and excruciating at their hands.

* * *

Past

Sherra

My tenth birthday had come and gone unremarked by my father, who was visiting his friends when I returned home from my lessons. Pottles wouldn't know it was my birthday either; I'd never told her.

Nevertheless, she'd welcome me into her small home and talk while I cooked whatever she'd haggled for in the market.

Her back door was little more than rough boards held together with string and bits of rusted wire, while the front looked marginally better—that's where she bought and sold pots and utensils from those in the village and outlying farms.

Metal was hard to come by; therefore, used pots were prized, even if they'd been repaired and the handles replaced many times.

The Rose Mark

"What's this?" I'd walked in the back door, through the small, two-room home and out the front door, which was open to allow the afternoon breeze to cool the house. I was asking about the wooden crate blocking the front door—the one filled with junk that Pottles had purchased while I was still in class.

I'd asked her many times to wait until I could see what was brought to her—Pottles was blind and could only feel what she bought with fingers and hands rough from harsh living over sixty-nine years.

"I think you should look through it and tell me what it is," she said. "The farmer was very poor and needed a cooking pot."

"Well," I squatted next to the crate to look. "Two pottery cups, one chipped," I set those two out of the way first. "Four wooden spoons that need sanding," I set those beside the cups—too much handling would result in splinters in fingers, I decided. "Three loose-weave sacks that smell like potatoes," I laid those out. "A bunch of carrots," I set those in a special place. Carrots were good raw or cooked. "A cabbage," I added, setting the small head next to the carrots. "And a book."

"A book?" Pottles frowned. "Why would he trade a book to a blind woman?"

"No idea."

"Is it something you want?"

I hadn't really looked at the title—the book was small, with thin, fragile pages. The title had disappeared from the cover long ago, and the lettering was almost worn off the spine, too.

"What does it say?" Pottles asked.

"It's almost worn off," I touched the spine with my fingers, as if that would make the letters clearer.

4

Chapter 1

I jumped and almost dropped the book when a shock went through me, and I fell backward off my knees and onto the dusty doorstep. It took a moment to get the fire-vision out of my brain.

The Rose Mark had been printed in white letters on the spine and the cover, far in the past. If I hadn't touched it, I'd never have known what it was.

"It looks like a book of tales," I improvised. "Like Varnon tells on feast day."

"Hmmph," Pottles expressed her opinion of the book. "If you want it, keep it."

"Thank you," I breathed and hastily stuffed the small book in a trouser pocket. I'd work out why the book had shocked me later, when I had time to consider it fully. "Do you want me to put the carrots and cabbage on to cook?"

"Yes. I have a bit of meat from the butcher—add that and we'll have soup for supper."

"I will."

"Set the other things back in the crate. I'll decide what to do with them later."

"Yes, mum."

Ten years later, after I'd read that book so many times I'd memorized most of it, I placed it carefully in a clay pot, sealed the lid on it with my fire and then went looking for a safe place to bury it. I'd learned when I was fifteen that the book was forbidden, and others like it had been confiscated and burned long before my birthing.

* * *

Present
Sherra

The Rose Mark

"You only need one set of clothes," my father snapped at me as I laid things on my narrow bed. "As an honored one with the mark, they'll provide for you."

He intended to sell my things the moment I was gone.

I wouldn't be back for them; we both knew that.

Honored.

What a false pile of horse dung.

Outcast and ignored—if you were lucky.

So far, I'd been extremely lucky that way.

"It's coming," I heard a boy's voice in the street. He meant the truck coming to collect me. Snatching up the patched and threadbare leggings and tunic off the bed, I stuffed both into a cloth bag and turned away from my father.

There would be no tears from him; only a hand held out for ten gold pieces when I boarded the vehicle.

There would be no good-bye either—from him or anyone else in the village. They'd said good-bye to me eighteen years ago, when I was two and cringing from the pain of the needle as a Diviner's artist tattooed a black rose over my pulse.

* * *

The journey to North Camp was hot and dry—as dry as the ocean of sand four hundred miles away, where the enemy's border lay. Or so I'd heard.

Sixteen women rode in the vehicle with me to the training camp—ours was one of four that dotted the King's lands, one for each direction. All those camps were built for a single purpose—to train the warriors and the women who'd serve them.

When we passed the high, wood and metal gates into North Camp, a sigh escaped my lips.

My life was over; my body merely hadn't realized it, yet.

* * *

Chapter 1

Kerok

I stood with Merrin as the trucks rumbled along the dirt road between stunted evergreen trees. This year, the crop of young women was sparse. The King was discussing a raise in the payments to common folk if they produced a daughter who'd wear the black rose.

Already, common boys outnumbered girls, and there was no immediate relief for that malady. Boys with the warrior's gift were becoming almost as sparse as the black rose girls.

The idea that we should breed the two had already been suggested.

The King always said *not yet*.

Soon, I think his mind would be forced to change, or we'd fall to the barbarians. Yes, it would be barbaric to breed those able to fight the enemy.

Falling to the enemy would be worse.

Sacrifice a few to preserve the many, as those who'd proposed the idea had said. I couldn't say whether it was a good idea, or merely an expedient one.

Blank, empty stares from the young women on the next truck rumbling through and raising dust forced a sigh from my lips.

Marked early—for service and death.

For most of them, anyway.

* * *

Sherra

"Undress, leave your clothing in this pile and go straight to the showers. I want the stench of the villages washed off you in half an hour."

I and my fellow trainees stood inside a tile-floored, low-ceilinged building that housed communal showers on one end and a laundry on the other. The scent of washing soap and

7

starch blew through the open area, announcing that laundry was done here every day instead of once a week.

The woman who spoke wore no rose tattoo. Instead, a solid block of black ink covered her left wrist. She was short, wide and angry as she shouted at us, her close-cropped, brown hair bristling as her eyes narrowed at us in disgust.

I understood then that the clothing we wore would not be washed and returned to us; it would be burned. I'd caught the stench of other piles burning as we were ushered from the truck into the long building.

The training compound was huge; large enough to house and train fifteen cohorts. Dry grass and dirt made up most of it, with fences made of posts and strung wire forming large rectangles to separate the buildings housing the cohorts.

My group was one of six cohorts, and none of the six was full, if my guess were correct. A cohort could hold as many as fifty; I doubted many of the six had half that number.

So far, I'd barely made eye contact with anyone else, including the woman who barked at us as if we were thieves assailing her house. Bowing my head, I watched my numb fingers automatically untie the strings at the throat of my tunic.

"You'll find soap, a cloth and a comb in the showers. Use all of them. Clean your hair well. If we find insects, the hair will be shaved from your head. After the shower, comb your hair and leave no tangles, as it will be cut at your shoulders and kept at that length. Do you understand?"

Nobody spoke.

"I said, do you understand?"

"Yes, Lady," several of us murmured.

"Good. I expect a response when I give orders. Do you understand?"

Chapter 1

"Yes, Lady."

"Good. Go clean up. You stink. All of you."

"Yes, Lady."

Small, pale-brown tiles covered the three-sided cubicles of the showers, which were lined up one after the other. No doors were provided, but why should they be? We were nothing compared to the warriors, and no private space would be afforded us. A mere fuel source was all we were; why should we have privacy?

The water in the shower was tepid at best—the boilers were overworked to bathe so many at once, in addition to providing water for the laundry. I'd combed my hair before leaving my father's house, but I stood in front of the dull, metal mirror on one wall and dutifully combed it again after washing it three times.

A shower was a luxury only afforded twice a week in the small village where I'd lived with my father, as water was scarce and precious, there. This shower was far from a luxury in my mind, as it marked me further as an outcast.

Some of us wept as the water enveloped our bodies, hoping the sound of the spray would hide our sobs. At least the tears went down the drain with the soapy water, whether sobs were muffled or not.

* * *

Kerok

"Don't." I held up a hand to keep Merrin from speaking his thoughts. He'd been prepared to speculate on which girls we'd end up with. We and many others had gathered at the top level of the high seats surrounding the main training field, to watch as the young women were marched out after showering and dressing in their uniforms.

The Rose Mark

All were clad in training fatigues provided by the Crown—sand-colored and loose, for ease of movement. Extra tunics and trousers would be issued, just as the male trainees wore.

This camp trained women only; the warriors were trained elsewhere. It made it easier to keep virginity intact until the women were assigned to a warrior. Afterward, if they were so inclined, sex could be offered between those two, but only between those two.

With their hair cut to the tops of shoulders, most of the trainees looked the same. Wet-haired, thin and mostly ignorant, the latest cohort lined up as the Bulldog shouted at them. Hers was the last of the cohorts to make it to the field, too. The Bulldog liked to cause a stir every time, either choosing to go first or last.

The women were required to learn how to read and write before their arrival at a designated camp. Most villages barely spared them that much. I heard that several villages were reported during the last training period, because they hadn't bothered to teach the black-rose girls.

Some warriors, like Merrin, had steeled their hearts against these, knowing they'd be instrumental in their deaths. They were merely curious, because of the *connecting*. They looked forward to convincing their black rose to have sex with them—with great pleasure.

The Bulldog's shouting drew my attention back to her cohort; every woman's eyes were trained on her as a result—they likely didn't realize there were warriors lining the top benches, watching all of them.

"Small batch for us this time," Merrin observed. "I heard East Camp got twice as many."

"Hmmph," I grunted.

Chapter 1

"Maybe a few good ones. Depending on washouts, not every warrior may get a black rose."

He always said that. "Think they'll last more than a few seasons?" he added.

"Shut the fuck up," I growled.

"Yes, Commander."

* * *

Sherra

Already, my drying hair had begun to curl and now looked much shorter than shoulder-length. It didn't matter; several others had curly hair, too. We'd been lined up naked after drying off and marched through a line of drudges who handed out shirts, trousers, unders, boots and socks.

The barking woman instructed us to dress quickly and form six lines to march onto the training ground outside.

Only a few women had shaved heads after a thorough inspection; they'd also been given treatment for scalp infestation, so they wouldn't infect the rest of us.

Still, we hadn't spoken to one another.

Like the villagers I'd left behind, we knew we were dead already; it was merely training and battle that waited until death claimed us.

I glanced up at the top row of benches lining the stands outside the training grounds.

They waited there—the warriors, dressed in dark brown instead of the trainees' sand-colored fatigues. I jerked my head down again after that brief look; no sense drawing their attention by staring at them.

I didn't want to know them. One of them would end up killing me, after all. The dog-woman lined us up last of all, while five other cohorts waited on her to make us presentable on the training field.

The Rose Mark

"While you are here," the dog-woman barked, "You will follow the commands of your superiors. If you do not, you will be punished. While you are here, you will eat what is served to you. If you do not, you will be punished. While you are here, you will not copulate with anyone except the warrior you are paired with, and then only when he asks and you consent. If you do not follow this command, you will be executed. Do you understand?"

"Yes, Lady," we said in unison.

My stomach churned at her last order; I worked to keep from dry heaving. My meager breakfast had long since vanished, leaving an empty, rumbling belly behind. Dog-woman's comments about food made me want to laugh; any food would be welcome, if not enjoyed—until her last command.

The connecting. It was something I'd refused to think on until now; copulation with the one who'd kill you eventually. It was the worst of the insults offered by the King and his infernal book.

Chapter 2

*K**erok*
"I'd like to be there when those girls find out they won't be fed until they can produce fire," Merrin chuckled as I stomped down the back steps of the high stands. Clenching my fists, I ground my teeth until the retort cleared from my mind.

"Oh, right. Shut the fuck up. Yes, Commander."

He'd obviously seen my jaw working, if not the fists I'd made to keep from turning and twisting his collar in my grip.

He and I—we'd been friends since childhood. Only in the past year had I begun to see him differently.

He'd walked off the last battlefield, angry that his black-rose escort had died on him in the middle of a fiery blast.

The Rose Mark

I'd walked off the battlefield half an hour later, knowing my escort was also dead.

The differences were these; I walked back with Grae in my arms, tears in my eyes and deep wounds on body and soul.

Grae and I had worked together for six years. I buried her ashes in my father's flower garden when I returned home, searching for healing and eventually, another black-rose escort to continue the fight.

Merrin's escort's ashes were buried with many others in a mass grave on the battlefield. She and Grae had been friends.

Merrin and I had been friends. He thought things hadn't changed.

I learned from a tutor once that opening your eyes, no matter how long they have been closed, will bring you to enlightenment.

He didn't say that enlightenment also came with a heavy load of guilt and pain.

"Are we going to watch the march to trainees' mess?" Merrin turned to ask as we reached the bottom steps.

I didn't reply, choosing to toss a hand in that direction instead. We'd see what these women were made of.

In all, there were only one hundred thirty-five, from forty-six villages marching in to line up outside the mess hall. Many were so thin, I thought they might topple over before they reached the serving line.

Word would be carried to the King about their conditions. At least they were out of the unforgiving sun, lining up as they were along the side of the mess hall. Drudges had recently replaced the roof and painted the stucco-and-brick building the usual color of sand, just like everything else.

Chapter 2

The Bulldog appeared at the head of her cohort while Merrin and I watched. They halted obediently at her command.

"You will make fire in your palm," the Bulldog shouted. "If you do not, you will not eat. If you fail to make fire tomorrow morning, you will not eat. If you faint during your training tomorrow, you will be wakened and put back in your training group. Do you understand?" The Bulldog's hands were on her hips as she shouted.

"Yes, Lady," the women chorused.

"Do I have a volunteer?"

Three hands raised. "Good. Step forward and show me fire."

* * *

Sherra

Several of my group went to bed hungry that first night. I was one of them. Not because I couldn't make fire—but because I refused to do it.

Pottles, the blind pot seller in my village, befriended me when I was six. She was an old woman even then, whose callused hands felt the pots brought to her so she could determine a price to pay. Once I began to describe the color and condition of those pots to her, she'd feed me after my early lessons.

I learned to cook from her, too; she sat near the stove and described to me what to put in the pot and how it should sound while cooking. Cooking for her meant at least one good meal a day.

I learned from her what the black rose really meant—my father didn't bother to tell me. She'd lost a sister that way, long ago. The book she'd given me told me how to use what I'd been born with—the power warranting the black rose on my wrist.

The Rose Mark

Her name was Doret, although everyone called her Pottles. Eight months ago, Pottles died. In normal circumstances, I might have been given her things. Instead, because I wore the black rose and Doret had no living family, the village divided her belongings and I was left to grieve for the only friend I'd had.

For Doret and her sister, I refused to make fire that first night.

* * *

Kerok

I stood against the wall, watching as the girls who'd produced fire the night before were allowed into the trainees' mess for breakfast. Some were even beginning to chatter quietly among themselves.

Those who hadn't made fire were lined up along the opposite wall, waiting to make their second attempt as the others walked past them.

Nine from the Bulldog's cohort stood in that line.

Last in line was a tall, curly-haired youngling who stood at attention, like the others. The only difference I saw in her was the fire in her eyes.

The Bulldog hadn't seen it.

Couldn't see it.

I imagined for a brief moment that her gaze could burn the Bulldog to a cinder. That's when she dropped her eyes to the floor and the fleeting image left me. Merrin joined me, then.

"Captain," I acknowledged his presence.

"Anything interesting?" Merrin asked.

"Find out—discreetly, of course—the name of the curly-haired one at the back of the Bulldog's second-try line."

"May I ask why?"

Chapter 2

"No reason. She just reminds me of someone."

"It will be done, Commander," Merrin jerked his head in a mock salute. He didn't say it, although he thought it. Grae's hair had been dark and curly.

There, the similarity ended. Grae had been a tall, graceful water bird among hawks and pigeons. She'd had few friends, but only because she was wary of most people. I'd worked very hard to gain her trust, and there was love in her eyes when she gave me everything she had at the last.

I blamed myself for that, and many other things. "Have the information for me before midday," I instructed as I continued to watch the girl.

"It will be done."

This one was neither hawk nor pigeon. This one was wildfire in a fierce wind. She didn't speak with anyone while I watched her, and I kept my eyes on her while the Bulldog went down the line, demanding that each girl produce fire or go back to the barracks to await training.

Merrin and I watched as three of the second-tries became third-tries.

The curly-haired woman wasn't one of them.

* * *

Sherra

I learned her name was Yasa, but she preferred to be called Bulldog instead of dog-woman. Close enough, to my thinking. Everyone else referred to her as *the* Bulldog.

The second morning before breakfast, she glared at me as I made a small fire in my palm when commanded. Three of those in line with me went without another meal.

I wanted to bring them food. I couldn't, or I'd be punished. What I could do, perhaps, they hadn't made a rule against. The moment I could, I intended to work with them so they could make fire.

That morning, after breakfast, we learned to march in formation and turn on command. Dry grass crunched beneath my boots during endless steps and turns. Sweat ran down my face and between my shoulder blades as I kept the next woman's shoulders in my line of sight. That enabled me to stay in step as the Bulldog called the drill.

By midday, the dust was so thick from the trampled ground I thought we would choke on it. The rest of us were sent to a midday meal; those who hadn't made fire were given water and nothing else.

Whispers filtered through the trainees during the short meal break. Those who stood outside were called second and third-tries. A few trainees called them worse. I noticed that two of the three who'd volunteered for the Bulldog the night before were the source of those derogatory terms.

The Bulldog was already culling her favorites.

I learned what being in the second and third-try line meant when we were released to our barracks after a day of physical training.

Six beds had been shoved against a far wall. Adjacent to those were three others—for the third-tries.

Already, they were evaluating us. I was relegated to the second-try section. Would they let the last three starve if they couldn't produce a flame? I was determined not to let that happen.

* * *

"Come," I whispered to a third-try after touching her shoulder gently. Lights had gone out and I'd waited for what felt like forever, before making my way to the nearest of the third-tries.

Chapter 2

"What?" she spoke aloud.

I clapped a hand over her mouth. "Quietly," I whispered against her ear. "You want to eat, don't you?"

I felt her nod. "Good. Come with me." Pushing back her thin blanket and dropping legs nearly as thin over the side of her cot, she rose and followed as I moved in the darkness to the next bed, then the next.

"They'll see," one woman, cross-legged on the floor beside my bed, hissed when I placed a shield about us and made a light in my palm.

"They'll hear us," another hissed.

"We're shielded, you can talk now," I said. "You've never tried to use your power, have you?"

All shook their heads. "That's what I thought. Close your eyes. Take a deep breath and hold it for six counts. Release," I said when it was time. "Keep your eyes closed. Rest your hands on your knees, wrists up."

They did as I asked. "Now," I said, "Take another deep breath. Hold it for six counts. When you release, imagine that your breath is fire."

I smiled when six hands bloomed with flames. "Open your eyes and see," I said.

Two of them cried. One laughed with joy.

That night, amid the barest of whisperings to three hungry young women, I taught them how to look within themselves and find their fire.

* * *

Kerok

"Sherra, from Merthis," Merrin dropped a scrap of paper on my desk. He'd listed her parentage, too; a living father and deceased mother. "You don't need a second-try," Merrin offered when I didn't respond.

"Her education appears to be adequate," I said.

"How did you find that out?"

"I looked at the forms she filled out yesterday. I looked at all of them, actually. Hers was the best-written of the lot."

"Why did you send me after the information, then?"

"Because I wanted it at midday, not just before lights out."

"I had to bribe someone to get that," he gruffed, pointing at the scrap of paper. "All you have to do is walk in and demand the forms."

"A wager, then?" I blinked at Merrin.

"Depends," he said.

"I wager ten golds that the third-tries will get breakfast tomorrow."

"Done," Merrin agreed immediately.

* * *

Sherra

All three of my secret trainees made fire and went to breakfast the following morning. It made me want to shout at the Bulldog for not providing proper training for them, but that would invite punishment.

My mouth stayed shut as a result. Our beds never moved, however. In this crop of trainees, we'd always be the second and third-tries.

* * *

After the first ten days of physical training, in which we were commanded to run, jump, climb under and over barricades, carry heavy packs and march in formation, our training began to include that associated with an escort's actual work—that of wielding the power we were born with.

I thought of it as the curse we were born with, but never said it.

Chapter 2

Some of my group had begun to make tentative friendships with one another; that meant the barracks became noisy at night before lights out.

The ones who wanted to speak with me came hesitantly at first; all of the third-tries wanted to be friends.

Tera, Misten and Wend began to stand near me for our exercises, too—and sit near me for our classes. If they failed to understand any power moves described during classes, I made sure to explain them better after lights out.

I hoped we wouldn't be discovered—I worried that someone would attempt to stop me from helping them.

Yes, I understood about shields and put up the best I knew how, but someone could detect it if they were determined enough.

So far, lessons on shielding had not been given, and I wondered at that. After all, I'd read about it in the presence of a blind woman, who never knew what I was actually doing.

Or, if she did, she never said it to anyone. If the villagers had learned of it, they'd have been afraid of me. Instead, they barely offered a glance whenever I arrived at Doret's modest home to help her buy and sell pots.

Fear does strange things to people. The barbarians were afraid of us; therefore, they wanted to eradicate all traces of us from the planet we walked. By attacking us, they created the very thing they feared—those who could wield power and destroy their machines of war.

However you looked at it, I was caught in that vicious, painful vortex, with no road of escape open to me—or to anyone tattooed with a black rose.

* * *

Kerok

"How did you know?" Merrin slumped onto the chair next to my desk.

"Know what?" I stopped calculating expenses and looked at him for a moment.

"Know that the third-tries wouldn't wash out and be forced to serves as drudges?" he asked.

"I didn't."

"Then why the fuck did you bet on them?" Merrin blew out a frustrated breath.

"I didn't bet on *them*."

Merrin frowned deeply for a moment.

"Oh."

He knew the who, now. He merely didn't know the why. He hadn't seen the fire in those dark eyes, as I had. "You lost more money, didn't you?" I guessed.

"Yes. Fuck yes. I bet they'd wash out by the third week. Instead, they're getting along in all the classes."

"Hmmph," I snorted and went back to my figures. "You make that sound like a bad thing. Drudges we have plenty of. Those able to act as escorts—you know how we're being drained in that area. I recall reading something about actual black roses teaching power classes instead of drudges—that happened in my great-great-great-grandfather's time," I pointed out. "When the enemy took more land and forced more races to bow to them, their armies became larger and more deadly. We barely beat them back last season."

"What can a black rose teach that a drudge can't? They're still the same, even after the tattoo is covered over."

"Yes, but remember those drudges never really did the work of an escort. There is no substitute for experience."

Merrin made a rude noise in response. "I have my eye on one or two already," he admitted.

Chapter 2

"Good." My sarcasm was meant to convey to Merrin that I wanted the subject dropped.

"The connecting," he began, ignoring my tone and intent. Immediately, I held up a hand to stop his words.

"Merrin," I said.

"Yes, Commander?"

"Get out."

* * *

Sherra

Over the course of several weeks, I learned that the continual use of power made us hungry. Our rations increased as a result. It became apparent that no black rose trainee would ever be overweight—after a full day, we were drenched in sweat and drained. Occasionally, one of our number would faint.

None of my third-tries were victims of such—else it would have alienated them further from the others. It warranted a shower every day, too, before we went for our evening meal.

I waited for the day when a handful of girls would begin tossing insults at the others—those girls had pleased the Bulldog with their talents and would probably get away with such against the rest of us.

Those were always the ones chosen to go first, whenever a new talent was required. I slogged along, doing what was necessary to pass the trials and nothing else. The Bulldog hadn't earned my respect in any way, and it was clear she was prone to picking favorites instead of treating all the same.

I hadn't failed to notice the black block of ink on her wrist—all our instructors wore those. Perhaps it was a way to differentiate them from us; I didn't know for sure. The Bulldog wore long sleeves most of the time, though, to keep her ink covered.

The Rose Mark

"Today," the Bulldog announced as my fellow trainees took chairs at the four long tables inside the classroom, "We will talk about shielding."

Wend shot me a glance before turning back to the Bulldog. It wouldn't do to let her see the thirds turning to me first.

With my left forefinger, I tapped my right thumb. It was the signal to stay quiet in this. As I'd covered us with shields while teaching Wend, Tera and Misten before, they had a firm idea of how I'd formed my shield.

I'd wager they could fashion their own, if they wanted.

"Now," the Bulldog went on, "Proper shielding requires plenty of space. That means we'll have this lesson on the training grounds. Everyone follow Ura and Veri—in an orderly line, please. We may have an audience for today's work, so be prepared to do your best."

She'd named her two favorites to lead us; they'd go first, too, to make a good impression. I had the idea that the warriors would be our audience, and I had no desire to be laughed at by the likes of those.

Tera was about to burst with the question of how we'd be tested, but knew better than to talk. The others filed out after the leaders; seconds and thirds would be last. I made sure to be at the end of the seconds, and the thirds followed me.

* * *

Kerok

I could see it in their eyes the moment they walked onto the training ground; these young women thought we'd be watching from the stands.

Instead, we waited for them to form four lines of six each at the Bulldog's command.

24

Chapter 2

Perhaps thirty yards separated us. I stood near the back, although my men had spread out so I could easily see everything.

The Bulldog wasn't capable of testing shields—it required someone with talent to do that. Someone with enough talent to temper their blasts against an untried trainee's shields.

Like Merrin, I'd once enjoyed this.

Already, I could see the Bulldog's favorites—they stood first in line, waiting to be tested. Six years earlier, I'd seen other favorites from the Bulldog's cohort. She hadn't changed for the better in that time; anyone with any sense could see that.

The men I'd brought with me would test the trainees—with stronger blasts each time, until the shield was breached. They knew to gauge the distance carefully, so as not to cause harm to the trainee. I nodded to the Bulldog, letting her know we were ready to begin.

"Veri," the Bulldog barked, "Up first. Make a shield."

Veri walked half the distance between her and the warrior who'd stepped forward, before putting up her hands in the proper stance. It didn't surprise me that the Bulldog had coached her favorites ahead of time. In this it didn't matter—at least the others coming after them would know what was expected.

The warrior hurled his first blast, which bounced against Veri's soft, weak shield before dropping to the ground and fizzling out.

"Do better," the Bulldog shouted. Veri strengthened her stance before the warrior launched a second blow. This one bounced better, but the shield still bent. On his third try, the warrior broke the trainee's shield.

"Not bad for a first-timer," Merrin said softly at my shoulder. I guessed then that Veri was one of the two he had his eye on.

"Ura," the Bulldog snapped as Veri walked to the back of the line and the others moved forward one spot.

Another warrior launched a blast at Ura's shield. Her first held up better than Veri's had. "Nice," Merrin breathed. It took four tries before Ura's shield broke.

I watched carefully as each of my men stepped forward to test a trainee's shield. There was only one I was truly interested in, however. I waited for her to reach the first position.

* * *

Sherra

"Sherra," the Bulldog called out, after a dismal showing from the other second-tries. One of those had broken down at the first blast launched at her. With tears streaming down her face, she strode, head down, to the back of the line.

It made me angry that some of the warriors and at least two of the trainees snickered at her tears.

I walked forward, fury burning my heart.

"I'll take this one," I heard a warrior's voice from somewhere in the back of the pack. I didn't care who it was. I intended to put out a full effort on this one. None of the trainees had lasted longer than Ura's four tries.

I was determined to do better. To make the Bulldog and every fucking warrior there sit up and notice the seconds and thirds.

Fuck them.

Fuck all of them.

I put up my hands, as the others had done, although I didn't need that bit of show to create a shield.

26

Chapter 2

He stepped forward confidently while I glared at him. He wore a deep scar on his face; I didn't care that he'd been wounded in battle. Perhaps he thought me weak, just as the Bulldog and the others did.

"Whenever you're ready, Commander Kerok," the Bulldog dipped her head as he took his stance.

Commander?

Even better.

Come on, jackass, I mentally goaded him.

In a blink he launched a blast my way. It hit my shield so hard it exploded with a boom and a flash of fiery stars.

Almost before I could blink, he'd launched another, and another, each harder than the last.

Six blasts.

Seven.

Nine.

Fifteen.

Come on, jackass, I can go all day, I mentally taunted.

"Enough," he held up a hand and walked toward me. I released my shield. Yards away, the Bulldog stood with her mouth hanging open.

When he stopped in front of me, Commander Kerok nodded and said, "Well done, trainee." *It's never wise to call the Commander a jackass*, breathed into my mind before he turned away.

* * *

Kerok

"I'll set it up and you can lob blasts at her," I said when Merrin took the chair, looking as if he were ready to pop like a shaken bottle of wine.

"No, no," he held up a hand. "I felt the backwash of power on that last one. No thank you," he said.

"Did you lose money again?" I asked.

"Yes."

"You really ought to stop betting. It's costing too much." I shuffled things on my desk; my way of telling him he needed to leave. He ignored it. I lifted a letter from my father and began to read, attempting to shut him out.

"I took your example and bet on the thirds, though. I won on them."

"Nobody thought they'd get a shield up to begin with?" I lifted my eyes and locked gazes with him, then.

"Yes. It's really odd, too. Under normal circumstances, I would have bet against them. What are you going to do about the girl?"

"What do you mean?" I stopped reading my father's letter for a moment.

"Well, it's obvious she's been holding back," Merrin began.

"Hold on," I said and pulled a sheet of blank paper from a stack. I scribbled a hasty message on it and folded it before handing it to Merrin. "Take that to the Bulldog."

"What does it say?"

"It says if she punishes the girl, I'll punish her."

One of Merrin's eyebrows rose to a new height. "It will be done," he said and left my office in a blur.

* * *

Sherra

As expected, the Bulldog didn't appreciate a trainee holding back. Her crop was in her hand as she paced back and forth in front of the bench where I sat. I considered blasting her to a crisp again, but that was merely a favorite fantasy.

Chapter 2

The other trainees knew what was coming, too. The Bulldog's chosen were giggling about it, and she hadn't called them out.

If the Bulldog thought I hadn't received bitter humiliation before, she was mistaken. My father had taken his frustrations out on me many times. In this, I merely waited to see what form it would take.

That's when a warrior walked into the barracks, a paper note in his hand. With an angry scowl, the Bulldog lifted it from his fingers.

He waited while she read it, and the color drained from her face. With a furious grunt, she shoved the note back in the warrior's hands and stalked from the barracks. The door slammed shut behind her.

"Sorry," the warrior didn't bother to hide his grin. "There'll be no entertainment tonight, Commander's orders." With that, he left, too.

I went still. The Commander knew she'd punish me in some way and had stopped it.

Why?

How had he heard my thoughts?

I'd called him a jackass. That thought made my cheeks burn.

Thank you, I said, hoping he'd hear my words. At least I wouldn't have a sore back or legs in the morning, from running, carrying and climbing, or whatever the Bulldog planned for me to do the entire night as punishment for holding back.

Instead, I slept and felt refreshed when we were called to exercise in the morning.

* * *

Kerok

The Rose Mark

I allowed her words and her gratitude to soak into my mind like parched ground absorbing rainwater. Even Grae had never had that connection with me. It took more talent than most black-rose trainees possessed.

I didn't say anything in return, however. The Bulldog had her pets. I refused to single anyone out this early in their training. It could cause them more grief than it was worth.

Chapter 3

*S*herra

   That night, after lights out, I had four at my bedside instead of three. The trainee who'd wept at her failure came, too.

   I put up my shield and went to work, touching fingers to each one in turn, showing them while we were touching how I built and strengthened my shield.

   "In my mind, I see it as a wall of fire, keeping everything out," I whispered as the image appeared in each of their minds. "Take the fire you created on your first day or two, and feed it until it is an inferno that will burn anything thrown at it."

   "I see it." Jae, the one who'd wept, had a fire in her eyes that night; I could see it myself.

The Rose Mark

When we were done, I had only a few hours of sleep, but I felt better about the four I'd stayed awake to teach.

Jae outclassed many of the firsts on our second day of shield training.

This time, Commander Kerok was missing from the complement of warriors who'd arrived to test us again. Captain Merrin took me on that day, and he hit me with twenty blasts before stepping back and dipping his head to me.

The best anyone else could do was eight, and Ura did that.

The Bulldog didn't hide her anger, either; her mouth was a grim, straight slash across her face as she watched me defend myself. It didn't take long for me to realize that somehow, she would get back at me. I'd caused her embarrassment before her trainees, and she would never allow me to forget it.

Because the Commander sent a note.

Perhaps he should have left it alone and allowed the punishment; I'd been prepared for it. His desire to protect me from a vindictive instructor would only cause me trouble later. I wondered where he was, but shut that thought down immediately.

* * *

"I heard some of the laundry drudges gossiping earlier. They said six from another training group were sentenced to drudgery," Wend whispered at evening mess. Jae sat beside her, listening quietly while Wend spoke.

I lifted my head to stare at her across the narrow, plank table. "What?" I began.

"They washed out in shielding class. They have to serve the instructors or do menial work in the camps or on the

32

Chapter 3

battlefield, now. Their rose will be obliterated by black ink. Haven't you ever seen the Bulldog's wrist?" Wend hissed.

My eyes widened as the truth hit me. We were being trained by those who'd never made it through their own training.

Now I wanted to spit on *The Book of the Rose* and then burn it. I kept my words behind my teeth. They were blasphemy, and that could get me beheaded.

Like a mother hen, I wanted to gather those other chicks to my nightly training sessions, but that could never be. With a sigh, I allowed my shoulders to slump. "At least they'll be safe enough in the long term," I said.

"Yeah, but I heard they were all crying about it anyway," Wend said. "It means they'll never get to—you know."

"What?" I failed to understand what she meant.

"Have children. Get married, you know—be with a man."

I considered telling her that living without a man might not be the worst thing I could think of, but she was clearly upset by it, so I kept my mouth closed on the subject. "I think that's what's wrong with the Bulldog," Wend lowered her head and her voice to impart that bit of speculation.

Jae stifled a laugh.

Tera elbowed Jae, but she struggled to hide a grin, while Misten pretended to drop something so she could duck her head.

"Anything wrong?"

The Bulldog appeared at our table as if she'd been called.

"No, Lady," I said.

The downward curve of thin lips told me she failed to accept my words as truth. Narrowing, anger-filled eyes promised trouble to come, however.

For me.

The Rose Mark

Her shoulders squared above her stocky body as she strode away, fury stiffening every step. I considered that the Bulldog's disposition had soured long before my arrival, and the Commander's note had only stirred the stench of it.

* * *

Kerok

"I've had word from Hunter," I told Merrin as he stepped up beside me on my way to the evening meal. "Fourteen vehicles were captured, and they have none available to shield them and take them to the King's City."

"What do you intend to do?" Merrin allowed his curiosity free rein.

"I've offered to take some of mine, here, along with a few escort trainees to shield the vehicles so they can be driven away from the battlefield."

"Do you have your choices made already?"

"Yes—I worked on that earlier. They'll be notified tomorrow."

"Is Ura one of your choices?"

"No—she is on a par with one or two others, and I dislike taking one of the Bulldog's favorites—her favoritism annoys me greatly, and I admit I should have done something about it six years ago when I witnessed it the first time."

"I'd like to see Ura tested in the field, Commander," Merrin breathed.

"Why?"

"To see whether she is as good as the Bulldog believes."

"What do you think?"

"I think she's better than you think."

"File a proper written request, and I'll consider it," I said.

"I'll have it on your desk before lights out."

* * *

Chapter 3

Sherra

The following morning, after training exercises, we had new classes to attend and a new instructor, who ignored the Bulldog standing in a corner of our classroom before clearing his throat and announcing his purpose.

Yes, it was a male instructor instead of a female one, as we'd had in all our other lessons.

"I am here to teach you the geography of our land, such as it is, and some history of it," he announced. "I am warrior Geb, retired from the army, as you may imagine from the color of my hair."

He was right—his hair was iron gray and thin atop his head. I had no way to guess his age, however, although my book said their power enabled warriors to live beyond the years allotted to a common man.

It said nothing about the years allotted to those who bore the rose mark. We died early and young, in my estimation, so there were none who'd retired bearing the rose tattoo.

"This is our land," he held out both hands, forming an image that hung in midair beside him. I heard a few gasps around the classroom—they hadn't known this was possible.

My book had described the talent, but not how to perform it. I watched warrior Geb closely, hoping to learn something of it from him. He quickly drew our attention to the map instead.

"Here is where we are—in this valley," he pointed out our location on the map. "You see the mountains here," he pointed out the mountains to the north and west of us. A dense forest lay to the west, and several lakes who owed their existence to winter snows.

Water for several villages and our training camp came from those lakes, but as they were finite sources, the villages were forced to use it sparingly. Most of the water went to crop production to feed us.

"You see here," Geb pointed far to the north, "The peninsula formed six centuries ago by the End-War."

The *End-War*. Not much was taught about it. We only knew that what happened then changed everything. Crippled everything.

Destroyed almost everything.

What remained was now underwater or a poisonous desert—except for a few areas. Ours had survived, because someone with power had stood against the End-War and saved what they could.

None recall who that was. Perhaps there was more than one, and their names were lost through the years. It could be that the King knew, and kept the information to himself.

"Now, here is the continent we are a part of," Geb enlarged the map. It was easy to see the vast desert that covered most of the center part of it, with a wide split down most of the middle.

That split was a great river that had become saltwater instead of fresh after the End-War. As a result, the upper continent resembled two broken, sandy mud pies made by a child. Far to the south, that continent was separated from another by a wide stretch of water. Pottles always said that both had been joined together before the End-War. Now they were isolated, and rough edges separated the lands of both from the water surrounding them, as if they had been hacked haphazardly by an uncaring hand.

"See, to our south," Geb's map enlarged and moved again, "There is more desert and waters cutting us off from a lower continent. Word has it that this continent is much smaller than it once was and islands have formed about it, which were tall mountains long ago."

Pottles told me once that the world had drowned in war and water, and there was little to be done about either. "For the enemy," she'd added, "War is their only reason to live. Without it, they are empty. Nothing. Hate keeps them alive."

"Hate?" I'd asked her.

"Their hatred for us. They believe they will not have a comfortable afterlife if they fail to kill as many of us as they can."

"The war is about an afterlife?" I was confused.

"It's what they believe. Sometimes, that is the hardest war to fight."

"The End-War destroyed other continents across the waters," Geb's voice brought me back from my memories. "What land remains there is poisoned and unlivable. If we could find our way there, it would only be to die."

"How was it destroyed?" Ura raised her hand. My eyes cut to the Bulldog; a smug half-smile stretched her thin mouth. She'd planted the question—I could see it easily.

"That is a very good question, trainee," Geb nodded at Ura. "Long ago, dreadful weapons existed, that could cause destruction of land as well as lives. Much was lost in the End-War, and there are no written records of how much was destroyed. An extreme and terrible winter followed, then came the rising waters and what we have now—an enemy who gathers here," he pointed toward the northeast of our twin mud-pie continent. "They bring their war machines across the wide desert," he mapped a trail with his hand to the southwestern edge, where we were.

The Rose Mark

"Az-ca survives because of our warriors and their escorts. Our enemies in the lands of Ny-nes have the ability to build their machines of war—we have the power to defeat them."

"Where do our vehicles come from?" Ura raised her hand. Another planted question by the Bulldog, who was all but glowing in her corner.

"They come from the enemy," Commander Kerok walked into our classroom.

"Yes—that's right," Geb sounded flustered at the Commander's sudden appearance. "We take them when we defeat the war machines in battle." I imagined Geb wanted to wipe moisture from his brow as he answered Ura's question, but refused to allow the Commander to see it.

In her corner, the Bulldog glowered at the Commander's back as he strode to the head of the class. Geb stepped aside, his map still hanging in midair beside him.

"That's why I'm here," the Commander said. "We've taken vehicles recently, but we don't have enough warriors and escorts available to leave the battlefield and get the machines taken to the King's City. I am enlisting the escorts-in-training with the best shielding ability to do this task with many of my unassigned warriors." A few gasps were heard around the room.

"You will not be assigned to a warrior," he held up a hand immediately to quell the reaction. "You will be providing your best shields to get the vehicles back to F'nexscot—the King's City."

Ura and Veri, seated on the front row, turned and smiled at one another. I waited to see what Commander Kerok had to say about those chosen to go.

"I have selected four from this class," the Commander announced. "Those four will pack for a few days' journey and

Chapter 3

meet my warriors on the parade grounds. Ura," he said her name first.

"Jae," he said next. I blinked—Jae had certainly improved her skills and was better than Ura in my opinion, but she'd had a poor showing on the first day and had wept.

Jae, whose eyes were round with a mixture of terror and happiness, blinked at me before rising to join Ura at the back of the classroom.

"Wend," the Commander announced next. Her reaction was very similar to Jae's as she rose from her chair and left our row. I fully expected to hear Veri's name next—if the Bulldog had made her choices known, she'd selected this way to punish me—if punishment it was.

"Sherra," the Commander said.

Veri yelped and turned immediately toward the Bulldog, whose frown was so deep it cratered her face.

"You four," the Commander ignored Veri's outburst to address those of us who now stood at the back of the classroom, "You will join six more trainees chosen from other classes. Meet on the parade grounds in half an hour. Be prompt, or you will receive demerits."

* * *

"I never thought I'd use this until we were done with training," Wend set her duffel next to mine on the parade grounds. Jae had almost reached us; Ura and four others hadn't arrived, yet.

Nearby were two trainees—strangers who stood together and spoke softly to one another. They hadn't approached us, although Wend had greeted them politely when we arrived.

I figured the Bulldog was busy giving Ura last minute advice on how to make herself stand out to the warriors, so she'd get a better selection when the time came. So far, the warriors hadn't arrived, with or without the Commander.

"We're sending four out of the ten," Jae whispered as her duffel joined Wend's and mine. "From six cohorts."

"Two cohorts aren't sending anyone," one of the strangers stepped toward us and held out a hand. "I'm Neka, from First Cohort."

"I'm Wend," Wend took Neka's hand with a smile. "This is Jae, and this is Sherra, all from Sixth Cohort. Ura hasn't arrived yet, but she's also from Sixth."

"I heard you didn't have any washouts in Sixth," the other woman came forward. "Caral," she introduced herself. "From Fourth. Second and Fifth had none strong enough to send."

"I'm Ura," Ura shoved her way past us to extend a hand to Caral. "The Bulldog says I'm in charge of those from Sixth."

"I think the Commander is in charge," Caral said, refusing to take Ura's hand. "My instructor said to follow his lead and obey his commands. I assume that should go for all of us."

Ura's eyes narrowed, but her cheeks flushed from the slight Caral offered. I wanted to warn Caral, but I expected that she'd learn soon enough how special Ura thought herself to be.

Two more women ran up to join us just before the Commander and his warriors appeared—*from nothing*.

* * *

I'd thought that part of the book was near-myth. *Stepping* had been outlined and explained, although I'd never thought to attempt it, as it carried the individual from one place to another, as long as that person was familiar with the place he wished to travel.

Chapter 3

If not, it was dangerous in the extreme and *The Rose Mark* warned against it.

"All here?" The Commander's second-in-command—Captain Merrin, stepped forward to ask.

"Yes, sir," Ura said immediately.

"No, sir—two haven't arrived," Caral corrected Ura.

"Can't count, eh?" the Captain grinned and lifted an eyebrow at Ura, whose face turned a deep red. Only eight of the ten had arrived and she'd have known that if she'd bothered to count heads.

"They're coming," Neka said, as both latecomers were spotted across the field.

"Good. Barely on time, but good enough," the Captain said.

He waited until the last two, breathless and one holding her side, dropped their duffels in the pile and stood at attention.

"We'll be *stepping* to a designated rendezvous point from here," the Captain announced. "I'm Captain Merrin, by the way, and there are ten warriors here who can *step* others. The rest can only take themselves, understood?"

"Yes, Captain," we replied.

"Good. When we arrive at the rendezvous point, trucks will take us to the vehicles. I warn you, there may be battles going on nearby. Do your job and close your mind to that. The warriors will be driving vehicles and providing firepower if needed. As you've likely guessed, vehicles cannot be *stepped*, so they must be brought back under ordinary means. That requires a driver, guards and a shield escort. Some of you may be asked to shield more than one vehicle. Is that clear?"

"Yes, Captain."

41

"Good. Formation," he barked at his warriors. They separated into ten groups swiftly. One group was short a man—I assumed that was the Commander's group. "Ura," he continued, "you're with my group."

Ura, pleased at being selected first to join a group of four warriors, hurried to take her place with them.

Commander Kerok appeared, then, gave a nod to Captain Merrin and took charge of us. Swiftly he placed the other women with this group or that, until only I was left. "Sherra, you're with me," Commander Kerok snapped. I followed him, his wide shoulders my focus as he strode toward his group. Arms linked within the group—I found one of my arms linked with Kerok's, the other with a man I didn't know.

"*Step*," Kerok commanded the moment we were in place.

Everything went dark.

* * *

Some of the women were on their knees when my vision cleared; I struggled to draw air in, just as they did.

"It's best to take a big gulp of air before you *step*," the warrior I didn't know grinned at me as he disengaged his arm from mine.

I realized then that he'd kept me on my feet; Kerok had dropped my arm and walked away the moment we'd arrived. "I'm Levi," he introduced himself with a wry smile. His skin was the color of dark, polished wood, and his smile was engaging.

"Sherra," I nodded to Levi. "Thank you for not letting me fall."

"No trouble." His smile turned into a grin. "Now, our vehicles are waiting just over that ridge," he pointed. "Everybody has time to get their breath back while we walk there."

Chapter 3

"Come," Kerok raised his hand from feet away. The warriors snapped to attention. I did likewise, as it appeared to be expected. I marched beside Levi as we took first position behind Kerok and followed him toward the gentle rise over sandy, dry ground, sparsely littered with desert plants.

* * *

Kerok

I wanted to growl at Merrin—he was paying too much attention to Ura and not enough to his men. I should have been more reluctant to grant his request to take Ura; she would have stayed behind if I'd followed my own advice.

For the thousandth time, I wished he could speak mind-to-mind, but that would never be and was a waste of a wish. Perhaps it was just as well; lately, all I wanted to do was chastise him, when I'd been very like him not that long ago.

Nevertheless, I growled at him mentally, just to soothe my temper.

Don't get her killed, I snapped. She was needed on the battlefield, not in his bed. I topped the rise first, the others right behind me. Three transport trucks waited there for us.

"Come; every moment we dally could be a moment to save lives," I said and made my descent toward the vehicles.

* * *

Sherra

"He always says that," Levi breathed as we made our way down the sharp slope toward three waiting trucks. "Commander doesn't like losing lives, on or off the battlefield. We'll take these three trucks to the others," he added. "*Stepping* past this point can be risky, so we don't do it. War changes the landscape too often to make it safe, and the Commander doesn't take foolish risks."

The Rose Mark

I didn't say it, but my opinion of the Commander rose slightly. I hoped his sentiments included the women who fought beside the warriors, but I'd wait to see that for myself.

I didn't miss the looks Wend and Jae sent me as they were loaded onto a separate truck; the one I was pointed toward held Caral and Neka. Each of us stayed with our assigned pod and were placed in the middle on hard benches in the back of the truck. I imagined it was to allow for full effect of an escort's shield for the men.

Levi sat on one side; another man who nodded at me sat on the other. "That's Armon," Levi nodded toward the other man, while a hidden dimple appeared in his cheek. Armon's skin was paler, although it had darkened with exposure to the sun.

I'd already suspected, too, but this solidified my opinion. Those two—Levi and Armon—were together. It happened sometimes and bothered me not at all. The women assigned to either would remain virgin. It was the way things worked.

"Pleased to meet you," I nodded to Armon, who grinned suddenly. I think he was waiting to see how he'd be treated. If anything, it made me like him more.

"It'll take an hour to get to the location," Levi informed me. "You'll probably hear sounds of battle when we get there."

I drew in a breath at his words—he'd seen and heard this before. I had never been exposed to it. So many questions crowded my mind—questions I wanted to ask him but was afraid to do so.

"Go ahead; I see you're curious," Armon spoke.

"What's it like when they die?" I turned to him and asked. The truck lurched forward, then. We were on our way.

* * *

Kerok

44

Chapter 3

I didn't miss hearing her first question, and it was the one I didn't want any of my pod to answer.

"I can't really answer that," Armon said, causing my shoulders to sag in relief. I'd instructed all the warriors on that question—*do not answer it.* I should have known Sherra would ask it first. "What else would you like to know?" Armon filled the silence that came immediately after as Sherra blinked at him.

"How do you assemble for battle? Does the escort stand beside you?" she asked. It was an excellent question and the one I'd have asked myself, if I were in her place. The instructors hadn't gotten that far in the training schedule yet, and it was a very good thing to ask a warrior, as he'd have first-hand experience on the field.

"The escort stands six paces behind—close enough to shield," Armon replied. "It leaves them far enough away that they don't interfere with our work, while keeping us safe."

"It's a two-step process," Levi broke in. "You shield while the enemy fires at us; we give you a signal to drop the shield long enough to level a blast against the enemy's war machines, then you replace the shield. It's hard work, turning it on and off like that."

"So we have to be fast," Sherra nodded.

"Yes. That period of your training will come soon, and you'll be paired with different warriors who'll work beside you, leveling very weak blasts, in case you don't lower your shield properly when the signal is given. You don't want to know what happens when a full blast is fired and the shield doesn't drop in time to release it."

"Messy," Armon sighed. "Two deaths, instead of one."

"Unless the blast destroys the escort's shield," I broke in. Sherra's head jerked in my direction. I sat behind the cab of the vehicle, not far from my pod, and could listen easily to their conversation.

"What," she hesitated, as if she wasn't sure she should speak to me. I gave her a nod to continue.

"What happens to the escort?"

"If the initial blowback doesn't kill her and her warrior, she is emptied and sentenced to drudgery, for miscalculating." I gave her the hard answer—she may as well know the truth of it.

"Commander?" Caral, who sat on the other side of the truck with her pod, raised a hand.

"Yes, Caral?" I turned toward her, although I hadn't missed the brief glimpse of concern in Sherra's eyes.

"How long are the escorts and their warriors expected to fight?"

"Good question. How long can a battle last?" I asked. Caral bit her lip and pressed her back against the side of the truck, as if she were attempting to retreat from my answer.

Sherra turned her head away from me, then. I'd been callous in my answer. A part of me wanted to say *get used to it*. Another part wanted to calm her fears. That would be a false hope, and I was sick to death of false hope.

Every escort who ever traveled to the battlefield imagined they'd be the one to survive.

It always turned out the opposite. They wearied and died in protracted battles, after spending all their strength to protect and aid the warriors. Some lasted for years, but every subsequent season wore them down, until there was little left and they became brittle.

Fragile.

I wondered if the untalented women from every village ever wondered what sort of strength was required from the

Chapter 3

escorts to protect them from the enemy. Not only did they hold the shields, but supplied extra strength for the warriors to send their blasts against the invaders.

I couldn't imagine being nearly emptied that way, time after time, until there was nothing left and they died.

There must be a better way. Sherra's tentative, mental voice stunned me.

Find one and I'll listen, I barked back. I wasn't intending to sound so harsh, and she didn't reply. I didn't miss the hunching of her shoulders as she turned farther away from me, though.

Only fifteen minutes had passed and none spoke, now. The trip would seem longer than it was as a result, and it was my fault.

* * *

Sherra

I stayed silent the rest of the trip. A few spoke in hushed tones now and then, but there'd been no mistake that Commander Kerok had become unyielding and cold, shutting off the questions and the majority of conversation inside the truck.

Asking Levi or Armon for an explanation later sounded like prying, so I kept my fears and worries to myself and waited to be told what to do and when to do it.

"This is a blast bowl," Levi informed me as the truck dipped over the edge of the rough road we traveled. I could only see out the back of the truck, past the other pods who rode with us.

We'd certainly taken a steep dip—the angle of our descent was troubling. Glancing back, I saw the fear in Caral's and Neka's eyes, although their lips were pressed tightly shut.

47

The Rose Mark

The warriors appeared to be used to it, however, so I forced myself to lean back and attempt to control my unruly heart and ragged breathing.

A blast bowl.

A warrior created this crater, I reminded myself as I forced my breaths to even out. No wonder none of them had second thoughts about it.

At the bottom of the blast bowl, fourteen vehicles waited for us. I blinked—some had been manufactured recently, I could tell. There were few dents in the metal and the paint hadn't peeled or turned a paler color of its original hue from being in the desert sun for months or years.

Still, they were an ugly shade of yellowish-brown—camouflage for the areas where they'd be employed in the ongoing war.

When I climbed from the back of the truck to stand at the bottom of the bowl, I saw how high and steep its sides were and marveled that we hadn't turned over while going down it.

"We have to drive up it, too," Levi chuckled next to me. He'd read my thoughts as I stared at the crater in alarm.

"You could have saved that for later," I said before slapping a hand over my mouth. My words were disrespectful to a higher-ranking warrior, especially when spoken aloud while surrounded by others, including Commander Kerok. Levi and Armon laughed, though, which caused me to breath a relieved sigh.

Another truck descended into the bowl and Ura, Merrin and two other women spilled out of it, laughing and teasing with Merrin and a few warriors. Commander Kerok wore a frown as he strode toward Captain Merrin, who left Ura and the others behind to meet Kerok halfway.

Chapter 3

I didn't miss the look on Ura's face, however. Her eyes followed Captain Merrin closely, as if she already had her sights set that high. I didn't care, actually—I found Merrin lacking in something I couldn't define, and wished her well with the death awaiting at his hands.

A boom startled us as it sounded, shaking the ground with its intensity as the third truck rolled cautiously down the side of the bowl. Jae, Wend and two other women were inside it, and I hoped they wouldn't be frightened by the descent and the sound of battle that had finally reached us.

Commander Kerok whirled and shouted at the rest of us. "Pod leaders, load up—the battle is headed this way."

"Follow me," Levi snapped. I followed him at a run, while Armon raced beside me and four other warriors came behind. Armon flung the driver's door open and climbed into the seat before strapping himself in.

More booms sounded—closer, this time.

"Into the back, and put up your best shield around this vehicle and the one behind it," Levi told me. I nodded and immediately ran to the rear of the vehicle. I watched as three of our warriors ran to the truck behind ours. Two climbed into the front seat, while one trotted toward the back to act as a guard.

"Strap yourself in," the warrior with me commanded.

Pulling straps from a line of them inside the back, I snapped and buckled so I wouldn't be thrown out of the vehicle when it began moving.

Farther behind us, others were scrambling to reach the purloined trucks to drive them away from the blast bowl into safer territory.

Once all of ours were onboard and the warrior with me nodded, I placed my shield around both vehicles as commanded. Both lurched forward at the same moment, and our ascent to the top of the blast bowl began.

Several times, I was thrown as far as my restraints would allow during the rough journey out of the bowl, but what terrified me most was the blast behind us that blew a massive cloud of sand, rock and dirt skyward before the deafening boom ever reached my ears.

Chapter 4

Kerok

"That's too damn close," Merrin shouted at me from the back of our vehicle as another explosion shook the ground behind us.

I'd elected to travel with him on this leg, as he'd so blatantly ignored my warning not to engage or get involved with Ura or any of the other women on the trip out.

It was far too early for the women to form an attachment, and he could get one or more of them killed by bedding them. Therefore, he had an unwelcome chaperone while Ura, strapped in and sitting not far away, concentrated on forming her shield around this vehicle and the one behind it.

More blasts came from rockets fired by the enemy, some of which skipped off the escorts' shields on the battlefield and bounced away to land elsewhere. Elsewhere in this case turned out to be quite close to the blast bowl where we'd hidden our stolen vehicles. It couldn't be helped or controlled by our side—there was no way to predict the direction a rocket would skip or bounce.

I'd received a mental communication from a Colonel on the battlefield, who informed me they were taking heavy fire. So far, none of the troops had been lost and they were holding up well.

That same message also went to the King's advisor, who would record it for the archives, then draft it as a message to present to the King.

A blast hit parallel to our convoy, causing our driver to careen to the side before righting the vehicle and speeding forward again. I imagined the same thing happened several times over, too, as our convoy was a long one.

Are you still on the road? I sent to Sherra.

Yes, Commander. Her reply was curt, angry and proper.

I wasn't surprised at the formality she'd adopted. I'd barked at her before, when I shouldn't have. Perhaps I should have sent the message to Armon—he could mindspeak. I didn't want to distract him, however, and, if I were honest, I wanted to see how things stood between Sherra and me.

Merrin would argue that she was nothing and not to waste time worrying what she thought or how she felt. I knew better than that.

Now.

When the next rocket hit with a resounding blast, I knew it was too close, because we skidded away from the rutted road and bounced for neck-jarring yards across pitted, rock-filled land before the driver could brake properly.

* * *

Chapter 4

Sherra

Two trucks were overturned, and I wanted to weep as I struggled to unbuckle my restraints to get to them.

The trucks I shielded were unharmed, but a rocket had breached a shield over the last two, which caused brakes to squeal and both vehicles to reel and spin several times before coming to a bone-crushing, smoking stop—one vehicle on its side, the other upside down.

While I ran toward those overturned trucks, others joined me—men and women, as we raced to help.

"Incoming," someone shouted behind me.

He was right—I could hear the whine of the rocket getting close. Terrified, I skidded to a stop, my boots sliding across hard, desert ground. Turning swiftly, I gauged the distance from the front of the convoy to the back before forming a shield as fast as I could.

Don't fire, I shouted mentally at all the warriors. We didn't need to fry ourselves and accomplish the enemy's goal for them.

The whine stopped when the rocket hit my shield dead center, and I'll never forget the moment of calm silence before the ground rocked beneath our feet and our ears were deafened from the explosion above our heads.

* * *

Kerok

"Temporary deafness, I think," Armon shook his head at me when I asked him to report on Sherra. "No idea how much power she has left, either. That was a direct hit. She didn't know to angle and lift the shield so the rocket would skip off and land somewhere else."

"I doubt anyone else could have shielded the entire convoy and angled their shield at the same time," I pointed out.

"That's true," Armon frowned as he studied the length of the convoy. "Two or three trucks, maybe. Not the whole thing."

"At least things have died down for now. We lost two in the last truck—a warrior and the escort."

"Are we carrying the bodies with us?" Armon asked.

"Yes. We don't have time for a burial here. We need to get going. Leave the two wrecked vehicles behind and load the others where they'll fit. We have broken bones to be tended while we're on the road. Someone can scavenge the wrecks for parts later. Tell everyone to load up and head out."

"I'll take care of it," Armon agreed and trotted away to inform the others.

Merrin was noticeably absent; he knew I was angry with him. Armon and Levi were next on the command chain, so they'd see that things got done. We needed to be underway again soon, if we were to reach our midway point before exhaustion hit.

Less than half an hour later, we were loaded up and on the road again. I hadn't planned on losing a trainee or a warrior on this trip, but war was war, and nothing was predictable about any of it.

* * *

Sherra

I had difficulty hearing when someone spoke to me. That meant I struggled to read lips. Armon began to feed me orders by mindspeaking, and I was grateful. Those I could hear perfectly.

Chapter 4

I was also grateful that I only had two trucks to shield again—providing such a large shield and taking such a massive hit to protect the convoy had lessened my strength considerably.

Levi sat beside me now in the back of the truck, instead of the warrior I'd started out with. I was grateful for that, too, as Levi looked sympathetic, at least, as we bounced along the uneven, rutted track they called a road.

I had water in a canteen nearby—I'd already emptied two of them after the rocket hit my shield. I felt continually thirsty—as if the water had been sucked from my body along with my energy.

I suppose this is what it felt like on the front lines. No wonder the escorts failed and died after a while. The effort to shield so much was debilitating, and they only had continuous days of the same thing to look forward to when the enemy came to do battle.

Long past nightfall, we reached the midway point—a small, military post where wounded were often brought from the battlefield for treatment. Regular supplies came from farther down the valley, including food and medicines.

The survivors of the wrecked vehicles were unloaded carefully and carted away for better treatment than we were able to provide, while I unbuckled myself from the wall straps and rose stiffly from the uncomfortable bench I sat on. The two bodies were taken in a different direction—I hoped they'd get proper burial and their families notified.

"Need—help?" Levi spoke beside me. At least my hearing had improved somewhat during the trip; I heard part of what he said and guessed the rest.

"No," I shook my head, puzzled by the way my words sounded to my own ears—as if they'd been stuffed with buzzing fluff.

"Food," I caught Levi's word among several others, as he pointed to the lines forming nearby. Our fellow troops were lining up to march to the warrior's mess, it appeared.

With a nod, I fell in step behind him, while Armon took the position behind me. Flanked by both, we made our way to a long building, where the scent of food reached my nostrils and almost sent me to my knees in welcoming bliss.

* * *

Kerok

She hears less than half of what we say, Armon informed me as he and Levi made sure Sherra received enough food to replenish lost reserves.

Each pod sat at their own table; the last one missing a warrior and an escort. Ura and Merrin sat at the table next to mine; I sat at the table with the facility Commandant and his Chief of Medicine.

My eyes strayed often to Ura, however, who gazed longingly at Merrin before turning narrowed, jealousy-filled eyes toward Sherra.

It made me angry—Ura's life had been saved, along with that of the rest of our convoy, and she settled on hatred toward the one who'd saved her ass. I had no doubt that the Bulldog had encouraged this behavior rather than dealing with it as she should, and I considered reporting it now, instead of later.

Time would tell whether I actually followed through with that idea or not, but I resolved to watch Ura and the Bulldog closely from now on.

"You're lucky to be alive," Chief of Medicine Welton said, drawing my attention back to my dinner companions.

Chapter 4

"True enough," I agreed. "My father is understandably grateful. I sent a personal message to him, after the official report was delivered."

"Mindspeak is perhaps the best of gifts," Welton nodded.

"Mindspeak and a strong shield," I amended his words.

"Very true."

* * *

Sherra

Seasoned warriors often experience hearing loss after time spent on the battlefield, Armon informed me as I was escorted to the women's barracks. *Your hearing should be better in the morning, but it may take several days before it feels normal again.*

"Thank you," I said aloud, my words sounding tinny and false to my damaged senses. I only wanted to go inside the barracks, find my duffel and an empty bed. The first two things went well. The last one—Ura managed to fuck that up for all of us.

* * *

Kerok

I had no idea I'd be called from a deep sleep to handle a brawl that erupted in the women's barracks. I'd borrowed the Post Commandant's office to handle the impromptu complaints and make decisions, while four glowering trainees sat before me.

Ura's left eye was swollen shut and turning purple—she sat on her chair fuming and casting accusing glances toward Caral. Neka sat beside Caral, while Wend had scooted her chair away from Ura's to distance herself from all of it.

"Which of you can tell me, in the briefest and most honest way possible, exactly what happened?" I asked, practicing my best, low, calming voice. Not easy to do while seething inside at the foolishness I was faced with, when all of us should be asleep.

Wend held up a tentative hand.

"Wend," I nodded to her to begin.

"As you know, Sherra can't hear very well right now," she began, her voice and manner quite nervous.

"Understood—go on."

"The moment Sherra found her duffel beside a cot, she sat down to take her boots off. Ura went right up to her and started making fun of her mindspeak."

"In what way?" I cut my eyes from Wend to Ura and then back again.

"She said Sherra was a stupid bitch who thought she was so smart for being able to do it," Neka broke in.

"Did I ask for your input?" I snapped at Neka.

"No, Commander." She went silent and hung her head.

"Right. Wend, was that what Ura said?"

"Yes. She called Sherra a bitch, who was showing off because she thought she was better than anyone else."

"Has Sherra ever said anything like that?"

"I've never heard her say anything like that. She works hard and keeps her opinions to herself."

"What happened after Ura accosted Sherra?" I prompted.

"Sherra didn't understand all of Ura's words, so she asked her to repeat them."

"Ah. What then?"

"Ura spoke them more loudly, and called Sherra a mindless, hearing-impaired dolt afterward. Caral walked up, then, grabbed Ura's arm and told her to shut up because she didn't know anything, including how to count."

Neka looked away to hide a tiny smile.

"What was Sherra doing?"

Chapter 4

"Sitting on her bunk, trying to make sense of what was happening, I think," Wend explained. "She looked really tired."

"Go on."

"Ura pulled her arm away from Caral and tried to hit her. She missed, but Caral didn't."

"Did Ura fight back?"

"No, sir, she was unconscious on the floor after Caral's first punch."

I wanted to laugh. I didn't.

"Was anyone else involved in this altercation?"

"No, sir," Wend said. "I'd gone to sit with Sherra while Ura had her say. Caral and Neka came right after, and then those things happened."

"Neka?" I turned toward her.

"It's like Wend says." She didn't look up at me.

"Caral?"

"I punched her, sir. I'm prepared to take the demerits."

"Ura?" I settled on her last.

"Permission to speak freely?" she asked.

"You have that permission, as long as what you say is truth and not personal opinion or conjecture."

"Then I have nothing to say."

"Good. Caral—five demerits. That puts you in Fifth group to choose a warrior. Earn more demerits and you'll be in the last group, understood?"

"Yes, sir," Caral nodded at her sentence.

"Ura," I began.

"She injured me," Ura spat before turning toward Caral and attempting to swat at her.

"Levi," I snapped. He and Armon stood beside the Commandant's door, acting as guards while I passed judgment.

Levi stepped forward to restrain Ura, who still wanted to strike Caral.

"Ura," I said, weariness in my voice, "tonight you will sleep in solitary confinement in the lock-up. You have seven demerits."

"Nooo," she shouted as Armon stepped forward to help Levi haul her out of the office.

"The rest of you, go to bed. If I hear anything else out of the women's barracks tonight, I'll hand demerits to everyone. Is that clear?"

"Yes, sir."

"Good. Leave. Sleep. We have another long day tomorrow."

My hand went to the back of my neck when Wend closed the door behind them. *Fucking hell.* I knew better than to humor Merrin on bringing Ura along. I considered giving him demerits too, as I rose from the Commandant's chair before returning to my borrowed bed.

* * *

Sherra

I still had ringing in my ears the following morning, but I could hear better. That was and wasn't a good thing, as every woman in our barracks was whispering about the altercation between Caral and Ura the night before.

All because Ura was jealous and spoiled by the Bulldog into thinking she was better than she was.

Caral had received five demerits for punching Ura; Ura received seven for becoming combative again in front of Commander Kerok.

Chapter 4

That dropped her into the last group to choose a warrior from the list. While that wouldn't bother me, it would certainly bother her—she expected to be first to pick, with Veri second.

At the end of our training, the warriors would sign their names to the list of any escorts they were interested in. The escorts would then choose a warrior from that list. The farther down the round of lists you were, the more likely it was that the best warriors would be taken already. At the end of the rounds, there was often little choice remaining, as some warriors signed every list because they were least likely to be selected in the first three or four rounds.

Ura had hamstrung herself as far as choices went, and training wasn't over yet. Caral was almost as bad off.

"Come on—we'll be late for breakfast," Jae tugged on my sleeve as I smoothed the blanket on my made-up cot.

I followed her and Wend toward the door, grateful that Ura wouldn't be released from lock-up until it was time to leave.

She wouldn't be locked up when we went back to the Bulldog, however, and that concerned me a great deal.

The combined bootsteps of eight women echoed on the cobbled walkway as we made our way to the mess for breakfast. In moments, the warriors' steps matched ours, following behind us.

I didn't turn to look back, but kept moving. I'm sure they were as hungry as we were after the experiences of the day before.

Theirs, for the most part, had ended at bedtime. Ours had continued past it. Squaring my shoulders, I hoped to put it out of my mind and enjoy my meal.

* * *

The Rose Mark

Kerok

Jae and Sherra marched at the back of their group on the way to breakfast. I studied both—Jae was slightly shorter than Sherra, and not quite as thin.

That meant nothing to me. I intended to speak with others who waited in the capital city regarding the events the day before, and how we'd escaped with our lives through the talents of a half-trained escort.

We'd lost two, but that was prior to Sherra's actions to save the entire convoy from a direct hit. Had Ura not been prevented, things could have gotten much worse the night before. I considered that Caral's demerits were earned, but she'd also provided a shield of sorts where it was most needed at the time, to protect an exhausted escort.

The prospect of staring down the Bulldog, too, presented itself. She wouldn't appreciate the fact that one of her favorites had earned more demerits in a single incident than the entire training class had earned together up to now.

I'd been prepared to issue five to each combatant. Two more were tacked onto Ura's tally when she attempted to strike Caral during my interview. I'd never seen behavior like this, when Ura had to know there'd be consequences.

Cursing myself again for selecting her at Merrin's official request, I shut off that line of thinking and began planning the rest of the day.

* * *

Sherra

"Heard there was a bit of excitement in the women's barracks last night," Levi grinned as he set his breakfast tray beside mine. Armon took my other side before I could form a reply.

Chapter 4

"Maybe it would be excitement for you—I was still half-deaf and too tired to know what was happening," I grumbled and lifted my cup of tea to drink. "Besides, one of ours died yesterday. A fight wasn't the best way to deal with it."

Levi let out a breath before nodding his agreement. They'd lost one of theirs, too, although they were probably used to it by now. For us, we should have spent time in quiet reflection. Instead, Ura wanted to air her perceived grievances.

"I hope she thinks twice about doing that again," Armon said, spearing a chunk of sausage and placing it in his mouth.

It drew me back to my own plate of food, *which I should eat*, I reminded myself, to keep up my strength. Ura would do whatever Ura wanted, Armon's hopes aside, the moment she made it back to the Bulldog's barracks.

If she were wise, she'd know that where we'd gone the day before was perhaps the closest thing we'd seen so far of the reality of the war. Instead, she'd focused on the pettiness that was inside her, in total disregard of the deaths that came of it.

I hadn't been introduced to the trainee who died before we'd left camp; therefore, I couldn't put a name to the loss. I imagined there was someone in our group who knew her, however, and perhaps others would mourn her properly when news of her death arrived at North Camp.

"Did you know her?" Levi asked, as if he could read my mind.

"No." My eyes dropped to my plate while shaky fingers toyed with the fork I held. "I didn't get her name before we left—she ran up at the last, holding her side and out of breath."

"And things moved quickly after that," Armon nodded and broke open a piece of bread to swipe butter across it.

63

"Yes. I'm not sure any of us could have deflected that explosion—she had no real experience."

"I'm surprised the rest of us are alive and having breakfast," Levi grimaced before going silent.

Shoving thoughts on the matter away from my mind, I concentrated on finishing my food. At least Ura wasn't sitting with her pod, casting angry looks in my direction. Her absence would aid my digestion, if nothing else.

* * *

Kerok

I moved Ura out of Merrin's pod when the trucks were loaded for the final half of our journey; he was angry about it but I no longer cared. She'd caused too much trouble for me to humor his wishes where she was concerned.

Therefore, I loaded into the back of Armon's vehicle, where Levi, Sherra and two warriors from the wrecked vehicles sat. One of those warriors had a broken arm, which a post physician had casted and wrapped. He wouldn't be able to do anything for two weeks, while his arm began to heal. Partial duty and some blast-work could be handled past that. Good enough for the training courses coming soon.

Sherra was buckled in near the back of the truck, so she could shield it and the one behind it when we rolled away from the post.

I wanted to ask her how she felt—how the weakness affected her and whether she was capable of shielding the entire convoy a second time, should the need arise. I kept my questions to myself, fastened the straps around me and swayed with the others as the truck creaked and bounced through the gates toward the road.

* * *

Sherra

Chapter 4

The ride was a long one, and more than once I wanted to sleep. Levi, sitting nearby, kept a close watch to make sure that didn't happen. Perhaps it was expected, when an escort expended so much power the day before.

Weariness blurred my vision near the end of our journey, but I snapped fully alert the moment the track changed to smooth road, the truck's wheels making an even, monotonous whine on paved ground.

"We're nearing the royal city," Levi explained as I turned toward him, an unspoken question in my mind. "The roads are maintained from this point."

Kerok must have listened in; he sent mindspeak to me, then. *The outer roads are left rough to discourage the enemy from traveling them, should they break through our lines of defense. We travel several tracks here, to confuse them, too.*

"Food and a bed are waiting," Levi continued, unaware of Kerok's mental explanation. "We'll have three days to rest before we return to the training camp."

Thank you for the explanation, Commander, I replied. *I wondered what would happen should the enemy succeed.*

They will kill us all, if the army fails to hold them back. His reply was simple and honest. I appreciated that.

"We're coming to the domes," Levi interrupted.

"Domes?"

"The domes covering the King's City," Levi grinned. "You'll see soon enough."

From my seat in the back of the covered truck, I could only see what we passed and not what we were headed toward. That's how I saw the large concrete pipes first.

"What are those?" I asked Levi.

"You see there are separate pipes—one larger, one smaller?" Kerok answered my question.

The Rose Mark

"Yes," I said aloud, although with a small amount of hesitance.

"The larger pipe carries sea water into the desalination and purification plant. The smaller pipe carries the brine back to the sea. This is how the King's City gets its water, as there are no nearby lakes to supply enough water for those who live here. Sun and wind provide the power for the pumps, you understand."

He was right—the King's City lay in the midst of a desert, and was far from the nearest source of fresh water. The sea was much closer—according to the few maps I'd seen.

I hadn't heard about domes in connection with the King's City before, but then few in my village cared about the King's City. Their days were taken up with the normal toil of survival—maintaining a modest home and feeding themselves and their families.

I doubted any of them had gone more than a few miles away, and that was either to grow or purchase food, find wood to burn or build, and trade with their neighbors for things they needed.

"You may release your shield, trainee," Kerok said, breaking me away from my thoughts. "We are safe enough, here."

We'd just driven past a portal within a thick, clear wall. I breathed a deep sigh—I imagined the domes to be opaque and built of some sturdy material—concrete or the like.

"It's not glass, but a stronger simulation of it," Levi said. "Not that it'll withstand the bombs—if the enemy comes close enough."

When the trees, flowers and shrubs appeared as we drove along a smooth road, I felt awe that such things could exist. My eyes misted—I reached up to wipe the moisture away.

Chapter 4

Kerok

I'd been born in the King's City, and it held no wonders for me. When I watched Sherra brush tears from her eyes, however, I felt as if I were seeing it for the first time with her.

Until now, desert blooms were likely all she'd seen, and precious few of those. Here, there were plants, trees and flowers that existed in no other place. Their beginnings came from the before-times.

Before the End-War destroyed everything or changed it forever. Most of the population had no thought for what came before—as if their ancestry began after the End-War and not before.

No history of the before-times was taught anywhere. Very little history of the first century after the End-War was known to any. The King's library held records—some impossible to access, others impossible to read as the written languages had changed so much.

Six centuries is a very long time, after all, and those kinds of changes have happened all along. Most people were merely oblivious to it.

"Nothing higher than four stories exists under the domes," Levi informed Sherra, whose widened eyes took in everything she could see from the back of the vehicle. "Everything here is solar or wind-powered—those things we have in abundance," he added.

We were passing through the outer northern dome, which was mostly residential. Regardless, grass grew on some lawns, while others had been left natural. Chances were, Sherra had never traveled more than a few miles from her village all her life, until the truck came to haul her to the training camp.

The Rose Mark

Most trainees never saw the King's City. Some escorts did, but they had to survive their first season on the battlefield to do so.

My shoulders slumped at that thought. We were in enough trouble as it was, because the numbers of escorts and warriors was dangerously low. If something weren't done soon, well, I wouldn't think about that, now. I watched Sherra instead; if any trainee deserved to see the King's City, it was she.

* * *

Sherra

When we passed the fourth entrance, moving from one massive dome to the next, it was to enter the King's dome, which Levi explained was the tallest, central dome. "The barracks where we'll stay while here are on the southern side, so you'll see the palace on the way," he told me.

Palace. A word from tales and not from experience. An involuntary shiver took me by surprise. It wasn't pleasant, that shiver. Somewhere in the King's palace lay *The Book of the Rose*—the book that demanded my marking at a young age, and my death a few years later.

Chapter 5

*S*herra
    I blinked as our truck pulled up outside a long, three-story building made of concrete with little embellishment. Yes, we'd passed the King's palace, which was elaborately decorated and contained many windows. Surrounding it were large gardens, with flowers blooming in all colors—enough to take my breath away at the sweet scent of it all.

Bees in plenty buzzed in and around those blooms, intent on collecting pollen and nectar to carry back to a hive somewhere.

That meant the King had sweets whenever he wanted them.

"Come on, time to get food, a bath and a bed," Levi's hand dropped on my shoulder.

"Yes, sir," I said and fumbled with my buckles and straps.

"Commander Kerok, this is fine work," a man appeared at the back of our truck as we prepared to exit the vehicle. "We've never taken so many vehicles at once."

"Thank you, Hunter," Kerok smiled and moved toward the back. Levi and I moved out of Kerok's way so he could climb from the truck first.

Leaping down, as if he were fresh and not weary from a long journey, Kerok clapped Hunter on the back as if he knew him well.

"The King's Advisor," Levi said softly next to my ear. "Kerok sends reports for the King in mindspeak to Hunter."

They did know one another well, then. Squaring my shoulders, I nodded to let Levi know I understood, and followed him out of the truck.

* * *

Kerok

Dusk came quickly as I followed Hunter to the Command Center; the others would go straight to the barracks, wash faces and hands and then head to the mess for dinner.

I envied them—I had hours of duty left, making my reports in person and writing out the official records to coincide with the earlier, mindspoken messages to Hunter.

I'd have dinner while making my report to the King.

While I walked with Hunter, I could hear Merrin's voice and Ura's laugh behind me. I clenched my teeth and kept to my path.

Merrin would have to be disciplined, as I'd told him more than once to stay away from her. The moment my back was turned, he disobeyed my order. If he held mindspeaking ability, I'd blister his brain cells with my transmitted thoughts.

"The King especially wishes to hear the report regarding the shielding of the entire convoy," Hunter said.

"I thought he would," I agreed and put Merrin's disobedience out of my mind. "I've never seen anything like it before."

"What about the incident in the trainee's barracks afterward? Was she involved in that?"

"Not really, no. I'll explain that to the King when we have dinner."

"Good. I anticipate he'll have questions."

"I'll answer truthfully."

"You always do," Hunter sighed.

"Hunt," I said, "I speak honestly for myself, and not for anyone else. I couldn't live with myself otherwise."

"I know. I can't say the same thing about others," he said. "They embellish or omit, depending on which will gain them the most prestige with the King."

"I'm ultimately responsible for selecting the one who ended up causing the trouble," I pointed out. "As a favor to Merrin, who didn't deserve the favor. He will be dealt with later. She has already received demerits."

"Who trains her at camp?"

"The Bulldog."

"Ah."

Hunter didn't need to say more. The Bulldog's trainees were more trouble on the battlefield than any other instructor's. The most talented among them often required an *attitude adjustment*, as Armon was fond of saying.

I doubted Sherra would need such—the Bulldog clearly didn't like her, probably because I'd sent a note and not just because Sherra had held the full extent of her talent back.

She called you a jackass, I recalled and muffled a laugh.

"Something funny?" Hunter asked before reaching out to open the door leading into the Command Center.

"Just a memory," I replied. "I'll tell you later."

* * *

Sherra

Between laughing at Merrin's attempts at humor, Ura shot malevolent glances in my direction during dinner. After the first few narrow-eyed glares, I deliberately concentrated on my plate of food or Levi's and Armon's faces, depending on who was speaking.

At least I was two tables away from Ura, who couldn't reach me to strike a hit, no matter how much she wanted to do so. Between us lay Wend's table, and Wend pointedly ignored Ura's fake laughter and simpered words, just as I did.

"Pay her no mind," Armon said after a while. "Her punishment will come home to her when training is over."

That wouldn't make it easier on the rest of us in the Bulldog's cohort before then. I didn't voice my opinion aloud—Armon knew it as surely as I did.

* * *

"At least she knows to stay away from us," Wend whispered as she, Jae, Caral and Neka chose cots near mine.

Ura chattered away on the opposite side of our wide room, while those nearby put as much space between Ura and themselves as they could. Ura ignored any slight and went on talking as if they were all interested in her aimless prattle. Depending on the trainee, they either ignored her or feigned attention to her words.

72

Chapter 5

Here, away from the training camp, Ura had sunk to the level she deserved. Only Merrin and one or two other warriors from her pod paid any attention to her at all. Every trainee chosen for this assignment was talented—Ura wasn't one of a special handful, as she imagined herself to be.

"If Veri were here, they'd cause even more trouble, I think," Jae whispered.

"Who is Veri?" Caral came to sit beside Jae on her cot.

"The Bulldog's other pet," Jae mumbled. "They get away with things the rest of us would be punished for. She was mad because Wend and I were picked to come, and she wasn't."

"The Bulldog was mad, too," Wend pointed out. "Her face looked like a dark cloud when the rest of us were chosen and Veri wasn't."

"Lights out," Armon pounded on the outer door. A moment later, the lights went out, leaving us in darkness.

I was glad; it never helped to sit and worry the bone of mistreatment until it became filled with the disease of unrest. In the end, we were all dead—whether we were the Bulldog's favorites or not.

* * *

Kerok

Hunter read through my report a second time while I flexed my hand to rid it of writing cramp.

"Good," he nodded. "Concise and clear, as always. Come now—dinner with the King is waiting."

"Will Drenn be there?"

"That's my understanding."

I wanted to curse. I held it back and dipped my head in a nod. Following Hunter from the Command Center, we loaded into a vehicle driven by a servant to be hauled to the King's palace.

The Rose Mark

"Drenn," I dipped my head to the King's eldest son as Hunter and I walked into the less formal dining room for our dinner with the King.

"Thorn, welcome back." My father, the King, smiled and opened his arms as he stood at the head of the table.

Yes, I go by one of my lesser names in the field. In the King's palace, I am Thorn, the King's youngest. Drenn's frown didn't escape my notice as I moved past him to embrace my father.

Hunter calls it sibling rivalry. When I was young, I'd asked Hunter why Drenn disliked me so much.

Because you have power he will never have, Hunter replied. I pointed out that Drenn would have father's place someday, with power over all. Hunter merely shrugged and said, *people's emotions often get the better of their intelligence.*

I couldn't argue with that assessment, so I didn't.

"Welcome home," Father embraced me tightly and patted my back. "Your muscles are harder every time," he laughed and pulled away.

"It's good to see you, too, Father," I grinned at him. The only thing marring my welcome here was Drenn's presence, but that couldn't be avoided. Drenn did as he wanted much of the time, unless Father gave a direct command.

Drenn's biggest asset, in my eyes, was the fact that he loved Father as much as I did, and a rebuke from our only living parent made him mope for days.

Drenn didn't have the talent to mindspeak. Father did. Drenn was jealous of that connection between us—something he could never do. It probably made him paranoid, but that was none of my doing and I took no blame for it.

Chapter 5

I had the idea that Sherra's mindspeak could blast into his brain, just as it had into the minds of all in the convoy. That was something Father would no doubt be interested in, along with the ability to shield a convoy of twelve vehicles.

"Sit, sit," Father gestured for Drenn, Hunter and me to join him at the table. Beer and water were served with the first course.

* * *

"How many others in North Camp have better-than-average talents?" Father asked.

"A handful. I selected the best of the lot to take with me on the vehicle run. One took a direct hit, as I explained before, and is now dead."

"Are any of them as good as the one you call Sherra?"

"Not that I've seen, although I will say this; three of those I selected weren't firsts—two are seconds and another is a third—all from Sherra's cohort."

"So they came from behind, then," Father lifted an eyebrow at my explanation.

"Yes, and quite well." I didn't say that Sherra was one of the seconds.

"Who trains them?"

"That's what I'd like to speak with you about," I said. "They came from the Bulldog's group. One of those four is Ura, the troublemaker, as I said before. I don't think Jae and Wend received their training at the Bulldog's hand. I think Sherra taught them what she'd learned."

"That's remarkable," Father breathed. "I can't say that I've heard of such—that another trainee bothered to help her classmates. It could affect the lists, you know."

"I doubt the lists are foremost in Sherra's mind," I said.

The Rose Mark

"We haven't had an escort survive in two centuries," Drenn observed. Not only was he stating the obvious, it dampened Father's enthusiasm for the subject.

"There's something else," I said, pointedly ignoring my brother for a moment.

"What's that?" Father asked.

"There were no washouts in the Bulldog's cohort."

"None? That's unheard of," Drenn snapped.

"It's true," I said, toying with my empty beer glass. "All of them were able to form a sufficient shield."

"There are other trials to come," Drenn said. "We'll see if there are any washouts then."

"What about the Bulldog and her penchant for favoritism? I know you referred to it seven years ago, when you selected Grae from another cohort at the northern camp," Father said.

"It's still there, and perhaps worse than it was before, because it has gone unchecked."

"What do you want to do about it?"

"I want to wait and see how things turn out with Sherra in the group, helping the others. I'm interested to see whether there will be washouts at upcoming trials, or if the class will remain intact. Of course, the Bulldog could ruin my experiment, but I'll be watching carefully as things proceed. Ura will certainly be watched, as will the Bulldog's other pet, Veri."

"Do you have your eye on Sherra as your escort?" Drenn's voice was flat as he posed the question. He meant to get under my skin, one way or another.

I turned to him, then. "I want nothing to do with her death," I stated. "So the answer is no."

* * *

76

Chapter 5

"Perhaps you should reconsider your decision," Hunter began as he and I rode toward the warrior's barracks after dinner.

"What decision?" I asked absently. I was weary and ready enough for my bed.

"Not to take Sherra as your escort. Neither I nor your father wish to see you return again, wounded in body and mind," Hunter informed me. "This girl—Sherra—may be able to protect you better than the others."

"Hmmph. I meant what I said, Hunt. This way, when she dies as they all do, it won't hurt so damn much."

"I see."

I wanted to shout at him—tell him that he didn't see. *Couldn't* see. Couldn't understand. He'd never set foot on a battlefield. Had never watched escort after escort die giving him everything they had to support him in his efforts to turn back an insatiable enemy.

He'd never carried a dead lover in his arms, knowing he'd had a hand in her death. I wanted to bellow that to anyone who could hear me. Instead, I hunched my shoulders and remained silent for the rest of our short trip.

* * *

Sherra

"How long have you been a warrior?" I asked Levi at breakfast the following morning.

He looked at Armon for a moment before answering. "Seventeen years. Armon came along three years later."

I wanted to ask how many escorts they'd had, but Armon's pain-filled eyes and furrowed brow warned against it.

"No morbid thoughts, trainee," Levi gruffed before concentrating on his plate of food.

He was right, but I was filled to the brim with morbid thoughts. How could I not be? When the worst came—as it surely would, I wished to be prepared.

* * *

Kerok

She wanted to ask us about how many escorts died with us, but held it back, Armon's mindspeak interrupted my breakfast with two Colonels and Hunter.

Good. Let's hope she keeps holding it back, I said.

Most escorts had guessed eventually that there would be no sex with either Levi or Armon. Therefore, they often were accepted by the weakest or worst of the trainees. Levi had watched nine die; Armon seven.

"Something wrong?" Hunter asked. I suppose my eyes had unfocused for a moment.

"Just an update from Armon," I shrugged.

"I fully support your decision to demote Captain Merrin to Lieutenant," Colonel Kage said before taking an enormous bite from a piece of buttered bread. He'd been on the battlefield for years before coming to my father's city to train new warriors. The battlefield habit of consuming the most food in the least amount of time had never left him.

"You told him he was responsible for his actions in this?" Colonel Weren repeated a question from an earlier meeting.

"Yes. Ura was on a par with two others. Merrin asked me to select her over the others, to test her mettle. I have his original written request, which you have seen already. As you know, he promised to observe only. Instead, he has engaged in conversation many times, and none of it was official business or the answering of allowed questions."

"It wouldn't be the first time an officer had his eyes dazzled by a trainee," Kage pointed his fork at Weren.

Chapter 5

"Merrin's actions, however, have set him apart in this. He has flaunted his authority before, and don't say he hasn't."

"Who will be elevated to Captain?" Weren nodded and went back to his plate.

"Armon. He can mindspeak, and I find that more than helpful on the battlefield."

"Good enough," Kage said. "I support that decision."

"As do I," Weren agreed. "I will have the letter delivered to Merrin this afternoon. If he isn't expecting it, then he's a bigger fool that I already imagined."

"What will you have the trainees doing for two days?" Kage asked, changing the subject.

"Light drills. Some shielding practice. Armon and Levi already have those orders."

"I'd like to see the one you spoke of," Weren lifted his head so his eyes would meet mine.

"Then come tomorrow. She's still recovering, and I won't allow a testing until then."

"Fair enough."

"Be harsh when you word Merrin's demotion papers," I said, placing authority in my voice.

"Do not fear, Prince Thorn. It will be as you say."

* * *

Sherra

Armon and Levi snapped the drill as I and my fellow trainees marched and turned in a small formation. At least the commands weren't spoken as a belittlement, as they were from the Bulldog.

From the corner of my eye, I caught sight of Commander Kerok, Hunter and two other, older men who joined Levi on the side of our practice ground. Here, we marched on flat, smooth concrete instead of dry grass and sandy dirt. It made a difference in dust accumulation and the occasional sneeze.

Warrior trainees were being drilled not far away; I could hear someone shouting similar commands as they marched and turned.

It made me wonder what their lessons were like, and how they were taught to use their power.

Warriors didn't receive their tattoos until they successfully completed their training, and then something resembling a fireblast was tattooed on an upper arm. It was a verification that he had passed all tests and was capable of combating the enemy in the field.

"Keep up, Sherra," Levi snapped at me. I did as instructed quickly, chastising myself for allowing my thoughts to get in the way.

Stop thinking and let your body take over, Armon mindspoke. *It knows what to do.*

He was right. I shut down my thoughts and let body memory take me through the drills.

* * *

Kerok

Sherra moves gracefully, even when she shifts to catch up, Hunter informed me in mindspeak.

I doubt she cares how she moves, I responded. *How do you feel about Merrin's demotion? You're his uncle, after all.* Hunter wasn't giving up on his mission to pair me with tall, slender Sherra.

And you're his cousin, Hunter retorted. *Merrin's had it coming for a while, don't you think? The last time he got in trouble, he almost revealed your true status to warrior trainees. While his aunt, your Mother-Queen, was alive, he liked to flaunt that, too. It isn't becoming to one of his rank.*

Chapter 5

Drenn will likely be upset about it—it's why I didn't bring it up last night. He and Merrin like to drink together and exchange horror stories about me, you know.

Drenn isn't in charge of the army, and neither is Merrin.

I snorted a laugh at Hunter's unspoken words.

"Would you like to see how the warrior trainees are doing?" Kage asked.

"Yes, Colonel, I would," I replied. Hunter and I turned to follow Kage and Weren away from the smaller practice ground.

* * *

Hunter left after a while, but I watched as trainee after trainee leveled blasts against a brick wall. So far, none had breached it. I didn't expect them too—they were early in their training; practice and focus would eventually hone the abilities of the best of them. Then, they'd learn finesse or they'd wash out.

"Would the Commander join us for lunch in the trainee's mess?" A Sergeant approached and dipped his head to me.

"The Commander would greatly enjoy that," I agreed.

"Fall out," the Sergeant turned smartly and shouted. "Corporal, march them to mess."

Kage, Weren, the Sergeant and I followed the troops, who marched together toward a welcome midday meal.

* * *

Sherra

At least Kerok and his companions didn't stay long to watch us. In such a small group, any mistake would be magnified. Mortification plagued me now, that I was the one shouted at during his presence.

The Rose Mark

I suppose that in the passage of time it would no longer matter, because I would die and be forgotten like so many others before me.

We marched in formation to the trainee's mess, and I was surprised to see that we had a small space set aside in the warrior trainee's mess.

Officers on duty barked at any who were curious enough to look up from their meal as we walked to the line to be served.

"Are those the warrior equivalent to drudges?" Wend whispered beside me as she stared at the men behind the serving line, waiting to assemble our plates of food.

"I don't know," I whispered back. "They don't have their wrists tattooed, like ours do."

"You could ask Levi," she replied as we moved closer. Ura had placed herself at the front of the line, which failed to surprise me. I watched as she took her tray and headed for the two tables reserved for us on one side of the large room.

This trainee's mess hall was built to hold many more than it currently did, and I imagined that the numbers of warriors could be dwindling, just as those of the escorts were.

"I'll ask Levi," I agreed absently. There was a larger problem staring us in the face here, and I surely couldn't be the only one to notice it.

Something wrong, trainee? Kerok's voice entered my mind. He was here, somewhere, I just hadn't seen him among the warrior trainees.

The numbers are down—here and in the escort camp, I said bluntly.

Sherra, I hope I don't have to order you to keep that to yourself, he gruffed back.

82

Chapter 5

Do you think I want to frighten the others? I retorted. *They have enough to be afraid of as it is.*

Wise decision, he fired back. I still hadn't seen him and refused to look as I lifted my tray and strode to one of two tables set aside for us in the warrior's mess.

Ura, sitting at the other table on one end, was unnaturally silent. I wondered at that as Wend pushed the butter plate toward me.

"What's wrong with Ura?" Jae whispered from across the table.

"Huh?"

"She hasn't said more than a few words, today."

"I was grateful for the silence," Caral mumbled before stuffing a chunk of bread in her mouth.

"Why are Armon and Levi sitting at her table?" Neka whispered.

They were—I merely hadn't paid attention as yet, as my mindspoken conversation with Kerok had left me somewhat rattled.

"They usually sit with Sherra," Wend nodded. "At least the food is good—better than what we get at camp."

"This is the King's City. It doesn't surprise me that the rations are better," Jae pointed out.

"Commander Kerok is walking this way," Neka stuttered.

* * *

Kerok

Shortly after my silent conversation with Sherra, a corporal delivered a private, written message to Kage. Kage read it swiftly, then passed it to me.

Colonel Kage, the message began, *blood was found on Captain Merrin's sheets when a drudge came to make up his bed. I called the King's Diviner, who says it is virgin blood.*

83

He then tested the blood itself and has put a name to the woman—trainee Ura. He says Merrin stepped *into the women's barracks and took her away with him, then returned her later. The Diviner is leaving this in your hands as to what you wish to report to the King. Please advise if you need further information—Corporal Carle.*

Sit at Ura's table, I barked mentally at Armon. *Levi, too*, I added. *We have trouble, and she and Merrin are at the bottom of it.*

"Our letter will be revised," Kage stabbed a chunk of meat with his fork.

Fury clouded my mind and almost forced curses past my teeth. I had to wait while those feelings dissipated before I reported the note's contents to Hunter, who would pass them to the King at his earliest opportunity.

With Merrin involved, I sincerely hoped Drenn wouldn't weigh in on the matter, as it could show favoritism, when none was warranted or deserved.

Ura already had demerits. This would exact the worst punishment for her. *Fucking hell* entered my mind—Hunter had replied after taking a few moments to digest the information.

For Hunter to employ profanity meant he was disgusted and likely just as furious as I was.

Ura was a selfish, foolish brat, and Merrin knew better. Did he think to get away with this? Whether the blood was found now or later, Father's Diviner would have been called unless Merrin bothered to clean the sheets himself.

He could have found another woman to satisfy his needs—there were places for that sort of thing.

The rules regarding escort trainees were in place for a reason. Centuries in the past, escorts had allowed warriors they didn't like to be killed, so they could be with another. In my understanding, the laws were changed after several such incidents.

We'd already lost one trainee on this trip. Tossing the napkin on my plate, I stood and made my way toward Ura's table, where Levi and Armon waited for me.

* * *

Sherra

Kerok was clearly furious as he stopped beside Ura, who dropped her fork onto her plate and refused to meet his eyes.

Opposite me, Jae blinked in terror. All of us felt it, somehow; something had happened and trouble was coming.

"Commander," another man joined Kerok. "The Diviner wishes to speak with you in private." The man handed Kerok a note.

I watched as Ura lifted her head, then. Her face had gone quite pale as her eyes met mine. I'd never seen such a look of terror before. In that moment, all her petty jealousy had fled, and she was begging me with her eyes to help her.

I had no idea what she'd done, and, as a trainee, I had no authority to do anything for her.

"Armon, Levi," Kerok barked, "Take this trainee to the lock-up. Kage, take two others and place Merrin in custody. I'll meet with the Diviner at the palace." Kerok *stepped*, then, disappearing from the mess hall.

"Stand," Armon ordered Ura. She stood, visibly trembling.

Caral cursed under her breath—she understood this better than I did. I watched in horrified fascination as Ura was led from the mess hall by Armon and Levi, while the other— Kage—did as Kerok did and *stepped* toward his destination.

The Rose Mark

On the other side, all the warrior trainees had gone silent, leaving a hush that hung heavy in the air. The only sounds heard were the noises coming from the kitchen behind the serving line, where plates and pans were being washed and readied for the next meal.

* * *

Kerok

Father looked gray. He'd already heard from his Chief Diviner, Barth, and Barth's words hadn't sat well with him. I hadn't heard the full story yet, however.

"Drenn was with Merrin last night," Father's labored sigh broke into my stunned silence. Barth stood nearby, his face a mask. He'd brought the previously unreported news to the King—that was obvious.

"I asked him to make the report himself," Father admitted. "I already knew Drenn was out with Merrin last night; I merely had no idea what they were up to."

"Fucking hell," I breathed, repeating Hunter's mindspoken curse. "Barth, was the girl forced or coerced?"

"Not forced, my Prince. She was willing, although an offer of protection was made by both Merrin and Drenn."

"Father?" I turned to him, then. If these acts were committed by any other culprits, the heaviest punishment would be levied. With the Crown Prince's involvement, it was up to the King to place judgment.

"Thorn, my heart is involved in this," Father said.

"What do you say, Barth?" I turned to the Diviner.

"I say that this should remain a matter between father and son, as far as the Prince's involvement goes. As for Merrin, he should take responsibility, as he was the one to do the *stepping* to get Drenn out of the palace to begin with, and to remove the girl from her barracks."

Chapter 5

"Will you speak with Drenn, Father? Whatever Merrin's final punishment, he will be removed as Drenn's enabler." I didn't want Drenn to feign innocence in the matter or escape punishment, but that was Father's decision to make.

I also didn't want to take Drenn's place as Crown Prince. I was happier where I was, instead of being stifled inside a palace covered by a dome.

"I will speak with Drenn, and he will be placed under house arrest until such time as I deem he has been punished enough," Father said. He sounded defeated in this, as if Drenn's punishment was also a punishment to him.

It is, I told myself after a while. This deed would harm Father more than it would ever harm Drenn.

"What punishment for Merrin?" I asked.

"Banishment, after his power is burned out of him," Father mumbled before striding from the room.

Banishment. I couldn't say whether that was a lighter punishment than the swift death that Ura would receive. Where Merrin would end up, there was nothing, and no way for him to escape, once his power was removed.

He would die of thirst and radiation sickness in a matter of days.

"On days like these," Barth admitted, "I desperately hate my talent."

"Truth is a hard thing to deal with, my friend," I told him. "Far better that, than the lies which began the End-War."

Chapter 6

*S*herra
     Execution and banishment. Two sides of the same coin. Ura died at the hands of the King's executioners, in a terrible blast that she had no defense against.

We were not forced to witness it; Armon and Levi told us afterward that it was done. Merrin had been banished to the poisoned lands after his power was removed, where he would die a horrible death.

Armon informed me in mindspeak that Merrin cursed the King's Diviner, the King and the Crown Prince before he was *stepped* away.

The Rose Mark

I had no idea how this affected Kerok; I felt empty and only wished to be left alone. Instead, Wend, Jae and the others crowded about me, feeling lost and confused.

We were two trainees down, now. How had Ura thought she might get away with bedding someone? It was forbidden by law, and the penalty was death. How would the Bulldog react to this news? Would she take her anger out on the rest of us?

"It'll be all right," I lied and wrapped my arms around Wend, who wept silent tears.

Armon had been named Kerok's second-in-command after Merrin's banishment—I had no argument with that. My argument was with the laws, the King, *The Book of the Rose* and the infernal, cursed enemy who forced these things upon us.

* * *

Kerok

"Your command?" Armon ventured to ask after a protracted silence on my part. I sat in an empty office at the Command Center, attempting to force the day's events from my mind.

I'd *stepped* Merrin to the poisoned lands myself. He had no kind words for me before I left.

"Your brother hates you, you know," Merrin had barked a laugh. "Maybe you'll find my bones when he sends you here one day."

"Perhaps I will, but it won't be because I disobeyed the King's laws," I'd snapped before *stepping* back to the Command Center. Merrin was a dead man and he knew it—if I'd stayed longer, he may have bargained for his life.

Chapter 6

I had no desire to listen. He and Drenn were responsible for a trainee's death, and I wouldn't forgive either of them for that.

"Order a night march," I said, rising from my chair. "They won't sleep unless they're exhausted. We'll remedy that."

"I'll see to it." Armon walked out of the office; I watched him go. *I'll come with you*, I mindspoke. *It's only fair.*

* * *

Sherra

"The Commander has ordered a night march," Armon entered our barracks, Levi right behind him. "You have ten minutes to dress properly. Meet Levi outside; he will lead you to the starting point."

"Are we being punished too?" Jae whispered.

"I don't think so," I mumbled. "Get your gear on. We'll get through this."

What followed was a grueling six-hour march, from dusk until the small hours of the following morning. By that time, we'd reached the first of many domed, southern farms outside the King's City.

If I hadn't been exhausted, I'd have asked many questions. As it was, I saw sheep for the first time in my life—while they were sleeping.

There, a truck waited to haul us back to our barracks. Most of us were asleep when we reached that destination.

Only Armon, Levi and Kerok were fully awake during the trip back; all thoughts of the previous day's events had left us, we were so tired.

"Clean up and get in bed," Levi barked at us when we stirred to climb out of the vehicle. "Breakfast will be served at the usual time. Be prepared for drills and exercises afterward."

The Rose Mark

I heard soft grumbling as we walked toward our barracks, shepherded by Levi and Armon. Kerok didn't follow; instead, he *stepped* away, perhaps to his own shower and bed.

* * *

Kerok

We didn't call a halt until more than one had staggered in the march, which took longer than I imagined it would.

There'd been no complaints, either—Levi and Armon kept a close watch on their charges while I marched behind them.

More than once, my eyes strayed to—and stayed on—Sherra. Throughout the long march, her back had remained straight and she never stumbled. By the time Armon called a halt, we were all covered in sweat and dust. I didn't fail to notice that the trainees gathered around Sherra while we waited for our vehicle to arrive to take us back.

If we were lucky, we'd get four hours' sleep before breakfast. My exhaustion was the reason I considered firing a fireblast at my brother, who waited beside Hunter when I returned to my private quarters.

"Father says I have to apologize," Drenn refused to meet my eyes.

I'm not sure I'd ever exploded at Drenn—not like this, anyway.

"Apologize?" I hissed while he hung his head. "Apologize to me?" I thumped my chest. "You should be apologizing to every escort trainee who came here. You killed one of theirs. I don't give a fuck whether she was the worst of the lot—she was a shield for our warriors. A weapon against the enemy. A woman who could mean the difference in whether we stand or fall. Apologize to me? Go and apologize to every warrior and warrior trainee in this city, and on the battlefield, because they may have to wait to get a shield. You crippled us in a way you can never fix, brother. Apologize to me? Fuck you, Drenn. Get out of my quarters and out of my sight."

Hunter only lifted an eyebrow in my direction as he ushered Drenn from my quarters. At that moment, I didn't care if I ever saw my brother again. The laws should apply to him as much as they'd applied to Merrin.

Drenn found himself protected by the privilege of birth.

Fuck that.

* * *

Sherra

Our group was quiet at breakfast. Yes, we were still tired from our night march, but there was an empty space in our company—two actually.

Eight of the ten of us remained. I wondered if Kerok had known that some of us wouldn't be returning to North Camp when he made his selections. Neither he nor the others had warned us of that possibility, but then I'd finally realized that some information was deliberately withheld from us, as if the questions answered were by design and preapproved in some way.

I wanted to ask Kerok about that, but it was a question better kept to myself. He was just as capable at barking in mindspeak as he was aloud.

Everything came back to the *why* for me—the *why* of Merrin's actions, when he knew what the consequences would be.

As for Ura, she knew better, too. The Bulldog had shouted the rules to us on the first day, and on many days afterward, as if she were afraid we'd forget.

Had Merrin done this before? I wondered. *Had he gotten away with it, so he decided to try it again?*

You're thinking too much again, Armon warned in mindspeak. *Finish your breakfast. We have drills to do.*

Dipping my head in a silent nod, I went back to my food.

* * *

Kerok

"I told Kage to come to the training camp in a few weeks if he wanted to see the shielding lessons," I told Armon, who stood beside me at the edge of the training field while Levi called drills for the trainees before the midday meal. "None of them are up for it right now."

"Hmmph," Armon snorted a laugh. "When we started this trip, I thought deaths were the remotest of possibilities."

"Merrin fucked up," I stated baldly.

"I heard from one of the warrior instructors that they're having a hard time stopping rumors among their trainees. They should never have been exposed to even the barest of hints about this sort of thing." Armon shook his head at the worrisome complexity of the situation.

He only had half the story, too. What would happen if they suspected my older brother was shoulder-deep in Merrin's duplicity? That Drenn was just as guilty as Merrin?

I think what bothered me most, however, were the lies they'd told—that they could protect Ura, when nothing was further from the truth.

She'd died for it, and Drenn's hands were just as bloody as Merrin's in the matter. "What will you tell the Bulldog when we get back there tomorrow?" Armon asked.

"I've given it some thought. I think a letter from the King ought to take care of some things, don't you?"

"That would certainly convince me. Do you think Merrin is dead?"

Chapter 6

"Yes—if not now, then soon. He was dead the moment I left him there, and he knew it."

Armon's jaw worked for a moment, as if he wanted to say something else. "Speak your mind, Armon," I said. "It will go no further."

"Do you think he did it before, and thought he could get away with it again?"

"It's possible, and that troubles me a great deal." Armon would never know that I silently included my brother in that answer.

* * *

Sherra

My legs ached when we finished morning drills and marched toward the mess hall for the midday meal. It was a relief just to sit down for a while to eat.

Levi and Armon were showing signs of wear, too, but I didn't mention it. Armon would only say I was thinking too much again.

"Lieutenant, when will we leave tomorrow? To go back to camp?" Wend pointed her question to Levi, who sat at the end of our table.

"After midday meal," Levi replied. "Commander Kerok has appointments in the morning, so we'll leave afterward."

I hunched my shoulders at the news; I wasn't looking forward to seeing the Bulldog again, especially after one of her pets had committed a crime and died for it.

Yes, I thought it unfair. Only the King's black rose trainees and warrior troops were sentenced to death for this crime—civilians could have sex with anyone they wanted, although the usual issue of jealousy often cropped up and caused problems of its own.

The Rose Mark

My mixed feelings on Ura's death plagued me, too. Why did it matter so much that she be virgin when she chose a warrior to protect? As for Merrin, I couldn't think on him without seeing my darkest anger manifest.

He was an officer—a Captain in the King's army. He knew better. He knew what the consequences could be, yet he did it anyway.

He deserved his fate—or worse, in my opinion.

I was staring into space, not seeing anything when Armon rapped on the table next to my plate. It startled me and I let out an involuntary yelp.

Thinking too much, he reminded me. I nodded before scraping potatoes off the plate with my fork and shoving the food in my mouth.

* * *

Kerok

Lilies were scarce this time of year; nevertheless, I'd gathered the few I could find to lay on Grae's resting place in Father's private garden. Only a tiny, blue-flecked lump of granite marked the spot where her ashes lay.

Lilies were Grae's favorite—I'd gifted them to her on her birthdays while she was with me. The rest of her belongings had been returned to her family after her death—I imagined they'd been sold or given to this one or that, as luxuries were hard to come by in most of the villages.

I thought about keeping a few things, but realized it was to assuage my guilt and pile unnecessary expectations onto the one who took Grae's place.

I'd seen all the trainees, and my only decision so far was that Sherra would go to someone else, because I couldn't bear to watch her die.

Chapter 6

"Hunter tells me you spoke plainly to your brother," Father came to stand beside me. "I knew you'd come here before you left today."

"He deserves worse," I pointed out.

"Yes. I just couldn't bear the loss," Father admitted. "Those who know—besides Hunter and my trusted advisor, are standing in this garden. That information will stay where it is."

"Father, there is no need to worry," I sighed. "Drenn's life is safe." *Although it shouldn't be*, I mentally added. "Just don't ever tell me that the girl's life was less important," I snapped when Father opened his mouth to speak.

"I won't." He looked away, as if I'd pointed out a flaw in him. Perhaps I had. He'd never stood on the battlefield, either, or had to worry about protecting as many of our troops as possible.

We had bodies to fight with; the enemy had machines—and the tools and facilities to build more.

My grandfather, when he was still alive, said it was shortsighted on our part to build only farms instead of manufacturing concerns more than six hundred years past. It didn't matter how many times you might wish for things to change in the past; they never would.

"What are you thinking about?" Father interrupted my silence.

"Past mistakes and irrational enemies," I replied. "I must go, Father. Do your best to keep Drenn out of future troubles." I *stepped* away before he could respond.

* * *

Sherra

The Rose Mark

We were *stepped* back to North Camp two hours after the midday meal, and found ourselves in the same place we'd met only a few days earlier for our impromptu mission.

Ura and one other were missing from our group; Captain Merrin and another warrior I didn't know were no longer with the warrior's group.

Across the field, I could see the low building that housed the classrooms. Somewhere inside, no doubt, the Bulldog was presenting her lessons as she usually did, with no idea that one of her pets would never return.

"Wend, Jae, Sherra," Armon joined the three of us. "I have a letter for the Bulldog, from the King. It explains recent events." He pulled the message from a wide, side pocket of his trousers. "I'll walk with you and deliver it personally."

My shoulders sagged in relief; I'd worried that he'd ask one of us to deliver it, which would draw the Bulldog's wrath upon any messenger Armon chose.

Instead, he'd chosen himself for this task, and I was more than grateful. We walked toward the classroom building with Armon, while Caral, Neka and the others followed. I hoped the others would be welcomed back; I held no such hope for myself.

"Wait," Kerok trotted up beside us. "I'll come with you."

I released a heavy sigh. The Bulldog's reaction was unpredictable in this, and even more so after Kerok and Armon left us with her.

* * *

Kerok

The Bulldog's head jerked in our direction the moment Armon knocked on her classroom door.

"Yes?" She sounded short and impatient—until I stepped up beside Armon. Sherra and the others waited to the side of

98

Chapter 6

the door after Armon placed them there. There was no need to announce Ura's absence early to the class. Already, Veri, sitting at the front of the class, craned her neck to look around Armon and me.

"We lost two trainees on the mission," Armon stepped into the classroom. I followed, after motioning for the trainees to come in and take their seats. "One of them, unfortunately, was one of yours," Armon continued. "I have a letter from the King, explaining Ura's death."

Veri's gasp was audible throughout the room—others whispered to their neighbors until the Bulldog barked at them to stay silent.

Armon held out the letter; the Bulldog moved forward to snatch it from his fingers. I cleared my throat—there was no need to be rude to Armon, who'd had nothing to do with any of this.

The Bulldog only knew me as Commander Kerok. Few knew my real name and rank. My father gave her some leeway in his letter. I'd see her dismissed myself if she continued down the path she'd chosen.

I was filled to the brim with my disgust for favoritism, and that started at the top with my brother and fell down the lists, until it landed on Ura and the Bulldog.

"This can't be right," the Bulldog shook the letter at Armon after reading it.

"It is right—the King's Diviner discovered it, and the King enforced the laws in the matter," I answered before Armon could. I wasn't willing to listen to more whining. Not today— or any day in the future.

That's why I chose to address the Bulldog's class while she stood by, fuming in silent disagreement. "Ura will not return to this class—she was executed after it was discovered that she'd had sex with another—an officer among the warriors. He is also dead—left to die in the poisoned lands for his misdeeds."

Trainee's faces went pale as I spoke the truth to them. "It will behoove us all to obey the King's laws and work hard to protect our lands from the enemy. No trainee or warrior will be spared if they run afoul of the rules. The other trainee who did not return perished during an engagement with the enemy. She died with honor beside one of my warriors. She is honored by the King and the death toll has been paid to her village."

Swift glances were exchanged at those words. There were two ways to die, once you were taken into the King's army— with honor, or without.

"See to the proper training of your students," I glared at the Bulldog before stalking from her classroom, Armon right on my heels.

* * *

Sherra

I don't know what else the King wrote in his letter to the Bulldog, but I think something broke in her that day. No, she didn't stop hissing and snarling at me; Wend, Jae and Tera became bigger targets for her malevolency afterward, as if she blamed us for Ura's indiscretion.

Veri certainly blamed us for Ura's death, and made that known to us after classes were over for the day. "This is your fault," she snapped as I strode through the classroom door. She'd waited there for me, instead of heading toward the mess hall to eat, as she should have done.

"Ura did this to herself," Wend hissed at Veri. Jae and I held her back; I imagined she wished to take a swing at Veri for her accusation.

Chapter 6

Veri hadn't been there through any of this. She may have been in pain over a friend's death, but that remained to be seen. Ura had been a compatriot and a fellow pet for the Bulldog, and those two had armed themselves against the rest of us.

Now there was only one to make our lives miserable, and it appeared that she would cover for the loss of the other, by doing twice the damage she normally did.

"Do you know what it's like?" I said, causing Veri to stop as she turned to walk away from us.

"What?" she retorted, as I'd had the temerity—in her mind—to speak to her.

"What it's like to be under fire?" I asked. "To wonder whether you're going to live through the next few minutes, because the enemy's bombs are bursting against your shields and all around you?"

"So?" She began to turn away again.

"You learn how unimportant you really are," I said. "When nobody can save you during those moments except yourself."

Her mouth dropped open for a moment before she shut it and narrowed her eyes at me. "Shut up," she said. "You don't know anything."

Veri almost ran to get away from us, then. I was grateful to watch her leave. The Bulldog wouldn't be on the battlefield cheering her on after she finished her lessons, or to feed her needed information ahead of time.

Veri—like the rest of us, would live or die by her talent and quick thinking. Eventually, like the rest of us, she'd die. The warrior who fought beside her would gain a new black rose and the cycle would begin again.

The Rose Mark

Kerok's mental reprimand came back to me then, after I'd told him there had to be a better way. *Find one and I'll listen*, he'd said.

Would he really listen? I hoped so, because I was now determined to find a better way, with or without help from anyone else.

* * *

After dinner, we walked back to our barracks. I worried that Veri or someone else would sabotage our beds and belongings, but during our absence, sheets and dirty clothing had been gathered, laundered and placed back on our beds.

Drudges had done that for us. Usually we changed the linens ourselves and piled the soiled ones in a cart that was gathered by drudges while we trained and learned.

They'd become almost invisible to us, and I realized that those trainees who'd already washed out had joined their ranks.

Sadness filled my mind, as they could have been taught— I felt it in me as surely as I could feel my heartbeat. If they'd had better teachers other than failed trainees, then perhaps things would be different for them.

A seed of an idea began to form in my mind, but it would require a great deal of thought and stealth if I were to fully consider it as an alternative. In the meantime, I had to deal with the watchful eyes of both Veri and the Bulldog, who'd settled blame on my shoulders for something I had no hand in.

It would also require that I lose my fear concerning a certain talent, if this were to work at all.

Resolving to try it the following evening, I placed the clean uniforms inside my trunk and sat on my bed to consider how things were, and how they might be improved.

Chapter 6

Kerok

"Commander." Armon set a bottle on my desk. After the days away, I was behind on my written records. A drudge had brought my meal and I'd worked while eating.

"What's this?" I looked up at Armon.

"Something Levi and I thought you should have."

I turned the bottle until I could read the label. "Whiskey?" I was surprised.

"We were supposed to be out for a long drive, and weren't really expecting the worst of all possible outcomes from it," Armon said. "Either way, that's yours, now." He turned to leave.

"Armon?" He stopped when I called his name.

"Yes, Commander?" He turned back to face me.

"Thank you. And thank Levi. It is much appreciated."

"You're welcome. Good-night, Commander."

"Sleep well, Captain."

* * *

Sherra

If I thought the Bulldog was bad before, barking at everyone who displeased her, I hadn't considered facing her cold fury.

Only a minimum of commands were given as we went through our morning exercises on the field, after which the Bulldog sat alone in the mess, choosing to cast hate-filled glares at this trainee or that during the meal.

She refused to look in my direction. Somehow, I knew that wasn't a good thing. Following the Bulldog's lead, Veri chose a table not far from our instructor's, and only two others had the courage to sit near her.

103

The Rose Mark

Something was bound to explode in one or both of them; I simply didn't have an idea when it could happen. All I and the others could do in the meantime was struggle to be perfect, lest we face the Bulldog's ire or punishment.

"What are we going to do?" Wend whispered as we walked toward our classroom for afternoon lessons.

She didn't need to say more—I understood she felt the Bulldog's icy anger as well or better than the rest of us.

"I don't know," I replied. I'd been marked before we'd left North Camp to shield vehicles. Upon our return, and with the loss of a pet and the receipt of a letter from the King, things had worsened for all of us.

Except Veri.

The last thing I wanted to do was inform Armon—this was our problem and I didn't want to run to the warriors every time something wasn't going our way. Besides, if the Bulldog found out, heavier punishment would land on our shoulders.

That night, we found out what our punishment would be—a night march.

As if some of us hadn't already had one in less than three days. It galled me, too, that the Bulldog allowed Veri to call the drill as we marched from one training field to another, until two hours before dawn.

I almost didn't see the drudges when we were herded into the showers by a smirking Veri; we'd caught them right as they'd finished cleaning up and doing laundry.

Several I knew were from the current training class, and already their eyes were empty and devoid of hope.

If I'd been more awake, I'd have pondered whether it was worse to die on the battlefield or face the rest of my life as a drudge for the King's army, with no other job than to cook,

Chapter 6

clean and wash, unless you were fortunate enough to act as an instructor.

The why of some drudges acting as instructors still baffled me, and I wanted to ask Armon or Kerok about that. How were they chosen to instruct others—did they have a talent for teaching? If so, I'd never seen it in the Bulldog.

Armon would probably tell me I thought too much and refuse to answer. Kerok would likely bark and refuse to answer.

The Bulldog?

I wished to stay as far away from her as possible. My question would go unanswered, because I was afraid to ask it.

Jae fell asleep at breakfast; Wend woke her so we could march to the field for regular drills.

The Bulldog had crafted her revenge well—more than half of our cohort fell asleep during our midday meal. The master stroke came after that, however, when the Bulldog proceeded to impart necessary information in a monotonous drone during class, where heads were nodding and women struggled to keep eyes open.

There was no talk after the evening meal in our barracks; covers were pulled back and trainees slept with the lights still shining over our heads. I cursed the Bulldog mentally, calling her as many names as I'd learned in my village and from the warriors on our short mission away from camp.

Veri, however, was still smug, and I wondered at how she'd remained awake and alert all day, while the rest of us struggled to do so.

* * *

Kerok

"It helps to have spies here and there, no matter where you are," I said, handing the note to Armon, who sat before my desk. I'd called him in, after asking Levi to guard the door to my temporary office at the training camp.

My father would laugh and call this space rustic. I wondered how he'd view the barracks, which were worse.

Neither he nor Drenn had ever slept in such a place, let alone the barely-covered ground with only a tent over their heads on the battlefield.

"It's no secret about the night march, or that the Bulldog is setting her other pet up to command the rest of her cohort," Armon nodded while he read the note. "Giving a marching draught to a trainee is a violation of the rules, however."

"I figured she'd react in some way to transfer her anger, and a night march is harmless enough," I shrugged. "The other is certainly cause for dismissal."

"Are you planning to do it?"

"At the end of training, because we don't have anyone ready to take the Bulldog's place," I said. "In the meantime, we'll keep watch and wait. I doubt the Bulldog will try anything blatantly against the rules. She's angry and taking it out on her black roses, just as I imagined she would. Hunter is already going through the records, searching for a replacement for next season."

"We have become complacent, haven't we?" Armon asked. "Letting things go, because our numbers are falling. The Bulldog should have been given the boot years ago."

"Yes." I considered Merrin in all that, too. Perhaps I should have asked Father's Diviner to dig deeper into his misdeeds before I left him in the poisoned lands. I blamed myself, too, for being a friend instead of his commander for so many years.

"You're thinking about Merrin, aren't you?" Armon asked.

Chapter 6

"You always have better insight than most," I agreed. "For now, leave me with those thoughts—I haven't finished chastising myself, yet."

"Don't be too harsh on yourself—sometimes we fail to see the owls for the cactus," he said.

He was right. Small owls often nested in the tall, long-needled cactus that dotted the King's lands. Most only saw the cactus and didn't look closer to see the owls that made a home within.

Merrin was a strong and successful warrior; he'd had faults, however, and I'd missed them—or ignored them—far too often in my past.

"We live by a different code, Commander," Armon rose and dipped his head to me. "It isn't difficult to see the necessity of it, most times."

"Thanks for the advice, Captain. Have Levi place one of the others outside my door."

"Yes, Commander."

Chapter 7

*S*herra
"What do you know about the drudges?" I whispered to Wend at breakfast. "Is their power removed when they wash out?"

"I heard that," she dipped her head in a slight nod. "At least with the ones who wash out early. I only got to talk to one of them, while I was in the showers one day."

I felt deflated and defeated, then. My plan was now no plan at all. I needed information and there was nobody with real knowledge instead of hearsay and rumors to answer my questions.

Well, there was one way, although I wasn't anxious to be slapped down and told it was a foolish idea in mindspeak.

"What are you thinking?" Wend hissed at me. I'd stopped eating in favor of staring into space.

"About foolish notions," I admitted and dipped my fork into the pile of beans on my plate.

* * *

More shield training awaited us after breakfast, only this time, it was an exercise as to how quickly we could form and remove a shield.

High on the stands near the parade fields, the warriors had gathered to watch. This was the beginning of our training to raise and lower a shield, to allow a warrior to send a blast before protecting him from falling bombs and shrapnel again.

Yes, it was effective on the battlefield—and exhausting.

I thought it far from efficient, too. There had to be a better way.

"Ow," Jae yelped as the ball the Bulldog hurled hit her squarely in the shoulder before she could reconstruct a shield. Wend, standing beside her, had tossed a ball outward after Jae removed her first shield to allow it through.

The Bulldog had thrown her ball immediately after Wend's, giving a trainee new to the idea no time at all to react.

Surely the warriors on the field could time their blasts better than that.

The rest of our cohort waited our turn to be embarrassed or coddled by the Bulldog in this newest exercise. Here, we played with hard, wooden balls that would leave marks and bruises. On the battlefield, I imagined we'd wish for wooden weapons to hit us instead of rockets carrying explosives.

I doubted the Bulldog had ever come close to those weapons. In that respect, some of her trainees were already more experienced than she would ever be.

Chapter 7

Jae was hit three more times out of the four the Bulldog required before moving on to the next trainees. I waited as patiently as I could while my mind worked furiously on the problem of dealing with incoming and outgoing balls, which represented incoming and outgoing deaths.

Wend's turn came next, and I didn't like the spiteful expression on the Bulldog's face as she prepared to throw. Tera, who was tossing the ball near Wend, looked terrified. The Bulldog hit Wend hard in the chest on the first throw.

* * *

Kerok

We'd watched two other classes deal with raising and lowering shields before the Bulldog's turn arrived. So far, nothing out of the ordinary had happened.

I waited for one particular student, however. How would she deal with this—and how hard would the Bulldog's balls be thrown at her?

In all my forty-five plus years in the army, I'd never seen a trainee not get hit on their first day of this exercise. The instructors knew not to aim for the head; they'd be punished if a trainee came off the field with a head wound. They also knew not to cause serious injury—this was training, after all, and we were supposed to be on the same side.

"The Bulldog is throwing harder and faster at the ones she doesn't like," Armon pointed out. He and Levi sat beside me on the top tier of the stands, watching the exercises on the field.

The other warriors sat below us, assessing the trainees and mentally ticking off names for the lists they'd enter.

This was life or death for them, in actuality. The ability of an escort translated to the warrior's ability to keep his life—unless they were extremely talented or lucky.

111

Armon and Levi were better at many things than Merrin had ever been; therefore, both were still alive. They'd risen in the ranks slower than others, too, because they often received the least talented among the black roses.

Perhaps things would change—for Armon at least. He now held a Captain's rank, and that was often much sought-after.

"Sherra!" The Bulldog's bellow from the field below us tore me from my thoughts.

"Here we go," Levi breathed from his seat beside Armon.

Sherra stepped forward; the one called Misten moved forward with her. Misten would toss the ball outside Sherra's shield area when Sherra lowered her shield.

The Bulldog intended to hit Sherra on the first try—I could see the determined set to her shoulders as she gripped the ball she held tightly.

"What's she doing?" Armon asked as Sherra took the ball from Misten for a moment, handling it as if it were on fire before passing it back to Misten, touching Misten's hand as she did so.

"No idea," Levi shrugged in reply.

I had no comment; I was just as mystified as Armon by Sherra's actions.

"Place your shield," the Bulldog barked.

"The shield is up," Sherra replied, just like the others before her.

"Throw the ball, Misten," the Bulldog shouted.

As expected, the Bulldog launched her ball at the same moment Misten did. Misten's ball sailed high—clearing Sherra's shield space easily and landing near the edge of the practice field fence.

Chapter 7

The Bulldog's ball hit Sherra's shield so hard it bounced far past Misten's, landing in another cohort's practice space. "I'll be damned," Armon breathed beside me before standing to get a better look.

"They crossed the line in midair—I swear it," Levi said. "The balls crossed the line at the same time."

"Wait for the next attempt," I said, motioning for Armon to sit. "It's probably coincidence and nothing more."

"Yeah." Armon sat heavily beside me, keeping his eyes on the field as if he were afraid of blinking.

"She's handling the second ball," Levi said as Sherra lifted it from Misten's hands. That's when I knew something was happening during that step. I merely had no idea what it could be.

"Armon, if she does the same thing all four times, then I want a word with her—and Misten—when this is over."

"Of course, Commander. I'll *step* to the field afterward and inform the Bulldog."

* * *

Sherra

My shield recognized itself—that's what I intended. I'd had no idea whether it would work when the Bulldog called my name. It was a hasty plan, as I had no doubt that the Bulldog would attempt to harm me with one or more of the balls she hurled in my direction.

In between, I passed hasty mindspeak to Misten, who would be up next. The Bulldog would hit any of us she could, because she hated me and anyone associated with me.

She'd already put bruises on Wend's chest—I knew that when Wend walked back to the other trainees, one arm crossed over her heart.

"Instructor," someone shouted behind me.

The Rose Mark

I turned swiftly to see that Wend was on the ground—and turning blue.

"No!" I ran toward her, even as Commander Kerok appeared on the field with Levi and Armon right behind him.

Wend's shirt was torn open, revealing a spreading, purple bruise over her heart where the Bulldog hit her.

"She's not breathing," Jae wept as Kerok knelt beside her, shoving the remnants of her shirt aside. With Levi's and Armon's hands on his shoulders, Kerok's hands filled with light and power before he released it into Wend's body.

Her body jerked upward immediately, while she coughed and gasped for breath. That's when the Bulldog walked up, casually asking if there were anything she could do.

"You're done," Kerok rose to his feet and hissed at the Bulldog. "I've had enough of this. You'll receive your dismissal papers from the King this afternoon. Your trainees will be portioned out to the other instructors—I'll see to it myself."

"It was a stray blow," the Bulldog snapped at him. Kerok took a step toward her—and then another.

The Bulldog quailed before his fury. "Go to your quarters and wait there. Do not go anywhere else or speak to anyone else. Is that clear? A list of all the charges against you will be given to the King. Perhaps, if you're lucky, you'll be serving on one of the farms for the rest of your days. You have no business training black roses. Go now, before I do worse than vent my anger."

The only one who wept as the Bulldog walked away from us was Veri, and none attempted to comfort her.

"Sherra," Kerok turned toward me, then. "Armon will come for you and some of the others tonight. You will be questioned in this—for the official record, you understand. Armon, see that Wend is taken to the infirmary. Levi, take

Chapter 7

these trainees back to their barracks, and I'll determine who goes to which cohort by dinner tonight."

"Yes, Commander."

"Wend?" I knelt beside her before Armon could lift her up. "Are you all right?"

"I just—my heart wouldn't beat like it should," she whispered.

"The physician will take care of you," I said.

"Why don't you help me take her to the infirmary?" Armon asked. "I can get you to the barracks afterward."

"I will," I said. Together, Armon and I lifted Wend to her feet. Armon then *stepped* us to the infirmary on the far side of the training fields.

* * *

"Bad bruise—very bad," the physician shook his head after leaving Wend's bedside and coming to speak with us. "I'll have someone at her bedside through the rest of today and tomorrow, too. They'll be ready to give compressions if her heart stops again."

"It shouldn't have stopped to begin with," Armon said.

"I've said for years that those balls should be softer—these are first-timers and that should be taken into consideration," the physician observed.

"I'll ask the Commander about it," Armon said. "Send a message if anything changes."

"I will. Go now—she needs rest, I think."

Armon jerked his head toward the door. I followed him out of the infirmary. "Tell the Commander that I—am grateful—for Wend's life," I said.

"I think that makes two of us," Armon agreed and *stepped* me to the barracks.

* * *

The Rose Mark

Kerok

"We have five cohorts and twenty-three women," I said, tapping the paper on my desk. "I'd like to keep Sherra, Misten, Tera, Jae and Wend together," I added.

"Then look at one of the cohorts that lost the most in washouts," Armon suggested.

"I am. Fourth lost three, Second lost six."

"Second it is," Armon began.

"Hear me out on this," I said, holding up a hand. "I think those five should go to Fourth."

"Why?"

"That's Caral's cohort. Caral has already formed something of a bond with Jae, Wend and Sherra. I think that would mean they'd be more welcome there."

"Possibly," Armon agreed. "It wouldn't go amiss to see a friendly face."

"Besides, Lilya is a decent instructor, and fair in her treatment," I pointed out.

"Something those girls haven't seen much of as yet," Armon nodded.

"As for the others, I say we send six to Second, that makes eleven of the twenty-three.

"We could send four each to the other three cohorts, and that will take care of the rest," Armon suggested.

"Good enough," I began writing names onto cohort rosters. "I'll write notes for the instructors, and the trainees will join their groups in the morning. Wend will have to join them later—the physician wants to keep her under observation for three days."

"What the bloody fuck did she think she was doing?" Armon asked, meaning the Bulldog.

Chapter 7

"Taking revenge for perceived slights and mistreatments," I said. "It's moot, now—Hunter is sending someone after dinner to take her to the potato farms. If she misbehaves there, it'll mean banishment, I think."

"I suppose she'll have to mind her manners, then," Armon shrugged.

"Couldn't happen to someone more deserving," I said. He chuckled.

* * *

Sherra

"Shut up, Veri," one of the firsts—Hayla—snapped. Veri had spent much of the afternoon sniffling and bemoaning the fact that the Bulldog had been taken away from us.

"She didn't deserve," Veri began.

"She deserved it and more, or did you not notice she almost killed one of us?" Hayla snorted.

"What's going to happen now?" Veri's eyes filled with fresh tears. I'd had enough of her antics and chose to sit on my cot, which was far away from hers. If Kerok hadn't come with Armon and Levi, we'd be mourning Wend's death instead of wondering what would happen to us after the Bulldog's removal.

"I figure we'll be parceled out to the other cohorts—they all had washouts," someone else spoke up.

That was my assessment as well, so I remained silent. My hope was to see a friendly face when I arrived at my new destination. It could be too much to hope that those faces would belong to either Caral or Neka, but a familiar one would be nice.

I also hoped that Wend and Jae, at the very least, would end up in the same cohort, but that was wishful thinking and usually stayed within that imaginary realm.

117

"I think we'll receive our new assignments at dinner," Hayla spoke again. "Probably be sent to them in the morning, after breakfast. Our training will continue, just under a different instructor."

"Fall out for the mess hall," Levi walked inside our barracks and announced. Here it was—time to learn what news there was over a meal, and then go for questioning with the Commander.

It reminded me of something Pottles used to say—*ain't life a bitch, sometimes?*

* * *

"You four and Wend will go to Fourth," Armon said. Jae, Misten, Tera and I sat at our usual table in the mess hall, but were only picking at our dinner, for the most part.

My breath caught. "That's Caral's cohort," I stuttered after a moment's consideration.

"Yes it is. Mind your manners and obey Instructor Lilya's commands."

"Yes, Captain," we chorused as he left to go to the next table over.

"Oh, my gosh, Wend will be so happy." Jae looked as if she'd been given the best gift ever, her smile was so wide.

"Who is Caral?" Misten asked.

"One of the trainees who went with us on our mission," Jae explained. "She decked Ura for trying to hurt Sherra."

"Does this mean that Ura was already in trouble before she ah," Misten didn't continue.

"She received seven demerits, putting her on the last list," Jae shrugged. "The other thing she did was so—disturbing— that we sort of left that part out."

"What about Caral?" Tera asked. "If she hit Ura."

Chapter 7

"Five demerits," I said. "Ura received the same—until she tried to hit Caral in front of Commander Kerok. She got two more demerits for that."

"Damn," Misten whispered.

"Did you just curse?" Tera grinned at Misten.

"I guess I did," she laughed.

* * *

Kerok

"I'm not going to ask you about the Bulldog," I told Sherra when she took a seat in front of my desk. "I've heard the same story from eleven of twelve trainees already, and one of the twelve, as you've likely guessed, was Veri."

She blinked at me in surprise, curiosity evident in eyes that were as dark as her hair.

"What I want to ask you about instead, is what you were doing on the training field today. I've never seen a trainee react that fast the first time a projectile is lobbed their way."

"It wasn't a reaction." Sherra hung her head.

"What was it, then?"

"Cheating."

I sat back in my seat, feeling dumbfounded. "You cheated? I find that difficult to believe. How did you cheat?"

"I placed a shield around the balls Misten picked up. My outer shield will recognize another of my shields, thinking it's a part of it—or so I hoped. That's why Misten's shielded ball sailed right through, while the real shield never fell. The Bulldog's ball couldn't get through and wouldn't ever get through."

My stunned silence was so long Sherra shifted uncomfortably in her seat. She thought she was in trouble. Nothing could be further from the truth.

"I have another question," I said after clearing my throat. Sherra lifted her head; her face was as pale as I'd ever seen it, and I'd seen her exhausted before.

"What's your question?" she asked.

"Do you think you could do the same thing with a warrior's blast—they start out small, you know, and grow larger the nearer they come to the target."

"I don't know—perhaps if I touched him to feel the fire he holds."

"Would you attempt that with Armon while I watch tomorrow morning—before breakfast?"

"If that's what you want."

"His blasts will be little more than weak fire—I don't want either of you toasted in front of me," I frowned.

"That's fine," she agreed. "It's worth a try, I suppose."

"Good. Armon will arrive shortly after dawn, and we'll see what you can do. You're dismissed."

"Commander, I have a question," she said, hesitation in her voice. She worried I wouldn't hear her out.

"Go ahead," I told her.

"The uh, washouts? Has their power been removed? I know they're acting as drudges now, but," she didn't finish.

"Their power will be removed at the end of training, when the Diviners come to do their final assessment of the trainees."

"I have a request." She'd sat up straighter, and a hopeful gleam appeared in her eyes.

"What's that?"

"I want to train them," she said. "Please. You're down several already. What if I can get them where they need to be? Will you reverse their status?"

Chapter 7

I drew in a breath. Here was proof of what I'd thought before—she had been teaching the seconds and thirds in the Bulldog's group. There were no washouts as a result.

Leaning over, I pulled a folder from a bottom drawer of my desk. "This," I tapped the folder after setting it on my desk, "is the list of washouts. I'll give you two hours every afternoon for three weeks to bring them up to speed on what they've missed. Anyone not able to form a sufficient shield will be kept where they are. Anyone who succeeds—I'll change their status myself—after their testing, of course."

"Thank you."

I'd never seen someone near tears from happiness before.

"Do what you can—this is an experiment only. Will you need assistance? If so, I give permission to select up to six other trainees to help you. Armon and Levi will be in charge of your group and report to me regularly. Now you're dismissed."

"Commander," she said, her voice hushed as she rose from the chair. "I've never been so happy in my life."

* * *

Sherra

"What happened?" Jae demanded as I joined her and the others who waited outside Kerok's office. I was wiping tears away, and she probably thought I'd been upset by his questioning.

"I'm not upset," I held up a hand. "I'll tell you later, all right?"

"All right."

"Commander Kerok says he has all he needs, so Levi and I will *step* you back to your barracks. Sleep well, and do well in your new assignments, trainees," Armon said when he appeared in the doorway.

The Rose Mark

Kerok had mindspoken Armon, I'm sure, because he'd *stepped* from wherever he'd been to take us to our old barracks—for the last time. The following evening, we'd be sleeping elsewhere.

* * *

Dawn had barely reached the eastern horizon when Armon arrived at the barracks in the morning. I dressed quickly and followed him out the door—some of the others were still sleeping.

He *stepped* me to the farthest point of the training camp, where rock-covered mountains loomed around the small lake that supplied our water.

Kerok and Levi were already there, waiting for us.

"Now," Armon said, "I realize you're barely awake, but what is this you need to do to get in touch with my fire?"

"I just need to touch your fingers," I said. "It's not invasive or painful—it's how I could tell that Wend and the others had their fire to begin with."

"Ah," he said. "My hands, you say?" He held them out to me. I came forward and gripped his fingers, gasping at the amount of fire contained within him. Closing my eyes, I ventured further into his power, attempting to get a feel for it so I'd recognize it—and my shields would recognize it.

After a while, I nodded, dropped his hands and opened my eyes. "You have amazing fire, Captain," I informed him. "I think I have its feel, now."

"Then shall we?" I seldom saw Armon smile. He was smiling, now.

"Remember, only a little," I cautioned. "I don't like burns."

"Only a little," he agreed.

122

Chapter 7

"I'm forming my shield," I said. "All right, it's up. Fire your blast, Captain, and good luck to both of us."

* * *

Kerok

That morning, I felt as if I were seeing into the future. Levi stood nearby, ready to fire a blast at Sherra's shield, should Armon's get through it.

Armon's weak fireball sailed straight through, as if nothing were there.

Levi's blast splattered into thousands of sparks against the shield—it hadn't recognized his fire.

"Try it again," I said. "Stronger, this time."

I watched with hope in my heart as the same results occurred six more times, with stronger blasts each time.

This experiment would be continued each morning, until I felt confident enough to inform my father. I desperately wanted to celebrate, but it was far too early for that.

* * *

Sherra

"Are you joking? He's going to let us try?" Jae's eyes were round with wonder as I told her and the others at breakfast what we were about to attempt—training washouts so they'd have a chance to catch up with the others.

"We have three weeks to get them to the shielding exercises," I said. "They'll be tested just as we were."

"What if we fail?"

"This is an experiment," I reminded her. "If we fail, then we fail, and nothing changes. I'm trying to make a change," I said, lowering my voice. "Have you not noticed that our numbers are down? We can't afford to lose anybody who's talented—unless we want to die at the enemy's hand."

"Some will say that this will dilute the lists," Misten pointed out.

"Fuck the lists," I hissed. "Lives are on the line—your villages are on the line. They can't protect themselves. That's up to us."

"True," Tera agreed. "I don't mind, actually. I think it's fair."

"Did you curse?" Misten's dimple appeared in her left cheek.

"I believe I did," I replied.

* * *

Kerok

"How are you doing today?" I asked Wend. I'd found her sitting up in bed having breakfast when I arrive.

"Better. I was really scared, Commander. My heart started beating strangely, and the more scared I got, the worse it became."

"A hard blow to the chest can cause that," I agreed, pulling up the chair at her bedside. "The Bulldog has been sent to the potato farms for harming a trainee."

"What does that mean?" She dropped her eyes and picked at her eggs.

"It means I've sent the others from the Bulldog's cohort to other cohorts. I've portioned them out as best I can."

"Where will I go?" she asked, refusing to meet my gaze.

"To Fourth. With Sherra, Misten, Tera and Jae."

Her head popped up, then, and she stared at me in surprise. "I—thank you."

"Not to worry. I'm hoping the rest of this training period will go smoothly. Oh," I continued, "Don't be surprised if you're added to a special project that will take place during the next three weeks."

Chapter 7

"Special project?"

"Sherra can tell you—she knows more about it than I do." I gave her a smile and rose from my seat. "Heal quickly, trainee. The others are waiting for you to join them."

* * *

Kerok? Hunter's voice came to me the moment I settled at my desk. I had communications from the Colonels on the battlefield to attend to, so breakfast would be eaten in my office.

Hunt? I replied. I hadn't missed the tinge of worry in his voice.

That woman—the Bulldog? She escaped last night. They're searching for her, now. If she's caught, she'll be banished unless someone speaks for her.

Foolish bitch, I responded. *No second chances, Hunt. She almost killed a trainee yesterday, and I'm done with this. Relay my thoughts in the matter to Father.*

I will. We have to find her first, though.

Keep me informed.

Of course, my Prince.

* * *

Sherra

Lilya was an opposite to the Bulldog in many ways. Yes, she expected her commands to be followed, and she was strict about the rules, but there the similarities ended. Every trainee was treated the same as we went through shielding exercises similar to those we'd had the day before. Balls were thrown, always aiming for arms or thighs. Some would have bruises, but not dark ones.

This I could live with, although the Commander had told Lilya already what was expected from me in this.

125

"Show me what the Commander saw yesterday," Lilya commanded. She was taller and thinner than the Bulldog, and her pale hair was forced into a topknot on her head so it wouldn't blow into her face.

"Yes, Lady," I dipped my head to her. The trainee beside me wasn't someone I knew as yet, but she handed the ball to me when I asked. The other trainees gasped when her ball sailed through my shield while Lilya's hit and bounced away.

"Trainee," Lilya said after the third time, "Do you think you can show the others here how you did that?"

"I can try," I replied.

"Good. Everyone, line up for your turn with trainee Sherra."

* * *

"Good to see you again," Caral spoke in a low voice as she came forward. So far, half the trainees had been successful in their lesson with me. Some laughed with joy when their shield held against Lilya's balls while allowing their partner's to fly through it.

The others were anxious to try again—I could see it in the set determination in their faces. Lilya was more than pleased; it was obvious. We only stopped our practice to march to the mess for our midday meal, before going back and trying it again.

What I was looking forward to the most, however, was getting away two hours before the evening meal, where the washouts would be brought to me by Armon and Levi.

"Come with me," I invited Caral as Jae, Misten, Tera and I gathered for our special assignment. "Commander Kerok said I could have as many as six assistants."

"For what?"

Chapter 7

"We're going to train the washouts," Jae almost bounced with happiness.

"What?" Caral blinked at me in confusion.

"Come on—we have to be there in a few minutes. I don't want to be late on my first day."

We headed toward the classroom building, and found fourteen trainees waiting for us there. Two had been unable to make fire at the beginning.

Levi and Armon took seats at the back of the classroom to watch.

"What are your names?" I approached the two who'd failed at making fire.

"Bela," one told me.

"Reena," the other replied.

"All right. Reena, I'm going to touch your fingers first," I said, reaching out to take her hands. She had fire—the Diviner had seen it in all of them eighteen years ago.

"You have fire," I smiled at her. "Now, I'm going to tell you how to show it to the rest of us."

Chapter 8

*K*erok
     "It took her less than five minutes to coax fire into two girls' palms," Armon reported. "As if it were the most natural thing in the world. They cried, they were so happy."

"What about the other twelve?" I asked, leaning back in my chair.

"Caral worked with Sherra, to get a feel for what they were doing. Jae and Sherra's other assistants were already working with the shielding washouts on how to form effective shields. If things continue to go this well, you'll have fourteen trainees to add back to the cohorts."

"This—is remarkable," I said. "I never thought it possible, either. I have a report from Lilya after today's training. She says more than half of her cohort can do what Sherra can, after Sherra showed them how."

"That woman is a genius, and I think she has a touch of a Diviner's talent," Armon said. "She told me I had amazing fire after she took my hands."

"Why didn't the Diviner see that in the beginning?" I asked, leaning forward and resting my elbows on the desk.

"I doubt he was looking for it," Armon suggested.

"You could be right, although I've never seen her do anything other than what she did with you and those other trainees, which is see their fire. A Diviner can do so much more than that."

"Very true," Armon grinned. "Is there anything else, Commander? We've had a long day."

"Go to bed, Armon. I'll see you, Sherra and Levi on the field near the lake tomorrow morning."

"What if this changes everything on the battlefield?" Armon asked softly.

"Let's pray that it does. With our dwindling numbers, it's only a matter of time before Az-ca falls."

"I know your father stopped recording population numbers twenty-five years ago," Armon began. Yes, he knew who my father was, as did Levi.

"I know. I argued with him about it, but he and Drenn thought it a waste of time. At least Drenn did. I think Father became discouraged at falling numbers and preferred to shut it out of his mind. The Council went along with his idea, of course, and the laws recording births and deaths vanished overnight."

"No disrespect meant, but the Council is worthless," Armon said.

Chapter 8

"None taken, and I agree. Drenn leads them by the nose in most cases, because they're afraid of losing their position with all the benefits it entails. The next time they want to argue about warrior and escort pay, I want to haul all of them to the battlefield and let them see what really happens there."

"They'll never go—or if they do, they'll deny their own eyes," Armon snorted.

"You're right. It happens more often than not. There's not one among them I'd trust with three-day-old bread."

"At least I haven't been forced to witness it first-hand," Armon breathed a sigh. "You have my sympathies in the matter."

"It's a bag of mixed frustrations," I admitted. "I've never considered any part of it enjoyable. At least there are decent times to be had on the battlefield—between battles."

Armon laughed, which is what I intended. "Go to your bed, Captain. I'll see you in the morning."

* * *

Sherra

Wend joined us after the fourth day, and after two full weeks of training washouts, some were capable enough to pass the initial shielding tests, and getting better every day. Bela and Reena were also doing well, once things were explained well enough.

In between, Caral, who had a very good memory, taught them the classwork they'd missed after washing out the first week at camp. It was evident that they'd needed specialized attention, rather than an expectation that they automatically do what they'd never attempted before.

Levi and Armon were especially pleased, and carried reports to Kerok every day unless I missed my guess. So far, there'd been no orders to stop what we were doing, so I went

131

on, determined to get Bela and Reena ready for the shielding test.

As for the experiments with my shielding technique— those went on every morning, and Armon's and Levi's blasts were getting stronger against my shield. Kerok gave orders and took notes during these early training periods, while I performed the tasks set before me, including swift blasts from Levi and Armon.

Without my connection to Armon's fire, we'd both be dead by now, with the strength of the blasts Kerok requested.

I was grateful, too, that we did these exercises before breakfast, as sitting down for a meal allowed me some rest while I ate and readied myself for the next training periods.

Not only were we working on strengthening our shields and making our shield construction times shorter, we were expected to pass a final exam with the warriors lobbing heavy fire in our direction.

In other words, we were training for two different types of tests at the end—the old way and the new way. And, as I worked with Armon and Levi every day, I learned something about how their blasts were constructed, and how they'd hit against a shield once they reached it. I was hoping to learn more about bombs and how they hit, too, once I reached the battlefield.

"I think the problem is that you're imagining your shield as a thin barrier," I told one of the washouts later in the afternoon. "It's invisible, no matter how thick it is. The bombs the enemy sends will have no mercy when they hit. Make your shield thick and impermeable."

"You've seen bombs?"

Chapter 8

"She went with me on the Commander's assignment," Caral said. "We found ourselves directly in the line of fire. If Sherra hadn't shielded us at the last, we'd all be dead."

The trainee's eyes grew round as she blinked at us. "It was nothing," I brushed it off. "I want you to stay alive, and a thick shield is the way to do that. All right?"

"Yes. All right," she nodded, her words breathless. "I'll try again."

"Levi?" I turned back to him—he'd been lobbing weak blasts at this one while Armon supervised.

"I'm ready," he grinned and lobbed a blast at the trainee. It exploded against a better-constructed shield.

"That's it," Caral crowed. "Exactly. Keep it up."

The trainee laughed and put up another shield when I asked.

* * *

Kerok

"Three weeks left," Armon took his usual seat in front of my desk. "Next week, we test the washouts. Do you think they'll be ready for final testing when training is over?"

"Some of them," I said, consulting the progress chart I'd been keeping after Armon's daily reports. "Perhaps we can send the two early washouts through the next training class, so they'll be better prepared."

"That's actually a good idea," Armon nodded. "I can tell they're getting nervous about being behind all the others, when they'd be ready, I think, if their training hadn't ended the first week they were here."

"I think the same. I'll send messages to Father, asking for this allowance, and perhaps the same for future classes. These two—perhaps they can pass on to new trainees how to find their fire."

133

"Tutors. An excellent idea," Armon agreed. "Will your Father see it that way?"

"If he wants our numbers to increase so we're able to turn back the enemy. I'm going to suggest that we try it for the warrior trainees, too. Perhaps some of them only need more time. We have enough cooks and latrine diggers on the battlefield already. We need more warriors and escorts."

"Any news on the Bulldog?"

"She hasn't been captured—or seen by anyone," I said. "My guess is she went outside the domes thinking to escape, and fell victim to either her own foolishness or to wild animals."

"Not a good way to die, either way," Armon shook his head. "She'd be better off digging potatoes."

"I worry that she'll have revenge on her mind if she survives," I said. "I've informed Hunter that this one could cost us all if she isn't found—dead or alive."

"No village will take her in—not with that block of ink on her wrist. They'll turn her over to the King's guards for the promised fee."

"I'm sure she knows that," Armon agreed. "But I'm not sure she can survive in the wild very long, either."

"I trust Hunter to keep a watchful eye, and to keep me informed."

"Have you approached Kage and Weren about the new techniques?"

"Yes. They're coming to witness the testing, and we'll show them then. We are cautiously optimistic about this."

"Will we retrain the escorts on the battlefield if the King approves?"

"That's my hope—with Sherra's new method, the escort trainees don't tire so quickly. They're able to preserve their

Chapter 8

strength by maintaining a constant shield, instead of raising and lowering it between blasts."

"Already, the trainees are preferring the new method, as they don't exhaust themselves with constant raising and lowering. The men who've worked with them prefer the new method, too."

"As do I. I'm hoping for clear approval from the King when he arrives to witness the trials with Kage and Weren."

"He's coming himself?"

"Barth and Hunter will also come—Barth will act as our Diviner at the end."

"Barth is a good man."

"Yes, he is."

"The lists will be coming to the warriors soon," Armon reminded me. I'd chosen to ignore it, as I had no clear choice in my mind. Who I wanted at my side and who would end up there were two different people.

"Who will get your name, Captain?" I asked.

"You know, I usually put my name on all of them, as does Levi. This time, I may be more selective. Veri's list will certainly not carry my name."

"Will Sherra's list have your name?"

"And Levi's. We've never seen anything like her, before. Caral, too—and Wend, Jae, Misten and Tera. As far as Levi and I are concerned, they may be the best of the lot."

"Then I hope you get one of them," I grinned at Armon. "It is deserved."

"We worry about the other thing, though," Armon shifted uncomfortably.

"Ah. The other thing—yes. I suppose they'd want sex or love—in some measure."

"We can love them—but not in the ways they may want," Armon admitted. "Sex is out of the question."

"I understand. This has been a conundrum for others, you know. I've asked Father many times to bend his thoughts in that direction, but he always avoids the discussion, much like he avoids the discussions of a breeding program."

"I dislike that idea," Armon said.

"As do I, but Drenn and the Council think it a good one. They believe it will solve all our problems. If that were the case, they should have started it twenty years ago, because the first crop would come of age this year," I huffed. "The whole thing disgusts me and I've told Father that. Doing it now will only be a patch over a sinkhole that is rapidly disappearing into the ground. Eventually, our lack of numbers may destroy all of us."

"I know. I don't speak of these things because I don't want the rumors to start."

"Sherra's noticed it," I huffed. "I told her to keep it to herself."

"That doesn't surprise me—that she'd notice. I tell her fairly often that she thinks too much, but mostly it's an attempt to keep her from asking forbidden questions."

"I know. Look—in a week, we'll have lists. I'll make a decision then."

"Kerok, listen to me. There's one clear choice for you in this, and if I don't miss my guess, your father and uncle have already pointed it out to you. In this, I say follow their advice. None of us want our Commander falling on the battlefield. You have deep scars, in case you didn't know it already, from the last time. Levi and I loved Grae almost as much as you did, and her death was a heavy blow. Don't allow your grief to override your good sense." Armon's face was stern and set.

Chapter 8

"You've heard from Hunter, haven't you?" I frowned at him.

"What if I have? He can mindspeak; I can mindspeak. In this, we agree. Put your name on Sherra's list."

"Armon, I don't have any desire to carry the body of someone I love off the battlefield again."

"There are times," Armon said gently, "When I can't help but wonder if I'd even be able to walk if Levi fell. Still, we go out to the battlefield and do what we were trained to do with the best the lists will hand us. Don't handicap yourself, Commander. Without your steady hand, the King's army could fail—and sooner than you imagine it might."

"Your concern is noted, Captain," I snapped. "My decision on this particular matter is closed. You're dismissed."

"As you say, Commander." Armon turned on his heel and stalked out the door.

* * *

Sherra

Neka and most of First Cohort were pleased to see Fourth Cohort join them for training. Veri was there and bursting with jealousy and hatred—it was easy to read her thoughts in this.

Hayla, however, was more than happy to see those of us from her former Sixth Cohort, and bounced with happiness until Nina, their instructor, told them to settle down and move into formation.

We'd be marching to First's training field to work together. I and the others who worked with me would be showing them the new method of shielding.

That meant Armon and Levi were with us—to toss blasts at our shields. I'd heard them talking softly together behind us as Lilya marched us toward First, who were waiting for our arrival. Only a few of their words were understandable, as they'd hung farther back than they normally did to have their conversation.

"He has to make the proper decision," Armon hissed at Levi. Levi's response was unintelligible. Then, "Hunter says," came from Armon, before his voice dropped away again.

Hunter. Kerok's friend and an advisor to the King. What would he have to do with any of this? Perhaps they were discussing the new method we were teaching, and whether it was effective enough. The King would have to approve it—Armon told me as much.

The new method would save and prolong lives—I was sure of it. Without the King's approval, however, we'd go back to the old, exhausting way, which would surely cost us precious lives.

In this matter, all I could do was the best I knew how to do, and hope it would be enough. Levi and Armon were already believers; but they weren't the King. Squaring my shoulders, I waited for Lilya to call me forward. Neka and Hayla wanted what I could teach them.

Veri wanted nothing to do with me.

I waited to see how our day would go.

* * *

"She should have gotten demerits," Wend said while we ate our midday meal. "Acting like she didn't understand and almost frying Levi? That's not only stupid, it's dangerous."

"If Sherra hadn't shielded him," Jae shook her head.

Our topic of discussion was Veri, and how she'd intentionally botched her first few attempts at the new method. The moment Nina screamed at her after I'd shielded Levi from his own, ricocheting blast, Veri had straightened up and performed to expectations, like the others in her cohort.

Chapter 8

"She's going to kill somebody, mark my words," Caral said before biting into a buttered roll. "Out of stupidity and a thirst for revenge."

"She needs to learn that she's not as special as she thinks," Misten said. "The Bulldog didn't curb her jealousy, either, like she should have."

"At least Nina doesn't think Veri's so special," Wend agreed. "Did you see how embarrassed she was when Nina pointed out that she was the worst in the class after she almost fried Levi?"

"Levi's a friend, and doesn't deserve that treatment from anybody," Caral sighed. "Armon, too."

Captain? I sent mindspeak to Armon after taking a few moments to consider Caral's words.

What is it, trainee?

Put your name on Caral's list—and tell Levi to do the same.

We're not supposed to be discussing these things with escort trainees, he pointed out. *It's against the rules.*

Then forget I mentioned it.

Mentioned what?

Thank you, Captain.

Your thanks are noted, trainee.

"I think the lists will go to the warriors soon," Tera whispered after hunching down so other tables wouldn't hear.

"The final decisions won't be made until the day of the trials, when we'll be ranked into groups. The best students will be in First group, the worst in Fifth, since Sixth was disbanded. The warriors who are chosen by First group will be struck from the remaining groups' lists," Caral said. "Lilya says the warriors consider it a token of honor to be chosen by

139

First group. I'm already in Fifth group," she added. "I think all of you will have better choices coming your way."

"You may be surprised," I patted her shoulder. "Just don't let it bother you, all right? I will never forget the sight of you punching Ura in the face—it was very satisfying at the time."

"I don't regret it," she said and ducked her head to hide a smile.

* * *

"You'll be learning how to angle your shields, beginning today," Armon informed me after stepping both of us to the farthest training field. "Instead of repelling what's thrown at you, you'll be adjusting your shield to softly catch and cushion it, before forcing it away. Like catching an egg without breaking it, and then tossing it before it explodes in your face."

"We'll be manipulating what we make—interesting," I breathed. This bore thinking about.

"And that's why we want to try something new today," Kerok, who'd *stepped* in beside us, announced.

"What are we going to try?" I asked. Yes, his words made me curious.

"Instead of shielding Armon's blasts, I want you to catch them—whole. Then I want you to place a shield completely around them—if you can. Forcing them away from you is the next step, if the first two are successful."

"You want to lob those bombs back at the enemy, don't you?" I blinked at him.

"It came to me last night. I know some escorts are very skilled with their shields, and some may be capable of this. For the few talented enough, I'd like to make this an option."

"I'll do my best, Commander."

"I believe I'd like to see your best, trainee."

Chapter 8

That morning, he stood close to explain exactly what he wanted. Close enough that I could smell the scent of fresh-washed skin and see the curve of his chin and jaw. The scar on the left side of his face only gave it character, as he seldom revealed his emotions, other than the occasional frown if things weren't going the way he wanted.

I wanted to ask if the scar made it difficult to shave; he'd done that so carefully his face looked as smooth as any I'd seen.

"Ready?" Armon grinned as he prepared to launch a weak blast toward me. Kerok stepped away, then, taking his scent and nearness with him.

"Ready," I dipped my chin in agreement.

"Catch it like an egg," Levi reminded me as Armon drew power into his hands to form the blast.

The first three attempts were only partially successful. I'd never imagined using my shield to capture something, only to hold it back.

In this, I found I needed to thin the shield and make it pliable. The fourth time, I caught Armon's blast, and then promptly dropped it in my excitement. Levi laughed aloud as I stared at the fizzling blast in amazement.

"Do that again," Kerok barked.

"Yes, Commander." Armon tossed another blast. I managed to shove it away, but not far. Now, I was determined to do better. Armon fired, I caught and launched, until the last one we tried sailed far over the lake.

"Let your shield around it drop," Kerok shouted. I pulled it away, and the blast burst over the water in a shower of sparks, hissing and spitting as the fiery remnants hit the lake.

"Very, very good," Levi said. "That was perfect."

The Rose Mark

"Not perfect yet—that was a weak blast, Lieutenant," Kerok pointed out. "It has potential, however, and that's exactly what I wanted to see. Armon, get her to breakfast and make apologies to Lilya for her tardiness."

"As you say, Commander."

I was still blinking in amazement at the spot above the lake where the blast detonated, once I'd pulled my shield away. Kerok's idea was true genius, and I wanted to thank him. He'd already *stepped* away, however, when Armon took my arm to *step* me to the trainee's mess.

* * *

Kerok

Training is going very well, and we may have a few extra things to present to Father when he arrives, I informed Hunter. *Some may take more time to perfect, but their potential is worth the effort.*

Let me guess—Sherra is involved in all this, somehow.

She is, I hedged.

Have you changed your mind?

Hunter, no, I snapped at him. *Do not do this.*

Your father wants this, you know.

The law is that he cannot command me to choose one over another, I pointed out.

Then I still have two weeks to convince you.

You'll be wasting your time and effort.

It's my time and my effort, and I'll waste it if I want.

Hunter was as stubborn as they came, when he believed himself right in any matter. Father adored him for that quality. I often did, too, just not in this case.

You can be just as stubborn as your uncle Hunter, my mind, traitor that it was, informed me. *Face it—she smelled good. Felt good near you, too.*

142

Chapter 8

"Shut up," I snapped aloud and went back to my messages from the battlefield.

* * *

Sherra

Lilya gratefully accepted help in her attempts to explain shield angling to her cohort. I could see that this was a difficult task for someone who'd never done it themselves. I began to realize that perhaps the drudges who trained us had passed all their tests when they were trained early in their lives, before failing at this one last lesson.

It made me want to ask Lilya questions about her training, and then ask Kerok or Armon about the removal of the instructors' power afterward. I wanted to know why it was done, because they didn't have any power at all, now. I also wanted to know whether it could be restored.

Like the washouts Wend and the others helped me train, I imagined that I could do the same for Lilya and the other instructors—if it were possible to restore what they'd once had.

Power should only be burned out of those who couldn't be trusted—like the Bulldog. She should never have been placed in charge of trainees; it made me wonder how she'd managed to be chosen for that task.

"See the shield in your mind, catch the ball softly in it like an egg tossed at you, and then push it away gently," I told the trainee. "You can do this—I've seen you make excellent shields."

"I see it as making a hollow in my shield," Caral stepped up beside me. "A soft hollow, as if I were a mother hen protecting the chick inside her egg."

The Rose Mark

Caral had performed the exercise successfully from the start after I'd explained it to her. I was grateful for the early practice with Armon and Kerok.

I'd arrived at the training camp without hope.

Now—I had the glimmerings of hope in my mind. My determination to keep as many of these women alive as I could grew stronger every day.

Armon and Levi had it, too—a hope that they wouldn't burn out their roses in a handful of years. Kerok's face stayed shuttered most of the time, and I wondered about that.

Perhaps he'd seen too much death and preferred not to be involved, other than working to save his troops. I wanted to ask Armon about Kerok's last escort, too, but held back. I did and didn't want to know about her.

Either way, hearing of her death would be painful, and would present a glimpse into my future, when I, too, died beside a warrior.

* * *

Kerok

"We watched all the groups while they trained today. Lilya's was obviously the best," Armon reported. "With Sherra's help, and then Caral's, those women learned in half the time."

"How difficult will it be, do you think, for them to offer power to a warrior? I know that's reserved for Secondary Camp so it'll be fresh in their minds, but what could it hurt to test it now?"

"I don't see that as a hindrance," Armon shrugged.

"Then select several of our best, and arrange to have them on Lilya's training field tomorrow morning. I'll send a message to Lilya, explaining what I want. Tell your men to gauge the drawing of power and keep it to a small amount only, or punishment will be considered. This isn't a contest, and I expect you to make them understand that."

"I'll tell them, and have them blasted if they don't follow orders," Armon agreed.

"Ask Levi to handle Sherra, all right?"

"I will."

"Hard to believe we'll be back on the battlefield in two months or so," I sighed.

"I know. Every day is a new day, Commander."

"You have the truth of it," I conceded.

He was right. Once the trainees passed their final tests and made choices from the lists, they would serve a final internship at another camp—where they'd get to know their warrior partners and work with them every day, to get used to working with each other and hone their skills.

Some called it a honeymoon period, because they'd eat together, train together and, if desired, sleep together.

I wanted nothing to do with the last one, and intended to tell my escort the truth straight away.

Training only, meals perhaps, and *nothing else.*

You'll be watching Sherra and whomever she chooses, a small voice reminded me. "Shut up," I growled.

"What's that, Commander?" Armon asked.

"Nothing—certainly not meant for you," I said. "I believe you'd say I was thinking too much, Captain."

"Then stop," he grinned. "I'll go tell the others." He turned and left my office. I released the breath I was holding before going back to the messages on my desk.

"A message from the General," a courier from the battlefield *stepped* into my office. He placed a sealed note on my desk.

"Here." I handed him two messages for General Linel. "Everything all right at the front, Dayl?"

"Yes, Commander. Awaiting your return, as always."

"I'll be there in two months, and will likely visit in between," I said. "Feel free to tell the General that."

"I will, sir."

"Anything I should know, soldier?"

"The General looks weary. That didn't come from me, sir."

"I'll be in and out, then, when the trials here are finished."

"Thank you, sir."

"You're dismissed."

He *stepped* away while I watched him disappear. Couriers were more than capable of *stepping*; they'd merely failed in their blasting lessons. It was a position offered to the best students who'd never become warriors; they were allowed to keep their talents, such as they were, to carry messages and other written records.

General Linel didn't have mindspeaking talent, more's the pity, or I'd have saved the couriers time and effort, passing written messages back and forth. More often than not, the messages came to me first, and were passed in mindspeak to Hunter immediately after.

Yes, I could inform my father directly, but I wasn't aware of his schedule and could be interrupting something important.

That's why Hunter was the King's advisor—he'd not only preserve a temporary written record of the communication, but would pass the message to Father the moment he could.

He was my mother's only living brother, now—Merrin's father had died early and Merrin was raised by his mother and grandmother.

Chapter 8

Talent ran strong in both families—it was one of the reasons Father married Mother. Drenn, unfortunately, had no talent. I, on the other hand—Hunter said once I'd gotten both measures—mine and what should have been Drenn's.

I'd studied warfare from the moment I could read a sentence. Even then, Father had plans for me to command the army, placing a Prince at its head—something that hadn't happened in nearly a century.

War was complicated, and it was difficult enough making sure the army was supplied with food, water, uniforms, supplies, medicines and everything else. Much of what was grown under the far southern domes went to the army.

As for warriors and escorts—those were produced in the scattered villages, and they were dwindling.

Since Father stopped the census, I had no idea whether the regular population was falling in numbers, either.

If Drenn had any sense, I'd ask him to quietly send out couriers to speak with heads of villages about how their numbers were holding up, and whether there was enough food grown and available water to support their populations.

Drenn would not only refuse, he'd go straight to Father about it, just to cause trouble between us.

"Fuck," I grumbled softly. As Armon said, I was thinking too much, and it was only frustrating me more.

I've been away from the battlefield too long, I told myself and slipped a finger beneath the seal of General Linel's message to open it. If Grae were here, she'd smile at me and take my hand, leading me away from my desk and the infernal paperwork atop it.

Those memories didn't crop up often, but I was reminded of Grae's loss every time I looked at myself in the mirror. The scar no longer looked red and angry, but it was deep—a lasting postscript from a terrible, soul-crushing day.

As for replacing her—I wanted someone competent who was self-sustaining, wouldn't get in my way and wouldn't mind if I ignored her most of the time. I had no idea whether there were any like that in this crop of escort trainees, and I'd be forced to select one of them or stay away from the battlefield for another six months.

Fucking hell.

Chapter 9

*S*herra
    Lilya was smiling at our noisy tables at dinner. All her trainees were discussing the new methods and how to better themselves. If nothing else, they spoke with hope in their voices—perhaps for the first time since they'd begun their training.

The Bulldog would have shouted at us to shut up, and frowned at anyone who made noise while they ate.

I didn't miss her.

Perhaps Veri still missed her, but she could be the only one.

Whenever Fourth worked with First, too, Veri always sent nasty looks my way, although she knew better than to slack off in her training—her instructor kept a close watch on her every time.

"I heard the lists went to the warriors today," Wend elbowed me before leaning in to give me the information.

"How do you hear all these things?" I frowned at her.

"Drudges," she grinned. "Besides, while you're working with the two early washouts every afternoon, I ask what's new of the others—who are still working as drudges outside our training classes. They know everything."

"Of course they do," I said. "Does this mean they will or won't be ready for their testing tomorrow?"

The warriors were coming to test the washouts we were training, and Armon said there was something else in the works, too, but didn't elaborate. I figured it was something Kerok wanted, so I forced myself not to ask further questions.

"They're ready—they can do so much more than we were able to do that first time," Wend agreed. "Levi is very happy with their abilities."

"It's too bad we didn't get this much attention and special training before we were shoved in front of warriors," Jae observed. "Things would have been so different."

"I know." She'd wept after failing the shielding test the first time. That had probably stayed with her, and could affect her choices with the warriors.

I hoped that wasn't the case—Jae was more than capable, and I'd pick her over most of the others. Only Caral, Wend and I could form better shields, in my opinion.

Jae should be given third pick in First group, if there were any fairness left in that ranking process. Caral was already sentenced to Fifth group because of the demerits levied against her, or she'd be in First group for sure.

Chapter 9

I wanted to blame the Bulldog for those circumstances, but I couldn't. How we'd been trained initially had likely been the standard practice for a very long time. The Bulldog was merely a symptom of the disease, not the disease itself.

The favoritism, revenge and almost-murder, however—those misdeeds fell squarely onto the Bulldog's shoulders. Armon told me that she'd been sentenced to work on a potato farm, but I'd heard nothing since then.

I hadn't asked, either, as I didn't really care. She'd harmed Wend intentionally, and I had no sympathy for anyone who'd do that.

I also considered that when I arrived at training camp, I'd been alone and friendless. Friends surrounded me now—friends I cared a great deal about, and I felt responsible for keeping them alive.

"You think you're so smart," Veri walked up to our table. "The Bulldog called you useless tripe. I'm calling you useless cow dung."

I blinked at her in shock—how had she gotten away from her cohort, to come and taunt me? First Cohort was at the other end of the mess hall, eating.

Somehow, Veri had escaped her instructor's eye.

"Trainee, you have two demerits for leaving your cohort," Lilya snapped from behind Veri.

"You can't do that; you're not my instructor," Veri hissed.

"Three demerits, and I just did," Lilya said. "Any instructor can level demerits. If the Bulldog were still here, I'd point out the demerits she leveled against trainees in other cohorts, just to make you and the other one stand out at the end."

Veri's face flushed deep red. "Go back to your cohort, before I level another demerit," Lilya said, her voice even.

The Rose Mark

Veri turned and fled, although Nina met her halfway. Most of us heard Nina ask Veri how many demerits Lilya had given her. Veri was forced to answer truthfully.

"Three," she hung her head to hide the embarrassment.

"Then I'm adding one more to the tally," Nina said. "Get back to your cohort, trainee."

"Yes, Lady." Veri walked as fast as she could toward First's tables.

"I'm sorry," Nina walked forward to apologize to Lilya. "It won't happen again."

"It has been remedied," Lilya nodded. "You have no need to apologize."

* * *

"I really don't want to talk about it," I said as I pulled covers back on my cot in Fourth's barracks.

"She's a spiteful bully, because Nina won't let her get away with everything, like the Bulldog did," Wend huffed.

"It's done," I shook my head at Wend. "She has four demerits, and that drops her down the lists. She did this to herself, and if she has any sense at all, she'll realize that."

"I wouldn't accuse Veri of having sense," Caral interjected. "Having no sense, however, appears to be her usual behavior."

"Lights out," Lilya called.

The lights went out moments later, and I settled onto my bed, hoping that sleep would come.

* * *

Kerok

"Lilya gave her three demerits; Nina gave her a fourth one," I handed the notes I'd received from both instructors to Armon, who sat in my office.

152

Chapter 9

"That drops her way down," Armon nodded as he read the brief messages. "I can't say it isn't deserved, either. She's pushed Nina to the limit too many times to tell."

"Nina says she only looked away for a moment, and Veri was already gone. I have no idea how she made it to the opposite end of the mess hall so fast."

"Little snipe can move quickly, eh?" Armon read the messages again before lifting his head to grin at me.

"Looks that way. I'll be watching her and her warrior in the field—you can bet money on that."

"I can help with that," Armon agreed while handing the messages back. "I'd trust a poisonous snake before I'd trust her."

"It's strange that you should mention that—Hunter sent mindspeak earlier. He says that the Bulldog's body was found just outside the southernmost dome, and she was dead of snakebite."

"How long ago?"

"Says the body looked fresh, and she wasn't filthy, as she should have been for being out on her own so long. The workers who found her said she appeared relatively clean."

"I've heard that tale before," Armon said. "Although it was a while back."

"I've heard it more times than that," I sighed. "I have no idea what this means."

"A mystery for sure, but at least she's dead and saves us the trouble."

"We know the snake didn't give her sanctuary," I shrugged. "But somebody did—before she was bitten there at the last. That troubles me, Armon. A great deal."

"Now that you put it that way," Armon frowned. "What did they do with the body?"

"Burned with a blast. Her ashes were scattered outside, as usual."

"Did they send a Diviner?" Armon thought to ask.

"Yes. This is something you can never tell anyone else, Armon. This time is like other times that I've seen—the Diviner says there is nothing to divine—as if everything about her, except her identity, is missing in some way."

"What can cause that?" Armon asked after thinking about my words for a moment.

"We don't know. Father doesn't like hearing about it, because it's something outside his control."

"You don't believe it's accidental, or just an anomaly, do you?" Armon asked.

"No. It wouldn't be the first time an instructor from one training camp or another has been found in the same way— some of them came up missing while still teaching a class. All of them were found later, in much the same condition as the Bulldog, only dead of a snakebite or some other, mundane reason."

"I've heard they'd just went mental for some reason and ran away," Armon began.

"And that's what you're supposed to think, so we don't have mass panic."

"All right—this is beginning to scare me," Armon confessed.

"It scares you? I've carried this around for years and it still scares me. You're the first one outside the palace who's heard this, and it's because I trust you more than anyone else."

"Are there records of this? Written records?"

"Hunter has them buried, but they're recorded," I agreed. "I asked him to do it, because Father didn't want it written down. Drenn doesn't care, one way or the other. Missing

Chapter 9

instructors and strange deaths don't mean anything to him. There's something else, too," I added.

"Don't start with ghosts—please," Armon held up a hand.

"It's not that—this concerns you and Levi," I said.

"What's that?" Armon was concerned immediately, the moment I said Levi's name.

"I'm giving you both a promotion. When we reach the battlefield again, you'll be Colonel Armon, and Levi will be Captain Levi, special advisors and attachments to the Prince Commander. I need trustworthy people around me, and we both saw what happened to Merrin."

"I'm—speechless," Armon breathed.

"Get over it. We'll have to hit the ground running when we get there, and I'll have you both up to speed by that time if things go as planned."

"As you say, Commander."

"Go. Give Levi the good news—I've already gotten the approved paperwork filed with Hunter."

"Out-fucking-standing," Armon stood while a slow grin spread across his face. "Thank you. I'll tell Levi straight away."

He didn't bother walking out of my office—he *stepped* away, carrying the good news with him.

* * *

Sherra

I'd brushed Veri's verbal attack aside with the others, but I couldn't shake it from my mind—as if it were a warning of some sort. Therefore, I slept fitfully, waking often and then falling into troubling dreams.

In one of those dreams, I smelled a choking, acrid scent of burning before waking to the reality of it. Smoke filled our barracks, and the popping noise of dry, blazing wood hit my ears.

155

The Rose Mark

Fire! I shouted in mindspeak before shouting it verbally, in case the women around me failed to hear the mindspeak.

Immediately, everyone threw back covers, their first, indrawn breaths filled with smoke and making them cough. Light cast by flames at the south end of the building reflected off rising levels of smoke inside our barracks.

"Get out of here," I yelled at everyone, before stopping to pull Wend and then Jae to their feet on my way toward the door.

"The door's locked," someone shouted at me.

"Windows, too," someone else called out, amid heavier coughing and rising hysteria.

"Get down low," I commanded. "The air will be cleaner there." I raced toward the door, where a coughing fit hit me, taking up precious seconds of our time. If we didn't find a way out soon, we'd die from the smoke alone, before the fire burned our bodies to cinders.

Armon, I sent mindspeak, *our barracks is on fire and the doors and windows are locked. We can't get out*, I sent while attempting to force the door open.

It didn't budge, and I was beginning to feel terrified.

"Shields," I shouted. "Shield yourselves and hold as much good air as you can inside," I said.

We're coming, a blessed reply came from Armon.

Get back from the door, Kerok's voice sounded in my head.

"Get back," I told the others. "Keep your shields strong."

The barracks door blasted inward, causing a massive fireball to explode and whoosh through the building, lighting bedding on fire and giving new breath to an out-of-control blaze. If our shields hadn't protected us that night, we'd have died the moment Kerok's blast blew down the door.

156

Chapter 9

Kerok

Barth sat near my desk, an angry expression etched deeply on his face. The fire had been set shortly before dawn. The intention was to kill everyone inside Fourth's barracks.

Two deaths were discovered when the sun's light hit the camp—Lilya and Nina were found murdered in their beds—both dead of burning.

Colonel Kage had brought Barth to me shortly after I requested it. Hunter came with him.

"Now we know who, the how and the why, but we don't know the where," Barth reported. "I can't predict where she is, now."

He spoke of Veri, who'd committed two murders and attempted so many more than that.

She'd killed the two best instructors at North Camp. I was furious, as were Barth and Hunter.

Armon and Levi, with assistance from Colonel Kage, had their hands full, attempting to calm the remaining instructors, their trainees and the warriors.

Nina and Lilya had no power to fight back against Veri, who'd used what she had to kill. I had a feeling that Nina had given her the news of the Bulldog's death, and Veri had taken her revenge. She was already angry with both instructors for giving her well-deserved demerits.

"Do you think anyone else from the Bulldog's cohort has murder on their minds?" Hunter asked.

He stood near the window in my office, looking out over the training grounds and the still-smoking ruin that used to be Fourth's barracks.

"No. I've already discussed that with Armon and Levi. They say the same."

157

"If they hadn't put their shields up, those trainees would be dead," Hunter pointed out.

"I know." I wanted to find Veri and blast her myself for this. We were almost at the end of training, and two cohorts were now without instructors. Those instructors were the only ones capable of submitting recommendations for their final trainee rankings.

"If Sherra didn't have mindspeaking talent," Barth began.

"They'd be dead for sure," I acknowledged. "Veri melted the locks on windows and the door so they wouldn't open. I had to blast the door down."

"Behavior such as this has never been recorded," Hunter said. "Ever."

"Not with multiple murders and attempted murders," I agreed. We didn't discuss the events two hundred years earlier—when a newly-trained black rose had been responsible for the Crown Prince's death.

Laws had been changed following that event. Much of the previous records had been destroyed, too, so those of us here and now had only a narrow view into those incidents.

The one thing I knew for sure concerned the law that was written afterward, which prevented a Crown Prince from serving on the battlefield. Other princes or princesses were allowed, but never the one who'd inherit the King's position.

Drenn would be exempt, even if he'd been born with talent.

Just as Father had been exempt—and his father before him, all the way back to my many-times great-grandfather.

"Commander—the report from the infirmary." Armon knocked on the open door before entering my office. He placed the physician's message in my hand.

Chapter 9

"What is your assessment, Armon?" I asked before opening the note.

"Smoke inhalation—a few bruises from being knocked around inside their shields. The physician says the damage is minimal—their shields went up quickly enough to keep them from lasting harm. He also says for them to refrain from strenuous activity for a few days—he'll check on them before they're cleared for further field training."

"In other words, some coughing, a few headaches and hoarseness," I read through the physician's note quickly.

"That's right."

"Tell the physician and his staff that the Commander is grateful." I folded the note and slipped it into my top drawer.

"I will." Armon turned to go.

"Armon?" He stopped immediately and turned back to me.

"Pull the washouts away from their drudgery and place them in one of the empty barracks with Fourth cohort. Divide First into three parts and place a third with Second, Third and Fifth."

"I'll see to it, Commander."

Carry a message to Sherra, I sent mindspeak. *Ask her and the others in Fourth to teach the washouts everything they can. Nothing strenuous on their part—only teaching, all right? Ask Levi to supervise.*

It will be done, Commander. Armon *stepped* away from my office.

"Will this affect the upcoming trials?" Hunter asked.

"I don't know," I answered honestly. "I'll know more when we get the ones from First and Fourth onto the training field again."

"What about our murderer?" Hunter asked.

"I've sent four out looking for her, but it appears Veri can *step*. I don't think she'd have gotten away, otherwise. There are guards posted outside the perimeter, day and night."

"I've questioned the guards and divined their answers—none saw or helped her," Barth supplied. "This adds to the Prince's theory that she can *step*—a rather brazen thing to attempt, when untaught."

"Then it's my hope she impaled herself wherever she landed," Hunter gruffed.

"She knows her own village well enough; that's why I sent two warriors there, first thing," I said. "If she's there, they'll bring her back for the King's justice in this. The other two are searching nearby areas—anywhere she could have gone by *sight-stepping*."

"Also a precarious thing to do, when one is unaware of exactly where one's feet may land," Hunter observed.

"Hunt, we'll either find her or we won't, and we'll certainly place more guards around the barracks in case she thinks to return and try again," I attempted to soothe his worries.

"Your life could be in danger next time," Hunter blew out a frustrated breath.

"I can take care of myself against a trainee," I said. "Stop worrying."

"I'll stop worrying when they find her body and not before. Every building here is made of tinder-dry wood. Melting a metal lock is diabolical; setting fire to the building afterward is murderous in the extreme. Don't pretend it isn't."

"Frying instructors in their beds is worse," Barth grumbled. "If we're not careful, that story will spread like wildfire and we'll have an epidemic of murders on our hands."

Chapter 9

"I think you're both taking this to the farthest extremes," I said. "This is an isolated incident, and should be treated as such."

"Thorn," Hunter frowned at me while using my proper name—something he seldom did outside the palace, "This comes too close on the heels of the unusual circumstances surrounding the Bulldog's death. I don't like it at all."

"Now you're just being superstitious. Yes, I think Veri heard the Bulldog was dead, and frankly, we should have guessed she'd try something. Just not—this." I swept out a hand.

"Have you made a choice in the lists?" Hunter asked. I should have known he'd get around to asking that question.

"The paper isn't filled out, if that's what you're asking," I grumbled.

"You know your father's feelings in this. And mine," he added.

"Make that mine as well," Barth said.

"I won't have you three making a choice for me—it's against the rules," I reminded them.

"Thorn, you need someone to protect you as fiercely as Sherra worked to protect her cohort last night," Hunter said. "I remember your arrival at the palace after being wounded on the battlefield last time. The King's physician says it's a near-miracle you survived that attack. So many others didn't."

Hunter turned back to the window at that admission. I knew he spoke the truth—on both counts.

"Hunt, I'm still here," I said softly. "The choice will be mine to make."

"Then make it the right one."

* * *

Sherra

The Rose Mark

Most of us were still having occasional coughing fits, after inhaling smoke the night before. Armon explained as much as he could—some of it in mindspeak, so as not to alarm the others.

Veri had done this. She'd murdered Nina and Lilya in their beds by burning them with her fire, when they had no defense to raise against that sort of attack.

Then, she'd melted the locks on the door and windows of our barracks, before setting it on fire, too.

Armon said she'd escaped after that, and it was suspected by Kerok, the Diviner and the others who'd come from the King's City that Veri could *step*.

Warriors were looking for her now.

Armon warned me to speak carefully about the cause of the fire and the deaths the night before, so as not to frighten everyone more than they already were. That didn't stop the rumors from running wild inside the infirmary, where Fourth waited for our relocation to an empty barracks building.

"We're moving you to the barracks nearest the warriors," Armon *stepped* into the infirmary—not far from where I was sitting. The long bench I occupied also held Wend, Caral and Jae—the others were up and wandering about. We stood the moment he arrived.

Everyone else stopped to listen as Armon made his announcement. "The washouts will be joining you permanently, and have been instructed to meet us there. For the next three days, you will be training them. No strenuous activity on your part—let them do the work. Is that understood?" he went on.

"Yes, sir."

"Good. The drudges have been working to air out your new barracks and replace burned uniforms and such. Things

Chapter 9

should be in place well enough to move in. Levi is waiting outside—he'll march your cohort over."

"Will we have a new instructor?" Misten asked.

"The commander is considering that, now. You'll be informed when a decision is made. In the meantime, begin teaching the washouts full-time, and show them everything you can, all right? News will come later, I'm sure."

Armon stood aside while Caral took the lead and walked out the door, the others falling in line to follow her. I waited to go last, to make sure all were accounted for.

Levi and I will be supervising Fourth, Armon informed me as I passed him on the way out the door.

Thank you, I replied.

* * *

"Catch it gently," I called out to the trainee. Reena was responding faster than anyone expected to her extended training period. I'd asked Levi to make a game of tossing small fireballs at the trainees, who were laughing as they went after the randomly-tossed flames.

Reena was doing it—catching fireballs some of the other trainees were missing, by moving about and carrying her shield with her instead of staying in a fixed position.

"That's great," I encouraged when Reena captured the latest one. "Now, toss it away."

I watched as she made the motion with her hands, and her shield obeyed, tossing the fireball toward the opposite side of the field. It fizzled out and became harmless before it ever hit the ground.

We'd had enough of burning, and had no desire to put out fires on the field.

Mostly, I gave credit to Levi, who could gauge the fireball's life-span before he ever released it.

The Rose Mark

On nearby fields, I could hear the commands of our three remaining instructors, as they worked with a few other warriors while training with both the old and new methods.

I hoped that we'd be ready to show the King enough that he'd approve and implement the new method, and see to the training of other instructors to train to it in the future.

"See how fast you can do it, this time," I told Reena, who turned to me with a smile and a nod before looking to Levi to fire off another small blast.

Levi flipped the fireball high and to the side, while Reena raced toward it. I held my breath as she captured it with her shield and then flipped it away immediately, toward open, empty ground.

It fizzled with a pop just before it hit.

"Perfect," I crowed. The other trainees behind me clapped their appreciation for Reena's efforts.

This—this was what they'd needed all along—encouragement, more one-on-one training, and the knowledge that they were accomplishing the goal—not just for the cohort, but for themselves and for the lives in the King's army.

"Dinner," Armon arrived and called out. "Form your lines and we'll march in together."

"I love this part," Reena trotted up beside me. "Going in *with* you, instead of watching from the laundry or looking up from a scrubbed floor."

"You should have been there all along," I said and smiled at her.

"Thank you. That means a lot—to all of us."

* * *

Kerok

Chapter 9

"Commander, the washouts are blooming into roses," Armon grinned as he took the offered chair in my office. "One of the fire washouts has actually drawn ahead of the others, with the intensive training we've been giving them."

"Good news," I nodded. "Will they all be ready for the testing?"

"I believe they will—now that they're almost up to speed with the other classes."

"That sounds fine. Good work."

"You seem preoccupied," Armon's grin disappeared.

"Veri's body was recovered earlier today—near the spot where the Bulldog was found."

I watched as Armon went still for several seconds. "Tell me," he said after a few moments.

"Clean for the most part. Dead of snakebite, like the Bulldog. There's one big difference, however."

"What was that?"

"A dark handprint—as if she'd been slapped hard—before she was bitten by the snake."

"This is worse than ghost stories," Armon turned his head away. "The ones about the vengeful ghosts."

"I can't say how worrisome this is—coming so soon and so close in proximity to the incident with the Bulldog," I grimaced. "We have no idea how to explain any of it, and since Barth can't get a Diviner's reading off the victims, that only makes it worse."

"Do you think the enemy?" Armon began.

"No." I shook my head. "They'd torture any of ours, and not bother to send the bodies back. I have no idea what this is, and it concerns me a great deal."

The Rose Mark

"At least the one or ones responsible have only targeted those who deserve what they get—or seemingly so," Armon sighed.

"That's something else," I toyed with a pen on my desk. "Those who have disappeared unexpectedly in the past—we don't usually find out about their misdeeds until after the bodies are discovered and the Diviners start asking questions of those around them."

"Do you think we may have a very talented, rogue Diviner on our hands?" Armon suggested.

"I think he would need help—many of those taken were men, and a few had power—like Veri. That didn't appear to help them in the end."

"You think someone—or more than one—has appointed themselves an alternative source of judgment, outside that of the palace?"

"Right now, I don't know what to think, but things are pointing more and more in that direction. My question is this—if what I think is true, how did we miss finding someone with this sort of power? How did they slip past our notice? We have enough problems facing the enemy—we don't need somebody attacking us from the side, too."

"Or from the inside."

"Armon, stop scaring me." I didn't admit that I'd considered the same possibility, and that worried me even more. "We've never had two this close together, either," I said. "Usually, the incidents are years apart. Besides, if they were on the inside, with the power to confound other Diviners, we should have discovered that when they were young, don't you think?"

"Let's hope so," Armon agreed. "I'd hate to think the one living in the next tent could have that kind of ability."

Chapter 9

"Go to bed, Armon. We have another early day, and it'll be difficult enough to sleep after this conversation."

"You have the right of it," Armon said while standing. "One last question," he said after a moment. "Have any of the bodies showed signs of torture or abuse? Other than the handprint on Veri's face?"

"None. It was as if this time it had become personal, when all the other times it wasn't. Good-night, Colonel."

Chapter 10

Sherra

On the fourth day after the fire, we were allowed to go back to our training schedule. The washouts were training alongside us by that time, under Armon and Levi's watchful supervision.

Yes, Lilya's and Nina's deaths still affected all of us, and on the third night, we were allowed to hold a memorial for them after the evening meal. The other instructors paid them tribute, and a small glass of wine was poured for each of us.

We drank to their memory at the last, before we were herded to our barracks. I imagined at this point in other training classes, the trainees would be considering the lists and discussing them at length.

The Rose Mark

This training class had seen tragedy after tragedy, and any talk of the lists was subdued.

We spent the following morning doing shield training after Levi took us through our normal drills. After the midday meal, we were marched toward the classroom building. I wondered what Levi would be teaching us today—he was unusually quiet as we made our way over parched, dusty ground to new lessons.

"I wish it would rain," Wend sighed as we walked through the door to take our seats in the classroom. "We haven't seen any since we came."

She was right—it hadn't rained here for nearly three months, and that was unusual. Normally there was at least a smattering here and there, although it never lasted long.

"Fall is coming—surely it will bring some rain," I said, hoping to lighten her mood.

"I know. I heard the enemy increases their attacks in cooler weather."

"I think that's why they train us in the summer—when the attacks are lighter," Caral whispered.

"Take your seats," Levi commanded as he walked into the classroom last. All of us pulled out chairs to sit right away, and conversation hushed.

Armon arrived, then, and walked to the back of the room, where he pulled out an empty chair to sit in a corner. He nodded to Levi to begin. I turned back to see Levi, who looked as uncomfortable as I'd ever seen him.

"Today's lesson is about the lists, the choosing, and the vows," he began. "As you probably know, the lists of trainee names have already gone to the warriors. Those lists will be turned in after you are tested at the end of your training. Once you have passed your tests, you will be ranked according to

170

your performance in the field and in the testing. Are there any questions so far?"

"What if we fail the tests at the end?" Reena raised her hand.

"Your performance in your training sessions will be taken into account," Levi said. "Usually, your instructor will have a preliminary ranking already, for all her students. Only a few will be shuffled after the tests, according to their final performance, you understand. After Lilya's death, Armon and I have taken those things into account, and we have put a list together as best we could, to substitute for Lilya's. Of course, any here with demerits will also be taken into account."

Caral shifted in her seat beside Wend.

"If you'd failed in your training, you'd have washed out already," Levi almost smiled as he continued. "Yet here you are, listening to me."

His words drew a few giggles from the former washouts—he'd quieted many of their fears.

"Any other questions about the testing?" Levi asked.

"Do you think the King will approve the new method?" Misten asked.

"Ah. The same question we keep asking ourselves," Levi nodded. "It is our hope that he will, but much will depend on how everyone performs during the testing. Be confident. We've seen you master it, time and again."

"How do you feel—personally—about the new method?" I asked. "You've been on the battlefield, and know what it's like to use the old way. How confident are you that this will be more effective and less tiring for the black roses?"

"The answer I am about to give you is a personal opinion only, and cannot be taken as the opinion of other warriors, the leadership, or the army as a whole," Levi stated. "I would much prefer the new method. I've watched you trainees, and I'm sure you've noticed the difference yourselves—you're exhausted after working the old way, while you remain fresher and more alert longer with the new method. I imagine it has to do with the fact that you're not constantly raising and lowering your shields."

He received nods of agreement throughout the classroom. I think that's why we wanted the new method approved—we would last longer on the battlefield, and ultimately keep our lives longer.

"Any more questions on the new method?" Levi asked.

Nobody raised their hands.

"Good. Now—on to the lists," he said, although he sounded less enthusiastic about this subject. "As you've probably determined by now, the lists that go to the warriors contain all your names. From those names, they make their own list—of those trainees they ah—find competent and who they would prefer to work with. This warrior list is called a preliminary list."

"So—they sort us by looks and then by ability?" Caral raised her hand.

"I can't guarantee what their criteria is when they put a preliminary list together," Levi hedged. "They've watched you work—during the shielding exercises, of course, and at other times."

"You'd think they'd want to keep their asses safe," Caral followed her own question with a sarcastic observation.

"Trainee, I will issue a warning," Armon said from the back of the room.

A warning. It could lead to more demerits, if Caral didn't keep her tone respectful.

"Understood, Colonel."

Chapter 10

Yes, Armon and Levi had received promotions. I thought them deserved, but hadn't discussed the subject with them or any of the others.

"After the preliminary lists are made—which are mostly for reference purposes, you understand," Levi continued, "The warriors attend the testing. Some of them are selected to participate, as you may have guessed. Afterward, while the rankings are considered by leadership in attendance, and compared to the rankings of the instructors, the warriors will finalize their choices, and place their names on individual trainees' lists for consideration."

"Is it possible that names could be added to their preliminary lists after the testing?" Wend asked.

"Yes, although it doesn't happen often, especially with seasoned warriors."

In other words, they were looking for either sex or protection, depending upon the warrior. I didn't say it aloud, however. I felt Caral was thinking the same thing. If Captain Merrin were still here, he'd be looking for sex; that was a given in my mind.

"When the warriors have added their names to the trainee lists for consideration, those lists come back to you, the black roses-in-waiting. You will be given a day to consider the warriors' names on your list and make decisions. If you are ranked first among the trainees, congratulations. You will be given your first choice. That warrior's name will then be struck from all subsequent lists, so other trainees may have to adjust their choices, until all trainees have had their pick. Those final decisions will be announced at a feast at the end, where each of you will be allowed to sit with your chosen warrior and have dinner with him, although the pairing will not come until you arrive at our secondary training camp and take the vow of faithfulness."

"Secondary training camp?" Bela raised her hand.

"Yes. It is six weeks of intense training, where you work every day alongside your chosen warrior—to learn his battle methods and preferences. You must be able to successfully work together on the battlefield, or you could die quickly. Do you understand? This is to preserve your life, if nothing else."

"What is the vow of faithfulness?" Someone else asked.

"That is a vow you take with your warrior, that you will remain faithful to one another while you both live," Levi said. "A proven violation of the vow will result in a death sentence for the one violating it."

"Faithful?"

"In a sexual context," Armon intervened when Levi hesitated. "As you've probably guessed by now, Levi and I are life-partners. Any rose accepting either of us will not be given sex. It's nothing against you—he and I are bound by our own vows. That doesn't mean we won't care for you, because we will. Just not in that way."

"And what about roses who prefer their own sex?" Caral spoke. Yes, I'd understood that about her for a while.

"That is not ours to decide—the King rules in this, and roses are bound by their vows."

"But you and Levi," another pointed out.

"That rule was handed down by the King nearly a century ago—that warriors who are bound may stay faithful to one another. Their roses must understand this when they make their choice for either. On the lists, there will be a designation by each of our names—the letter indicating we are already bound to another warrior. It affects how we're chosen, more often than not."

Chapter 10

"But the same rule wasn't given for the roses." Caral sounded angry, now.

"I'm sorry to report that it's true," Levi admitted. "You have no idea how regretful I am about that."

"Not your fault," Caral sighed and ducked her head.

"What if a rose chooses to be celibate?" Misten raised her hand.

"Then it's my suggestion to look for a bound warrior," Levi shrugged. "Easy enough, don't you think?"

"That would certainly solve the problem," she admitted.

"These are things for all of you to think about," Levi said. "Consider who may keep your best interests at heart. Those may be the ones who aren't as handsome or charming, perhaps. I'm sure you've made your own assessments when you've worked with the warriors in your training sessions. Make the best choice for yourself, understand? This isn't a popularity contest—or it shouldn't be."

"The warriors get to see our rankings," I raised my hand a second time. "Will we get to see theirs?"

Levi drew in a breath at my question.

"It's not done," Armon spoke behind me. *You're thinking too much again*, he reminded me in mindspeak. "If they're an officer, that will be listed with their name. That's all you'll receive."

"Captain Levi?" Tera raised her hand.

"Yes, Tera?"

"Why are some born with the power, and some not?"

"That is a question for the ages," Levi admitted. "We don't know. Even the Diviner-scholars don't know, and they've studied it more than anyone else."

175

"Was that the King's Diviner who was here after the fire?" Jae asked. "Will he be the Diviner who examines us after our testing?"

"Yes. That is Barth, the King's Chief Diviner and head of the scholarly branch of his profession. Barth is trustworthy to a fault, and the King relies heavily upon his judgment."

"Has Veri been found and held accountable?" Wend asked.

"That's off-topic, trainee," Levi said. "Keep your questions related to today's class."

"Yes, Captain."

"What if you're afraid?" Reena raised her hand timidly.

"Of what?" Levi didn't understand. I did. I think all of us were afraid.

"Of being hurt the first time, or anytime afterward," I answered for Reena, who'd turned bright pink and dropped her eyes.

"The Prince Commander works tirelessly to see that doesn't happen," Armon said quietly. "All officers know to watch for bruises and other—signs. No warrior wants to be brought before Prince Thorn and a Diviner to be questioned about such. It is also your right to take these concerns to any officer, who will carry your message to the Prince. You'll receive more information regarding this before you take the vow."

Thorn—the Prince Commander. We hadn't heard his name mentioned before, although everyone knew he was in charge of the King's army. Like me, I think all the trainees imagined he was so far-removed from them and what they'd be doing, that he'd have no interest in any of us.

Like the King had no real interest in us. I'd been surprised when I heard that he'd be coming to watch our

Chapter 10

testing, and wondered if that were something he often did. We knew that Thorn was the King's younger son; Drenn was the King's eldest and heir, who would never be sent to the battlefield. There was a law in place that prevented it.

The King had no trouble sending any woman who wore the black rose to the battlefield and their ultimate death. Some men, like the King, were born to privilege. Others, like the black roses—decidedly not. Did the King honor the tattooed women, as it said in the book he kept in his library, or were they mere conveniences, so he could keep his life of privilege?

I dared not speak of that book to anyone—I'd read about *The Book of the Rose* in *The Rose Mark*—the forbidden book an old, blind woman had inadvertently given me when I was ten.

Perhaps the warriors we chose would treat us well until we died—I could only hope that they would.

As for my choices—those were narrowed to three already. I wondered how surprised Armon and Levi would be that they accounted for two of those three names. The third was a long shot, as things either went well or didn't between us—but I trusted Kerok well enough to respect my wishes in most matters.

Yes, they were all officers, but Armon and Levi wouldn't be on many lists because of the vows they'd given one another. I could live with that honesty between us. I'd worked closely with Levi, and many times with Armon. We were familiar with the others' methods and ways, and I'd felt their fire. Understood it, too.

"Are there any questions?" Levi asked, interrupting my thoughts.

There were none.

"All right, let's walk you through the testing schedule," he said. "First thing after breakfast that morning, each cohort will be called upon in numerical order. That means Second will be tested first, since First no longer exists. While Second and Third are being tested on the field, Fourth and Fifth will go through their interview with the Diviner. Fourth and Fifth will face their testing after the midday meal, while Second and Third are interviewed by the Diviner. The rankings will be discussed afterward, while you go to the showers and clean up before the evening meal."

"You have five days to prepare yourselves," Armon stood and stretched. "Make them count."

* * *

Hunter Lattham
King's Advisor

"Pour yourselves a glass," King Wulf pointed to the bottle of wine on his desk. Barth, who was just as confused as I about this late-night meeting, lifted the bottle and poured his, first.

"May I ask," I began.

"When you have your wine in hand," he waved away my question.

Barth passed the bottle to me; I reluctantly lifted it and poured half a glass of the dark liquid for myself.

The vintage was good—the best the southern domes could produce. As for Drenn's absence, I didn't mind that the Crown Prince wasn't here. It did tell me, however, that this was a private matter and the King wished to keep Drenn out of it.

That didn't happen often.

"This is about Thorn," the King sighed before sipping from his own glass. "I have the reports from you and Barth regarding your conversation with him at North Camp. He is being stubborn about this, and I wish to entertain suggestions on how to change his mind—through any means possible. I have no desire to lose a son to the barbarians."

"Are you suggesting blackmail or threats?" Barth asked. His voice was steady—he had no qualms about following the King's commands in this.

I agreed—up to a point. There were two lives involved here, not just Thorn's. I thought the girl would be foolish to turn down Thorn's offer, but he had to make an offer, first.

I wasn't naive enough to think that some warriors, when they tired of their escorts, wouldn't pull away excessive amounts of power just to have a change. I'd heard Merrin boast of it once, but I'd kept quiet on the matter, as that was only one example of what I perceived as a much larger problem.

I'd never taken that knowledge to Thorn, either, but that could change. I disliked placing more weight on his shoulders, but in this—we would fall sooner than later without sufficient escorts to support the warriors.

"I don't care what it takes. Dig farther into her past if needs be when you examine her—if there is anything we can employ to force both in the proper direction, then I wish to use it."

"And if there isn't?"

"I'm not above blackmail in this case. He has to see reason, you understand. I want the best for him, and this girl—Sherra, is the best."

"She certainly saved those others in her cohort by using the mindspeaking ability she has. That's extremely rare in black roses."

"I believe that when she helped train the others on shielding, it helped them maintain a strong shield under difficult circumstances," Barth offered. "Everything I hear about her is positive."

"And that's what the Prince Commander needs," Wulf pounded a fist on his desk. "He has to see reason in this and set his personal losses and feelings aside. He doesn't need an inferior, or even a second-best. He needs the best at his side. You know he's the strongest in a very long time, and he needs the same sort of strength to support him."

"Are we agreed then?" Barth asked. "To do whatever it takes to make this happen?"

"We're agreed."

* * *

Sherra

We were up early, as we usually were—Levi, Armon and I—to continue with our special training sessions before breakfast.

Today, Kerok came, when he hadn't in a while.

"We want to practice pulling energy away," Armon told me. "Don't worry," he said when I expressed fear and surprise at his words. "It won't be much, and this is usually set aside for the intense training after choices are made. This is a preliminary thing—just to see how well you respond. We'll decide whether to employ it with the other trainees afterward."

"What are you afraid of?" Kerok walked toward me, his voice low and reassuring.

"This is how we die," I said and lowered my eyes.

Kerok went completely still; I could see his feet and legs in front of me. After a moment, he spoke again.

"You have permission to speak your mind, trainee. Nothing will be held against you."

Chapter 10

"Do you care?" I lifted my eyes to him, refusing to wipe away the tears gathering and unshed. "Do any of you care that we'll die? I know the King doesn't give a fuck about any of us, and the villagers only look forward to the money when it comes. We're outcasts the moment the tattoos are placed on our wrists. Slavery isn't allowed in any other circumstance than this." I turned my back to him before wiping stubborn tears away.

* * *

Kerok

Even Grae had never had the courage to speak to me this way. Perhaps she felt the same, but never voiced it.

Nearby, Levi had moved closer to Armon, who placed an arm about his shoulders. After she wiped tears away, I watched as Sherra's arms came around herself, holding in sobs—refusing to let me see that.

"Your ideas can save those lives," I took a step toward her. "I know it. I've been on the battlefield for more than forty-five years, Sherra. I've never had as much hope as I do now. I can't speak for everyone, but every time an escort dies, a part of me dies with her."

"How can you be certain the King will agree to any of this?" she wept. "He doesn't care, remember? When I reach the battlefield, how much more of a battle will I have to fight to convince the other roses that the new method will help them? You've already seen what jealousy can do. Veri proved that."

"If the King approves it, the Prince Commander will order it done." I barely realized that my hands had gone to her shoulders. She stiffened at my touch.

Armon, I sent mindspeak, *Take Levi back to my office and stay there until I say.*

181

He and Levi disappeared.

"Hush, now," I pulled Sherra against me. "I didn't mean to upset or frighten you this morning. I'll wait for the power-pulling lessons at Secondary Camp, as I should have done." She shuddered against me, making me feel like a fool. How would I react in her place? I didn't have an answer for that.

Born with power and born to die young. She'd known her fate most of her life. "If I could change things, I would," I soothed as she trembled in my arms. "Life is seldom fair, and for some, it never is."

* * *

Sherra

"What happened?" Wend asked when I arrived at breakfast, my eyes still red from crying.

"Please don't ask," I whispered. "Some things are so hard for me to accept."

"I'll ask later, then," she said. "When you feel like talking."

"Stress," Caral said from behind me as we waited in line for our trays. "Trials are coming fast, and so much has happened to all of us already."

Perhaps it was stress. What had happened, however—I'd never expected such gentleness from Kerok. It skewed my brain and I could barely force a logical thought through it afterward. That in itself terrified me—I had to stay sharp to finish training washouts and prepare for the testing.

If I were honest with myself, I'd never been held by a man before. If my father had ever done so, I didn't remember it. Pottles had been the only one to soothe me when I felt alone and frightened. After her death, I'd felt more alone than ever.

Nobody in Merthis had spoken to me unless it was necessary. I wasn't lying about being outcast. Perhaps Veri

Chapter 10

and Ura, in their own way, were starved for attention, too, and had fallen into the Bulldog's way of thinking.

That mattered little now. Ura was dead and Veri, when they found her, would be just as dead. It didn't excuse her actions in my mind, however. She'd killed two, and attempted to kill so many others.

Trainee, stop thinking such terrible thoughts, Armon's mental voice sounded kind. I'd forgotten that he and Levi would be here, supervising and eating with us. *It's on your face and in the frown*, he added, as I wondered how he knew these things.

Any word on Veri? I returned.

Dead, he replied. *Found that way not long after her escape. I don't have details to share, other than that.*

Thank you, I said.

Don't tell the others—it could upset them at an inconvenient time.

I won't. He was right—we had enough worries, and some of the trainees were scared witless of the trials and what would come after—regarding the lists and the choices that had to be made.

Whomever they chose would watch them die—that was a given, and it still left a bitter taste of hopelessness in my mouth.

* * *

Kerok

Drenn wants to see you. Hunter's mental voice interrupted my thoughts on the morning's events.

What does he want? I didn't want to see Drenn. He probably knew that, as I hadn't had kind words for him the last time. He was a criminal in my mind, and if he didn't realize it, then he was a bigger fool than I imagined.

The Rose Mark

He kept his life because of our father's decision and for no other reason than that. *I don't know what he wants—he didn't explain and I know better than to ask*, Hunter answered my question.

Drenn wasn't the easiest person to deal with if anyone questioned his motives.

When? I asked. *Does Father know?*

I doubt it, but feel free to ask, Hunter said. The tone of his voice urged me to ask, but he didn't come out and say it. *Drenn wants to see you at dinner tonight, if it's convenient.*

It would have to be convenient—I was subject to Drenn's whims in most cases, just as the Council was, as long as it had nothing to do with the army or any decisions made regarding it. Only Father could supersede my decisions in that respect, and he generally deferred to my choices.

I'll be there.

Good. See me when dinner is over.

I will.

* * *

Sherra

All of us were covered with sweat and dust by the time our training was over for the day—a strong wind had whipped up, blowing sand and grit at us whenever we didn't have a shield up.

Dark clouds had formed to the north, and we could see rain—at least I hoped it was rain, although the water wouldn't soak into the ground at first—the drought we'd had would ensure it, and runoff could shift to low-lying areas and flood them.

The camp was in a low-lying area, between mountains and not far from the lake that provided our water supply. I wondered if it had ever flooded before.

Chapter 10

"Get cleaned up and then get in formation to march to the evening meal," Levi ordered as a rumble of thunder sounded in the distance. Rain began to fall before we'd finished with our showers.

* * *

Kerok

"Drenn," I nodded as respectfully as I could to my older brother. I'd been ushered into the small dining room adjoining his private suite in the palace. His valet dipped his head to Drenn before backing away.

Food and drink were already on the table, and I heard the door shut behind Drenn's personal servant.

"Why the privacy, brother?" I asked as he pointed to the empty chair at the table.

"It's a delicate matter." Drenn seldom expressed real happiness in his smiles; therefore, they were more of a self-satisfied smirk. I hated it, but Father either didn't notice, or chose to ignore it.

"What delicate matter is that?" I reached for the open bottle of wine and poured for him first, before filling my glass.

"I'm sure you know I have, ah, informants," he began, the smirk firmly pasted on his features.

"Your spies, you mean?" I lifted the wineglass and drank. "Good," I saluted him in his choice.

"I suppose you could call them that—for expediency's sake."

"Good. Glad that's cleared up," I said.

"This involves you—and a plot Father is hatching with Barth and Hunter."

"There's a plot? What if I don't believe you?"

"You'll believe me when I tell you what it is."

185

"Then tell me." I lifted my knife and fork to cut into the fowl on my plate.

"They intend to blackmail you—and that Sherra woman, to put you together. Father told Barth to look deep into her past to find something he could use, or go so far as to fabricate something that would place her in danger if she didn't choose you."

"You heard what I had to say on the matter," I pointed my fork at Drenn. "If I don't offer, she can't refuse me."

"But you're included in their diabolical machinations," Drenn's smirk widened. "I didn't know what they planned for you until recently—that's why I didn't ask to see you until now."

I drew in a breath and released it slowly, so I wouldn't reach out to punch Drenn in the face. My anger at him from the defiling of a trainee hadn't abated, and now that flame was fanned to an inferno at hearing that he'd spied on our own father.

No, I didn't appreciate Father's plan in this, but I believed it came from his love for me and nothing else. Drenn only wished to drive a wedge between us, and I knew that better than anyone.

I couldn't let him know this, however. He was too clever, and he'd find a way to make me pay. "What is Father's plan?" I expressed anger in my words. Drenn wouldn't realize they were meant for him and not Father.

"That new method you're perfecting?"

I went still. That would be the ultimate blackmail. If Father refused to approve it, lives would be lost—I was more than sure of it. And, after the events that morning, it didn't sit well with me at all.

Chapter 10

"What's your advice in this, then?" I asked. Drenn loved to be asked for advice—it made him appear wise—in his own eyes.

"The girl's a goner anyway, and you said yourself you don't want any part in her death. Let Father decree her death for you. I can suggest that it be quick and as painless as possible. Problem solved." He lifted his knife and fork to cut into his meat.

"Why would Father decree her death?" That wasn't logical at all.

"Because my spies have been working overtime, you understand."

"Overtime? What the hell is that supposed to mean?"

"I have this." He leaned down beside his chair to lift something. In his hand, he held a small book. "She learned to do what she does with this." He pushed the book in my direction.

"Go ahead, take it. Look inside—it won't explode or cast a spell."

Warily, I reached out to lift the book, unsure of why Drenn would present such to me. *The Rose Mark* was printed on the cover, the title outlined by square lines of gold leaf, and a red rose had replaced a single letter in the title.

"Open it," Drenn sounded gleeful.

I opened the book and almost dropped it when I did—a spark of power and a vision of fire went through me before I could even read the first page.

The forbidden book. I had no idea why it was forbidden, I only knew that it was.

"It was hers, as near as I can tell," Drenn chuckled. "I sent my spies to Merthis to ask questions. A few villagers reported seeing her at times with a small, black book in her hand. My men had to do some digging to find it, you understand."

"Drenn," I kicked my chair back and stood, my body stiff and my anger seething. "If you've told this to anyone else, I will fry you here and now, and then announce to all what you did to that trainee. I have witnesses, and Barth will certainly testify against you. Any other Diviner is welcome to test your ashes, to see for themselves. What will it be, Drenn? Answer quickly, as I have no patience for you or your schemes."

"I only wanted to give you a way out of all this," he cowered in his chair. "You said you didn't want any part of her death. I was making it easy for you."

"You make nothing easy. I will take this," I shoved the book into my pocket. "I will see it destroyed and if you ever, ever speak of this, I will see you dead."

I slammed the door behind me when I left Drenn's suite, and that's when I received Armon's message.

The camp is flooding, he reported. *From an unexpected, heavy rain.*

Chapter 11

*S*herra

"I think I can shield the camp, but I need a way to push the perimeter of my shield into the ground," I shouted at Levi while thunder growled over our heads and lightning lit the sky to the north.

This wasn't a swift-moving storm that would be over quickly; dark clouds covered everything as far as we could see whenever lighting lit the skies.

"Armon?" Levi turned to his partner, whose frown was deep and the worry in his eyes troubling.

"If we send up blasts, do you think you can tilt your shield to send them tumbling down the sides to the ground?" Armon asked.

The Rose Mark

"Maybe," I nodded as more thunder came and rain pounded harder. The three of us stood outside the mess hall, where a thin layer of water already covered the floors. In the distance, our barracks was receiving the same treatment, and the water would only get higher as the storm progressed.

"Let's try it," Levi agreed. "We'll have to stand in the rain to do this—we can't fire blasts beneath any roof."

That meant we'd have to move away from the covered walkway outside the mess hall to do this. "I'll put up a shield—so our heads won't get wet," I offered.

"Go ahead," Armon half-shouted as louder thunder broke over our heads. I raised a shield to cover the three of us as we strode toward empty ground; our boots splashed and splattered as we walked through rising water.

Normal mud would be sucking at our boots. This wasn't mud. This was baked-dry ground that only held the water on its surface.

"Here is good enough," Armon raised his voice to be heard against the pounding rain.

"All right. I'll have to cover every occupied building," I warned.

"Let us know when you have it done."

"It's done," I reported. My shields recognized Levi and Armon's blasts, and would allow them through. Levi nodded briefly at Armon before they both lifted their hands and prepared to send out blasts.

Gauge them carefully, Kerok's voice sounded in Armon's and my mind.

We will, Armon included me in his reply. I wondered briefly where Kerok had been, but turned back to the emergency at hand.

190

Chapter 11

Blasts were fired; I tilted my head to watch them fly upward. This would take a finesse I hadn't employed before. Mostly, I hoped to keep us alive while I experimented with this new technique.

* * *

Kerok

I'd shoved the book into a desk drawer before *stepping* toward the mess hall, where Armon and Levi worked with Sherra. Other warriors waited inside the mess hall, in case a full evacuation was necessary.

I barely arrived in time; Sherra was raising a shield to cover North Camp—or most of it, anyway.

"They're trying to sink the edges of Sherra's shield into the ground, so the water will flow around it," Caral had to raise her voice so I'd hear her over the rain and thunder.

It was a brilliant idea—if it worked. That's when I sent mindspeak to Armon and Sherra, to gauge their efforts carefully.

Four blasts were fired straight up, until they cleared the top of Sherra's shield—I could see where that was easily; the rain was hitting it and bouncing off with a great deal of noise.

It helped Armon and Levi gauge their blasts, as I'd asked them to. The blasts cleared the shield dome; Sherra moved her shield to capture the blasts, then sent their dripping flames down the sides of her shield.

Would they accomplish their goal? I wondered.

"Look—she's moving the bottom of the shield, too," Caral pointed out.

I watched in awe as the blasts flowing down the sides were redirected just before they hit the ground, sending them in a trail around the edge of the shield dome.

"I have chills," Caral admitted as we watched Sherra release the part of her shield directing the blasts around the perimeter.

They melted into a fiery ring around the base, and I physically felt the shield lower itself by nearly a foot.

"She did it." Wend had joined us, and was now bouncing and laughing.

When the lightning bolt struck Sherra's shield, we were all thrown to the ground by the impact.

* * *

Sherra

"I'm fine, stop fussing." I attempted to push Levi and Armon away. "I'll have trouble holding the shield if you do that."

Both wanted to put their hands on me to check for damage, to make sure I was all right after the lightning strike. If I'd known it was coming, I'd have waited for it to envelope my shield and dig deeper into the ground around it.

My shield had sunk two more feet after it hit.

At least no rain was pouring into the camp, now—unless you counted the empty barracks that I hadn't bothered to shield. I'd also adjusted my shield to allow air in and keep the rain out.

"Everything all right?" Kerok joined the three of us.

"I'm fine," I repeated. "It just—scared me for a minute."

"Can you detach from the shield and leave it standing?" Armon asked.

"I think so," I nodded.

"Then do it," he said.

Forcing my breaths to become even and steady, I disengaged from the shield while leaving it in place. It was advanced work, but not impossible.

192

Chapter 11

The moment I nodded to Armon, letting him know it was done, I was lifted in his arms and hugged hard enough to crack ribs.

"Armon, what are you doing?" I asked, smacking his back.

"Hugging you," he set me down with a splash. We still had standing water, but it wasn't enough to worry about. The bulk of the flood was now flowing around the perimeter of my shield.

"Excellent effort," Kerok offered a brief nod. "I worried you wouldn't be able to pull it off the first time."

"I worried the same thing," I admitted.

"Come with me—you're probably thirsty and starved after that," Levi took my elbow.

"I am," I agreed. "It's been a long day."

* * *

Kerok

I'm surprised she can stand, let alone walk after that. We should have been fried, Armon said as we walked toward the mess hall behind Levi and Sherra. *Have you ever seen anyone do that?*

No. I have no idea how she did it, either.

Well, that wasn't exactly true. I had a book in a desk drawer that might explain it, but for me to know for sure, I'd have to read it myself. If it was her book, how had she come by it? To my knowledge, all copies had been destroyed long ago.

"We haven't had a flood like this in fifteen years," Ana, Second's instructor, said as she joined our party inside the mess hall. "We had to replace almost everything back then, the water got so high."

"How high do you think it'll get this time?" I asked.

193

"I can't say—the more it rains, the worse it'll be."

"Sherra," I called out.

"Commander?" She stopped and turned toward me. She looked tired.

"Are you sure of your shield?" I asked.

"Yes, Commander. Even if I sleep, it should hold."

"Good. Armon, post extra guards inside the shield perimeter. Make sure they wake us if anything changes. If that happens, I want everyone ready to *step* the trainees away."

"I'll see to it, Commander."

Sherra nodded her understanding—this was a precaution, and she was just as concerned about the lives in the camp as I was.

"Levi, make sure she eats and gets to bed."

"I'll see to it, Commander."

"Good." I *stepped* away, then. I had an appointment with a book, and I didn't want to be late—or caught while reading it.

* * *

Sherra

They didn't wake me early the next morning. In fact, when my eyes blinked open when the others in the barracks began to stir, I jerked upright in bed, sure that I'd missed Armon's mindspeak to get me up before the others for early training.

Armon? I couldn't keep the bewilderment from my mental voice.

We let you sleep in—Commander's orders. Until the trials, you'll be working with your cohort only. Oh, and the rain has stopped. When we march to breakfast, you can bring down the shield. It isn't needed, now.

Thank you, Colonel.

Chapter 11

You are welcome.

When Levi arrived to march us to the mess hall, it was to find that the rain from the night before—what had stayed inside my shield, anyway, had finally soaked into the ground.

In two days, dry grass would be greener—for a short time. During the early morning hours, drudges had set many things to rights, including the floor of the mess hall, which was dry and clean when we walked into it.

I'd released my shield the moment we walked out of the barracks, and the early morning sun shone down hotter immediately. Levi grinned at me, but didn't say anything.

Until last night, neither of us had guessed that my shield might hold up against lightning. I was grateful to be alive, actually, and imagined that the whole thing had to do with splintering the lightning as I'd done with Armon and Levi's blasts. It allowed the fractured bolt to slide down the sides of the shield before burying itself in the ground.

It was something to think about for the future, if it were ever needed again.

* * *

Kerok

Why did someone ban this book? That question kept hammering at my brain as I worked kinks out of my muscles in the morning. If all the trainees had a copy, it would surely help them.

It did contain information about *stepping* and blast-work, but nothing that would compete with what the warrior trainees did.

I intended to hide it somewhere, so I could find it again. Had Sherra done the same thing? I still didn't know whether Drenn had the truth in this—he could have gotten the book from anywhere.

It troubled me, too, that he held information that could harm Sherra, should he level those accusations.

I wasn't lying when I threatened retaliation, either. He'd never gone this far before, and I'd never threatened him before.

A part of me wanted to tell Father. Another part of me worried that it would be a mistake. If Sherra had the book at one time, he could order her death and nothing I said could change his mind.

Why was the book banned to start with? That question returned to me. Why? There was nothing dangerous in its pages. In fact, in many explanations and writings within, it sounded as if the black roses were held as equals to the warriors, capable of living full lives.

When had that stopped?

When had things changed so drastically?

I didn't have answers, and I wanted them.

Perhaps if I went through Father's library, I could find missing information regarding the book. The laws were all recorded there; I'd merely have to read backward until I found the one concerning the book.

Meanwhile, I had to find a safe hiding place for it. Sherra—or someone—had buried it. Drenn told me they'd had to dig for the thing and I believed that much, at least.

This time, I had a better idea. *Stepping* away was the first thing on my agenda. It wouldn't take long to find a resting place for the book. I'd be back in plenty of time for breakfast, too.

* * *

I was eating breakfast at my desk when Hunter and Barth arrived in my office. "Sorry I didn't stop to see you last night— we had an emergency," I said.

Chapter 11

"We saw that when we got here," Hunter lifted an eyebrow. "Can you explain the narrow ditch that's running around the camp?"

"It'll fill in," I shrugged.

"What caused it?" Barth's smile told me he already knew.

"Most of it was caused by Sherra and a bolt of lightning," I admitted. "To keep the camp from flooding, you understand."

"A guard told us that the silt and water line was more than half his height this morning before the shield was dropped," Hunter said.

"Nice. I didn't even think to measure it."

Hunter cleared his throat, then.

"What is it, Hunter?"

"Why did Drenn ask to see you? Your father is curious, too."

"He thought to be helpful in making my selection from the lists," I said.

"How so?" Barth asked. I pointed him and Hunter toward chairs on the opposite side of my desk while I searched for a suitable answer.

"He pointed out ways to get what I said I wanted."

"And what did you tell him?"

"I told him to mind his own business."

Barth and Hunter turned toward one another and exchanged a glance.

"Let me guess—you have spies, too."

"Well, ah," Hunter sounded uncomfortable.

"Don't worry—I'm not completely naive," I held up a hand. "Just because I spend a lot of time on the battlefield doesn't mean I've let my mind rot."

"Then perhaps we can begin this conversation again?" Barth asked. "What did you do with the book?"

"It's where it will never be found."

I hadn't realized that Hunter was holding his breath until he released it in an audible sigh.

"Do you believe that it was hers?"

"I don't know. I only have Drenn's word on this, and frankly, I have no idea whether to believe him."

"Ah. Good," Barth nodded.

"You don't think it's hers?" I asked him. He was the Diviner—he'd be the one to know for sure.

"I care not," he said, shocking me. "In my knowledge, no other book has ever been banned in this land, and I have my own doubts as to the reasons in this case. However, your father's job is to uphold the law, and I worry that Drenn will cause you trouble, somehow."

"He's one to cause trouble, when he should be," I didn't finish, but waved a hand in the direction of the poisoned lands.

"That may have ramped up his—less than rational behavior of late," Hunter told me. "He knows he got caught, and he knows he owes his life to the King's love and generosity where he's concerned."

"We understand that much," Barth agreed. "But he's still the Crown Prince, and can still cause trouble, big or small, in the long term."

"What kind of trouble, do you think?"

"I believe he knows you have sympathy for Sherra. Therefore, he's doing his best to keep you two apart, when she's the one who can keep you alive."

"You think he's aiming for my death?" Neither answered. Hunter dipped his chin and refused to look at me. After a

Chapter 11

moment's reflection, I realized that Drenn wouldn't shed a tear if I fell.

He'd have all of Father's attention and love, then. Why he thought he didn't have his share now befuddled me. "This bears thinking about," I held up a hand.

"Think quickly, then. The trials are in two days, Thorn. I will protect the girl from whatever I read in her, but you have to make the right choice, too." Barth's eyes bored into mine.

That's when I saw that he was afraid. Afraid of what the future held—not just for me, but for Father and the country as a whole, when Drenn took Father's place. Drenn had a penchant for pettiness, and it hadn't abated—rather, it had grown with the years.

"I'll do what I can," I said, flexing my hands as if they were cramped.

"Good. Are we sure about the girl?" Hunter asked. "Will she make the right choice in this?"

"I have a feeling she'll have three names in mind," I admitted. "Mine, Armon's and Levi's. I can't predict which one of us she'd choose."

"There is Prince's privilege," Barth suggested.

"I've never exercised that option," I growled. "It's not fair," I added.

"What's fair about Drenn making everyone in the palace fearful and uncomfortable?" Hunter asked. "What's fair about his attempts to get rid of Sherra so you'll not have the protection you may need?"

"She'll have rank immediately if you declare Prince's privilege," Barth pointed out. "Lieutenant or Captain, whichever you choose. Don't you think it's deserved? She's already saved lives—and the camp, too."

"Stop pressuring me," I held up a hand. "Let me think about this, all right?" I turned my gaze away from them and stared, unseeing, out the single window in my office.

"Thorn, don't think too long—too much is at stake, here," Hunter breathed softly. I heard them get to their feet, followed by silence. Barth had *stepped* them away.

I couldn't shake the feeling that things were happening in the King's City that I wasn't aware of, and Hunter and Barth were attempting to deliver whatever blow it was as gently as possible, because I had enough worries on my plate.

Never had the enemy hammered us as relentlessly during the heat of summer as they had this year, and fall was coming quickly. If they stepped up the attacks, we needed as many able bodies on the battlefield as we could place there.

Father, in his usual way, could be ignoring what I'd recognized months ago. Somehow, the enemy knew we were in a weakened state, and were determined to exterminate us as quickly as they could.

Drenn, in his usual way, would ignore it for a different reason. He didn't care about the army as long as we kept the enemy away from the King's City. That way, he could continue his palace intrigues, bullying, and the occasional breaking of the laws.

Was he now plotting my death, as Hunter and Barth believed?

It was possible, after taking recent events into consideration. What I'd said to him during our last meeting, I thought was an empty threat spoken in the heat of the moment. Now, I realized I was serious the entire time.

* * *

Sherra
"Two more days." Reena sounded worried.

Chapter 11

"Hey," I said, causing her to lift her eyes from the plate in front of her for a moment. She sat across from me at our evening meal, Bela at her side.

"I have full confidence in you," I told her. "You've performed better on the training field than some who've been in training all along. Don't start doubting yourself now."

"I can't help but worry," she said in a small voice.

"We're all worried, because none of us has done this before," Wend said.

"You don't need to be worried," Bela snorted. "You're perfect at everything."

"I'm a second," Wend declared. Bela jerked her head up at Wend's admission.

"I'm a third," Jae said.

"But," Reena breathed. "You're one of the best—everybody says so. You went with the commander on his special mission."

"Sherra," Wend and Jae said at the same time, before laughing about it. "She wouldn't let us fall behind," Jae said. "She refused to let us wash out."

"And we're here for the same reason," Reena chewed her lower lip.

"Look, that's neither here nor there," I said. "Just do what you've done a hundred times—perform your duties. That's all this is, I think."

"With the King watching," Misten teased.

"I was hoping you'd leave that part out," I pointed my fork at her. "Look, I know this is a stressful time—I feel it myself. Just—don't lose confidence in your ability, that's all I'm saying. You've worked hard to get here, and you deserve to stand next to any other trainee in this camp."

"We're worried about the lists," Bela confessed. "That they'll only see us as washouts from the beginning, and pass us over because of that."

"Stop thinking about that, all right?" I attempted to comfort her, when my own gut knotted at the thought of it. The thought of going to a stranger, if I weren't given the choices I wanted, made me ill.

"What would you like to see in your warrior?" Caral asked Bela quietly.

"Somebody who cares about me," she sighed and dropped eyes. "That's all. Somebody who'll care at the end."

Silently I cursed the King and his laws, which forced women into these positions. Yes, we were needed on the battlefield, but there had to be a better way.

Had to be.

I wondered what would happen if I cursed the King's name aloud. Yes, it was considered treason, and depending upon the severity, the death penalty could be levied. I dreamed of a time when voices could be raised at what they saw as tyranny or unjust laws, in the hopes of making a change.

Especially regarding women, and specifically the black roses. I think I'd hated the King for a very long time; I'd just never voiced it aloud, or cursed his name to anyone other than myself.

Yes, I'd told Kerok that the King didn't care about us, but that wasn't the same as cursing his name. I'd been given permission to speak freely, too, and that should count for something.

"I think we all want that," Caral responded to Bela's statement. "Keep your chin up, trainee. You never know what the day will bring."

Chapter 11

In my mind, Caral was a natural leader. I hoped whomever she chose recognized and encouraged that, rather than feeling intimidated by it. Once again, I wanted her to take Levi or Armon—that would be the best fit, and neither would try to hold her back.

Are you thinking again? Armon asked. He and Levi sat at a table nearby, pretending to ignore our conversation.

Always, Colonel. It isn't like I can shut it off every time.

Understood, trainee. Finish your meal. You need to keep your strength up.

Yes, Colonel.

Call me Armon in mindspeak, Sherra. It's right—and fair.

Thank you.

Thank you—for keeping us from getting fried by lightning. Levi and I owe you a honey cake and a glass of wine.

I haven't had honey cake in a while. I'd take it, I replied.

* * *

Two days can pass slowly or quickly, depending upon whether there's hope or dread at the end of them.

For me, it was mostly dread, although I did want to get all of it over with, so my future would be clearer.

That's how I found myself waiting in line with the other Fourths, to be called into an infirmary examination room to be seen by the King's Chief Diviner, Barth.

On the training field, Second and Third were going through their final testing while the King, a few guards and advisors looked on. Levi didn't remark on the process; he marched us directly from breakfast to the infirmary.

Outside, Fifth cohort waited their turn with the King's Diviner.

The Rose Mark

I worried that those in Second and Third would be so nervous they'd botch their efforts with the new method. I worried the King wouldn't be impressed, or decide that trying something new wasn't a good idea.

Worrying causes wearying, Armon informed me.

He'd joined us late—walking into the infirmary now, when we were halfway through the cohort. So far, there'd been no news as to what the Diviner saw in anyone.

I wondered if that came later.

Three stood in front of me; Wend, Misten and Caral. Jae had already gone through, as had the former washouts. I worried about them, too. Would the Diviner find them unsuitable?

If he did, they'd be stripped of their power and thrown back in with the other drudges.

They didn't want that. I didn't want it on their behalf. So many things could go wrong with this day, and it terrified me.

"Stop worrying." I was pulled into Caral's arms. "Just stop, all right?" she whispered against my ear. "We're here. Make the best of it."

"All right," I mumbled as she let me go.

"Wend," the next name in line was called. I sighed.

* * *

"My name is Barth." He smiled at me as he introduced himself. This was the King's Chief Diviner, and I was terrified of him. He'd done a very thorough job when he'd been called to determine Merrin's and Ura's misdeeds.

He was about to put his hands on my face, and he'd see everything in me, too.

My hatred for the King.

My possession of a forbidden book.

I'd be lucky if I weren't executed on the spot.

Chapter 11

"Let's see," he placed hands on either side of my forehead as I sat on the examination table. Miri, instructor from Fifth, sat in a corner, giving every trainee from Fourth and Fifth as much comfort and support her presence could offer.

Barth never said anything while he worked; I watched as his eyes lost focus. If I hadn't been so frightened, I'd have wondered about his talent and how it worked.

"Well, now." Barth's eyes returned to normal. He was still smiling at me, although this time, the smile didn't reach his eyes. *If the King asks you a question, young woman, your answer should be yes. Understand? Your life depends upon it—as do many others.*

His mindspeak was loaded with authority—and with suppressed information that I had no access to. I had a good idea what that information was, though, and wondered why he wasn't calling for guards immediately. Perhaps the King would present the questions concerning my guilt himself, but how would that save my life and others, too?

My answer will be yes, I silently replied. I'm sure he recognized the fear in my mental voice, but I couldn't hold it back.

Good. Very good. "You're dismissed," he said aloud. "Call the next trainee, please."

Chapter 12

*K*erok
"I like this new method. Very much," Father said as Levi poured a glass of wine for him in my office. We'd stopped the trials after Second and Third had performed, so everyone could have a midday meal. I'd arranged a private meal in my office for Father, Barth, Hunter and myself.

A table had been brought in and covered with a fine cloth by drudges, who worked silently to lay plates and carry food and drink.

"You'll have to describe it to me, as I'll miss all of it," Barth mused.

"Come to Secondary Camp, Barth. You'll see it in full practice with the warriors," I invited.

"I'll do that," he agreed, holding up his wineglass in a salute.

"I think it's extraordinary," Hunter said. "A work of genius, no less. I predict longer lives for the escorts, if we're successful in retraining what's in the field now."

"That's what I plan to do, actually, while at Secondary Camp," I said. "I'll bring in one or two pairs at a time and show them how it's done. More, if possible, providing the enemy lets up somewhat."

"I remember when the Secondary Camp would be filled with new trainees and their warriors," Hunter said. "Most of it lies empty after new black roses are named."

"Has the enemy become that much stronger?" Father asked. I noticed he wasn't eating much, but didn't remark on it.

"No. It's not that," I said. "We've just become—fewer and weaker."

"If you find a way to change those things—without resorting to a breeding program because it's far too late for that, I'll listen," Father sighed.

"I may have answers for you soon, Father, but that may take some cooperation from Barth and other strong Diviners."

"What sort of help?" Barth was immediately interested.

"Is it possible to remove the blocking of a trainee's power, after they wash out? Male and female?" I asked.

"Yes, I think so. I've just never done it," Barth admitted.

"Good. Father, some of the trainees you'll see this afternoon were washouts. I challenge you to sort them from the others when they go through their trials."

Father's hand stilled as he gripped his wineglass. "What changed about them?"

Chapter 12

"Sherra. She was determined not to let them fail. And they haven't. At least one of them is quite talented with her shields, and can move them about, easily and under a warrior's direction, if necessary."

"And you say she washed out?"

"At the beginning, Father. She couldn't produce fire and was tossed aside with many others. Sherra and some of her fellow trainees took them in and showed them how to do the things they'd previously failed at doing. She can touch them and see their talent, I think, and then has the ability to let them see it, too."

"Outstanding," Hunter breathed, setting his empty wineglass on the table with a joyful thump. "If we can gather up all the washouts and release the power blocked within them, that would certainly increase our army."

"I want the same thing for the escort instructors," I said. "If they'd had some sort of power, I believe they'd be better able to teach trainees."

"I think that's how it used to be, before we needed every able-bodied and talented woman on the front lines," Barth said.

"Hunter, check the laws," Father waved a hand. "Give me the legalities on all this, please."

"Gladly," Hunter agreed. "The moment we return to the palace."

"I'd like the information, too, if you don't mind," I said.

"Include Thorn in all your communications," Father said, and that was that.

"Commander, it's time," Armon knocked lightly on my door.

"We'll be there soon," I called out. "Shall we?" I nodded at Father.

209

"Yes," he said, rising from his chair. "You've issued a challenge. I wish to see if I can solve it."

* * *

Sherra

I should have known they'd make me wait until last. It made sense—none of the others probably wanted to do their testing after I did mine, and I couldn't blame them for that. Armon was wise to keep the members of our cohort in the testing order he'd designated.

"They're doing well," Levi said. I stood beside him at the fence surrounding the training field. High on the stands, under a canopy, sat the King, his advisor, Hunter, a few guards and Commander Kerok.

The other warriors sat lower down—those who hadn't been selected to participate in the trials, anyway.

Caral was next to last, and she was performing very well. Blasts from the warrior who stood near her sailed straight through her shield, while those of her warrior opponent broke and spattered in clouds of sparks, smoke and loud booms.

We'd heard applause earlier for the first two cohorts. We received as much or more for our efforts. Even the washouts had successfully completed their trials, and walked toward the far end of the field with huge smiles on their faces.

I should have known Armon had something different planned for me, however. When Caral finished, she grinned and winked at me as she walked past to join the others from Fourth.

Levi urged me forward.

Two warriors came to stand beside me. Two more appeared farther away. I was about to see if I could allow two separate blasts through, while protecting the three of us from multiple attacks from the outside.

Chapter 12

"She has to touch both your hands," Armon stepped in to explain things.

"Armon?" I asked. Why were they singling me out for this, when I'd never attempted it before?

"Don't worry—I think you can handle this," he said.

I reached out to touch the first warrior's hands, searching for his fire. Once I located it and conformed mine with his, I turned to the other warrior and touched his hands, to do the same.

"Ready?" Armon asked after I squared my shoulders.

Who would ever be ready for this, with the King watching? "I'm ready," I said anyway.

Armon had barely stepped away before my shield was under attack—both adversaries were tossing blasts as hard and fast as they could.

The two beside me launched blasts of their own, which sailed right through, landing near the rock formations around the lake and blasting some of them to rubble. The sound of those hits carried back and rocked the stands behind us, causing the warriors to whoop.

I ignored them—in the interest of self-preservation. The onslaught continued for a time that felt like forever, until Armon sent mindspeak, telling me to capture the attackers' blasts and toss them away.

I did so, working to land them around the same distant rock formations already destroyed by the two beside me.

I imagined after the fourth or fifth volleys landed there that the rock had been pounded into sand, which resulted in high-flying geysers of small rocks, sand and dust, which blew away with the force of resulting winds.

The attacks went on—the booming sounds coming in a near-regular rhythm. The warriors in the stands laughed

211

every time a blast rattled the seats beneath them. I hoped the seats were sturdy enough to remain standing—especially if Armon didn't call a halt to this soon.

Even the warriors standing with me were grinning as they sent blast after blast—without having to wait for me to raise and lower my shield.

This—this was how it should be in my mind. It saved all of us time and energy, and, unless you counted our sweat from the heat of the sun overhead, we were still relatively fresh.

Still, I was grateful when Armon called a halt to my testing. Ignoring the applause, I walked toward Levi, who couldn't stop grinning.

"I knew you could do it," he said as I reached his side.

"A little warning would have been nice," I said as we headed toward the rest of the cohort. Fifth was ready to take the field after we left.

"Where's the fun in that? This is a test, remember?" Levi said. "You passed. Be happy."

"I smell," I said. I did. The top part of my fatigues was drenched, too, and I wanted a drink of water. A *big* drink of water.

"We'll head to the showers, now," Levi announced to the others when we arrived. "Water will be waiting there for you, and some fruit, courtesy of the King and the southern domes."

"I hope it's apples," Wend whispered as she came to stand in formation beside me. "I'd like grapes," Caral sighed. "I only got to taste them once."

I wanted pears, but I didn't say that.

Levi marched us to the showers, where he left us, after telling us to meet him outside when we were finished. "I'm proud of you," he added. "I don't think anyone could say you're not worthy of the black rose you wear."

Chapter 12

"This is so good," I moaned after taking a second bite of the juiciest pear I'd ever eaten. I leaned against a wall just inside the door into the showers, a cup of water in one hand and my pear in the other.

I'd cleaned up first, after getting a much-needed drink of water. Once I was dressed, I found a drudge-managed table laden with apples, grapes, peaches and pears.

"Are you kidding? These grapes are fit for a king," Caral came to stand beside me.

Eventually, the rest of the cohort joined us, eating their choice of fruit and licking juice from fingers, it was so good.

"Time to join Levi," I sighed when the last one finished her treat. Caral took the lead, while I waited for them to file out the door, taking last position as I usually did.

Levi led us back to our barracks, where he instructed us to wait until Fifth cohort was finished with their testing.

"Rest if you can," he advised. "The rankings and lists will come after the last trainee is tested. We'll march to the mess hall for those announcements."

"Were there any washouts?" I asked.

"None so far," he said. "Be proud. All of you. I think the King is very impressed."

* * *

Kerok

I was just as surprised as Sherra by the test Armon set for her. Hunter sat beside Father, his mouth open more often than not as he watched her trial on the field.

"I've never seen anything like that," Father shook his head when it was over. "I had no idea it was possible."

I'll need a moment of your time when the testing is done, Barth sent mindspeak.

213

I can arrange that, I replied. *Just me, or anyone else?*
Hunter, too.

That told me the unscheduled meeting involved Sherra and what Barth had seen in her. *Is there something we should worry about?*

Not concerning Sherra, no. It's something else, but I want to ask your thoughts—and Hunter's—in the matter.

I'll ask the instructors to show Father around, then. The crack in the soil is still there from Sherra's dome—I think he may be interested in that.

Good. I'll meet you in your office, then.

An hour later, after I left Father and his guards in the hands of Ana and Miri, I *stepped* to my office to meet with Barth and Hunter.

"What did you find?" I asked while offering seats to both men.

"Sherra received the book from a blind pot seller when she was ten, and had no idea at the time it was forbidden."

"A blind pot seller?" Hunter asked.

"That was Sherra's memory of the woman. Her memory also told me that a farmer traded the book, some vegetables and crockery to the pot seller in exchange for two cooking pots."

"You don't think a farmer had the thing, do you?" Hunter scoffed.

"No, and I believe I have a suitable reason. I believe the book belonged to the pot seller, and she knew exactly what she was doing when she offered a seemingly innocent book to a ten-year-old."

"What makes you believe that?"

"Her name," Barth said.

"Sherra's?"

Chapter 12

"No. The village called her Pottles, because she sold pots. Her real name was Doret."

"Coincidence," Hunter flung out a hand.

"What if it isn't?"

"Where is she now?" I demanded. "We'll find her and let you ask her yourself."

"She's dead. I saw that memory in Sherra, too."

"So. We have an old, blind woman with the same name as a kidnapped and murdered Queen from nearly two centuries ago. You have an active imagination, Barth." Hunter still wasn't buying Barth's explanation.

"I've never met anyone with that name, have you?" Barth wasn't giving up.

"Tell me how it's possible?" I rolled my shoulders to get kinks out of them. I'd been sitting most of the day, and the inactivity made me restless.

"I don't know," Barth shook his head. Hunter and I were wearing him down in this, I could see.

"Without putting your hands on the woman, you'll never know—and she's dead. If you want to visit her ashes, you'll have to find them yourself," I sighed. "Barth, it's a grand theory, but it doesn't hold up under scrutiny. Besides, she'd be ancient by now, and most women don't live that long."

"I know, but the woman I saw in Sherra *was* ancient."

"How old did Sherra believe she was?"

"Sixty-nine, but the images I saw," Barth argued.

"Barth, I think you're chasing rainbows," Hunter clapped him on the shoulder. "The woman's dead, regardless. We still have things to do, today. We can discuss old, blind women over wine some night, but not now."

The men have their lists prepared, and the rankings have been recorded, Armon informed me.

215

The Rose Mark

Meet us in the mess hall, then, and have the instructors bring the trainees.

It will be done, Commander.

* * *

Sherra

"It's time," Levi walked into our barracks, interrupting talk among all in Fourth cohort. Fear and excitement ran rampant, and I'd shut out the noise and occasional laughter, choosing to sit against the wall beside my cot and think.

"First of all," Levi said while I rose to my feet, "There were no washouts."

The former washouts squealed with joy and hugged one another.

"I think you'll be pleased, for the most part, as to how the rankings went. Now, assemble outside and we'll march to the mess hall, quietly and orderly, as becomes a black rose cohort. Is that understood?"

"Yes, sir," they all chorused.

I hadn't said anything. This would be where we learned our future—and our fate. Wend appeared at my side and hugged me. "Come on, we have things to do," I sighed after hugging her back.

The march to the mess hall was faster than I wanted it to be. Uncertainty clouded my mind and my future. I prayed that Armon and Levi had placed their names on my list, because more and more, I was leaning in their direction.

At least I knew what life would be like with them, and there would be no expectations of anything different. Friendship was a crutch I could lean on in the years I had left, and I considered both very good friends.

Chapter 12

Kerok—he was like the wind. He could be strong and violent, cool or hot. Frosty, too, at times, if he weren't pleased about something.

I'd only seen gentleness from him once, and that had served to confuse me more.

"The warriors are already inside," the whispers made their way back to me as Caral and the others in the lead walked inside the long building.

Behind us, I could hear Fifth being marched toward the mess hall. That meant Second and Third had already arrived.

Once my eyes adjusted to the dim light inside the mess hall, I saw that the tables had been removed, although the benches remained. Warriors occupied the benches on one side, while the trainee cohorts were being seated on the other side.

At the far end stood the King, his guards and advisors, Commander Kerok, Armon, Falia and Ana.

The King conversed quietly with Hunter and Barth; Falia and Ana were soon joined by Levi, who'd acted as Fourth's instructor. He'd done very well, in my opinion, considering the hardships and deaths we'd faced throughout the months of our training.

Kerok—his face was a mask. He wasn't looking around as the others were. He stared straight ahead as if lost in some memory, which made me wonder what he was thinking about.

* * *

Kerok

I hadn't seen a gathering since Grae had confirmed her black rose, and then chosen me from the others on her list.

I'd watched her during her training—always the quiet one, who observed carefully and executed deliberately. I think

217

The Rose Mark

I'd fallen in love with that, first, and her later. What would she say to me if she were here?

Would she urge me to do what I now understood I must?

In my short time with her, she'd never displayed jealousy; I'd never given her a reason. I didn't intend to give her memory any reason, either, but would lay out my truth to the one I ended up with and we would go on from there.

Were there any other warriors here, who now reflected on past partners—their escorts who'd protected their lives as long as they could?

I think Armon and Levi did, perhaps, because they'd been close friends with Nyra and Gale. How I wished that Grae had been taught the new method. I felt sure she'd still be alive if that had been.

My eyes wandered to the trainee responsible for the new method, and mourned the fact that she'd been born too late to save my love.

Fifth cohort began filing in. Once they were seated and Miri joined the other instructors, the ceremony would begin.

Black roses would be confirmed by the King, rankings would be announced, and then the lists would be given to the new escorts, who'd consider the names written on folded papers.

The following day, we'd gather here again, when the first-ranked black rose of a newly-formed First Cohort would make her selection, and those following her would make theirs, while names were struck off lists as warriors were chosen.

Then, following the first round, those black roses in the new Second cohort would make their choices—after some shuffling, of course. It would continue until all roses had chosen a warrior.

Chapter 12

Even with the fourteen previous washouts that had been added to the black roses, we still had four more warriors than we had black roses.

Any warrior not taken would be forced to wait until the following training period. Those men could still serve in some capacity; they merely wouldn't have a rose beside them.

More than anything, I wanted to *step* to my office and pour myself a drink from the bottle of whiskey Levi and Armon gave me.

There were things to do, though, and Father was here, expecting me to be nearby. I wouldn't disappoint him, no matter how much I wanted to be somewhere else.

"Now that everyone is here," Hunter stepped forward to announce, "It is the King's pleasure to announce that all in this trainee class have passed their final tests. Congratulations, you have all been elevated to the rank of an official black rose."

The warriors cheered and clapped—this was good news to them, as it meant more of them would be chosen by an escort.

"Now," Hunter went on, "after receiving input from your instructors and from the King and his advisors, I hold the final rankings in my hand." He held up a sheaf of papers.

This was it—I either spoke now or refused an opportunity to do what I saw as the right thing. "My King," I strode toward Father and bowed in deference, as was prescribed by the situation.

* * *

Sherra

Hunter, the King's advisor, held our rankings aloft—pieces of paper with a name and corresponding number on each. I assumed they'd begin with either first or last, depending on how they wanted to manage the suspense.

219

I just wanted it over with, so I could begin to plan my remaining years—if I were so lucky to last that long.

That's when Kerok walked toward the King and addressed him with a bow. The King's reply gave me the shivers.

"What is it, my son?" the King responded to Kerok's words. A gasp rippled through the black roses—there was no corresponding sound from the warriors—*they'd known.*

Still, my mind worked furiously, attempting to equate Kerok with the King. He only had two sons—Drenn and Thorn. There was no son named Kerok.

My breath was uneven as I struggled to follow the rest.

"Father, I wish to invoke Prince's privilege," Kerok said.

What was that? I'd never heard of it. What was Kerok saying? This had to be a mistake.

"Ah." The King appeared confused for a moment. "Tell me your choice, then," the King finally said. Something in his words held hope and dread—hope that the choice would be a good one; dread that it would be the opposite.

"Father, I, Prince Thorn Wulfson Kerok Rex, choose Sherra as my black rose escort. I ask that you and all others present bear witness to my choice."

If Wend hadn't gripped my arm with the strength of a coyote's jaws at that moment, I may have blacked out from shock.

"I approve your choice, my son," the King beamed at Kerok. "You know she must consent before I offer congratulations."

"I do," Kerok dipped his head.

"Sherra, get up." Levi was suddenly before me, urging me to rise from my place on the bench.

Chapter 12

The walk toward Kerok was a numb one, and I couldn't recall getting from the bench to his side afterward.

I had no feeling in my legs and little breath in my lungs as he and I stood before the King.

If the King asks you a question, young woman, your answer should be yes, echoed in my mind.

"Black rose Sherra, do you accept Prince Thorn's offer?" the King asked.

I froze. *Sherra, answer him,* Armon's voice commanded.

"Y-yes," I stuttered, as if my teeth were chattering from cold. Barth's words had held a warning. He'd said my life and the lives of others depended upon my answer. *What did he know?*

"You have the King's blessing," the King laughed as he held his hands aloft.

I felt as if I'd been punched in the gut.

"Now, Thorn, there is the matter of her rank," the King continued. I blinked at him in confusion. Rank no longer mattered—I felt as if I'd been forced to make this choice, whether it was one I wanted or not.

"I choose the rank of Captain for my black rose," Kerok said. "She came in first in the trainee rankings, and the elevation is deserved."

"Then it will be so written," the King declared. He was happy.

I was stunned.

Bow to the King, Armon instructed. Like a puppet, I did so. Kerok took my left hand, lifted it and kissed the black rose on my wrist.

The mess hall erupted into cheers as the room darkened about me.

* * *

The Rose Mark

Kerok

"A trying day, nothing more," the physician said after leaving my bedroom. Sherra sat up on my bed while Levi attempted to coax her to drink a glass of juice.

I'd waited outside for the physician's diagnosis; I didn't want to do more harm than I'd already done, blindsiding her as I had.

I had to tell her the truth, and I wanted privacy to do it.

"You'll inform Hunter?" I asked.

"Of course, my Prince. I am grateful to be able to call you by your proper title. Commander doesn't do your status justice."

"Hmmph," I snorted.

"You were always a humble sort," he laughed. "Good luck with that one in there—I think she's ready to take someone apart."

"Thank you for your help," I said. He nodded before walking out of my suite. Not far away, in the mess hall, the rankings and list distribution was winding down—Armon was keeping me informed through mindspeak. I wasn't sorry I was missing it—I had copies of everything on my desk and didn't need or want to see it in person.

Sherra's collapse had come at a fortuitous time; Father imagined she was overcome by her good fortune and dismissed us, Levi included, so we could tend to her.

I doubted Sherra considered anything about this shock as good fortune; I'd seen her face as she'd walked toward me, stiff-legged as a puppet.

I probably should apologize, before having an extra bed hauled into my quarters. She could sleep in my bed while I slept on a cot in the receiving area. I doubted I'd be getting much sleep until we headed to Secondary Camp, anyway.

222

Chapter 12

King's Palace
Drenn, Crown Prince of Az-ca

"Stop whining. I had to wait until Barth was gone for an extended period before allowing you here; he knows everything and snoops too much."

Merrin wasn't happy with my answer, but I was tired of his complaints. He should be happy to be alive, but had he thanked me once for ordering Father's assassins to allow him to keep his power?

Not even once. He should be grateful that those two were under my command instead of Father's.

"Those holes you call caves have nothing in them except blankets and rattlesnakes," Merrin failed to follow my advice. "Besides, you know as well as I do that there was no blood on those sheets—we looked. Somebody put it there."

"I just told you, Barth knows everything. He was waiting for us to make a mistake. He wasn't wrong in what he accused us of, either—Bray confirmed his findings." I named Barth's secondary Diviner. "Besides, I've learned a few things since your supposed death, you know."

"You could have sent better food and more water," Merrin grumbled. "This is the first time I've had a bath and clean clothes since Thorn dumped me in the poisoned lands."

"You're alive. Count your blessings," I snapped at him. "All you have to do is hold on until I become King, and then you can magically appear again, with a tale of survival in the poisoned lands to your credit. We can plot Thorn's death in the meantime, and you'll walk right into the Commander's position."

The Rose Mark

"What about Barth and Hunter? When you become King?" Merrin wasn't letting go of any loose threads; he toyed with them like a pet cat attempting to unravel the entire cloth.

"I will be King," I said. "I can dismiss anyone and bring in my own advisors. We can discredit them if you like, before I send them away."

"They deserve worse than that for framing us," Merrin growled.

"We weren't framed, remember? We did those things. Father didn't punish me—I knew he wouldn't, and I was able to keep you alive. Have another beer—it will cheer you up."

Merrin still wasn't finished with his complaints, but at least he poured another glass of beer for both of us.

"I have something for you," I said. "Maybe it will help you in some way."

"What is it? Say it's a decent bed, at least."

"No. Better," I said, pulling the book from a desk drawer and handing it to him. "I found this in the catacombs."

"What the hell were you doing down there with those dusty old bones?" Merrin demanded.

"Merely reflecting upon the ancient custom of burial as opposed to turning bodies to ash," I shrugged. "And that includes a penchant for asking that you be buried with items you've grown fond of—such as books. I've already handed one forbidden book to my brother to place doubts in his mind; you get the other one. Perhaps, since you hold power, it will be of some use to you."

He took the book, then, and studied the title. *Thorn's Book of Advanced Divination Techniques* was written across the front.

"Thorn? As in the ancient King named Thorn?"

Chapter 12

"The same one my dear brother was named after," I chuckled, "and destined to meet the same fate, although he won't be buried with his favorite things—I'll see to it myself. In your free time—which I assume you have plenty of, read that book and tell me whether you find anything useful in it."

* * *

Sherra

"I'm not an invalid." I frowned at Levi, who'd asked a drudge to bring a tray of food to me. Kerok—Thorn—was elsewhere; he hadn't bothered to speak with me after the incident in the mess hall.

"How did the rankings go?" I asked with a sigh. At least I was no longer on Thorn's bed—Levi allowed me to move to a corner chair with a small table beside it. The food tray sat on the table, while Levi waited for me to eat, arms crossed over his chest and glaring like a broody hen.

"Fourth came away with most of the highest rankings," the glare disappeared and a grin transformed his face. "Caral would have been second behind you, if she hadn't gotten demerits."

"How are they doing?" I asked.

"Fine. Armon has been checking on them, but they're all gathered tightly together, whispering about their list of warriors."

"Why?" I asked. I'd changed the subject, but Levi hadn't realized it.

"Well, that's what they do," he began.

"No, Levi." I rubbed my forehead. "Why weren't we told about Kerok—Thorn?"

"He didn't want special treatment. He hates it in the field, too. The Prince Commander fights on the front lines with the best of us. That's how Grae died."

The Rose Mark

"Grae?"

"His previous escort."

Chapter 13

*K*erok

I stayed away until late, hoping she'd be asleep when I got in. Yes, I was being cowardly about this, and I felt bad about it. Not bad enough to wake her, however, when I determined she was asleep.

There'd be time the following day, or perhaps when we arrived at Secondary Camp, for her to hear my truth. If she wanted to dress me down for my actions, then I'd allow her to speak freely.

Father, Hunter and Barth arrived safely at the palace; I received mindspeak from Hunter, letting me know. They looked tired when they left, but it could have been the extra glasses of wine I'd shared with them in my office.

Armon? I sent.

Commander?

Will you meet me in my sitting room, please?

I'll be there shortly.

He arrived seconds later, wearing a sleeveless undershirt, fatigue pants and boots. He'd dressed quickly, letting me know I'd pulled him away from his bed.

"I'm sorry," I waved a hand. "I didn't mean to wake you."

"I'm here. What is it, Commander?"

"Do you have any suggestions on how to tell Sherra about Grae? Sit, please," I offered a nearby chair.

"Ah. Well, Levi may have let Grae's name slip earlier—he told me because he was worried about it the moment he said it." Armon settled heavily onto the chair and gave me a nod when I held up my half-empty wine bottle.

"So she knows about Grae." I handed the bottle to Armon, who rose to retrieve a glass from the collection I kept in my sitting room.

"Only her name and that she was your previous escort." Armon reseated himself and sipped wine.

"Do you think she'll be upset?"

"I doubt it. She's very knowledgeable about these things. It would only make sense that she'd have predecessors. Sherra is quite practical, Commander. I doubt she'll have illusions about any relationship you may have with her."

"I hate that." I set my glass down on the side table with a thump. "I hate that she may be cheated of—well, many things."

"Then tell her that. Honesty works best, in my experience."

"I know. It's just—difficult to admit that I may be cheating her, especially since I really didn't give her much choice in the matter."

Chapter 13

"Wait until you talk with her about it," Armon suggested. "Stop worrying until you know there's something to worry about."

"You know, I'm grateful that you didn't suggest that I pretend anything with her. That would have been Merrin's advice."

"Hmmph." Armon sipped more wine.

"You saw through him, didn't you?" I asked. "It's all right—it took a while, but I finally did, too."

"Only interested in sex, that one," Armon didn't hide the contempt in his voice. "Talked badly about his escorts when he was away from them, too. They were just things to him—things that he would use up until they died."

"You know there are others like him," I said.

"I know. It makes me angry."

"With the way the laws are written concerning black roses, I don't see a viable way to change anything," I said. "Drenn, if he had any sense and wasn't as bad as Merrin about some things, could make a great deal of difference. He could present changes to Father, and perhaps push them through."

"Don't you have some sway in the matter?"

"Drenn will circumvent anything I suggest. He doesn't like me because I was born with power and he wasn't. Hunter says Drenn is filled with jealousy. He's had his way of digging at me since Barth declared me powerful."

"That can ruin a family dinner." Armon refilled his glass while I barked a laugh.

* * *

Sherra

Kerok's bed didn't sag in the middle like my cot in the barracks did. His bed hadn't been slept on by too many trainees to count, either.

229

I wallowed in the luxury of it when I woke, realizing that I'd probably slept later than I should have.

I heard stirring in the other room and quietly rolled off the bed. I didn't know who it might be, so I was determined to look. Putting up a shield, I walked toward the door, only to see it opened.

I jumped when Kerok's face appeared in the opening. I may have shrieked in fright, too, although my hand clapped immediately over my mouth.

"I just wanted to make sure you were up," he said. "There is a shower through that small door in the corner," he pointed behind me. "Clean up and I'll take you to breakfast with Armon and Levi."

"Th-thank you," I stuttered. No, I hadn't recovered from my fright, as weak as that made me feel. I doubted I'd get used to being in such close quarters for a very long time. He and I needed to discuss things, too, mostly concerning his being the Prince Commander and his high-handed method of circumventing any choices I'd had after my testing.

I could still hear Barth's voice in my head, however, telling me my answer to the King's question should be yes.

He had to know about the book, yet he hadn't pointed it out.

Did Kerok know about the book, too?

"Go," Kerok commanded. "We'll be late if you don't clean up now."

I turned and almost ran for the shower.

* * *

Kerok

I recalled how Grae used to look right after waking—tousled, with sleep still in her eyes.

Chapter 13

I'd startled Sherra; she'd gone into a defensive posture the moment I opened the door. I hoped that wasn't our morning routine from now on—I hated that she was afraid.

Armon, we'll meet you at the mess hall in a few minutes, I informed him.

* * *

Sherra

I washed and dressed in record time, and with my hair still damp, I joined Kerok in his sitting room. I couldn't bring myself to think of him as Prince Thorn; that way lay trouble.

"Ready?" he asked when I stopped next to him.

"Yes." I didn't—couldn't—meet his gaze.

He took my arm and *stepped* us away.

* * *

"How do you feel?" Levi asked first thing. Kerok had led me to a table, where Armon and Levi sat together. Instead of getting our own trays of food, they were brought to us by drudges.

"Strange," I admitted while utensils and drinks were set in front of us.

Kerok lifted an eyebrow but didn't comment. I hardly knew how to act while food was set in front of us. I'd always had to do those things myself.

"Strange?" Armon asked.

"I don't know what to say or how to act," I admitted. May as well tell the truth—I was out of my element, and that could be proven at any moment.

"You'll have officer training at Secondary Camp," Kerok said. I watched his hands as he broke a roll apart to butter it.

"Thank you," I whispered to nobody in particular.

Armon snickered; Kerok smiled slightly. Levi wore a face-encompassing grin.

"Eat your food—it'll get cold," Kerok tapped his butter knife against my plate.

Lifting my own butter knife, I broke my roll in half. Armon slid the butter dish in my direction. As a trainee, I'd gotten one small pat of butter at breakfast, just like everyone else.

This dish was full of butter, and I wanted to weep at the largesse.

"I think she likes butter," Levi said as I scraped butter across both halves of my roll and bit into a half with a sigh of pleasure.

"Butter and milk are scarce, and," I shrugged before taking another bite.

"And what?" Levi asked.

"They don't waste a lot of food feeding those who are only going to die anyway."

Kerok frowned and cleared his throat.

"What about your lessons? You're better at written answers and such than the rest of those here," Armon said.

"Hmmph. You can credit Pottles. Or blame her, if you want. My mother was dead. Pottles didn't care that my wrist was tattooed. She taught me a lot, and since she was blind, I'd read things to her from my school books. If I have good writing skills, it's because she corrected many mistakes when I was young."

"A blind woman?" Armon asked.

"She was the only friend I had. Everybody else went out of their way to avoid me."

"Because of the tattoo?"

"Like I had a terrible disease they were afraid of catching," I said. "I can't speak for any of the other girls, but I worry their experiences may be similar. If not for Pottles, I may have starved to death. She taught me how to cook by describing things to me, and I always shared her meal when it was done."

"What about your father?" Kerok asked.

"He ignored me, most of the time. My mother was dead already when the Diviner's tattoo artist marked me. After that, Father had no time or use for me. I could have disappeared and he wouldn't have cared."

"What would you change if you could, about your early life?" Kerok asked.

"I'd have asked to be taken and taught by a competent instructor much earlier," I said. "I'd never suggest marking children as young as two, either. Send the Diviner when they are eight, perhaps, and then take them then, to begin their education."

"Sounds like a lot of work," Levi said.

"At least there would be others like them in their classes, and they wouldn't be singled out as not worth feeding or educating," I said. "I may as well have been a ghost, except for Pottles."

"Where is she now?" Armon asked.

"Dead. She died eight months before the truck came to collect me."

"I'm sorry to hear that," Levi mumbled.

"Eat," Kerok reminded me.

I cut into my sausages and eggs.

* * *

"If you want, you can sit with your friends," Kerok told me. While we'd had breakfast, the cohorts had filed in, eaten and then waited to have their lists taken up.

The Rose Mark

Armon and Levi joined Falia, Ana and Miri at the head table at the other end of the mess hall, so they could announce choices and mark names off lists.

"Thank you." I left his side, heading toward the table where Wend, Caral, Jae and the others sat.

A flurry of whispers ran through black roses at other tables as I scooted onto the bench between Wend and Caral. Both hugged me while Jae, sitting on the opposite side, reached out to squeeze my hand.

My sigh of relief was silent; I worried that they'd treat me differently after being chosen by Kerok, who turned out to be the King's son and Prince Commander of the army.

"Before we begin with the lists," Ana announced, "We have a few promotions to announce. Those among you who will be designated as new officers will receive special training at Secondary Camp."

A hush went through the crowd of black roses. I'd been shocked by my elevation; it was evident that others would be as well.

"Named to the rank of Corporal are the following black rose troops," Ana went on. "Wend, Jae, Bera and Neka."

I clapped and cheered with the others at the announcement.

"As all of you saw yesterday, Sherra has been promoted to the rank of Captain. We have one other promotion to announce besides hers. Caral will be trained as a Lieutenant in the Prince Commander's army."

I whooped and hugged Caral, who appeared stunned at the news.

* * *

Kerok

Chapter 13

I watched everything from the back of the room. Before the choices were announced, the warriors filed in; Levi had *stepped* away to bring them. While they were still separated from the black rose troops, they'd have dinner with them tonight. Tomorrow, we'd head for Secondary Camp, sleeping arrangements would be sorted and the warrior-trainers would keep a close eye on the women, to ensure that they were treated properly.

I'd be leveling a sentence against any warrior who didn't follow the rules and the unwritten codes.

My eyes strayed to Sherra often, as I was curious how she'd react to the others' choices.

I hoped greatly that Caral would have the opportunity to choose Levi or Armon—she was suited to them and was a born leader—I'd pushed for her promotion, even with her demerits. She was officer material if I'd ever seen it.

It would also make it easier to fit into the dynamic formed by Levi and Armon as my trusted advisors at the battlefront.

The fact that she was good friends with Sherra didn't hurt, either. Sherra would need someone to lean on, when I couldn't or wouldn't be available.

Therefore, I hoped she'd take one of the two, and relieve my worries.

"The first warrior taken by Wend, who holds first place in the rankings, is Lieutenant Marc."

My shoulders relaxed slightly. Marc was an excellent choice, and I could see those two working together. He'd participated in the training much of the time, hadn't laughed at trainee failures and was more than helpful. He was usually passed over for a more handsome alternative.

Wend hadn't allowed a pretty face to sway her decision.

The Rose Mark

I watched Marc, then, who raised his arms in victory from his seat, while those around him slapped his back and congratulated him. To be chosen first was an honor and he knew it.

Other choices were made, then. I was happy to see Sherra's closest friends making well-considered choices—warriors who would protect and care for them. We were shocked, however, when Misten chose Levi. He'd been overjoyed and beamed at her as she shyly waved at him from her seat.

Then it was down to the last few roses. Caral was one of those, because of her demerits.

She'd have been ranked first after Sherra, without them.

Armon was still among the warriors waiting to be chosen. My body tensed as Ana began to read.

"Caral chooses Colonel Armon," she announced. The mess hall resounded with cheers.

* * *

Sherra

I didn't know it, but the warriors who were officers were allowed to take their black rose with them during their duties for the day. It was a way to get them accustomed to their new life and what would be expected of them. That meant Levi, Misten, Caral and Armon joined Kerok and me in Kerok's study.

Caral couldn't stop grinning. Misten wore an expression of bemused relief. I blinked when a messenger from the battlefield appeared in Kerok's office before his desk, in an empty spot there.

He'd sent mindspeak and now the messenger was here, handing off notes to Kerok. He'd done this the whole time I'd been in training, and I'd never known it.

Chapter 13

"Anything to report?" Kerok asked the man.

"Battle has been light the past two days, sir."

"Good. How's the General?"

"In better spirits, sir."

"I have this for him." Kerok reached into a desk drawer and drew out a sealed message. "I'll send for you when I have replies," he tapped the messages he'd received.

"Thank you, sir," the messenger dipped his head and *stepped* away.

"This is so exciting," Misten whispered.

Levi and Armon burst into laughter.

* * *

Dinner with Kerok that evening turned into a private dinner in his sitting room, rather than a public one, where I'd be in the same mess hall with the others.

"I have some things to tell you," he admitted as I lifted a fork and studied the thick cut of steak on my plate.

"All right." I watched as he cut into the meat expertly, then followed his lead.

"It's about Grae," he said.

"Levi said her name," I admitted. "That she was your previous ah, escort."

"She was my escort and my only love."

How do you respond to that? He'd said the words flatly, but there was a wealth of feeling beneath that smooth surface.

"I'm sorry for your loss," I said through numb lips. I was sorry. Sorry that she'd died. Sorry that he'd been hurt. Sorry that yet another black rose had been sacrificed to the enemy to keep the King safe in his city.

Kerok's father is the King, I reminded myself. When he said nothing, I spoke again. "I am under no illusion that I'll keep my life either, Commander. It is only a matter of time. I

237

will say this, however. You were to be my third choice—after Levi and Armon, because I felt I could express myself honestly in most circumstances and you'd listen. That's all I want or expect from you, Commander."

I felt cold after saying those words. There'd never been any hope for me. I'd learned it so young, too. There'd never be a husband or children—just battle, war and death.

"When I first saw Grae," he began after considering my words, "I envisioned a tall water bird, who walked among the others gracefully without disturbing them. She was a lake of calm for me, and I loved her from the beginning."

"She sounds like a wonderful person, and perfect for you."

"I thought she was, too."

"Look, I know you still miss her—it can't have been that long ago. Why don't we do this another night? Tonight, drink in her honor," I said, scooting my chair back.

"You know what I thought when I first saw you?" He lifted his eyes to me and gestured for me to sit down again.

"What did you think?"

"That you were wildfire in a fierce wind. I knew then that whatever you touched would be forever changed. This isn't the only scar I have," he touched his face as I sat uneasily on my chair again. "I have others that I received the day I lost Grae. They are constant reminders of my loss. I don't want you to feel insignificant next to a ghost, Sherra. I never want that. Whatever you want or need, within reason, I will attempt to provide. I just can't say that love will ever be a part of it."

"Commander, I've known since I was two that love would never come my way. I'm really not hungry. May I be excused?"

"Where will you go?"

Chapter 13

"I think I'd like to see the stars," I said, rising from my seat again.

"Don't wander too far, and certainly not past the perimeter."

"I can take care of myself, Commander."

"I know," he whispered.

* * *

Kerok

That certainly set the proper tone, I chastised myself. I had no idea whether she was actually looking at the stars or crying her eyes out, and I felt like a callous fool.

"Why is it that men think of gifts whenever they upset a woman?" Grae asked me once. That's where my mind had wandered—what to do or give to Sherra, to make this right.

I should just admit that I was an idiot walking unsteady ground and tell her I'd do better. At least that I'd *try* to do better. We'd be working closely together, and a relationship of some kind made things so much easier.

Merrin would say that I owed her nothing. Merrin had been the biggest fool I'd ever met; I just didn't know it for a very long time.

* * *

Sherra

I'd never attempted to *step*, because it frightened me. The book said it was possible, but somehow, there'd been no instruction on it during our training, and as a result, no trainee thought they could.

I could see the top of a rocky outcropping surrounding the lake at the far end of camp. It would be an experiment. If it killed me, then there would be no love lost between Kerok and me.

239

For a moment, I held the image of the highest rock in my mind and *stepped.*

Where are you? Kerok's voice came seconds later.

Sitting on the tallest rock next to the lake, I replied honestly.

I'll be right there.

I wanted to ask him why. He was the Prince and it wasn't done, as Armon would say.

The sounds of his boots against rock came seconds later. I refused to turn and look. He sat beside me, then, and held out a wineglass before uncorking a bottle held in the other hand.

"This is how it's supposed to be," he said, pouring wine into my glass. "A celebration of sorts, for where and when we are; a time when things are new and our prospects are brighter. Drink, Captain, and consider that I'm just a fool who chose the wrong time to hand you news that could wait."

"What would you have told me instead?" I snorted before lifting the wineglass to my lips.

"That it isn't all darkness. We will laugh, I promise. There will be times when things go well, and there will be victories— as an army and with just us."

"I'm sorry I don't share your optimism, Commander."

"What will make that change for you?" he asked.

"Change the world, Prince Commander."

"To changing the world, then." He clinked the wine bottle against my glass and drank from it.

* * *

Kerok

The night ended on a truce of sorts. I *stepped* her back, said good-night and watched as she closed the bedroom door

Chapter 13

behind her. I'd had her clothing brought from the barracks, although she'd be getting new officer's uniforms soon enough.

I'd also sent mindspeak to Armon, asking him to have a plate of cheese and bread delivered to my bedroom, in the hopes she'd eat something.

Anyone in the army knew how battle wore you thin if you failed to eat properly. We'd be leaving after breakfast the following morning, and I had assignments to sort for four warriors who hadn't been chosen.

I considered that the number should have been two, but the Bulldog had ruined two, who'd ended up dead.

It would do no good to curse her name yet again, but I wanted to. If she were still in charge and had Sherra not been there, I had the feeling several would have washed out of Fourth on her recommendation alone—because she didn't like this one or that. It would have meant more warriors would be unchosen in this training season.

All of the former washouts had placed well in the rankings, and had also chosen well enough. Again, we had Sherra to thank for that. She did change everything around her, and with the new method, I hoped for even better from her in the future.

Perhaps her fatalistic approach to everything is what drove her in these goals—a desire to make it better for the black roses, and make their lives longer as a result.

I certainly couldn't fault her desires or her determination. Grae would have been amazed at the fierceness in Sherra, because it was something she'd never had.

They would have been good opposites—the calm next to the storm—if they'd had the luck and opportunity to work together.

That would never be, and it made me weary thinking about it.

* * *

Sherra

There was a note from Armon and Levi set amid the cheese and bread plate on the bedside table. *Keep your chin up and your shields strong*, they'd written.

They were right. I couldn't let depression overwhelm me. Ever.

I'd fought for survival every day of my life. I would go down fighting. I merely had no idea when that day would come. Kerok and I—we had to make some sort of peace to work successfully together. He was right, too, saying that there was a ghost between us. All his dealings with me would be with her memory in the background.

A fight I had no way to win, because it involved love.

At least I had good friends—something I hadn't had before. Levi and Armon would continue to work closely with Kerok, and I would see Caral and Misten regularly, in addition to those two.

I had no intention of burdening them with my troubles, however, because that had never been something I'd do. People had enough worries of their own; I didn't need to add to the load they bore.

Thank you for the note, I sent mindspeak to Armon.

Eat, he gruffed. *We have a long day tomorrow. And you're welcome*, he added. *Remember, Levi, Caral, Misten and I love you. That counts for a lot, from my way of thinking.*

I love all of you, too. I'll see you in the morning.

Of course you will, his mental words conveyed a smile.

* * *

Chapter 13

Kerok

"Want breakfast here or in the mess?" I asked Sherra as she walked into the sitting room, fresh from a shower and dressed in clean fatigues.

"What do you want?" she asked. Morning sun sent shafts of light through the window nearby, and glinted on wildly curling hair about her face. The scent of soap and freshly-starched fatigues met my nose, making me recall past mornings that held smiles and stolen moments of intimacy.

"I don't care," I replied indifferently. "Wait, that sounds too much like an old couple," I held up a hand. "I need to see Armon and Levi, so let's join them in the mess."

"All right—that sounds fine." At least she didn't tack *Commander* onto the end of it. It was proper when we were in front of others, but when we were alone, it didn't matter. Levi and Armon didn't give a damn about that propriety, so it wouldn't be necessary with them, either.

I *stepped* both of us to the mess hall, where Armon, Levi and their escorts already occupied a table in our usual corner.

Levi had been teasing Misten—she laughed as Sherra and I took seats on the opposite bench.

"You look cheerful today," I remarked.

"We are. Cheerful. Commander." Caral's eyes held a light of mischief in them.

"What have they been telling you?" I asked, pretending sternness.

"About Garkus."

"Ah." I unfolded my napkin and dropped it on my lap.

"Garkus?" Sherra turned toward me.

"Drill instructor at Secondary Camp," Armon said with a straight face, while Misten struggled not to giggle.

"Garkus is big enough, and strong enough, to throw a boulder at the enemy and kill half of them," I said. Sherra's eyes widened at my explanation.

"He scares everybody," Levi said. "Including those who outrank him. If you don't do what he says, he's likely to react badly."

"Once, a rattlesnake threatened a cohort he was drilling," Armon said. "Now, I didn't see this myself, but those who were there swear it's true. He leapt onto the snake, crushed its head, jumped up and did a flip in midair, came upright with the dead snake in his hand and flung it over the far wall of the compound."

"That's creative," Sherra said. "I'd like to see that. Maybe I could duplicate it using shields as a cushion."

"That's an interesting observation," I said as a plate was set in front of me first. "If you determine how to do it, let me know."

"I'd form a shield around the snake and toss it away, like we do with the power blasts," Caral said.

"Much better idea," Sherra nodded at Caral. "Saves time, too."

"How about we practice that maneuver with large stones?" I asked. "Instead of snakes? Stones are easier to come by, and they don't bite," I added.

"You'll need a clear flinging space," Sherra pointed her fork at Caral. "So the rock won't land on anybody."

"That goes without saying."

"A rock could land on a snake. Accidentally," Misten snickered.

"We don't want unnecessary snake deaths," Levi teased.

Sherra laughed. I think it was the first time I'd heard her laugh, too. Something in me relaxed, I think. It *was* possible

Chapter 13

to see more than an occasional smile from her. Things were beginning to look up.

Chapter 14

Sherra

Secondary Camp was farther to the north, and much closer—by half, at least—to the battlefields that lay to the northeast.

High, wooden walls surrounded it, and it was quite large, so it had taken some time to build.

At the southern end, amid evergreens, lay small cabins. Each of those cabins would house a warrior and his escort. Half a mile away lay the mess hall, and on the farthest end lay the gate and the training fields close to it.

Rain had fallen before our arrival, and it was evident that rain was a more regular occurrence here than it was farther south.

The Rose Mark

On the east end lay the rainwater tanks, and between those and the other buildings was the purification and pumping shed.

Kerok's cabin was four times the size of anyone else's, and I blinked as we entered the dim interior. It would be much cooler here than the northern camp, because there were thicker blankets on the beds.

At least we each had a bedroom to ourselves—Kerok wouldn't be sleeping on the floor or a chair in a sitting room.

The room next to his bedroom held a long table and chairs—for meetings with other officers, I supposed.

That includes me, I recalled—unless the roses were excluded.

Are the black rose officers excluded from the warrior meetings? I sent mindspeak to Kerok.

Not often, he replied. I could hear him making himself at home inside his bedroom, so I didn't disturb him further. Instead, I walked across the hall to my own bedroom, which had a window with shutters and dark curtains drawn.

I opened them, discovering that trees and a few shrubs grew outside. Those served to provide a barrier of sorts between this cabin and the nearest one on my side.

I left the shutters and curtains open to let in light; I'd shut them again when night fell.

There'll be a meeting in the officer's mess in half an hour, Kerok informed me. *After that, you'll meet with the tailors for your new uniforms. Tonight, the vows will be exchanged.*

The vows. I was beginning to look forward to secondary training, when that ugly reminder was offered.

No, I couldn't be mad at him.

Well, I could. He had to know I found it upsetting, but then he was a Prince and his father was the King.

248

Chapter 14

The King that didn't care.

On the surface, he'd appeared to be reasonable. I only had to consider any black rose's fate to recall that appearance was often as thin and fragile as an eggshell. Anything could break it and show what lay beneath. In this case, it was darkness and death for any black rose, officer or not.

I'd seen aging warriors. I'd never seen an aging black rose, and therein lay the greatest distance—and difference—between the two. It made me want to hurl accusations against them. Demand to know how many women had died protecting them and emptying themselves of power to do it.

"You look angry."

I discovered that my arms were crossed tightly over my chest as I gazed out the window of my bedroom.

"I am. Not at you in particular," I let my hands drop and worked to keep from snapping at him. "Just at everything in general."

"Armon would tell you that you're thinking too much," Kerok offered. "Come with me; we'll walk to the officer's mess. Exercise helps clear my mind and releases my anger."

"It may take a really long walk for this," I mumbled and turned to follow him out the door.

* * *

Kerok

My reminder about the vows must have upset her—Sherra hadn't sounded angry when she asked the question about meetings.

She walked silently beside me; the officer's mess was in the northwestern corner of the compound, and perhaps a mile away from our cabin. Our boots crushed damp, fallen fir needles as we strode along; evergreens made up most of the trees in this part of Az-ca. An occasional seed-cone lay in our path; Sherra took care not to step on those.

I'd never gone out of my way to avoid them, and wondered why it was important to her. "Why do you avoid the cones?" I asked.

"Most of them are whole, or nearly so," she shrugged as she kept pace with me. "Who am I to destroy that? It feels like a disservice to them and to me, too."

"An allegory, perhaps?"

"If you'd like."

"Many trainees have no idea what an allegory is, or skipped over that part in their lessons," I pointed out.

"Hmmph. You never had to explain those things to Pottles and make sense while you did it. She was a better teacher than those in my village could ever be."

"Was she always blind?" I asked.

"No. She said she became blind late in her life. She could see perfectly well when she was younger, and described many things to me from her memories."

"That happens, sometimes," I agreed. Sherra was beginning to lose the stiffness of anger in her body; I'd watched carefully as she and I spoke while we walked.

"Pottles said the same thing," Sherra admitted. "She was never angry about it, though; at least not while I was with her."

"Do you think of her like a grandmother, perhaps?"

"I do, I suppose. A good friend who always had time for me. If that's how grandmothers are, then that's what she was."

"That's how my grandmother was," I said. "She was always feeding Drenn and me, until Drenn couldn't fit his clothes. Food was scaled back afterward."

"You didn't gain weight because of your power," Sherra said, hunching her shoulders. "It takes a lot out of you."

Chapter 14

"It's a proven fact," I agreed. "It's vital to keep warriors and escorts well-fed to maintain their energy."

"Were you ever envious of Drenn—that he wasn't put through the training like you were?" she asked.

"When I was younger," I confessed. "He was allowed to sleep late and drink with his friends. I always had lessons of one sort or another, and couldn't choose my activities as he did."

"I think I was envious of every other girl in my village," she sighed. "They could flirt and kiss and marry if they wanted. I wore a black rose and was outcast."

"I can't change any of that for you," I said. "And now that I know you a little, I would refuse even if it were possible. You're bringing a new method of fighting with you, and I wouldn't keep that from the army for anything. I can only say I'm sorry for your past suffering, and I hope things are better for you in the coming days."

She didn't reply; I didn't miss the tightening of her shoulders, however. We'd come full circle, she and I. If I were more adept, perhaps I'd have seen this coming and avoided it.

"What do they look like?" she asked after several moments of silence.

"Who?"

"The enemy."

"Much like us," I said. "Very much like us. They don't have power—none of them do. Our power is what they find repugnant, and fills them with hatred and a desire to eradicate us."

"I still don't understand that. We don't attack them; they come to us."

"Our existence offends them and what they believe."

"Pottles said they think their afterlife will be more comfortable if they kill us."

"I've heard that," I agreed. "I have no idea where these beliefs came from. I wonder if they know themselves."

"Do they speak our language?"

"The language is similar, but with many differences, too."

"Have you ever spoken to one of them?"

"We have seen prisoners from time to time. Occasionally, a few will infiltrate our camps in an attempt to kill us with small, hand-held weapons or explosives. Much of the time, a shield is placed around them until they decide to kill themselves with their weapon. Other times, they've tossed the explosive away before they're shielded. In either case, when the explosive is activated, everybody runs. Depending upon the escort who placed the shield, it may not hold. Many aren't practiced in providing a shield and then walking away from it while it continues to hold."

"What did they say to you—those that didn't die?"

"They call us names and try to spit on us. There is no useful information to be gotten from any of them, and it's a waste of time for the Diviners to look, because all they see is the hate. None of the prisoners are allowed to live, as you may imagine. They are executed quickly, as is dictated by our rules of combat."

"Do you think they have been conditioned for this?" Sherra asked. "Pottles called it being brainwashed once, but that term was strange to me."

"That is an interesting term—I wonder how she came by it," I mused. "And yes, I do believe it is conditioning—from a very early age. I doubt they have few independent thoughts that aren't dictated by their conditioning."

"What do they call us?"

Chapter 14

"Demons. Witches. Fire-devils. No matter which term is used, they consider us evil creatures."

"Those things are in children's tales," she scoffed.

"As we all believe. They think they're real and accuse us of being those things."

"Have we ever attempted to take the battle to them?"

"It hasn't been suggested, and would require *stepping* to a place we've never been. That alone could kill us; we have to know where to set our feet. Here we are." We'd arrived at the officer's mess. The meeting would take place, and the midday meal would be served when it was time, whether the meeting was over or not.

I led Sherra into the building; it was a far cry from the mess hall at the training camp. Here, walls were smoothed and plastered, with windows lining both long sides of the building.

A kitchen lay at one end; a separate corps of drudge-cooks prepared meals for the officers. The scent of cooking roast made my mouth water—perhaps a snack wouldn't go amiss.

"Let's ask for a snack." I grinned and took Sherra's arm to lead her toward the kitchen.

* * *

Sherra

I'd never dreamed of asking for food outside a meal. Kerok pulled me toward the kitchen, determined to do just that.

"Prince Commander," three drudges dipped their heads to Kerok the moment we arrived inside the kitchen.

"Have anything ready to eat?" he smiled at them.

"Of course. Cheese. Crispy wafers and grapes."

"We'll take it."

253

The Rose Mark

A plate was put together quickly; it was handed to me rather than Kerok. I may have lifted an eyebrow at him, but thanked the drudges for what they'd done and followed Kerok into the mess hall.

Seconds later, two cups of tea were set on our table. I pulled a grape off its stem and popped it into my mouth. The burst of sweetness on my tongue was delicious and welcome.

"Good?" Kerok asked, pulling a slice of cheese off the tray, laying it atop a crispy wafer and biting off half of it.

"The grapes are wonderful."

"Good." He pulled his own off a stem and ate it, followed by the rest of his cheese-wafer combination.

"Is there any left for us?" Armon and Levi arrived, with Misten and Caral close behind them.

"Get your own," Kerok laughed and ate more cheese and wafers.

I watched as Armon led his small group toward the kitchen, and then returned to our table, with Levi and Misten carrying plates of snacks.

"The grapes are really good," I said, pulling off another grape and eating it.

"Prince Commander, good to see you, sir." A man had *stepped* into the mess hall and walked swiftly in our direction. His fatigues were various shades of green—to fit with the forests of conifers surrounding the compound.

By the size of him—height and girth, I imagined this was the legendary Garkus. His skin was the color of dark tea—not as dark as Levi's, but his smile was much wider by proportion. With a voice as deep as a well, he greeted Levi and Armon, too.

"Good to see you, Garkus," Armon smiled back.

"I see you came away with suitable roses," Garkus said. "Must be the promotions I heard you received."

Chapter 14

"They'll need new uniforms to denote their rank," Kerok agreed. "Do you have something interesting planned for our first day of training tomorrow?"

"Why would I give my secrets away?" he chuckled.

"Will we be in trouble?" Misten turned to Levi.

Garkus' booming laughter filled the officer's mess.

*　*　*

Kerok

Garkus and Post Commander Alden spoke first, before I rose from my seat and went forward to address everyone. The first two talked of the training period and what was expected of the officers regarding new escorts—explaining that the beginning of the training was to get to know new escorts and determine how to work with them best. As officers, they were required to follow that protocol and ensure that the regular troops did, too.

"You may have gotten used to pulling power quickly from your escort," I reminded all present when it was my turn to speak. "I warn you now that these women have never had that experience. It is up to you to draw carefully at first, until they become accustomed to it and expect it. You know it can be painful to draw power if they are frightened and attempt to prevent it. Your previous escorts are gone. You are forging a new relationship. Start it properly. Reset your expectations. If any woman is harmed, I'll have a conversation directly with those responsible. Is that understood?"

"Yes, Commander."

I watched Sherra's face as I spoke those words, and saw that she'd gone pale. Levi rubbed Misten's back—Caral's hands were twisted in her lap.

For now, they were the only women in the officers' mess—the rest were warrior officers and it was a small group.

255

The Rose Mark

There's nothing to be afraid of, I told Sherra in mindspeak.

Says the physician before he removes the limb.

We'll talk later, I said. She turned her head away. I finished my speech and sat down; the kitchen drudges began serving the midday meal.

* * *

I sent Sherra with Armon and the others—they were going to the tailors to be fitted for new uniforms. Sherra needed those, too, and it was a way to speak privately with Garkus and the other resident instructors.

"I'm sorry about Grae," Garkus said when I joined him and three others at Garkus' table. I'd gotten a cup of tea from the kitchen so I'd stay awake after a heavy meal.

"As am I," I sighed. "I thought, well, you know."

"What about your new one?"

"If you have any doubts, I challenge you to take her on," I shrugged. "I opposed her on the first day of shield training. Her shield didn't break then and hasn't since."

"This is the one who protected a convoy," Garkus breathed. "Well done, Commander."

"I figured that would get out," I admitted. "We have a new method to teach you, too. You can have the morning to do your worst, but tomorrow afternoon, we'll provide a demonstration."

"You've been busy during your absence, then."

"Hmmph. It wasn't me."

"I'm waiting to see it, then. I take it your father approved?"

"If he hadn't, I wouldn't have said anything about it."

* * *

Sherra

256

Chapter 14

"What ranking for this one?" The tailor was male, but there were others who were women.

"Captain, and the Prince Commander's escort," Armon said.

"What does that mean?" I asked. "For the uniform?"

"It means you'll have the Prince Commander's insignia between your ranking stripes," the tailor explained. "You'll see. It'll go on your fatigues, too."

"It'll tell anyone else not to ride their high horse around you," Levi teased.

"You mean I can't just enclose them in a shield and toss them into a lake?" I teased back.

"Now there's a thought," Armon grinned. "Probably not a good idea with those who outrank you, though. I like clean bathwater, thank you."

"There's only one reason I'd toss you in a lake," I told him.

"What's that?"

"If you were on fire."

"Then I fully support that effort."

"Who would you have picked—if the Commander hadn't, you know," Misten asked. She and Caral had already been measured and stood nearby while my size was recorded.

"I had three names on my mental list," I said.

"Who?"

"Armon, Levi and the Commander, in that order."

"I'm at a loss for words," Levi laughed. "You were ranked first, before the Commander pulled rank, you understand. That would have been a coup for either of us." He clapped Armon on the back.

"It's good how it turned out. I couldn't have chosen better for Caral and Misten."

The Rose Mark

"We got what we wanted," Caral put an arm around Misten's shoulders. "Sherra's right."

What about what you want? Armon sent.

Armon, don't bring that up. Things are how they are, and I think you understand that.

He won't mistreat you. He may be aloof or abrupt, but never cruel. It isn't in him. He's still grieving. Give him time.

My time may be limited, I reminded him.

Understood. Live in the day, Sherra. Let tomorrow take care of itself.

He was right, but I found it difficult to turn off the worry that had dogged my every step for eighteen years.

* * *

We came away from the tailor's building with a uniform each, to wear to the vow ceremony later.

The dress uniforms were black; Caral's and mine had our rank displayed on our sleeves. Mine had the addition of a small crown between the stripes.

As often as I'd silently cursed the King, perhaps it was nature's revenge that I'd end up with his son. Armon was right—Kerok wasn't cruel. He could be indifferent, however, and that made me more than afraid to get to know him better.

Call it self-preservation, Sherra, I cautioned. *He'll hold himself away from you—you must do the same.*

* * *

Kerok

When Garkus outlined his plan for the following day in mindspeak, I felt a small shiver of concern. At least I'd be a part of it, and could call a halt if it were necessary. He'd been working this out during our more intimate meeting, and then informed me afterward.

It required my cooperation, or it wouldn't work.

258

Chapter 14

Are you sure of this? I can't predict, I began.

You can't predict the enemy, either. I hold the upper hand as senior training instructor, he reminded me. *Even in matters concerning the Prince.*

Then I have no further objections, I replied.

Except that I did.

Perhaps he needed convincing. I hoped he'd get as much of that as he wanted in the morning.

Meanwhile, I had the vow ceremony to prepare for; I'd be reading the group vows for the others. I'd decided to allow Armon rather than Garkus to read vows to Sherra and me.

Vows. I was still living by the vows I'd taken with Grae and that might always be. Yes, I felt the guilt of cheating a deserving black rose, but my heart wasn't cooperating. I was hoping a cautious friendship would be enough for both of us.

If the vows weren't a requirement by law, I'd dispense with them between Sherra and me. I trusted her well enough to do the right thing; I merely wished she didn't have such a morbid view of her life.

Every black rose in the compound—with the exception of Sherra—believed she'd be the one to survive and live to old age.

Statistics told a different story. I'd never seen one last ten years, and I'd served as Prince Commander for more than forty-five. I'd studied the records for the past century, too, and the tale was always the same.

I had thinking to do, so I walked back to the cabin instead of *stepping* there.

* * *

Sherra

The closer the time came for our vows and evening meal, the more my stomach churned. I wondered whether I'd be

259

able to eat anything at all when Kerok walked through the front door and interrupted my thoughts.

"Did you get a uniform for tonight?" he asked, his forehead wrinkling as he frowned at me.

"Yes."

"You look pale. I think I have a bottle of whiskey in my bedroom," he said. "It may help with any nervousness."

"I'm not sure that will help."

"Feeling queasy?"

I nodded at his question.

"Sit down." He took my arm and pulled me toward a nearby chair. "Now, put your head down between your knees and breathe deeply. Let me know if you need to *step* outside," he added, once my head was down and I was concentrating on my breathing.

Sitting that way for a few minutes helped—I no longer felt as if I were going to lose what I'd eaten at midday.

"It's a common occurrence," Kerok said, giving my back a rub and a pat. "Fresh air helps too, sometimes."

He'd done this before—for other black roses. Grae, perhaps. I resented it—that this was business as usual for him, and there was no affection in any part of it.

"I'm fine." I rose to my feet and walked toward my bedroom, shutting the door behind me.

* * *

Kerok

Something changed in Sherra the moment I said it was a common thing and patted her back. She stood and walked away, shutting her bedroom door to separate us.

Because you've done this many times, and this is her first, jackass, I called myself what she'd called me when we first met on the training field.

Chapter 14

I was beginning to regret telling Sherra about Grae; telling her I wouldn't love her and couldn't.

Hunter often said I was too honest at times, and I had only myself to blame for this. No part of this was fair, but I'd done it in an effort to save her life—I hadn't forgotten about the book and Drenn's knowledge of it.

As for other things—the laws regarding escorts hadn't changed in centuries, and I was in no position to make changes. Father didn't want to discuss those things and Drenn wouldn't listen to even the best advice if it came from me.

At least the book was no longer in his hands, and he had no real proof that Sherra ever had it. My proof had come from Barth, who would never say a word as long as Sherra served faithfully at my side.

Striding to Sherra's closed bedroom door, I tapped on it. "Are you all right?" I called out.

"I'm fine."

"Get your uniform on; it's nearly time to go."

* * *

Sherra

I combed my hair for a third time before giving up—it would curl however it wanted and there was no help for it.

Boots had been provided with the uniform—black to match the trousers. I'd never had such expensive clothing, yet it was something I'd have chosen not to wear had the choice been given.

I was marked as Kerok's escort by the tiny crown embroidered between my Captain's bars. I didn't feel like a captain or any other officer. Instead, I felt desperate and afraid.

261

The Rose Mark

Squaring my shoulders before the mirror in my bedroom, I released a breath and headed for the door. The sooner I started, the sooner it would be over.

I didn't realize Kerok wouldn't be ready yet; he walked past as I opened my door, seemingly deep in thought.

Without his shirt on. I received my first glimpse of the scars he wore on the rest of his body. A deep one down his right side; another on his back, disappearing into his trousers. Those kinds of wounds destroyed people.

What had killed his escort had almost killed him, too. The army had almost become leaderless, I realized in that moment.

He was the Prince Commander, and unless I missed my guess, he and Grae had been on the front lines during that battle. He wore two tattoos—one on each upper arm—the usual fireball every warrior wore on his right arm, and an entwined rope of thorns on the left, echoing his proper name.

Kerok turned, still frowning, only to discover that I was watching him. That's when I realized he was mindspeaking someone. I held up a hand and turned to go back into my bedroom—he could have the privacy needed for his mental conversation.

Instead, he waved me toward him. I went, although I had no idea what he wanted.

"Hunter is coming," he said, pulling me to his side. "One of Father's assassins has been found dead just outside the palace. He and Hunter are worried that we may all be targeted."

"Dead? How?" I whispered in shock.

"We don't know—the body was found half an hour ago by a palace guard. Father's physician is examining the body now."

262

Chapter 14

"This is terrible," I said. "You don't think someone is targeting your family, do you?"

"Are you confessing that you don't think they're all bad?"

"I didn't say that." I hunched my shoulders and drew away.

Hunter arrived then, curtailing further discussion. "You may need to post extra guards here," he said after greeting us.

"I'm not sure why you think I'm in danger," Kerok pointed out.

"Whoever killed Poul *stepped* in to do it. That means any of us could become targets," Hunter insisted.

"Nobody is allowed to *step* onto the palace grounds without permission from the King," Kerok said.

"Exactly my point. Barth has done his work and like ah, other recent deaths, he cannot find clues."

I knew something was wrong the moment Hunter hesitated over his words. I wanted to ask about other deaths. That could be a mistake.

"Do you suppose the same one," Kerok began.

"We do." Hunter shook his head.

"I can have wine brought," Kerok said and offered Hunter the same chair I'd sat in earlier to relieve nausea.

"I'll take it," Hunter nodded. "This is becoming much worse, and we have no idea how to fight a phantom."

"I doubt it's a phantom, Hunt. Armon is on the way with a bottle of wine."

Hunter's words chilled me. Kerok's answer didn't allay my fears.

What was happening?

Chapter 15

Kerok

"Armon is aware of the difficulty, Hunter," I explained after I let Armon in by the front door.

Sherra stood nearby, trying to make herself smaller, I think. The poor woman was tall and too conspicuous to be successful at it.

She was hearing the worst of things without the benefit of any explanations. Hunter had referred to the killer as a phantom, and Sherra had slapped a hand over her mouth to keep from speaking.

"Good. I trust you'll bring your rose into the tale? She needs to know, Thorn, that your life could be in danger, too."

"I've asked to have the vows delayed, and told Garkus to have the evening meal served now," Armon reported.

"Good," I nodded. "Hunter, my main concern is and always will be with Father. You know what could happen if he isn't guarded carefully."

"Hmmph," Hunter snorted. He knew as well as I what sort of chaos Drenn would cause after taking Father's place, and the least of those things would be rampant favoritism in his appointments.

I shuddered to think how the laws might be corrupted to suit his whims.

"Barth suggests tracing Poul's movements the past few days, and speaking with those who saw him."

"You mean he's going to divine those who had any dealings with Poul, to see whether he was friend or foe, don't you?" I asked.

"Yes. We've all seen what the victims of the past were. It's only right that we also delve into Poul's dealings."

"Then delve into Wendal's dealings, too. They're never far apart." I raked fingers through my hair in frustration after naming Father's second assassin. Poul and Wendal were responsible for dispatching Ura, and Poul was tasked with removing Merrin's power before I left him in the poisoned lands.

"Was it Father's decision only on Merrin's fate?" I asked.

"Drenn argued with him, but your Father said Drenn was in enough trouble as it was. I trust your father's decision wasn't swayed in the case, although I never asked Barth about it," Hunter replied.

"Will you keep me informed on everything you find?" I asked.

"That was Barth's suggestion, and I fully support it."

"What is the word coming from the Council's flapping mouths?"

Chapter 15

"They're fluttering around like sparrows, all worrying they could become targets," Hunter said.

"Drenn?"

"Has locked himself in his suite and only opens the door when food or drinks arrive. He doubled the guards outside, however, before locking the door."

That didn't surprise me. If Drenn thought his life truly in danger, he'd hide in any way he could.

"I'm hoping Sherra can do for this cabin what she did during the flood at North Camp," Hunter went on.

"You mean cover it with a shield and leave it overnight?"

"That's precisely what I mean. Barth insists, as does your Father."

"Sherra?" I turned toward her, then. Her eyes were wide as she blinked at me. We'd just dropped news of a phantom killer on her, and after her previous nausea, I worried she hadn't heard me.

"I, uh," she began before her voice cracked and she tried again. "I put up a shield the moment Armon came through the door."

"Excellent," Hunter beamed at her. "Most excellent. Young woman, I bring you the King's own words; *charge her with protecting my son's life at all costs.*"

"She'll have to touch you to allow you to leave the cabin," I said, my words dry. "Unless she lowers the shield, and I really don't want that to happen."

"Touch me?" Hunter was curious immediately.

"So she can communicate your presence, which her shield will then recognize and allow you to pass through it. Like the fireblasts at the final testing."

"Remarkable." Hunter held out his hand to Sherra. She took a step forward so she could touch it.

"You have latent power," she told Hunter before letting him go.

"The King wanted me as his advisor, therefore that is what I am," Hunter smiled at her.

"You could protect him, I think, if you put your mind to it."

"Fireblasts in the palace? No," Hunter shook his head.

"Shielding," Sherra said. "Here, let me touch you again, so you can see how it's done. If you worry for your King's life—or your own, this could be useful."

I watched as Sherra lifted both his hands in hers and sent mindspoken instructions.

"Now try it," Sherra backed away. "Yes, that's it—I can feel it," she said. "Make it stronger. Pretend it is a wall of diamond that nothing can break through."

"Wait," I said and reached out for Hunter's empty wineglass. Drawing back, I tossed it toward him.

It shattered against the shield he'd built. Sherra, mindful of the shards, captured most of them in a shield of her own and set them down on the table.

"I built a shield," Hunter grinned at me. "I built a shield."

"Don't forget to raise and lower quickly when necessary," Sherra reminded him. "Assassins are never slow—according to the tales I've read."

"Do you think you could teach me the same thing?" I asked her.

"I think so. It can't hurt to try, can it?"

* * *

Sherra

"Repeat after me," Armon said. "I Sherra, promise to protect Thorn, Prince Commander of the King's army, with all my power and all my being."

Chapter 15

I repeated Armon's words, but I never looked at Kerok as I said them. Keeping my eyes fixed on Armon and the small book he held, I determined to get through the vows without my voice breaking or tears forming.

"I promise to keep his secrets, and defend him against all enemies," Armon continued.

"I promise to keep his secrets and defend him against all enemies," I recited.

"Prince Commander, repeat after me," Armon turned to Kerok. "I, Thorn, will stand with you as long as you live," he said.

"I, Thorn, will stand with you as long as you live," he said, his voice even. I wondered how many times he'd said it before.

"I will keep your secrets and defend you against all enemies," Kerok echoed.

"I will value your life as long as you live," Armon read from the book.

"I will value your life as long as you live."

I had a problem with that last line, but this wasn't the time and there'd never be a place to voice that opinion. The King controlled the wording of the vows, and I doubted he'd listen to any escort's opinion on the matter.

"I pronounce you bonded," Armon said. Kerok lifted my left hand and kissed the rose on my wrist. I didn't watch and attempted to block the feel of his lips on my skin. I shivered anyway.

I'd already listened to the group vows read earlier by Kerok, and watched closely as my friends repeated their names as they made them.

A few in the room smiled at their warrior partner as the vows were made. Many others had hope in their eyes as they

269

spoke. A few were pale and worried, but like me, spoke the vows anyway.

What else could we do?

We were marked and the end stage of our lives had begun.

* * *

"Come to our cabin and bring wine," Kerok invited Levi and Armon, including Caral and Misten in the invitation.

"I'll grab plates of food for you," Levi offered. "You didn't arrive in time for dinner." He was worried that Armon hadn't eaten, either, but didn't point that out.

"Good idea, thank you," Kerok replied.

"I'll help," Armon offered.

"Will they all be able to get through your shield?" Kerok turned to me.

"Yes. Armon, *step* to the front porch, and then walk in, all right?" I told him. "My shield will allow you to walk in. I'm working to prevent anyone from *stepping* inside the cabin."

"How can you do that?" Kerok frowned at me.

"You use a certain energy when you *step*—I've felt it every time. I just have to block that energy with my shield. Nobody can *step* inside the one around the cabin."

"Father of warriors," Levi breathed. "That's—can we test that?"

"If you want to, but bear in mind you may bounce across the yard from the attempt."

"I may trust you on it tonight," Levi held up a hand and grinned at me. "We'll test it in daylight, so Misten can wrap a shield around me when I fall."

"We'll try that soon," Kerok agreed. "Let's get started— I'm hungry and we have a long day tomorrow."

* * *

Chapter 15

Kerok

"Show me how," Caral sounded excited as she and Misten asked Sherra to teach them how to prevent someone from *stepping* inside their shield.

"Hands, please," Sherra laughed and took a hand from each before closing her eyes. She'd had two glasses of wine on an almost-empty stomach, and was in the middle of eating leftovers from what should have been a celebratory dinner earlier.

"That's how you can tell," Caral breathed as Sherra released hers and Misten's hands. "I never thought about that."

"I'd suggest trying it with someone close to the edge of your shield, so they won't fall so hard," Sherra giggled.

I made a mental note to get her tipsy more often.

"Our turn," Armon grinned. "Show Levi and me how to make shields."

"That's so easy," Sherra waved a hand in the air. "Come on, let me have your hands."

She closed her eyes again after gripping their hands. Armon's eyes opened wider as information was given.

"That's—I wish they'd taught us that during warrior training," he breathed.

"Hmmph. I think I can make blasts," she laughed and let their hands drop. "After touching so many warriors and feeling their power."

I went still. Had that ever happened before? I couldn't recall reading anything about it in any of the history books, but what was available only covered the past two centuries or so.

"Tomorrow, I want to see you try that," I said. "Take my hand, now, and show me how to make a shield."

The Rose Mark

"May I ask a question first?" she asked before hiccupping.

"Absolutely," I attempted to hide my grin.

"The wall hanging put up for the vows shows a red rose. Why wasn't the rose black?"

"That's an ancient hanging, and they only get it out for the vows ceremony," Armon began.

"But the rose should be black, shouldn't it? Why is that one red?"

"Sherra, I don't know, but I promise to look into it. Take my hand now and show me what you showed Armon."

"All right." She reached out and touched my face instead of my hand, however, drawing a finger down the crevice of my scar. "I'm sorry that happened to you," she said. "I'll make sure it doesn't happen again."

While I drew in a breath at her words, she took both my hands. The shock of information I should have known long ago spread through my mind like lightning.

* * *

Sherra

I blamed the wine for strange dreams that night. I barely recalled Levi and Armon leaving, with Misten and Caral beside them.

I was grateful that those four were together; none of them had false expectations from the other. Kerok had given me strange looks after I'd touched his face and hands, but he had to realize I was mostly drunk and had no real control of my words or actions at that point.

I'd gone to bed shortly after our guests left, and sometime during the night, I'd dreamed of Pottles.

She kept showing me her left wrist, which bore a red rose.

I knew that was an alcohol-induced lie—I'd seen Pottles' wrists many times, and they were as empty as any other

Chapter 15

villager's had been. During the entire dream, I'd attempted to draw Pottles' attention away from what she showed me, so I could speak with her once more.

Her image in my dream remained mute, and when I woke with a slight headache the following morning, I recognized the dream for what it was—an attempt to go back to happier times.

Somehow, my question about the banner had insinuated itself into the dream, confusing me more than I already was.

"Sherra?" Kerok's voice was accompanied by a tap on my door.

"I'm awake," I called out. "I'll be out in a few minutes." I took the fastest shower my headache would allow, dressed quickly and walked out of my bedroom.

"Your new fatigues should be here either today or tomorrow," Kerok began.

"The drudges won't be able to come in," I pointed out.

"Good point. Go ahead and lift the shield until we get back tonight. We'll make sure there are no surprises waiting for us, and you can replace the shield."

"All right."

"Got a headache?"

"Yes." I hunched my shoulders.

"I'll have Armon bring something from the post physician when we meet at breakfast."

"Thank you."

"Sherra?"

"What?" I studied my boots rather than his face. Fool that I was, I'd touched it the night before. Now I regretted the impulsiveness.

"Thank you—for showing me things I'd never dream were possible."

"It's only fair," I replied. "Don't we need every weapon we have to bear against the enemy?"

"We do."

I looked up at him, then, and saw a rather crooked smile on his lips. "Come on or we'll be late for food," he said. "I'm starving." I followed him out the door; he took my arm and *stepped* us to the officer's mess.

* * *

Kerok

"Dissolve it in your tea, it'll help," Armon handed Sherra a folded paper containing powder from the physician.

She poured the powder into her tea, careful not to spill any of it. After stirring, she drank a healthy portion of the hot liquid, making a face as she did so. I knew from experience the powder was bitter; she was learning it for herself.

"Trust me—the bitterness is worth the relief," Levi said. "It helps to eat something, too."

"Does anyone else have a headache?" she asked.

"Not today," Armon chuckled. "This is what you get for drinking wine on an empty stomach."

"And you're telling me this now?"

I turned away so I could hide my smile.

"Why weren't you at dinner last night?" Misten asked Sherra.

"There was a small emergency—I had to speak with the King's advisor, and that made us late," I answered before Sherra had to make up an excuse.

"Oh. That's all right, then."

"While the Prince Commander was busy, that's when Sherra told me about shutting anyone out of her shield who tried to *step* inside it, and that I could probably form a shield myself if she showed me how." Armon was providing more information, which was mostly true—just not completely. He knew not to tell anyone else that Sherra taught Hunter how to form a shield in a matter of minutes.

Hunter could *step* and mindspeak, but he'd never trained in any of the other talents attributed to warriors.

Now, thanks to Sherra, he could form a shield to protect himself and my father if it were necessary.

"What will we be doing during our training today?" Caral asked.

"That's up to Garkus," Armon rolled his shoulders. "Could be anything."

I wanted to snort at Armon's reply. I knew part of what Garkus planned, and had no idea which way it might go. I had a part to play in it, but I was beginning to regret my promise to participate.

"Eat a full breakfast," Levi counseled. "It'll be a busy morning, and you've not had any training exercises since the trials at North Camp."

"I hope we get to see Wend, Jae and the others," Misten sighed.

"You'll see them," Levi grinned. "I promise. In fact, if you'd like to have the midday meal in the regular mess, I'll accompany you."

"As will I, if you wish to go, too," Armon told Caral.

"Sherra, if you'd like to go with those four," I pointed my fork toward Armon and the others, "You should be safe enough in their company."

"Why wouldn't I be safe?" she asked.

"Remember our conversation before the vow ceremony last night?" I reminded her.

"Oh. But what if—never mind. I'll go with you, wherever that is."

The Rose Mark

I blinked in surprise before considering that she'd meant what she'd said, tipsy or not. *I'll make sure it doesn't happen again*, she'd told me. I chose to ignore how gentle her fingers had been when they traced the scar on my cheek.

* * *

Sherra

Kerok didn't want to go to the regular mess for the midday meal. He preferred the smaller numbers in the officers' mess, perhaps.

Better food, too, I reminded myself.

I wanted to see Wend, Jae and the others, but would have to depend on Caral and Misten to relay any news from them. Perhaps we'd see them on the training grounds, but there'd be no time for social visits—we'd be put through our paces, and that would require our complete focus.

Whether I felt like eating or not, I'd finish my food. Employing power would drain it out of us by midday anyway.

Soon enough, we'd left the mess hall behind and began walking toward the massive training field northeast of the building.

He wouldn't know it, but I'd constructed a shield around Kerok and me. I hadn't forgotten the King's advisor's words the evening before. Kerok had viewed his personal danger with some skepticism—I knew him well enough to see it in him.

I, on the other hand, wasn't willing to let down my guard.

When the fireblast came from nowhere, it was easy enough to include Caral, Levi and the others inside the shield I'd already erected.

While there'd been no noise with the blast as there usually was, when it hit my shield it burst with a deafening

Chapter 15

boom, while sparks and dark clouds of smoke billowed everywhere.

Kerok had been knocked to the ground, and lay there, writhing in pain.

Armon and Levi, who'd also fallen, were being helped to their feet by Caral and Misten.

Separating myself from the shield I'd constructed, I went to Kerok immediately, terror filling every inch of my body. Frantic, I searched him for signs of a wound or injury.

"Kerok," I shouted to make myself heard over the second fiery blast that burst atop my shield. "What's wrong?" I begged him to tell me something.

"Get the physician," I shouted at Armon, who appeared to be unsteady on his feet and confused by the second blast that hit my shield.

It hadn't cracked and still held strong. Caral and Misten were attempting to find what was wrong with both Levi and Armon at that point.

All I knew was that the physician's cabin was not far from the regular mess hall. "Bring them here," I shouted at Misten and Caral to pull Armon and Levi toward me as a third blast hit my shield with the largest boom yet. Grass was beginning to catch fire around us when our attacker appeared nearby.

Garkus.

He'd attempted to *step* inside my shield, and hadn't been able to do so. With a smirk, he leveled another blast at us from very close range. Kerok stiffened and shuddered in my arms—was he having a seizure?

I'd never seen one before—I'd only heard about them.

Garkus' blast hit my shield, shaking the ground beneath our feet.

The Rose Mark

Laying Kerok down as carefully as I could, I stood up straight and glared at Garkus. *Leave it be*, I snapped in mindspeak. *Kerok needs the physician.*

What will you do, little whelp? His grin widened.

Are you the phantom? I queried.

Phantom? Is that what they call me? I heard his laughter as he prepared another blast.

I had no idea whether he meant his words or merely played along; either way, Kerok needed help and Garkus was delaying it.

Here's what the whelp can do, I said, and formed another shield before sending it flying through the one that protected us from his attacks.

Garkus formed another blast at the same time, and I hadn't realized it until it was nearly too late. Hastily, I enclosed his body inside a second shield, to protect him from his own fireball.

"Sherra," Caral screamed at me as fire bloomed inside the first shield I'd placed around Garkus. She thought he'd fried himself. I laughed, and for good measure, I sent the outer shield I'd thrown around Garkus bouncing across the training ground.

Physician, I need you, I shouted at full mindspeaking capacity. As for Garkus, we'd see how long he could hold his breath until his fire used up all the air inside the outer bubble and fizzled out.

* * *

Kerok

"She's not speaking to me—that's how things are," I growled at Garkus, who appeared none the worse for wear after I convinced Sherra to drop her shields around him. "She could have killed you," I added.

278

Chapter 15

"I doubted your word, Prince Commander," Garkus bowed to me. "I took her on and you played your part beautifully."

"Fine. You go and explain to her that it wasn't my intent to deceive and that it was just a training exercise," I said. "The physician says she almost blasted his brain apart with mindspeak. He didn't like it that his meal was interrupted, either, so he could make an unnecessary journey to the training field."

"I'll make it up to him," Garkus said.

"If I were you, I'd be more worried about making it up to Sherra. She was scared to death, and if I'd opened my eyes at any time during my performance, I'd have seen it."

"You're going to let her feelings rule your decisions from now on?" Garkus began.

I had his shirt collar in my fist before I realized it. "My father," I hissed into his face, "charged her with protecting my life. She saw your attack as a threat, and I added to that illusion by pretending to be affected. The next time you decide that her feelings supersede a direct order from my father, feel free to let me know." I shoved him away from me, then.

Garkus' eyes were wide; he was only now beginning to see the gravity of the situation. "My apologies, Prince Commander," he dipped his head.

"We're finished. Leave," I waved him out the door.

* * *

Sherra

"I'm not hungry."

Caral and Armon had come to the cabin with a plate of food and a cup of tea. I was sitting on the floor in my bedroom, knees drawn up to my chest and my forehead resting against my legs.

All of it had been fake.

All. Of. It.

Including Armon's and Levi's performances. I'd thought Kerok was having a seizure and called for the physician—unnecessarily, as it turned out.

Because Garkus wanted to test me.

Fuck him.

Fuck Kerok.

And Armon and Levi.

I could have killed Garkus, and he still didn't realize it—unless I was badly mistaken.

Jackass.

"Sherra, I said it was a bad idea, but here, Garkus rules the training sessions." Armon knelt beside me.

"I don't care. He taunted me while Kerok was having a seizure. A pretend seizure, as it turns out. If you think I can trust any of you after that—performance," I muttered angrily.

"Everybody in the mess hall is talking about how you responded to the attack," Caral sat beside me. "They all say it's a miracle Garkus walked away from it whole after blasting himself, and then bouncing across the training field until the fire went out."

"It'll just become another tale that will increase his fame," I grumbled.

"I know you're mad; I would be too," Armon twisted around to sit on my other side.

"And I'll be mad until it runs its course," I snapped.

"Sounds reasonable," Caral agreed. "Nobody ever stopped being mad because somebody told them to."

"Tell me he won't be training me from now on."

Chapter 15

"I can't say that. He should walk carefully around you, though, if he has any sense," Armon said. "Thorn isn't pleased about the whole thing."

"Hmmph. He should be a performer in the mummer's folk plays at harvest."

Caral snickered at my words.

"At least he isn't ill or injured in reality," Armon pointed out softly.

"That's the only thing I'm grateful for in the whole, sorry disaster," I huffed. "What would he be doing if I killed Garkus? I'd be facing death myself—isn't that right?"

"It's unprecedented, so I can't say for sure," Armon admitted. "Nobody has ever been able to do anything other than put up a shield against an unexpected attack from Garkus. He usually breaks through them, too. He couldn't put a crack in yours. Maybe we should have told him about the lightning."

"Is that what this was—a pissing contest, so he could assert his superiority?" I turned to Armon in disbelief.

"He has a habit of testing the best of every training class," Armon breathed a sigh.

"So I get blindsided, think Kerok is dying and fight back. Jackass."

"Who? Garkus?"

"How about both of them?"

"It was sort of like waving a red rag at an already angry bull," Caral patted my arm. "Maybe he'll be more cautious next time."

"Maybe he should be more cautious this time. Getting in trouble might be worth sending him bouncing across the field again."

"How is she?" Kerok *stepped* inside my bedroom.

"Considering insubordination," Armon said, rising to his feet.

"You haven't touched your food," Kerok pointed out.

"I'm not hungry," I insisted. I was, but I'd be damned before I touched food in front of him at the moment.

"Armon, will you and Caral give me a few minutes with Sherra?" he asked.

"Of course." Armon gave a hand to Caral to pull her to her feet. He *stepped* her away moments later.

Kerok took Armon's place against the wall, sliding down until he sat beside me, almost touching but not.

"I'm sorry," he said. "When Garkus told me his plan yesterday, that was before Hunter arrived and told us the news from the palace. I realize this had far more frightening repercussions for you than Garkus will ever realize. He doesn't know about the phantom and he won't hear it from me."

"I uh," I swallowed hard.

"You asked him if he was the phantom, didn't you?" Kerok guessed what I was reluctant to tell him.

"Yes. In mindspeak, when he kept hitting us with fireblasts."

"You didn't know and he'll never guess, so don't worry about it," Kerok sighed. "I didn't mean to frighten you, and now you probably distrust all of us."

"Yes." I didn't elaborate.

"I won't do it to you again," he said. "I can't account for Garkus, but I believe you'll be watching his every move from now on. Any respect he may have commanded will never come from the best black rose any camp has ever produced."

"Hmmph."

"Tell me what you're thinking," Kerok said.

"You don't want to know."

Chapter 15

"Yes I do."

"I'm imagining all the ways Garkus could have died, and they all make me happy."

Kerok threw back his head and laughed.

Chapter 16

*K*erok

        I allowed Caral and Armon to demonstrate the new method to Garkus during afternoon training.

It served two purposes—it kept Sherra away from Garkus until her anger settled, and allowed me to *step* to the palace when Father asked me to come for a meeting. Sherra went with me; this would be a first for her.

She wore her new dress uniform; I requested it as she did more than justice to it. As a precaution, however, I ensured that Drenn was still hiding inside his suite. I had no desire for him to see her, after he'd made threats.

As for the meeting, I expected an update on Poul's death, in addition to anything else Barth and Hunter could tell me.

The Rose Mark

Sherra would be with me as it was discussed. She needed the information if she were charged with protecting my life.

You're expected to dip your head to the King and reply to his greeting, I told her as she walked with me toward my father's private study. *Only a return greeting is expected for Barth and Hunter.*

She nodded; I noticed she looked pale.

There's nothing to worry about, I said. *You're with me.*

A guard stood outside Father's study door; he opened it when we approached to let us in. Father sat at his desk as we walked past the guard—Barth and Hunter, both looking agitated, stood nearby.

"What happened?" I demanded, dispensing with protocol.

"Wendal is dead, Thorn," Father sighed. He sounded weary.

"When?"

"Two hours ago. Like Poul, there was nothing for Barth to find in him, either. The phantom killer has struck again." Hunter answered my question while Father shook his head.

"Injuries on the body?" I asked.

"None on Poul or Wendal—the snakebite method has been abandoned. We don't know what killed either of them."

"Sit," Father waved a hand at Sherra and me. "Young woman, I regret that this will be your introduction to the royal palace. There is no help for it, I'm afraid."

"Hunter, have you spoken with Kage and Weren?" I asked before nodding to Sherra to take an empty chair before my father's desk.

"Yes. They know nothing. I've even searched all the trainees; they are not involved and have no knowledge of it. Everyone in the palace, likewise, has been questioned, except

Chapter 16

Drenn, and he is so frightened by the events he refuses to come out of his suite."

A real Crown Prince would be working beside Barth and Hunter to find the cause and the culprit in this, whispered through my mind. *Drenn chooses to hide from it. Why is he so frightened?* also breathed through my mind, but I shoved the thought away—he was a coward afraid for his own skin. Father was also afraid, yet he wasn't shirking his duties and hiding from everyone because of it.

"Who do we have as likely candidates to replace Poul and Wendal?" I asked.

"We were hoping you'd have someone in mind," Barth said. "I will provide your father with information on them regarding final approval, mind, but we need two replacements soon."

"I can't spare seasoned warriors," I began before it hit me. Perhaps Sherra's question to Garkus hadn't gone amiss after all.

"I suggest Garkus, then, and I'll look through the list of other trainers to determine a match for the position."

"Garkus—I can see that," Hunter agreed with a thoughtful nod. "Find another and bring them tomorrow. We'll have this settled quickly."

"Good. Very good," Father breathed before slapping his hand on the desk. "Hunter, have food and wine brought while Thorn informs us of the battles at the front."

* * *

Sherra

"I met with Linel before breakfast this morning," Kerok said as a servant poured wine for all of us.

I blinked at Kerok's remark—I had no idea he'd been up so early, or that he'd *stepped* away without me.

287

The Rose Mark

"What does General Linel say?" the King asked before waving the servant out of his study.

"There's been a lull in the attacks; perhaps the enemy is waiting for reinforcements or giving their troops a rest before the winter campaign begins," Kerok explained. "We've seen it before, perhaps ten years ago."

"Or they're waiting for bomb deliveries," Hunter's words were dry.

"That, too, perhaps," I agreed.

Why don't we step *where they are and attack them?* I sent my silent message to Kerok.

"*Stepping* into enemy territory is extremely dangerous," he turned dark eyes on me and answered aloud. "We have to know exactly where to place our feet, and wherever we land, imagine that you'll be surrounded by enemy. They can kill us with smaller weapons before we can fire a blast at them."

"What sort of weapon?" I asked.

"Here." I watched as the King pulled out a side drawer in his desk and removed a strange object from it. "This is called a pistol, young woman, although I can't determine why, or where that term came from. We have no ammunition for it, so it is harmless as it is." He handed the weapon to Kerok, who then handed it to me.

"It fires projectiles that pierce the body," Kerok explained as I turned the thing this way and that, attempting to determine how it worked. "If the body is pierced in a vulnerable spot, such as the head or heart, you can die instantly."

"That's frightening," I handed the thing back to Kerok.

"The enemy has many of these—and other small weapons besides the bombs they fling at us," the King said. "*Stepping* into their midst is a suicide mission."

288

Chapter 16

"Do you think my shield will hold against those projectiles?" I asked as Kerok handed the pistol back to his father.

"I think yours would, but you can't consider flinging yourself or others into that nest of vipers," the King said, his voice stiff and commanding. "Our attempts in the past have resulted in many deaths. We cannot risk losing warriors or escorts in such a foolish venture. Thorn and his army hold steady at the line—the one the enemy must cross to reach our lands. To the east lies unforgiving mountains and the poisoned lands, and to the west lies a great crater and water. Their army will be forced to defeat ours before they can enter Az-ca."

"So they are aware that we have no intention of attacking them," I said. "Meaning they know they can keep on attacking us as often as they like."

"Thorn has made that very argument to me time and again," the King snorted. "We fight with what we have, and that will be the way of it."

Stop arguing with him—you won't win, Kerok warned in mindspeak.

"My apologies, sir," I dipped my head to the King.

"Accepted. You are new and haven't seen battle, yet. I depend upon you to keep my son safe."

I didn't reply, although I intended to have a conversation with his son quite soon about *stepping* to the battlefront without me at his side.

Not long after, Kerok and I rose to leave the King's office, with Kerok repeating his promise to provide replacements for the King's assassins.

Did you not find anything on either assassin? I sent to Barth as Kerok embraced his father.

289

I'm still working on that, Barth admitted. *Rest assured, if there is something to find, we will get to it. Thorn will be informed if anything is discovered.*

Thank you.

Hunter walked out with us; Kerok didn't want to *step* away from inside his father's palace. Therefore, Hunter followed us to a garden outside the massive building.

I wondered at that, until I realized he was having a mental conversation with Kerok the entire time.

* * *

Kerok

Drenn will never consent to Barth's divination. He will argue until the end of time against it, even if Father asks, I told Hunter. *He has his secrets, and doesn't want Father to know how many Council members are kissing his backside already.*

We've gone through everyone else that we can think of, Hunter replied.

Trust me, Drenn is scared witless, I pointed out. *He's afraid he may be next on the phantom's list. I can't explain why Poul and Wendal were on it, so don't ask me to speculate*, I added.

If the phantom has stooped to random killings, Hunter began.

Hunt, I know what you're thinking, because I've already gone there. Yes, I've considered that the phantom, whomever that may be, can be leading us along until we think he's only after those who've done wrong. Until they hit us where it will hurt the most, and attempt to assassinate my father.

He could be doing this—getting closer and closer to your father, Thorn, in an effort to weaken you as the leader of the

Chapter 16

King's army. Have you considered that this may be a plot by the enemy?

I've never seen them act with such deviousness before, I responded. *Their conditioning to kill us has never been that amenable to complex thought.*

But you've only seen their lowliest warriors, unless I miss my guess. You haven't been in contact with any leaders, and certainly none of their women. Have you told Sherra yet what happens to escorts who are captured by the enemy?

Not yet—that's frightening, in and of itself, I said. *The time will come and I'll explain it completely to her.*

Make sure you do. She wouldn't have argued with your father about attacking the enemy, had she known of it.

Agreed. I'll tell her soon, I promise.

Good. She is a staunch defender and a credit to you and the escort program. I've heard about the incident with Garkus, Hunter sounded smug. *He was forced to report to me on the first day's training, as is customary.*

Garkus thought to test her and could have paid with his life, I said. *He's lucky to be alive, in my opinion. If she hadn't shielded his body inside the outer shield she constructed around him, he'd have fried himself.*

I wish I'd been there to see it.

I had my eyes closed while pretending to be ill, so I didn't see it either. Armon had to describe it to me.

Keep her alive as long as you can, Thorn. This one is quite sharp.

You think I haven't noticed?

Sometimes you have to be hit in the head with the obvious.

Thank you for your confidence in me, I sniped back. *No, don't walk that way*, I steered him down a different path. *Out*

291

of habit, I'd almost led us to Grae's resting place, and I didn't want Sherra to see it.

She walked beside me, realizing, I'm sure, that Hunter and I were having a private conversation. "We can *step* from here," I turned to Hunter. "Thank you for your support and honesty."

"Anytime," Hunter grinned. I took Sherra's arm and *stepped* us back to Secondary Camp.

* * *

"You're offering me a promotion?" Garkus sounded surprised. "I imagined I'd be placed on a list just below the enemy as to people you dislike," he grinned.

"Garkus, you are the obvious choice to stand as a guard, protector and assassin for my father," I said. "Why would I mistreat you? You had no idea how resourceful Sherra can be, and acted in your usual manner."

"The stories are already flooding the compound about me bouncing across the training field," he shook his head.

"And I'm sure you'll be able to spin that into another feat of heroism and renown," I said. "Your reputation precedes you everywhere."

"It does, doesn't it?" He grinned. "I will say this, after having a few moments to consider things," he went on. "That woman—I pity anyone who thinks to bring you real harm."

"You know—that's quite an accurate assessment," I agreed. "I'll let Hunter know that you'll report to him tomorrow morning after breakfast. *Step* to the warrior's training field; Weren and Kage will meet you there and take you to Hunter."

"I have a suggestion for the other position," Garkus said.

"I'll hear it."

"You're looking at instructors, correct?"

292

Chapter 16

"Yes."

"Ask Kage. He'd be very well-suited to the position, I think, and if what you're telling me about this phantom is correct, then Barth has already done his divination."

"Very true. I'll present that to Hunter, and he'll carry the suggestion to the King. It's a jolt to take away a second exceptional instructor, but the need is great and time is short."

"Exceptional? My gratitude, Commander," Garkus dipped his head.

"You're a legend, Garkus, and you don't mind telling everybody yourself," I laughed. He guffawed at my description.

* * *

Sherra

Kerok and I went to the evening meal together at the officers' mess. He'd already spoken to Garkus, after leaving me at the cabin for a short while.

"I have a request," I said as plates of food were set in front of us.

"What's that?" Kerok lifted his roll and broke it open so it could be buttered.

"Don't go to the battlefield without me again," I said. "I can't shield you if I'm not with you."

"But you haven't completed your secondary training, yet," he reminded me.

"Just as I'd never seen bombs or any other sign of the enemy before shielding a convoy of stolen vehicles," I countered.

"Good point," he said before stuffing half the roll in his mouth.

293

"What harm will it do if I'm standing beside you, making sure you're protected while you discuss things with the General?"

"You may hear things you're not quite prepared to hear," he began.

"I'll hear them eventually, don't you think? Now that I know you're sneaking away," he held up a hand to stop me from following up on that assessment.

"First off, I'm not sneaking away. I'm the Prince Commander, and I am merely doing my duty. In addition, you're not battle or officer trained yet, and may not be prepared for some of the things you'll see or hear."

"I still want to go with you," I said.

"Fine. I'll wake you at the ungodly hour I rise, then, and haul you with me next time."

"Thank you."

"It's not a gift, I promise you."

"It is if it stops me from worrying about your backside."

"Why would you worry about my backside?"

"I worry as much about your front side and your head, although your head may appear empty at times."

"Insults, my rose?"

"If you see it as such. I consider it payback for the training incident with Garkus. If that wasn't an empty-headed move, then I've never seen one before. Pottles would have called it bone-headed, although I never understood that remark."

He ducked his head to hide a smile and set about cutting into his meat and vegetables.

* * *

Kerok

Her cheeks were flushed pink as she scolded me about the incident with Garkus. She'd truly been afraid I was ill or

Chapter 16

injured, although her reactions, rushed as they were, had been carefully calculated.

Garkus still didn't realize how much danger he'd been in, choosing to ignore it since he'd survived the incident intact.

"Discussing the weather?" Armon and Caral sat beside Sherra, while Misten and Levi took the other seats beside mine.

"Absolutely," Sherra snorted. I tried not to laugh. It didn't work.

* * *

Sherra

"Wend, Jae and the others are fine," Caral reported. "They wanted to see you, but they heard about the incident during morning training. I had to answer questions all afternoon. Bela and Reena are anxious to see you at training tomorrow."

"Garkus will be leaving for the King's City," Kerok said. "Someone else will take the lead on training exercises. Armon, are you and Caral available for an early morning trip to the front tomorrow? Sherra and I will be going."

"I can do that," Armon agreed.

"Good. Levi, I'm leaving you in charge of the warriors and roses in our absence."

"I'll take care of it," Levi said.

"May I ask why," Armon began.

"Sherra doesn't credit me with enough sense to take care of myself." At least he grinned when he said it, so I wasn't angry.

"I'd say it's a good idea to take her, but not for the reason given," Armon said.

"What reason would you give?"

"I saw what nobody expected to see this morning, Commander. I saw a black rose achieve the impossible against Garkus."

"So, in spite of rumors coming from the front, you'd send her with me?"

"I would."

"What rumors?" I asked. Things had turned in a direction that worried me.

"They're not rumors," Kerok sighed, setting his napkin beside his plate. "Somehow, the troops got word on the new method before Linel announced that the King approved it, and there's been ah, pushback."

"In other words," Armon explained, "they may have received faulty information, and consequently they're afraid of trying anything new. Even if it would save lives."

"That's why you said I could hear things I shouldn't."

"It's possible," Kerok said. "Linel has told the officers to wait until the method is demonstrated before making their opinions known, but that's like stopping a boulder from rolling downhill."

"What about the black roses?" Caral pushed potatoes around her plate. "What do they say?"

"Most are in agreement with their warriors."

"That's too bad," Misten said. "If they could see it, surely they'd recognize the benefits."

"People will go to great lengths to avoid admitting they're wrong," Levi said. "Some would cut off an arm rather than acknowledge their mistakes."

"When were you planning to tell me this?" I asked Kerok. This was something I'd already feared would occur. I could see Kerok didn't like it any more than I did, and worried about how to proceed.

Chapter 16

"We can hold off if you want, but I'm not going to fight using the old method unless it's a direct order from you and the King," I added.

"Everyone in this training class will use the new method," Kerok sighed. "I'm thinking of allowing the rest to use either method. I believe that once they see the new version in action, they'll come around to it."

"It's foolishness to dismiss it without knowing the benefits, and people will probably die from their own stubbornness," Armon grumbled. "There may not be a better way to introduce it, though."

"I had hopes of going into the winter war with everyone trained," Kerok shook his head. I watched his face—he looked grim at that moment.

"Now it'll be one here and one there, while we're fighting battles," Armon agreed. "Not the best way to get things done."

"I'm not sure how the word slipped out and was allowed to fester among the troops, but it did. Linel met with immediate opposition the moment he announced it."

"Who could have carried the news back to them?" Caral asked.

"There's only the messenger, and I don't believe he'd do something like that," Kerok said. "I've been back and forth, but the only person I've discussed it with is Linel. He knew not to say anything until the King made a decision in the matter."

"No matter; we'll see things for ourselves tomorrow morning," Armon said. "Finish your meal," he told Caral. "We have an early day tomorrow."

* * *

"Will they know I'm responsible for the new method—for the most part?" I asked Kerok once we'd arrived at our cabin.

"I haven't heard any names mentioned, but I'm not privy to conversations between troops."

"This is so depressing," I breathed. Kerok frowned at my words.

"I thought I'd be saving lives," I confessed. "This just proves I shouldn't count on hopes and dreams, because they always turn to dust, don't they?"

"Don't look at it that way," he said, gesturing for me to sit down. "The new method is the best thing I've seen since I took command of the army more than forty-five years ago. Somehow, misinformation was spread through the troops, and now they're balking. Give it some time; they'll come around."

"How old were you when you took command?" I asked.

"Twenty-two."

"You still look almost as young," I said.

"It's the power within warriors," he said. "We have some who are nearly two-hundred still fighting. Linel is one of those, although this past year has worn him down. Part of that is my fault, because he's had to carry most of the weight while I recovered from my injuries and then waited for a new black rose."

I wanted to point out that the black roses didn't have the luxury of time like most of the warriors did, but we'd covered that ground too many times already. There wasn't anything I could do about it, either, unless I wanted to desert and have a death sentence leveled against me.

I ignored the small voice that informed me that Kerok was the one I wouldn't desert. That was news I wasn't prepared to accept as yet. Admitting that I was still in self-preservation mode against the ghost of his former rose was also not something I wanted to consider.

Chapter 16

Not now, anyway. Perhaps later I'd deliver the scathing news of his continued rejection to myself—when I was better able to handle it.

"I'm going to bed—will you let me know when it's time to get up?" I rose from the chair with a feigned yawn.

"I will."

"Good-night." I walked away from him.

"Good-night, Sherra."

* * *

Tents. Everywhere, there were tents—all in multiple hues of sand, brown and green, to match the surroundings of the army encampment. Many of them were nestled between small hills of sand and scrub, to hide themselves better.

No, I hadn't considered where the warriors and roses would sleep, eat or bathe. Tents were the option provided, as they were easy to take down, put up and move. Kerok and Armon had *stepped* Caral and me to a place outside General Linel's large tent and waited while a corporal standing guard outside alerted the General to our presence.

We didn't wait long before we were ushered inside—Kerok was Linel's Commander, too.

"I'm surprised and pleased to see your roses with you," Linel offered camp stools to all of us. Like Kerok said, Linel showed weariness in the lines of his face and the fading brown of his hair.

He wants to retire, my inner voice informed me.

"This is Sherra, and this is Caral," Kerok introduced us.

"It is an honor," I dipped my head to the General, as did Caral.

"I may have a partial answer to our recent rebellion against new practices," Linel said as we made ourselves

299

comfortable. "It appears that those few officers who regret Merrin's passing have ah, spoken out the loudest."

"I am not surprised," Kerok said after considering Linel's words. "Disappointed, yes, but not surprised. He had his friends and I should have expected this. What concerns me most is how they came by the information to begin with."

"They're not breaking any laws; they're only voicing their opinions," Linel sighed. "I'm anxious to see the new method in action, but it will have to wait until your official arrival to take command."

"I may take steps to hasten it, if your report about the enemy gathering is correct," Kerok said.

"Both our Diviners have said as much," Linel responded. "I don't doubt their findings."

"They're accurate," Kerok rolled his shoulders. "I can feel it."

Is that what the unsettled feeling is? I sent to Armon. *I thought it was the opposition to the new method when we arrived—as if massive hate was directed at us.*

It's the enemy—Thorn can feel these things—it's in his blood, somehow. He doesn't need to be a Diviner to know that something is happening with the enemy.

Can you feel it? How do you live with this constant barrage?

I don't feel it, and most people can't. I think we'd go crazy after a while if we did.

Kerok and I needed to talk. I had questions regarding whether this was how it usually was, less than ordinary, or higher than normal. I wasn't sure I'd be able to sleep with the overwhelming hatred aimed in our direction. My strongest shield was up and surrounding all of us in the General's tent, and still it found a way through to beat against my brain.

Chapter 16

"I'd like to inspect the battlefield, to determine whether we should move forward or fall back to make repairs," Kerok said, drawing my attention.

"I'll come with you," General Linel said. "I was hoping you'd make this decision so I wouldn't have to."

Armon rose, silently indicating that Caral and I should rise, too. The General stood next, followed by Kerok.

He'd officially taken command, it appeared, and this was protocol. Taking my arm, he *stepped* me away; we landed in an area that looked as if it had been scraped bare of anything living.

Not even a wary cactus thought to poke a spine or sticker above hard, sandy soil. Amid the barrenness lay dips and pockmarks—as if something hard had rained from the sky and formed those indentions.

"Not a smooth battlefield, for certain," Kerok shook his head as Armon and the others appeared nearby.

I noticed we'd landed on the southeastern edge of the large area. "This is where everyone *steps*," Kerok pulled me out of the small, unmarked square of dirt. "We'll have to pull back, General," Kerok turned to Linel. "Make the southernmost line the northernmost when you construct the new field. Complete shields are difficult to construct around these irregular spaces."

"I'll see to it, Prince Commander."

The terrible feeling—it's worse here, isn't it? I sent to Kerok, who studied the field around us in silence.

It is worse. This is the place they last knew we stood, so of course they target it with their hatred.

Is it always this bad?

No. Most times it's an unsettling feeling that you can ignore. This tells me that they're planning something big and working themselves into a frenzy over it. I worry that you feel it, too, he added. *The last time I felt it like this, I came away with severe injuries.*

What can we do? I asked.

I think Secondary Camp will be accelerated, he replied. *We may need all of them on the front lines in a matter of days. You won't get the officer training until later, but it can wait for now. This is more important.*

Where are they? The enemy?

At the moment, they're roughly ten miles to the north and east—at their nearest border. Close and far, at the same time. They can lob bombs at us from that location. If they pull back to regroup after heavy fighting, I send a few teams forward to look for vehicles we can take. We have safe stepping *points here and there along the way—that's how we spy on their movements.*

"Have you gone yourself?" I asked aloud. "To spy on them?"

"At times."

"Hmmph. Goes more often than he should," the General complained. "Always came back, though."

"How long—before they strike, in your estimation, Commander?" Armon asked.

"I give it five days at the most. We should get back to Secondary Camp, General. I think we're going to need everyone we can muster for what's coming."

Chapter 17

Kerok

"I'm depending on both of you to help. You've been through this process before, and know how to handle it. These roses are far ahead of any other class I've seen, so the acceleration shouldn't be too much for them to handle."

I'd sent Sherra to have a midday meal in the regular mess with her friends, so I could speak with Armon and Levi at a private table in the officers' mess.

"It helps that Sherra can just touch them and show them how to do something," Levi observed.

"I think that's what we need to do now—teach her, Caral, Wend, Jae and a few others, and then turn them loose on the rest of the roses. I think by the third day, they'll be ready to work with their warriors."

"The trouble, of course, is getting Sherra's cooperation when you pull power from her in the beginning," Levi pointed out. "I remember the last time we tried that."

"I know. That's why I'd like to teach her in private this afternoon, and then let her work with her close friends tomorrow morning. The rest should follow as quickly as they learn it."

"You know to proceed carefully?" Armon sounded hesitant. He didn't want to overreach, but he also wished to voice his concern for Sherra.

"I'll take care of her," I promised. "I understand how important she is—to all of us," I held up a hand before Levi could also voice his concern.

"I just worry that—she's getting shortchanged," Levi spoke anyway, before dropping his eyes to his plate.

"No more than I," I mumbled before rising and *stepping* away.

* * *

Sherra

Wend's shoulder was firmly pressed against that of Lieutenant Marc's. They'd be sharing meals with us in the officers' mess, except that one of Marc's duties was overseeing the troops in the regular mess.

Therefore, she ate with him.

Easy enough to see that they were connected already, with neither wanting the other out of their sight.

For now, I couldn't determine whether it was new love or new lust, but whatever it was, both appeared happy. Jae, Tera and Neka exchanged occasional glances and smiles with their warriors when they thought nobody was looking.

Chapter 17

Caral, Misten and I sat across from Wend and Marc; the others took up the rest of the benches on both sides.

"Commander Kerok says I can tell you, because you'll be in First group for the training," I began when conversation lulled and our meals were nearly finished. "It looks as if the enemy may be planning an attack very soon, and he wants us ready and on the battlefield when it happens."

"What does that mean?" Wend suddenly looked concerned, as did Marc.

"It means our training will be accelerated," Caral replied. "Sherra goes first, she teaches us, and then we train the rest. We'll be working alongside our warriors in two or three days if all goes as planned."

"So we'll get to train others again. I like that," Neka grinned.

"We have a short time to do it—the Commander wants us ready to go in five to seven days," Misten explained. "We'll have to hurry."

"If the Commander wants it done, we'll make it happen," Marc rubbed Wend's back. "I hate that our time here will be cut short, though."

"Tell them what you felt when we went to the battlefield," Caral nudged me.

"I felt what the Commander felt—the anger and hate of the enemy, even from ten miles away. He says it only gets this bad when they're planning a big attack, and with what I felt from them, I don't think it will be otherwise."

I didn't say that I was looking forward to working with Kerok in the afternoon with a high degree of trepidation—I didn't want to hand my fears and insecurities to any of them.

With Kerok, I'd have to swallow my fear and allow him in—to take whatever power he demanded.

305

It terrified me.

"Captain Sherra?" A warrior tapped my shoulder.

"Yes?" I turned to see who it could be; so far, nobody had addressed me by my rank. Standing beside a tall, thin man was Reena, and behind her stood Bela and another warrior.

"We just wanted to thank you—for our roses," the tall, thin one offered a smile. "Warrior Beckley," he introduced himself. "This is Harnn," he introduced Bela's warrior. "We, ah—usually it takes more than one training class for a rose to choose us," he added.

"Then you are doubly lucky," I stood so I wouldn't have to twist uncomfortably on the bench. "Bela and Reena are strong with talent, as I'm sure you've discovered already."

"Thank you," Reena flung arms around my neck, making Beckley chuckle.

Bela hugged me too, and Harnn dipped his head to me before they walked toward the mess hall door.

"I should probably find Kerok," I told the others. "It was so good to see all of you again."

Where are you? I sent to Kerok. *I'm finished with my meal.*

Meet me at our cabin, he replied.

* * *

Kerok

She walked toward the cabin by herself; I should have thought about that before sending her in this direction—that she'd be alone.

Not that she couldn't take care of herself, but I still felt concerned. As Sherra came closer, I saw she looked pale.

This scared her, when nothing else I'd seen had really done that.

Chapter 17

Except when she thought I was dying, I reminded myself. I'd heard the panic in her voice as she fought Garkus and begged Armon and Levi for help.

You're a fool for thinking she doesn't care about you, a small voice informed me.

Too many times, I'd heard Hunter tell me I was too honest for my own good. I'd lay money on there being several warriors who only pretended to care about their roses, to get what they wanted from them at night.

Or in the mornings, before breakfast.

Yes, I felt stirring in my own body at the thought of it, but chose to stifle the urges. Sherra and I had work to do, and she was frightened enough as it was.

"I've heard from Hunter," I said as Sherra stepped onto the porch where I waited. "The warrior trainees are facing their trials today, under Father's supervision. If all goes well, I'll ask for the names of their best students, and have them report here instead of to General Linel. I have an idea," I said. "If it works, we'll be more effective than ever."

* * *

King's Palace
Crown Prince Drenn

"They'll be out all day, stop worrying," I waved an arm at Merrin, who fidgeted in his chair.

"You don't know what it's like," he mumbled. "I feel as if I'm constantly being watched. That's why I move around so much."

"The phantom's elimination of Poul and Wendal means nothing. Nobody else inside the palace knows of your continued existence. It's only you and me, cousin. Tell me what's been happening with your allies in the army—and your forays among the enemy camp."

307

The Rose Mark

"My allies are ready to follow me whenever you make me your selection for the Commander's position," he grinned suddenly.

"Ah, there's the Merrin I know," I said. "Pour the wine and we'll drink while you tell your tale."

"Through my efforts, Thorn's new method is being met with opposition, as you may have heard already," Merrin began. I hadn't heard it, but nodded anyway. "This means only the new arrivals will be using it, leaving the others vulnerable when they tire. And they *will* tire, my Prince. Wait and see."

"You've whipped the enemy into a frenzy, then?" I felt elated at this revelation.

"Oh, yes. You should be pleased at how efficient I've become at *sight-stepping* at night. I've attacked their camp several times. Five times I've cooked one or more captives, before leaving blackened bodies for the guards to find. The last one, though—I tortured him until he was near death before killing him. I asked for information. I got nothing, but it was fun while it lasted."

"Did he say anything at all?" I asked.

"Oh, he went off his head after a while, covered in burns as he was. While he still had moisture in his body, he spit at me near the end and said I couldn't fly."

"What an odd thing to say," I observed.

"I told you he was off his head. I finished him shortly afterward and dumped his body in the enemy camp, just like all the others. They're so angry, the camp is buzzing like a hive full of hornets. They'll attack soon, mark my word, and it won't go well for those defending the front line."

"Where Thorn will most certainly be," I laughed. "Too bad, brother. You'll get what you deserve after all this time."

"Oh, Thorn has it coming, all right," Merrin chortled.

308

Chapter 17

Sherra

"You have to let me in," Kerok sighed. "I won't fight you, and I won't hurt you. You have to trust me in this."

We'd already tried it twice, and both times, something in me deflected his attempts to connect his power with mine.

My fear had only ramped up; I was beginning to feel sick and shaky.

"Sit down," he came to take my arm. "There's enough grass and evergreen needles to give some cushion here."

Here was on the southeastern side of the compound, where only trees and a nearby stream wandered through the property. He'd chosen it because it was private, so I wouldn't be put on display for everyone to see when I balked.

And I *was* balking; there was no doubt of that.

Lowering myself carefully to the ground while his hand remained on my arm, I drew my knees up and pressed my forehead against them, drawing in slow breaths to control the nausea.

Kerok settled beside me, not bothering to keep any distance between us. I jerked when one of his hands rubbed my back, and then again when his fingers moved to the back of my neck to massage it.

"So tense," he breathed beside me.

"I'm sorry," I mumbled.

"I know it scares you. Like someone is showing you your death," he said, his voice calm and even. "I will tell you this—I don't ever want to carry another rose off the battlefield, Sherra. I will do everything in my power to keep that from happening again."

The Rose Mark

While he spoke, his thumb rubbed stiff muscles in my neck and upper shoulders, using even, circular strokes that were meant to soothe.

"It's not you," I muffled against my knees.

"You can't take the blame for this; I understand that you've lived with this fear and dread all your life."

"Armon would say I'm thinking too much."

He snorted a laugh. "Armon would," Kerok agreed. "Why don't we try this," his hand moved down my back again in ever-widening circles. "You touch me and feel my fire. Then let your fire attempt to connect with mine. If we can't do it the usual way, maybe the opposite will work."

"You'd let me try? I think I can do that easily enough," I lifted my head to blink at him.

"Perhaps letting you take control will make you feel safer—at least at first, until you get used to me finding your power in exchange."

"All right." I moved to get my feet under me.

"Not just yet—you're still shaky and I can hear your breaths. Let me tell you a story, first."

"What story?"

"About Kyri, the Diviner," he said. "My mother used to tell me this tale at bedtime. She said her mother and grandmother told it, too."

"I've never heard about him," I said.

"Her," Kerok's mouth curved into a smile, lending laugh lines to his face. "Kyri is a tale about a Diviner who was also a woman. It's a wonderful bedtime tale."

"So she really didn't exist," I said.

"Who knows. There's nothing in any of the history books, but those only go back so far."

"Then tell me," I said.

310

Chapter 17

"You know how Diviners work now—they have to touch you or something from you, to know how things are?"

"Yes." My memory of Barth at North Camp was still fresh in my mind.

"Well, the tale of Kyri says that she was so powerful as a Diviner, that she didn't have to touch anything. She could see into the future as well as the past. In fact, she was so good at what she did that the King asked her to marry him."

"Did she?"

"She refused. He banished her for it and thought that was the end of things. But all during his life, he received messages from her, telling him whenever something was going to happen that he should attend to. Many times, in my mother's tales, Kyri saved our lands through her messages to a King she'd refused to marry."

"That's a nice story. Why wouldn't she marry him?" I asked.

"I don't really know. The reason wasn't given in any tales my mother heard. She speculated often that Kyri had seen the King's death, and didn't want the pain of losing him."

"That's a sad speculation," I said.

"I thought so too, until Grae died. Then I understood it perfectly."

"And here we are." We'd come full circle, Kerok and I. We were back to the ghost that stood between us.

"Remember, I told you that anything you wanted, I would do my best to provide?" He put both arms around me, now. "I don't know how to love anyone else. Not now. Perhaps never. That doesn't mean I don't care about you."

"I suppose you told all your other rose escorts that they'd always be in second place?" I didn't hide my sarcasm.

"I didn't know anything about that until Grae came along, and she was the most recent," he defended himself.

"You're saying I'm the only one in second place? Or is it farther down the line than that for me?"

"You told me once to change the world," he said. "I'm trying to change the world—with you—because of you and what you've shown me is possible. Don't rush my heart, or tell it what to do. It's not nearly that easy, my rose. Love and affection can't be turned on and off like the switch for the lights."

"Let's get this over with." I moved away from him before standing and dusting off the seat of my trousers.

* * *

Kerok

Armon would call me a fool—a fool sending mixed messages to a woman who deserved so much better.

In her eyes, she'd die deserving more without ever getting it.

"I know about the book," I blurted. Her back was turned to me already, but she visibly stiffened when I said those words. "Barth told me," I added lamely, making a decision to leave my brother out of it for now.

"Then kill me now and get it over with."

She turned toward me; I watched as a tear made a track down her left cheek.

"That's—the reason you're not—this isn't coming out right," I rubbed the back of my neck while searching for something to make the situation better. "Only Barth, Hunter and I know," I stumbled over the words, still leaving my brother out of the conversation.

"So you all hold me hostage, now, is that right?"

312

Chapter 17

"None of us are holding you hostage," I countered. "We recognize your worth, and something you received at a young age before you knew it was outlawed shouldn't be held against you."

"But let Sherra step out of line once, and it will suddenly and conveniently matter," she snapped before turning away from me again.

"I only told you this because I had to take you to save your life," I retorted, understanding that it was the worst thing I could have said the moment the words left my mouth.

"So you were blackmailed by Barth and Hunter into taking me. That's what you're saying."

"No. On the first warrior's grave, that's not what I meant. I meant that I wanted to save you. Yes, originally I intended to take someone else—someone I would never care for and who wouldn't hurt me when, well, when the time came. Then you came along, and things stood on their head around you. Change for the better happened to everything you touched. You changed everything and everyone around you, Sherra. What I'm saying—badly—is that I care about you. I care what happens to you. Can we leave things there for now, until my heart is no longer a grieving mess?"

Her head and shoulders drooped while I watched; as if she'd given up on something. That something was likely me. "Let's get this over with," she repeated, her voice barely above a whisper.

* * *

Sherra

His face was a mask, as if he'd withdrawn from me as much as I'd withdrawn from him. I'd been foolish. I'd begun to love him, and that turned out to be the biggest mistake I'd ever made.

He'd said I changed everything around me—except him.

He was what I couldn't change, and for the rest of my life, I'd be forced to work beside him while my failure taunted me.

"Take my hands and reach for my fire," he instructed. I took his hands. His fire, a lake filled with the inferno of it, was easy to connect with.

When he made the first attempt to reach into mine, I sobbed.

I didn't stop him, however, and he reached further, until I felt as if I'd burst with his presence.

Then, he pulled part of my power away with his, sending a huge, fiery blast sailing high over the compound's fence, where it exploded against stone and rock far away.

I wanted to shove all of it at him, then. Give it to him and empty myself. This was what it was for, after all.

One day, he would empty me and I'd die. He'd go looking for a new rose, then, and she'd probably hear his tale of a dead lover, too.

He fired three more blasts, employing my power to do so before he stopped and walked away from me.

"We'll show the others tomorrow," he said. "I'll take you back to the cabin, now, so you can bathe and go to the evening meal."

"You can go on; I can *step* myself," I mumbled and did so before he could stop me.

* * *

Kerok

"She's at regular mess," I explained to Armon and Caral, as they sat at my usual table after asking about Sherra. "She's—upset."

"I worried that she'd have difficulty," Armon began.

314

Chapter 17

"That's not it," I held up a hand. "I'd prefer not to talk about it," I added. If I'd had a script of everything wrong I could possibly say, I couldn't have done a better job at alienating her.

Should Levi and I, Armon sent mindspeak.

I doubt it would help; I really messed things up.

Will she be able to teach the others?

Yes. She won't back away from that—not if I know her at all. She will do everything she can to save lives, including mine.

"I hate this," Armon spoke aloud.

I snorted my response.

* * *

Sherra

"At least give us a preview," Wend begged. We'd finished our meal and now sat outside in a circle beneath a tall fir with low-hanging branches. Warriors had allowed us to sit and talk, while they remained inside the mess hall, doing the same thing.

"All right. Link hands," I instructed, grasping Wend's fingers on one side and Jae's on the other. Closing my eyes, I connected with everyone in the circle and showed them what I'd learned.

"That's it?" Neka breathed.

"Yes. But know this, too," I relayed more images to them. Images of the levels of their power. *This is where your line is,* I informed each of them. *If you are drained below this line, you will die. Remember this. I am going to show you how to stop the drain at that point. If you choose to allow your warrior to have more of your power after that, it will be your own choice and not his. Understand?*

"Yes," they all whispered.

See that line? Memorize it. See it whenever you close your eyes. Now, place a shield at that line, hear me? One no warrior can break through, understand?

"Yes."

Good. Protect them, but protect yourselves, too. Never forget. If you are sacrificed, it will be of your own choosing and none other's.

"Thank you," Reena breathed when she opened her eyes and blinked at me. Dusk was falling, but I could still see her face clearly.

I saw all of them clearly—as if their very essence was tattooed on my mind. "I love every one of you," I said. "I refuse to let you go to the battlefield without a defense for yourselves."

Yes, I'd just taught them a defense I'd created while stewing in my bedroom. My training period with Kerok hadn't gone as well as he'd have liked, and he had nobody to blame except himself.

Nobody in their right mind should ever send troops to the front lines to perish like the King and his son sent the black roses out to die. I was tired of accepting my future death at Kerok's hand. Tired of thinking and dreaming about it, too.

It was time to take a stand. If the King didn't like the ultimate result, then he could have me killed.

In fact, with Barth, Hunter and Kerok in possession of the knowledge regarding a certain forbidden book, I was dead anyway. They only had to choose the time and place to release the information against me.

I may as well save as many lives as I could in the interim.

As for the roses already on the battlefield, I considered what had turned them away from the new method, which could surely prolong their lives.

Chapter 17

Had any of them been friends with Merrin, or was it only the warriors who found in him something to admire or aspire to?

Any one of them, committing the same crime as Merrin, would have met the same fate. Did they condone his breaking of the laws? Did it bother them at all that he'd gotten a trainee killed by the King's assassins?

"You've stopped talking," Wend bumped her shoulder against mine.

"Just thinking," I released a heavy sigh.

"Armon says you think too much," she laughed.

"Armon is probably right," I agreed. In truth, I thought that people had carried that attitude for far too long, and it was more than time for somebody to think—about the enemy. About dwindling numbers in the army. About trainees being taught by those who had little knowledge of the power a trainee held and certainly had no way to train from experience, because they'd never had that in their lives.

Somebody should think about the completely idiotic laws governing warriors and escorts.

"Marc is walking toward us," Wend breathed before standing up.

"Everyone, remember what I taught you," I said while standing beside Wend. "I'll see you on the training ground tomorrow."

* * *

Kerok

When I walked through Sherra's shield around the cabin, I felt as if claws were scraping against bare flesh. So much so, in fact, that I felt my face and hands to check whether they'd been scratched.

317

The Rose Mark

She'd allowed me in, but hadn't missed the opportunity to let me know how upset she was. Had any other black rose accomplished something like this?

I seriously doubted it, as I'd read a history of escort innovations during the past two centuries.

It wasn't a large book, if book you could call it.

Hunter had already written twice as much on Sherra's accomplishments within a matter of months.

Where are you? I asked Sherra.

In my bedroom, she replied stiffly.

Would you like something to drink?

No, thank you.

What can I do to make things better?

Change the world.

* * *

Sherra

Another dream about Pottles came that night—likely because of my anger at Kerok. She was motioning for me to follow her to a strange place.

A line divided us—on my side, desert, where only scrub and cactus grew.

On her side, it was green and lush—a sight I had never seen in reality, but one which, once I'd seen it, I wanted more than anything.

Behind Pottles lay a floor made of tiny, square, colored stones, depicting a huge, red rose, surrounded by trees I'd never seen.

Catalpa trees, the words whispered into my mind. Certainly not Pottles' voice; it was a strange one to me. I studied the trees, which were in full flower with the most magnificent pink blooms. *You are invited*, more words followed.

318

Chapter 17

Come, Pottles mouthed the words as she continued to beckon. *Remember the red rose. Find your way here,* the strange voice begged.

Sherra, time to wake—we must go to General Linel immediately. Kerok's voice disturbed my dream and woke me with a gasp.

Shaking, I tumbled off the bed in complete disorientation, as I'd just been elsewhere in my dream.

Hurry, Kerok's mindspeak sounded close to panic.

I hurried.

* * *

Kerok

We hadn't had a murder at the battlefront in six decades, yet I studied the burned bodies of a warrior and his escort inside their tent, which hadn't been singed anywhere. Judging by the severe burns on the bodies, the murder had occurred elsewhere, and the bodies dumped in their tent afterward.

Who could do this? Sherra, standing nearby, was more than upset. I'd already sent a message to Barth; he would arrive very soon.

Had the phantom struck again? That was my first thought, although in the past, bodies had been left outside camp after a visit from that elusive entity.

This time, the dead had been dumped inside their tent and easily found by those from nearby tents when the call came for early breakfast.

I don't know; I hope we'll have better information when Barth arrives, I responded to Sherra's question.

The phantom hasn't burned anyone before—has he?

No, my rose. This is a first.

This looks like—torture.

319

The Rose Mark

I know. Perhaps it was. It is my hope that Barth can find something—some clue—in all this tangle.

"I am here, Prince Thorn," Barth pulled back a tent flap and entered before drawing in a shocked breath at what he saw.

"I need you to touch them," I said. "I know it's horrible, but please try."

"I will."

* * *

Sherra

Barth knelt beside the bodies, both burned horribly, as if someone with fire had toyed with them before allowing them to die.

If I'd had breakfast, I may not have kept it down. Instead, I felt queasy as Barth, kneeling near where Kerok and I stood, reached out to touch one of the least-burned parts of the warrior's feet.

Barth's body stiffened, causing me to jump. And, because he was kneeling precariously, he looked as if he would topple over. Quickly, I reached out to steady him with a hand on his shoulder.

The visions that came through Barth made me wish to scream in anguish.

Chapter 18

Kerok

Kerok

I'd never seen Barth so shaken before. Sherra had experienced Barth's visions when she touched him, and I was still waiting to sort that out with Barth, who held a cup of tea in his hands while wrapped in a blanket and sitting inside Linel's tent.

Barth shivered, as if he'd been so cold it would take hours to warm up again.

"Barth, what is it?" I laid a hand on his shoulder. "Tell me what you saw."

He turned his eyes toward me, blinking to keep the horror at bay, I imagined.

"I," he began, his voice so cracked that he was forced to clear his throat before continuing. "I saw some of it, before something blocked the vision. The moment Sherra touched me, it was as if the block had been removed and allowed a flood of images to come."

His next words chilled me to the bone.

"Merrin is alive. He did this, my Prince, and I believe he has his sights set on killing you and many others before he's done."

"Are you saying Merrin is the phantom?" I couldn't accept that—couldn't take that in.

"He's just as afraid of the phantom as anyone else," Barth snorted before sipping tea. "The other thing I have is this; Merrin was saved by Poul and Wendal's interference." *With help from your brother*, he added in mindspeak.

My rapid intake of breath let Barth know how shocked I was at that revelation. This gave another reason for my brother's locking himself away—he'd convinced Poul and Wendal to save Merrin's skin by pretending to remove his power. I had no knowledge of that when I'd left Merrin in the poisoned lands—he'd *stepped* away the moment I left.

This will kill your father, Barth informed me.

Which will leave Drenn in charge, and if he's in charge, he has enough support in the Council to change as many laws as he likes, and one of those changes will be to exonerate himself of any crimes committed, I sighed.

He'll have to kill you, Hunter and me, too, Barth pointed out.

After this, I flung out a hand, *what's to keep him and Merrin from succeeding?*

Kerok? Sherra's mental sending was hesitant.

What is it, my rose?

Perhaps Barth should look at Merrin's friends and supporters?

Chapter 18

She'd waited outside Linel's tent, keeping a shield in place while Barth and I talked.

I cursed—she was correct.

"Linel," I snapped, bringing the General into the interior swiftly. "Gather Merrin's friends and bring them to me. Now."

* * *

Sherra

The moment they learned of Kerok's summons, three of Merrin's friends deserted the army, two of them *stepping* away and leaving their escorts behind. The third had taken his escort with him; whether she went willingly, we didn't know.

Two others, a Lieutenant and a Sergeant, had been forced into Linel's tent, where Kerok waited to question them with Barth at his side.

I was grateful I wasn't asked to witness it, especially when Garkus and Colonel Kage appeared nearby and were ushered into the tent by the General.

After I'd drowned in visions through my contact with Barth, I knew of the Crown Prince's guilt in the matter. Not just for keeping Merrin alive, but for his participation in Merrin's taking of Ura's innocence.

I wanted to vomit every time I considered it. Both had known what the results would be should they be caught. They'd promised Ura that they'd protect her. That promise had been as empty and fragile as a discarded eggshell.

I couldn't complain about Drenn not receiving punishment, unless I wished to be a hypocrite and surrender myself for the forbidden book I'd been given.

The difference, of course, was that my reading of an outlawed book had resulted in no deaths. Drenn's and Merrin's actions had done exactly that—several times over. What little I'd seen of Drenn through Barth's reading had painted him as a vile, jealous, self-serving royal who saw his younger brother, Thorn, as a rival in some way.

I feared for the people if Drenn took the throne. For now, the only thing standing between Drenn and that high seat was his love for the King and the King's continued existence.

I wondered when even that might be set aside to serve Drenn's ambitions.

My rose, we are stepping *away to perform executions,* Kerok informed me. *We will return shortly—my father has already decreed this punishment.*

I—understand, I replied. *I am dropping my shield to allow all of you through. I want no part of touching those two,* I shivered as I revealed that information.

Sherra, you know it is deserved—the two who are dead attempted to inject reason into this madness, and paid for it with their lives.

I know, I whispered in mindspeak. *I saw it through Barth.*

We will speak later—I am sorry you saw any part of this.

As am I, but perhaps it's better that I know what we face. I keep your secrets, remember?

As I keep yours.

If it were only Thorn who knew my secrets, then it might not matter. Others knew, too, and that meant my life hung in the balance.

Drenn wanted Kerok dead.

He also wanted me dead.

The blood of innocents would wash through Az-ca, should he take the throne. Who needed the enemy, when someone destined to rule would achieve their goal for them?

Chapter 18

Less than ten minutes later, Kerok announced his return. I allowed him and Barth to *step* through my shield.

* * *

Kerok

I stood nearby when Barth examined the two escorts left behind. *They know nothing of this*, Barth informed me silently.

Then I'll take them back to Secondary Camp with me; it's obvious they're upset by all this. They can help the drudges until they recover somewhat and something else can be decided.

"Good enough," Barth sighed aloud.

"You'll come with me to Secondary Camp," I told both women.

"They're dead—aren't they?" One of the women wept.

"Yes. Treason and murder carry a heavy price," I replied. "You have been found innocent of those crimes. Therefore, I will take you to Secondary Camp, where you may grieve in private and help the drudges there if you want. A decision as to where to place you will come later."

"Thank you, Prince Commander," the second woman mumbled, her head bowed.

Her warrior helped Merrin in the killing of her friends, Barth informed me. *She sides with you on this issue.*

And the other?

Still angry at everyone, but mostly at her warrior for leaving her behind. Work with that, if you can. He deserted her, after committing crimes.

All right.

"Come," I said aloud. "My rose will help you get settled at Secondary Camp."

* * *

The Rose Mark

Sherra

Here were two who'd followed their warriors' lead, in discounting the new method—something they'd judged before seeing it for themselves. I didn't say anything about it, however.

Both were in mourning, and we were behind on our training.

Kerok still worried that the enemy would strike very soon—as was I. Even with everything else going on at the front, I'd still felt the hate and revulsion billowing into the encampment in waves.

"Do you wish to stay together, or have separate quarters?" Kerok asked the two grieving escorts as we landed outside a cabin in Secondary Camp. Nearby was another empty cabin, should they require it.

"Together, please," one begged after turning to the other. They could lean on one another when the pain of loss was too much.

"You've been here before; you know where the physician's cabin is. Meals are at regular times, but I will ask a drudge to bring you something today. Join the others at regular mess tomorrow—I believe they will welcome you," Kerok told them.

"Why would they do that?" one of them whispered.

"Things are changing," I said. "We stand together, here. We have a common purpose. Forget the jealousy and divisiveness you've known in the past. And, if you ask, any rose here can show you wonderful things."

"You're the one—the one they were all talking about. The one my warrior said would fail and die in the first battle because you didn't know what you were doing," the angry one accused.

326

Chapter 18

Kerok stiffened beside me, prepared to come to my defense. I placed a hand on his arm.

"Come to training tomorrow and see for yourself whether you think I'll fall," I said. "Come and tell me afterward what I'm doing wrong." I'd said it as gently as I could—issuing an invitation rather than a challenge.

"I will come," she declared.

Here was the challenge. She'd see for herself and pass judgment. That judgment would be most harsh, because her mind was already made up. Her warrior had done a very good job turning others against me.

"Join the others at breakfast. Ask for Wend or Jae—they'll guide you to the proper table," I said. "What is your name? So I can tell them you're coming," I added.

"Hari," she responded. "This is Lera," she nodded to her companion.

"Good. I'll see you in the morning," I said. "I'm sorry for your loss."

"Your cabins will be guarded," Kerok added. He didn't need to add that they would be guarded in case either thought to attempt escape—I think they both understood that quite well.

* * *

Kerok

By the time Sherra and I reached the officers' mess, they were serving the midday meal. "How did training go?" I slouched onto a chair opposite Armon's—he, Levi and their roses had already arrived.

"Much better than expected," Armon grinned as Sherra took the chair next to mine. "Whatever Sherra taught them last night after evening meal made things run smoothly from the beginning."

"I wouldn't expect these levels of ability after three weeks of training under normal circumstances," Levi admitted. "It's a miracle."

"Hmmph," Misten snorted and bumped her shoulder against his. He laughed.

I wanted to pull Sherra into a rib-cracking hug; she'd done this, even when she'd been angry enough with me to spit.

She'd done it for them—the black roses—and for Levi, Armon and likely for my own thin skin, too.

She was determined to save lives. Only now was I beginning to see that as clearly as I should have in the beginning. This was no selfish act to save herself—if it were, she'd never have passed her knowledge on to another.

"You are too generous, my rose," I mumbled before leaning in to kiss her temple.

You should see her eyes right now, Armon sent. *They are as wide as I've ever seen.* I laughed and kissed her a second time.

* * *

Sherra

My shock at Kerok's action disappeared quickly when he informed me that we were expected at the palace to make a report to the King. Hunter had probably been briefed already; he merely needed Kerok's written record while the King wanted a personal report.

I hoped we wouldn't come in contact with Drenn; yes, we could all point fingers at the Crown Prince, but the troubles that would come of it were many. Not least was the fact that he deserved a death sentence, and Kerok was needed at the battlefront rather than sitting in his father's palace as the new heir.

Chapter 18

That was the law—the Crown Prince couldn't serve on the battlefield.

If Kerok wasn't on the battlefield, then I wouldn't be on the battlefield, either, and in some way, I knew we needed to be there.

When one trouble comes, many others follow, Pottles used to say. She was certainly correct this time.

"What are you thinking about?" Kerok asked as he guided me past two bowing guards who stood at the wide door leading into the palace. He'd *stepped* us while I'd been deep in thought.

"About simpler times, when finding a pot without a hole in it was a good day," I lied.

"You make me laugh," he said. "Thank you."

"Thorn," Hunter made a turn from an adjacent hallway to join us.

"Hunter," Kerok acknowledged him.

"Tread carefully," Hunter warned.

"I know."

That's when I understood Kerok was thinking the same as I—that pointing a finger at Drenn could cause much more trouble than leaving him where he was for the moment. I didn't miss the frown on Kerok's face, however, or the determination in Hunter's eyes.

If Drenn wasn't prepared for the day of reckoning when it came, he could be very much surprised at what might happen to him.

For now, no accusations would be leveled.

My concern, though, which surprised me greatly, was for the life of the King—a man I'd reviled during most of my existence. As for Kerok and I; our lives had been vastly different, with each being perilous in its own right.

I would not have traded places with him for all the comforts in the world.

* * *

Kerok

Father looked pale, and that worried me. No word passed my lips concerning Drenn's involvement in the murders and treason committed. I chose instead to tell him that the sentences had been carried out against the two we'd found, and that we were still searching for three missing warriors and one escort.

"Does anyone know where they could be?" Father asked, lifting a cup of tea to drink.

"We're checking home villages and other likely places, plus guards have been doubled at Secondary Camp. Escorts have been advised to keep strong shields up at all times if possible."

"I hadn't considered that they'd strike there, but you're right," Father agreed. "I worry for your life, Thorn."

"Then stop worrying so much. I have Sherra beside me, and if they can get past her, I'll be much surprised."

"I've heard Garkus' tale," the memory drew a smile and added more color to his face. "Young woman, that was quite a performance, as I understand it."

"I'm sure Garkus was exaggerating—I've heard he excels at it," Sherra replied, bringing a wider smile to Father's face.

"Very well, then," Father set his teacup down. "I have full faith in you, Son. Keep Hunter advised of new developments. If you locate the escaped warriors, I'd like to speak with one of them before the execution takes place."

"As you say, Father," I dipped my head to him.

You know that can never happen, Hunter's voice sounded in my mind.

Chapter 18

I'm aware, I replied.

* * *

Sherra

Kerok *stepped* me back to camp, to find training in full swing. He gripped my arm as we stared in amazement—warriors in unison were flinging fireblasts far over the compound's northern wall, while escorts held their shields in place, strong and steady.

Each escort was lending her power to the warriors, and there were no weak blasts coming from any of them.

"I never thought to see this," Kerok breathed beside me.

"Look," I said. "They're here, watching."

Far outside the training area, Hari and Lera sat, watching the exercise.

"If this doesn't convince them, nothing will," Kerok growled.

"If I felt better about either of them, I'd suggest sending them to teach at the next training camp. With their attitude about the new method, though, they'd do new trainees a disservice."

"Agreed. They could cause damage," he said. "We'll wait and see about those two before making a final determination."

"Hari's standing up," I pointed out. "Do you suppose she's made up her mind already?"

"I know what I'll say if she disagrees with any part of it," Kerok grumbled. "I was fighting battles before she was born. She can argue as much as she likes and I'll tell her how things really are."

"Because she isn't in charge of the army," I smiled up at him.

"That is so very true. Oh, they're walking this way. I'm not in the best mood to handle insubordination," he admitted. "Perhaps they should have stayed in their cabin."

It didn't take long for them to arrive. I decided to let Kerok handle whatever they wanted to say—because he was the Prince Commander.

"Will you teach me?" Lera begged. "Please?" Her words were directed to me and not to Kerok.

"I wish to learn, too," Hari's eyes were downcast and color flooded her cheeks. "They've been doing this a long time, and they're not even tired."

"Wend said this was their first full training exercise," Lera breathed. "We thought we'd see all the mistakes we made when we were here to train. I—this—I don't know how they're doing it so easily."

"The warriors are tossing blasts massive enough to destroy the enemy," Hari admitted. "Not the weak ones that would fizzle out when we didn't lower our shields fast enough to let them through."

"Come to the training grounds tomorrow morning," Kerok said. "I have some of the best newly-trained warriors coming to join us. Many of these roses can shield well enough to protect several warriors. I won't allow them to pull energy away from an escort, but they can certainly fire blasts until they're depleted. They can step to the back of the line, then, and rest while others battle on. Sherra can show all of you how things work at the same time, and perhaps you can practice with them."

"I want to," Lera said. "Hari?" she turned to ask.

"I will. I appreciate this, Commander. It will take my mind off—other things."

Chapter 18

"You may continue to watch if you want," Kerok said. "My rose needs something to drink—she's had a long and weary day."

While they dipped their heads to Kerok, he *stepped* us to our cabin.

* * *

"Just one—the evening meal will be ready soon." Kerok poured two glasses of wine and corked the bottle. "Go ahead and sit." He gestured toward one of the two chairs in the small sitting area.

His chair creaked as he sat, after handing a glass of wine to me.

"This tastes like berries," I said after sipping it.

"Blackberries," he agreed. "One of my favorites. This one isn't too sweet; I prefer it that way."

I leaned my head against the padded chair back and closed my eyes. Kerok and I—we'd risen long before dawn to get to the army camp. The day had gone on forever, and still there was plenty of it left.

"It's the stress as much as anything else," Kerok rumbled. "The last camp murder happened before my time. I've never seen one until today. If I could get my hands on Merrin," he added.

"Don't let him get to you," I opened my eyes and turned my face toward his. "He'll be found, I think."

"But what sort of wickedness will he commit in the meantime? You saw those bodies, my rose. I wish it could have been otherwise, but you are with me now and there's no way around terrible truths at times."

"I know. You have been made a target, and me with you. Perhaps it is best that I saw it with you—so I know what we're fighting against. From outside and inside."

"Go ahead and drink your wine—we both need it," he said.

"Yes." I lifted the glass to my lips.

* * *

Kerok

Today had driven home a truth that I'd not considered before. If Grae had been at my side and seen burned bodies as Sherra and I had, she wouldn't have taken it well at all. I doubted she'd be able to stand at my side and build a shield afterward while Barth and I examined guilty warriors.

Grae had been so quiet. Willing to stand behind me wherever I went, but we'd never witnessed murders of our own. The deaths at the enemy's hand had been difficult enough for her.

This—Grae would have needed my support to get through the day.

Sherra had stood with me all the way, including a meeting with my father, and even managed to put a smile on his face during a trying time.

Grae was seldom brave enough to speak to him.

I considered that what I needed today, I'd had beside me. No, I hadn't stopped loving Grae, but I was coming to recognize Sherra as something more. There could always be a gap between what I wanted and what I needed, but that didn't mean I couldn't recognize both those things.

Lifting my glass, I swallowed a mouthful of wine and prayed it would work its magic quickly. I needed to be calm and in control before going to the evening meal, where Sherra would sit beside me and my traitorous, misbehaving body.

My injuries more than a year earlier had likely played a part in the reeling in of certain urges, but they were returning now with a vengeance. Father's physician told me things

Chapter 18

would return to normal, but I'd brushed his words away—they'd meant nothing after losing Grae.

Therefore, I had a new method of torturing myself over Grae's death. I suppose it was time to face my inner demons and admit that I was not only responsible for her death, but that I felt a terrible guilt, because I didn't die beside her.

"What are you thinking?" Sherra asked. "You have such a sad and bewildered expression on your face."

"I'm thinking I don't deserve what I have," I replied without opening my eyes.

"I can't fix that for you, Kerok," she said softly. "I think you're the only one who can."

"We should go, they're likely waiting for us to arrive before serving the meal." My eyes opened and focused on the opposite wall in the dimming light.

"Commander?" Sherra stood and held out a hand to pull me to my feet. The rose tattoo on her left wrist was partially revealed as she reached for my hand. I grasped her fingers in mine without thinking, and drew her forward to place a kiss on the black rose tattoo.

Sherra drew in an audible breath before pulling me to my feet.

"Food," I touched her face with my free hand. "They're waiting for us."

With a sigh, she released my hand and nodded. I *stepped* us to the officers' mess, where Armon, Levi and their roses sat at our usual table.

* * *

Sherra

Armon wore a huge grin as Kerok and I sat down. Drudges rushed out with plates of food to set before us; Kerok hadn't been wrong that they'd wait for us.

335

"Today's training went very well," Levi said as I lifted my fork. "Things are so much better than I could have ever expected."

"If we had to go to the battlefield tomorrow, we'd be ready enough," Armon agreed.

"I've seen far worse show up at the front after full training," Kerok agreed while discreetly pushing the butter dish in my direction.

There was plenty for everyone at the table, so I took a generous portion for my roll and slathered it across warm bread.

Kerok didn't turn at my sigh of appreciation for the first bite, but the corner of his mouth curled into a smile.

"Armon says we'll get our first pay soon," Caral said while I savored a second bite of bread. "He says we can spend it on treats, fruit or clothing, all we have to do is ask a merchant's messenger for what we want. There are retired warriors who now work for merchants to bring those orders to the army's camp."

I stopped chewing. *There's pay?* I directed at Kerok, because I didn't want to speak with my mouth full.

You'll receive a rose captain's pay, he replied. *Enough credits to buy pears and butter, among other things—if you want.*

I swallowed while blinking at him. "Pears," I breathed. "Nice, ripe ones."

"We may be able to get some of the latest picking," Kerok said. "And a few apples, too. I'll ask Hunter."

I was imagining a basket full of pears that I could eat myself when Wend's frantic voice filled my mind.

Chapter 18

Without thinking, I hauled everyone at our table toward the regular mess, where three missing warriors had arrived to kill two escorts they'd left behind.

"Shields up," I shouted at every rose inside the mess hall the moment we arrived. Kerok was already bellowing at warriors to fire at the three who stood in a corner, attempting to blast through shields that Wend, Jae and Neka had built around themselves to protect Hari and Lera.

Those two cringed at the table in fear, while the roses and warriors around them worked to protect them and everyone else.

"Sherra, get me close," Kerok turned toward me as the fireblasts flew and more than a few wooden beams in the ceiling began to catch fire.

Close? I sent mindspeak. *How close?*

Very.

It will be done, Commander. Forming the strongest shield I could, I grasped Kerok's arm and *stepped* us toward the fugitive warriors.

That wasn't all I did, either. The moment Kerok and I appeared right in front of them, I enclosed all of them in a second shield. If they didn't burn themselves to death at their first firing at Kerok, Kerok's return fire, which sailed easily through both sets of shields, took care of whatever remained of them.

"Get buckets of water, quickly," I heard Armon shouting somewhere behind me as I dropped the shield around three dead warriors.

"Sherra?" Kerok's voice was calm in the din as others took up the call to bring water. The mess hall would burn to the ground if something wasn't done soon.

"Kerok?" I turned to blink at him as the fire bloomed and sparked around us.

"I love it when you say that name," he said.

There, amid crackling fire and a fervent, reigning chaos to put it out, he took my face in his hands and gave me my first real kiss.

Chapter 19

*K*erok

"They tried to kill us," Lera wept.

Hunter stood nearby as I questioned both women inside the meeting room at my cabin. Sherra was outside in the sitting area with Wend, Marc, Jae and a few others.

The fire at the regular mess was out, now, but the building was so heavily damaged it required extensive repairs. During the rest of our stay, the officers' mess would have to serve everyone.

"Do you believe that, too, Hari?" I asked. "That they were trying to kill you?"

So far, she'd remained silent while Lera wept and told her version of the tale. Hunching her shoulders, Hari nodded.

"They yelled terrible things," she admitted. "Said if we told you anything we knew, we were dead anyway."

"Hunter, will you bring Wend and Jae in?" I asked. I'd get their verification in this matter. If Hari was correct, I assumed they'd become Merrin's new targets. They knew nothing—Barth had already verified it.

Merrin wanted them dead anyway, perhaps as a deterrent for anyone else in the army who'd seen or heard something that could damage him or three other warriors who'd died earlier.

Wend and Jae walked in behind Hunter, and took seats at the meeting table opposite Hari and Lera.

"Tell me what happened," I said. I trusted these and knew I'd hear only truth from them.

"Those men *stepped* into the mess hall and fired blasts directly at us," Wend began. "If we hadn't been trained to react quickly, we would have died then—they weren't holding anything back."

"So you put up shields?"

"Yes. All the roses at the table did, except, well," Wend hesitated.

"We didn't," Lera wiped tears away. "We were so shocked that we froze."

"Understandable—you knew those men," I nodded. "Go on," I turned back to Wend.

"When they didn't kill us with their first few blasts, they kept firing and started shouting. Calling Lera and Hari terrible names and saying they'd die. No matter where they thought to hide, they were marked for death."

"They were shouting *die, bitches, you'll never be safe no matter where you go*," Jae provided the unvarnished truth.

Lera sobbed as the words were repeated.

340

Chapter 19

I wondered why the men hadn't *stepped* away the moment I appeared with Sherra.

Perhaps that was the point, I cautioned myself. They thought to kill us, or make an attempt to do so.

They'd never seen Sherra work; they'd only discounted her new methods. *Sherra*, I sent mindspeak, *when you placed a shield around those men, did you keep them from stepping away?*

Yes, came her succinct reply. *I placed that shield the moment we arrived at the mess hall. I placed a second, smaller shield when we approached them, so their own blasts would take their lives quickly.*

They'd been unable to escape. So much the worse for them. *Thank you, my rose*, I replied.

"I believe Hunter has enough information to take to the King," I said, feeling weariness settle over me like a heavy blanket. "Hari, Lera, I'll have extra guards around your cabin tonight. Neka and her warrior will escort you there."

"Thank you, Prince Commander," Hari rose from her seat.

"Yes. Thank you. Thank you, Wend and Jae, for saving us," Lera wiped more tears away as she stood to follow Hari.

"We would do the same for any of ours," Wend said.

Once they were out the door, I turned to Wend. "I heard you—as did Sherra. Perhaps it was desperation, but you can mindspeak, Wend. I cannot tell you how pleased I am about that."

"I don't really know what to do with it," she confessed.

"Ask Sherra tomorrow morning at breakfast. I think she'll have you communicating in no time. Ask her to teach you how to *step*, too. She's quite adept at it."

"May I try?" Jae asked.

341

"Of course. You'll be able to *step*, unless I miss my guess," I told her. "As for mindspeak, it's rare enough among warriors, but you and the others are more than welcome to attempt it."

"Thank you, Commander."

"You're welcome. You're dismissed, Corporal Wend, Corporal Jae." I nodded to both as they rose to leave.

* * *

Sherra

Although I bathed after everyone left our cabin, I couldn't get the smell of burned wood out of my nostrils.

Sherra? Kerok's mindspeak interrupted as I pondered what to do about it.

I'll be right there, I said. I was dressed in a clean undershirt and sleep-pants, but everything, no matter how freshly-laundered, smelled of smoke.

He stood outside my door when I opened it, still dressed as he was earlier. He held a bottle of wine in his hands.

"Want to share?" he asked.

"Yes. Maybe it'll clear away the smell of smoke," I said.

"Good. Let's go."

"Wh-where?" He gripped my arm as if we'd be *stepping* somewhere.

"To our rock."

"We have a rock?"

"Yes, we do. I've placed Armon in charge, and asked him to mindspeak us if we're needed."

With that, he *stepped* us away, and I found myself standing beside him on the same rock we'd sat on near the lake at North Camp.

"I didn't bring glasses, so we'll have to share the bottle," he grinned.

Chapter 19

Moonlight on the lake cast eerie reflections on us and the rock, as Kerok sat down before motioning for me to join him. Out in the scrub, far from camp, a coyote howled and was answered by another. Pulling the cork from the bottle with a familiar, hollow-sounding boop, Kerok handed it to me, first.

"We'll drink to a fucking long day," he said.

In total agreement, I tilted the bottle back and drank.

* * *

King's Palace
Crown Prince Drenn

"You shouldn't even be here," I hissed at Merrin, who stalked about my suite in an agitated manner. "Barth is here, you fool. He could discover us at any moment."

"My allies are dead," Merrin snapped at me. "Only the whining escort is left, and if she doesn't cooperate, she'll be dead, too."

"I told you it was stupid to send them after those escorts."

"I couldn't take any chances that they'd heard something. I blocked information from the dead ones, so Barth has no idea I'm involved—unless you've heard otherwise."

"Hmmph. Father knows nothing, or he'd have told me already," I said. "You're safe enough, but stupid moves like sending them into Secondary Camp could get us both killed. We'd be questioned already if I hadn't found Thorn's book for you. That's the only reason you knew how to block information from a Diviner."

"Yes, that's been very useful, and something the phantom already had. We can commit murder and lay it all on the phantom, now. Besides, your father will never allow anything to happen to you, now will he?" Merrin sounded bitter. "He didn't give a shit about me."

343

"I'm the Crown Prince," I reminded him. "Father loves me and Thorn's too busy playing soldier to involve himself in politics. He hates all of this anyway, so I'm Father's only choice to serve."

"I'm still counting on you to put me in charge of the army."

"And you'll get there if you stop doing stupid things. Any new word on the enemy, and when I can expect their attack?"

"They're building some kind of strange road," Merrin scratched his neck. "It's short and just—stops."

"You haven't brought fleas into my suite, have you?" I accused as he continued to scratch.

"What? No," he denied my words while scratching an arm.

"Fuck. You've brought fleas in here. Get out and take them with you."

* * *

Sherra

"Here." Kerok scooted closer so he could wrap his arms about me. I was shivering in the night air, wearing only a sleeveless undershirt and thin sleep-pants.

"Relax, I won't bite. I'm just keeping you warm," he breathed against my hair. "You smell nice," he added.

While we'd passed the wine bottle back and forth, the moon had risen higher in the sky. Night insects buzzed low across the lake; an occasional fish leapt from the water to capture one for a meal. Resulting splashes were occurring regularly, and I found it restful and entertaining.

Kerok's arms about me were warm. For that small window of time, I felt safer than I ever had. And, after sharing wine with him, I felt as close to being cared for by Kerok as I ever had.

Chapter 19

Tomorrow, I'd remind myself of the ghost who stood between us—a rose who hadn't been prepared to protect herself in addition to protecting her warrior.

The rose Kerok grieved for above all others.

Tonight, I'd take the comfort he offered, as we'd shared the events of a trying day, along with a bottle of wine at the end of it.

"Ready to go back? We have an early morning scheduled." Letting me go, he stood and stretched before reaching out a hand to lift me to my feet.

"I suppose," I grumbled. After standing, I swayed unsteadily for a moment, wanting more than anything to press my body against his again for the warmth it provided. "I probably shouldn't drink," I hiccupped.

He chuckled and *stepped* us away.

* * *

Kerok

"News from the General," Linel's personal messenger appeared inside the officers' mess at breakfast the following morning.

"Good morning, Dayl," I said, taking the sealed envelope from his hand. "What can you tell me before I open this?"

"We sent scouts as you requested. Things are quite— busy—at the enemy camp."

"Have you had breakfast?"

"Yes, Commander."

"Good. I'll send a reply later today," I tapped the edge of the envelope on the table.

"Thank you, Commander. I'll let General Linel know."

"If he wants a private conference, I'll come," I said.

"I believe that is contained in your letter," Dayl grinned.

345

"Then tell him I'll be there tonight for the evening meal, unless it's an emergency."

"I'll inform him right away."

Dayl *stepped* away while I set the envelope beside my plate and continued eating. Armon and Levi had watched the exchange, both wondering, I'm sure, what Linel had to say.

Sherra eyed the envelope as if it were a snake about to strike. If I were alone, I would likely do the same.

Busy. The enemy camp was busy, as Dayl put it.

Ready to strike, in other words. I wondered what they were waiting for. We needed this day, at the very least, to prepare the warriors and new escorts for battle.

I worried we'd lose some in a vicious attack from the enemy. I worried that they had something terrible planned, and we wouldn't be prepared.

We stand or fall together, Armon informed me. *As it has always been.*

"As it has always been," I lifted my cup of tea in a salute to my first personal advisor.

"To us," Armon replied.

"Lift your cups," Levi said. "In a salute to those who stand beside you, when battle comes."

* * *

Sherra

Caral, Misten and I lifted our cups with the others, while other tables took up the chant—*We stand or fall together*—*as it has always been*, until the entire officers' mess was filled with voices.

"To our King and the Prince Commander," someone from the far end shouted. It was repeated until the building echoed.

A part of me was grateful at the omission of the Crown Prince. The others wouldn't know of his misdeeds, and I was

Chapter 19

sworn to keep Kerok's secrets. The crimes and treason Drenn had committed would remain with me.

If Drenn harmed a hair on Kerok's head, however—he should guard his back carefully from then on.

Kerok rose from his seat once the voices died down. "I know you're expecting this," he announced. "We'll be moving to the front tomorrow. The enemy is planning an attack, that much is plain. Use your training today to hone your skills and ready yourselves. Battle will come soon enough to all of us."

* * *

Sherra

"*Step* only where you have clear memories of the place," I told my trainees. Caral, Misten, Jae, Wend and several others—the highest-ranking ones from North Camp—had been allowed the morning off from training with the warriors so I could teach them how to *step*, and hopefully to discover whether any besides Wend had mindspeaking ability.

"Marc talks about *sight-stepping*," Wend said.

"I'm not as familiar with that," I said. "It would probably be better coming from Marc," I explained. "*Sight-stepping*, as I understand it, is *stepping* to a place in the distance that you can actually see. It's still dangerous, as you may not notice the snake waiting in the distance, or the hole in the ground which can twist or break an ankle when you land in it."

"That's why they always say to be careful where you place your feet," Misten sighed. She'd already had a conversation with Levi before coming to training.

"If you've noticed the General's personal messenger when he comes, he always *steps* to the same spot in the officers' mess," I went on. "That spot is reserved for *stepping*. The Commander and I land there every time."

347

"That makes sense—you could land on somebody if you picked a random place to land," Jae giggled.

"True. I think the warriors get extensive training in *stepping*, and this is only a rushed lesson, so I'll repeat their words—be careful where you set your feet."

"What if we need—well, a place to escape," Wend asked. "If your warrior is wounded away from the battlefield or something?"

"You should know at least two places where a physician is," I answered. "Here, and at North Camp. Kerok says the physicians, instructors and drudges are at training camps year-round, to maintain the training grounds and buildings. Either place would work, I think. Plus, you're very familiar with North Camp and know every inch of it, too."

"The battlefield has a corps of physicians," Kerok announced as he walked up to our group. "Sherra's right, though—if you're away from the battlefield, go someplace you're more than familiar with—in times of emergency, you're usually not thinking clearly and a familiar place is the best."

"I think it's time to try it," I said, struggling not to smile at Kerok as he came to stand beside me. "Wend, you first," I said.

She came forward and offered her hands so I could transfer the images and information to her.

When I let her go, she grinned and *stepped* away, appearing moments later with a cup of tea from the officers' mess in her hand. She handed it to Kerok with a giggle before moving away.

"Thank you," Kerok said. "Hot, too, just as I like it." He drank from the cup as Caral came forward.

* * *

Kerok

Chapter 19

Every rose Sherra trained that morning could *step* when it came time for the midday meal. Wend, Caral and Tera could mindspeak. I'd never seen Caral so excited—she and Armon would be able to communicate silently, and that was a gift to them and to the army.

We needed mindspeakers desperately, and I wondered whether Sherra could search the new warriors coming in for that particular talent.

I'd mention it to her during the meal; she'd worked hard with her small group of trainees and needed rest and food.

"Everyone knows how to *step* to the officers' mess, now—go in groups of two," I ordered while smiling at Sherra's group. "Your warriors will meet you there."

Sherra looked at me, her eyes shining as the trainees disappeared two at a time. *You've made a miracle,* I informed her.

"They already had the talent, I just showed it to them," she replied.

"Come on, then, I'm hungry," I slipped an arm around her shoulders to *step* us away.

* * *

King's Palace
Crown Prince Drenn

The conversation I'd had the night before with Merrin played and replayed through my mind. "You know what you have to do—the enemy will strike soon and I want to be in charge when that happens," Merrin had growled as he handed me the weapon and the projectiles he'd stolen from the enemy camp.

"Your father is ill, or haven't you noticed?" Merrin had gone on, making me draw in a shocked breath. "He has

349

months at best, and the last of those months will make him suffer greatly. Do the right thing and end it now."

Merrin—he'd made me more than angry, telling me things I had no desire to learn. His own desires were beginning to wear on me, and I considered waiting until he came back to fire the weapon at him.

Perhaps it was just as well he'd *stepped* away immediately, or I may have loaded the weapon while he watched and then killed him with it.

During the night, I'd had time to think. Merrin was becoming a bedsore on my ass. If I were in charge, I could order Father's new assassins to search for Merrin after I leveled a death sentence against him and had someone else placed in charge of the army.

Yes, I still wanted Thorn dead—when I took the throne, he'd be my heir until I could get one of my own. I wasn't willing to wait for that to happen. If I waited to pass a death sentence on Merrin, then he could take care of Thorn first, then I could name him an enemy of the state and have him actively hunted for execution.

Yes—that was the best answer.

The trouble, of course, was Father's life and role in all this. If I took him down, I'd be forced to take down Barth or Hunter with him, as one was always at his side. At times, both were.

Both.

I needed to kill all three, or one would call Thorn and bring him into this. That I didn't want—Thorn had already threatened me. If I killed Father, he'd waste no time taking me down.

Better to do this now and blame it on the phantom. I hadn't had dinner with my Father in weeks. I'd ask to have an evening meal with him, Barth and Hunter. I merely had to be careful so Barth wouldn't suspect anything.

* * *

Kerok

While Sherra and I sat at our usual table with Levi, Armon and their escorts, Wend and the others had taken tables nearby. All of them were laughing and discussing newly-discovered talents with their warriors.

This is how it should be, I told myself. *The excitement of new discoveries, instead of more somber discussions of how to survive on the battlefield.*

"I haven't seen this much enthusiasm in—well, I've never seen it," Armon admitted.

Thorn? Father's mindspeak interrupted my thoughts. He seldom contacted me directly, just as I didn't contact him. We each realized we could be interrupting something important. That meant what he had to say was significant.

Father? I sent my question back.

Drenn has asked to have dinner with me tonight. I was thinking about issuing my own invitation to him—and you— soon. I need to see both my sons, as well as Barth and Hunter. Leave your rose behind; I wish to speak with all of you privately.

I'll be there—is it the usual time?

Yes. I look forward to seeing both my sons at the table tonight.

It will be good to see you, I responded, although I didn't want to see Drenn. He had much to answer for, and I had no desire to sit across the table from him while he made jabs at me.

He'd gotten away with too many crimes in my estimation, and didn't deserve a place at Father's right hand.

351

The Rose Mark

He deserves a proper sentence, a small voice informed me. For the crimes he'd committed, he deserved death—just as Merrin had.

Both were still alive, due to Drenn's interference. Warriors and at least one escort were dead because of Merrin, too.

Stop thinking about it—you're only making yourself angrier, I sent a warning to myself.

"I'm having dinner with my father tonight," I turned to Sherra. "He wants a private meal with my brother and me. Will you be all right by yourself?" I asked.

"We'll make sure she has someone to sit with," Caral smiled.

"I'll be fine," Sherra said.

* * *

Sherra

I spent the afternoon with Armon, Levi, Caral and Misten. Kerok told us he had paperwork to do and sent me to the training field with the others.

Hari and Lera arrived to learn what they could, so I worked with them while Armon and Levi practiced with Misten and Caral while supervising some of the others.

"I can feel your fire," I said after touching Hari's fingers. "Now, you do the same for me."

She drew in a breath as we connected that way. "If you work with another warrior, do the same thing so your shield will recognize his power as your own and allow his blasts to go through unscathed," I told her.

"Why didn't anyone think of this before?" Lera asked.

"I don't know. Perhaps they did. I was lucky that the Prince Commander was willing to listen to my ideas."

352

Chapter 19

"Narris was so adamant that the new method was a waste of time," Hari let my hands go and dropped her eyes. She'd named her warrior—the one the King ordered executed.

"Where are the roses for those two who died in the mess hall fire?" I asked.

"Still at the army camp," Lera replied. "They were sent to work with the drudges, there. Ours were the ones convicted and executed, so we were allowed to leave to mourn their loss."

"I wonder if those escorts have been notified of their warriors' deaths?" I mused.

"I don't know—probably not unless the Prince Commander has informed General Linel."

"I'll ask about that later," I said. "Are you ready to try this? I can get Armon and Levi to fire weak blasts to test you."

"I'd like to try," Lera breathed. "I feel as if I've been set free, for some reason."

"I think maybe you have," I agreed and smiled.

* * *

Kerok

Send them to North Camp, I wrote to General Linel. He'd asked what I thought should be done with two escorts whose warriors were now dead after attacking Secondary Camp.

Dayl, Linel's messenger, waited in the sitting area of my cabin while I hastily scribbled a note to the General. As I wrote, I considered that Dayl could be taught other things. Sherra could touch him to see what he might be suited for.

Sherra? I sent mindspeak. *Will you come to the cabin for a few minutes?*

On my way, came the reply. Moments later, she *stepped* into the sitting area. Rising from my seat, I folded the note in my hands as Sherra blinked at me in curiosity before turning toward Dayl.

"Teach him how to shield himself, if you can," I told her.

Dayl drew in a breath at my words. "Stand up, Dayl," I told him. "Sherra needs to touch your hands."

* * *

Sherra

Dayl did very well at forming a shield; Kerok wouldn't let him leave until he'd done so. Kerok asked about Lera and Hari afterward.

"They're doing very well," I said. "I left them with Levi and Armon, to practice their new shielding techniques. Caral and Misten are helping them along."

"In your opinion, are they a threat to anyone here, or to the army as a whole?"

"No. Not after they were targeted in the mess hall. Before that, Hari was uncooperative, but that's changed."

"So you trust them?"

"I do. I think they still need a bit of gentle handling, but only because they lost their warriors and under such bizarre circumstances."

"Do you think they might consider working with some of the newly-trained warriors who arrived today?"

"I suppose—I think they could prepare them for what battle is, and what to expect when they get there."

"That sounds good. I'll leave that to you and Armon while I'm having dinner with Father."

"I think we should ask the new warriors to join their table with ours, then, and see how they all get along," I said.

"Good enough. I should get dressed," Kerok said absently. "I just sent two escorts to North Camp—the two

Chapter 19

whose warriors died in the mess hall attack. They'll be taken care of there until we can determine what to do with them."

"I hope they don't cause trouble," I said.

"Why do you think I asked you to teach Dayl how to shield?"

"Perhaps I should go with him," I began.

"No, I asked Linel to send Dayl and two unattached warriors with them. The warriors will stay there, and I've given orders for them to take care of things if the escorts step out of line. Barth did his divination when we were there, but they've had several days to stew about things."

"Things can certainly change," I agreed. Kerok was wise to take such precautions.

"Yes, they certainly can," he acknowledged. "Go back to your training, my rose. I'll dress properly for dinner with my father."

* * *

Kerok

"Drenn was the one to ask first," Hunter informed me. He and I walked along the hallway leading to my father's private dining room. "Your father took the opportunity to ask both of you; Drenn doesn't know you'll be there."

The last time we saw one another didn't go well, I informed Hunter. *I may have threatened him, too, before going back to North Camp to see about the flooding.*

You were supposed to see me afterward, Hunter said.

I remember.

What did you have words with your brother about? Hunter asked. *You didn't know then that Merrin had survived or that your father's assassins were compromised.*

It's nothing you don't know already, I said. *I'll explain later, if you're interested.*

I am.

We'd reached the door to Father's private dining room; the guards bowed and opened the door for us.

As usual, Drenn hadn't arrived. Father stood next to the far window with a glass of wine in his hand, looking at the gardens below.

"There are late roses blooming," Father turned to me with a smile. He looked weary. I worried that he knew about Drenn's misdeeds and it was taking a toll on his health. "Come, sit with me," he held out a hand, indicating my seat at the table. "Hug your father first," he chuckled as I made my way toward my chair.

Barth, as usual, stood nearby, nodding his approval as I embraced my father.

"Sit, sit," Father said when he pulled away. "Tell me how the training is going while we wait for your brother."

"Training is going extremely well," I said, reaching for the wine bottle and pouring a glass for myself. "I am more than satisfied with this crop of trainees."

"Is your rose one of those you're satisfied with?" Father had a gleam in his eye as he asked the question.

"Sherra is exceptional, but you know that already," I stated. "I have no complaints."

"Good, good," Father said, setting his glass down so I could refill it. "Ah, here's your brother now. Drenn, join us in a glass of wine," Father invited.

I turned to watch as Drenn approached the table.

"Ah, brother. How good of you to save me time and trouble," Drenn laughed as he pulled the weapon of the enemy from a pocket and fired it at me first.

Chapter 20

erok

     Had Sherra not taught Hunter and me how to shield, we'd all have died. Drenn intended to kill Father, but as I was there, he wanted to dispatch me, first.

Two times he fired the weapon, in swift succession. The first pellet glanced off my shield and hit a tall, precious vase that had belonged to my mother. It shattered while I widened my shield to include Barth.

The second projectile bounced from Hunter's shield to mine, then ricocheted with a whine off my shield and hit Drenn squarely in the forehead. In total shock, Father, Barth, Hunter and I watched Drenn die instantly in front of us, a victim of his own malicious intent. He was dead already by the time his body crumpled to the floor.

357

The Rose Mark

* * *

Father was in bed, asleep after his physicians administered a sleeping draught. Barth, Hunter and I sat in Father's sitting room, drinking wine after Barth had done a divination on Drenn's body.

"He knew your father was ill," Barth released a weary sigh. "From Merrin."

I'd guessed at it months earlier; I'd merely waited for Father to tell me himself. Evidently, Drenn hadn't known until Merrin the miscreant told him.

"So—Merrin told Drenn that Father would suffer and handed the weapon to him. Having a working weapon and ammunition for it means Merrin's been to the enemy camp to steal those things. No wonder they're all stirred up." I gulped a mouthful of wine and shook my head.

"I've checked the weapon," Barth nodded. "It has certainly passed through Merrin's hands."

"This leaves us in a very precarious position, Thorn," Hunter pointed out.

"You mean telling the populace—and the Council—of my brother's demise?" I lifted an eyebrow at Hunter.

"Not just that," Hunter said. "You are now the King's heir, Thorn. You know what that means."

"No." I set my wineglass down with a thump. "The enemy is preparing to attack. I cannot desert the army now and leave them leaderless."

"Linel is there," Hunter reminded me.

"Linel is old and tired," I snapped. "He doesn't need this. Not now, if ever."

"The first thing you need to do while your father still lives, is clean out the Council," Hunter said. "Immediately. Your father let Drenn have his way far too often with that den of

358

Chapter 20

vipers, and they'll revolt unless you tell them now that their services are no longer required. Then go looking for their replacements—men who can be trusted."

"Hunter—leave him be," Barth said softly. "He can deal with politics tomorrow. Tonight, he has to come to terms with many things, and one of those is his family. One is dead, the other dying slowly. Leave him be."

"Hunter?" I lifted my eyes to Father's advisor.

"Yes, my Prince?"

"Call Sherra, Armon and Levi. Have them come as soon as possible. I need to speak with them."

"Shall I have Armon and Levi's escorts come as well?"

"Yes. Please."

"It will be done."

* * *

Sherra

Hunter led us toward the King's sitting area, where Kerok and Barth waited for us.

Armon was worried—I could see that easily. Levi had a hand at Armon's back, while Caral and Misten walked together behind them. I followed those four as Hunter strode ahead of us.

Something had happened. *Something has gone wrong*, I told myself. Too terrified to mindspeak Kerok, I followed obediently behind the others, waiting to learn what happened directly from the Prince Commander.

When I entered the lavish sitting room, Kerok sat there beside Barth, drinking a glass of wine. He looked haggard.

They both did.

I drew in a breath. *Had something happened to the King?*

Once, I wouldn't have worried about that.

Now, I did.

The Rose Mark

"Drenn is dead," Kerok rose to his feet. "By his own hand, after attempting to kill Father and me."

Misten's gasp was the only sound to break the ensuing silence.

* * *

"I'm almost sure that Merrin had something to do with the impending attack by the enemy." Kerok nodded when I silently offered to refill his wineglass. "Sherra and I saw the bodies of a warrior and his escort that Merrin tortured before killing. I believe he's developed a taste for it, and now the enemy is furious and planning a large-scale attack."

"This brings up a difficulty we all face," Hunter intervened. "Thorn is now the Prince-Heir, and according to law, cannot return to the battlefield, even though he wants to." Hunter frowned at Kerok, who wanted more than anything to argue with that assessment.

I wanted to argue, too. We needed Kerok to stand against the enemy. He had the knowledge, authority and battle experience necessary to see us through the coming days.

"Father is ill," Kerok raked fingers through his hair. "I've spoken to his physicians after they gave him a sleeping draught. He has perhaps a year, with no stress aggravating his illness. They say the last few months he will be unable to serve as King."

"He was prepared to abdicate in favor of Drenn tonight," Barth admitted, causing Kerok's head to turn swiftly in his direction. "I divined it while touching your father in his bed earlier," Barth held up a hand. "Had Drenn waited only a little, he'd have gotten what he desired most and we would all be lost."

"Barth, have you not noticed that we're lost anyway?" Kerok snorted. "I hate the political climate in my father's

360

palace. I'm much better suited to the battlefield, where most people know not to fight with one another. We have a common enemy, there. Here, enemies are everywhere."

"Perhaps a short visit to the battlefield will bring them around," Armon suggested quietly.

"With what's coming, they'd likely end up dead," Kerok muttered, his words bitter.

"I think that, too," I agreed. "I just—something awful is coming."

"What do the General's Diviners say?" Barth asked.

"Linel says they're seeing a flash of light so bright it is blinding, and then darkness. I don't know what to make of that—do you?" Kerok shook his head.

"Has that ever happened before?" Hunter queried.

"They've seen the usual bombings—that's not out of the ordinary," Kerok shrugged. "They admit they've never seen anything like this and have no idea what it means."

"What is your command, my Prince?" Armon stood and dipped his head to Kerok.

"Go back to Secondary Camp and make the move to the battlefield tonight, under cover of darkness. I'll send messages to Linel—you and Levi will act as his right hands in this, with assistance from Sherra. Armon, stay in contact through mindspeak as often as possible."

"But," Hunter protested. I knew then he wanted me to stay with Kerok.

"She's needed at the front, Hunter," Kerok sighed. "I'm needed at the front, too, but this is how things are," he tossed out a hand in resignation. "We can't both leave Linel to fend for himself. He was expecting to step back and allow me to handle this attack."

"Very well," Hunter growled. "Sherra must return to the palace when this threat is dealt with; you know you need her at your side in the coming days."

"Hunt, don't tell me what I already know."

"I'm right here," I said, causing both to turn swiftly in my direction. In all my life, I'd never considered that I'd end up in the King's palace for any reason.

It sounded wrong, somehow. As if events hadn't gone the way they should have and I was still waiting for someone to say they weren't really true.

"I'd like a few moments alone with Sherra before you go back," Kerok rose stiffly from his chair.

"Come," Barth motioned for the others to follow him as he walked toward the door. Kerok waited until the door closed behind them before coming forward to take my hands. "I was hoping for a different ending to this night, and planning to move everyone from Secondary Camp tomorrow morning after tonight's dinner with Father was over." He leaned his forehead against mine.

"I'm sorry about your brother, although I would have been much sorrier if he'd succeeded in his attack. He'd likely have died anyway, the moment I found him afterward," I mumbled. "I care not that it would cost my life—that has always been a moot issue anyway."

"I," Kerok began before closing his eyes with a sigh. "I don't believe I've ever had anyone say they loved me—not in such a roundabout way."

"Hmmph."

He opened his eyes, then, drew back a little way and offered a wry smile. "Stay alive on the battlefield, my rose," he said, his eyes searching mine for a promise of such. "Perhaps we can change the world in some way after all, if you do."

Chapter 20

The kiss that followed his words took my breath away.

* * *

Everyone from the camp had gathered inside the officers' mess at Armon's command. It fell to him to report the evening's events and to tell them to pack for travel to the front.

"The Crown Prince is dead, after a terrible accident," Armon announced once the room quieted. "This means the Prince Commander has been elevated to that position, and his father, the King, has demanded that he stay at the palace. Therefore, he has issued a command through me—to pack and leave for the front tonight, under cover of darkness. He and the Diviners agree that the enemy is plotting and will strike soon. Our help is needed; therefore, we will go. We stand or fall together, as it has always been."

"Sherra," Levi said as the crowd began to file toward the door. "We'll meet you at your cabin in half an hour. Pack your uniforms and anything else you have—I know it won't be much. You'll be reporting directly to me, Armon and Linel."

"All right," I agreed. "I'll be ready." I didn't add that I felt strange without Kerok with me, but that would surely pass.

* * *

Kerok

"Do you wish to send the body to the catacombs, or have someone reduce it to ash for burial?" Hunter asked as I walked toward the suite I kept at the palace. Drenn's suite was reserved for the Crown Prince and was much larger, but I had no desire to take it—now or ever. I'd have Hunter clear it out eventually, to determine whether there was anything that should be kept or returned to the treasury.

"Barth?" I stopped in mid-stride, causing both my companions to slide to a stop as well.

"What is it, my Prince?"

363

"Would you mind going to Drenn's suite in the morning and making a determination as to whether Merrin may have been there? He had to be meeting with my brother somewhere, and as Drenn locked himself away for weeks, his suite would be the logical place."

"It will be done."

"Good." I strode forward again, forcing them to come with me. "Hunter, put the palace on notice—any sight of Merrin should be reported. Any guard or assassin with the power to do so should kill him on sight. Is that understood?"

"It is."

"It only makes sense that if he could steal one weapon and the projectiles it requires, he could as easily have stolen a dozen," Barth pointed out.

"You're not making me feel better about this," I grumbled. "If that gets out, nobody inside the palace will be able to sleep."

"He is more than dangerous, and once he discovers that Drenn is dead," Hunter began.

"Hunter, here, in front of Barth, I name you my heir," I said. "You and Father are my only family now; Merrin should be dead already and has no claim."

"I will wait to record that in the morning, when you've had time to sober up and think more on it," Hunter said. "Here's your suite. I'll have reliable guards placed outside. Shield yourself, Thorn; I will be doing the same."

"What about you, Barth?" I turned toward him. "Shall I teach you how to shield yourself?"

"I was hoping someone would," he replied, his words dry as paper.

* * *

Sherra

Chapter 20

"This portion hasn't been occupied for three decades," Linel showed me separate sleeping quarters inside his large, five-room tent. "That's when my last escort died, and Thorn honored my request not to have another. As his second-in-command, more often than not I've depended upon others to keep me shielded while I sleep."

His smile was tired, and his hair looked grayer than when I'd seen him last, which was only a day or two earlier.

"You'll have a shield tonight, General," I told him. "I only need to touch your hands to get a feel for your power, so my shield will recognize it."

He held out his hands; without thinking, I gripped his fingers with mine. The touch sent a jolt through me.

He, like the King, was dying slowly. He knew it, and held hopes that with Kerok's return, he could leave the army and spend the rest of his days in peace.

Depending on how things went, he could die from his disease while still attempting to fight back the enemy.

His power was weakened as a result; he didn't want anyone else to know it, either. Without remarking on what I received through his touch, I nodded to let him know he'd be able to come and go through my shield.

"Get some sleep, escort. The days start early in this tent."

"I will."

Linel left me alone to survey the small cot covered in fresh linens—he'd had someone make up my bed for me. More than anything, I wanted Kerok here so I could tell him of Linel's condition, but that would only add more troubles to an already burdened set of shoulders.

I'd tell Armon in the morning, and ask him to keep the General's secret. Perhaps Armon could take on more of Linel's duties without being obvious about it—to give Linel some much-needed rest.

* * *

Sleep was long in coming, but Pottles appeared in my dream. It was a disturbing dream, as I watched her mouth words at me from her place among the catalpa trees. In my confusion, I asked her many times to speak louder, only to be met with image only and no sound.

At the end, before Armon woke me with mindspeak, however, the strange voice intervened again.

Let it fall, the voice said. *Send everyone else away. Place your shield over it before it hits the ground. Step to the rose where Doret stands. Come away before it lands. You are invited.*

Yes, Pottles stood on the same tile-formed red rose I'd seen when I dreamed of her last, until the voice told me to *step* away before whatever it was met the ground. A vision of fire and blinding light came then, frightening me terribly.

Why? I shouted back to the voice as the light threatened to overtake me, only to hear Armon's mindspeak, telling me that it was nearly dawn and to get up to have breakfast with him and General Linel.

* * *

Merrin

I didn't take the news of Drenn's death, well. The evidence currently lay at my feet; I'd blasted the whiny escort bitch with a fireball that fried her instantly.

Thorn was at the bottom of this—most certainly. He'd made threats against Drenn; Drenn had told me himself. If Thorn didn't kill Drenn outright, then he'd had his two hand-picked assassins do it.

Drenn, dead of a self-inflicted wound? That was bullshit.

Chapter 20

It was fortunate I still had friends in the Council—and the army. My friends in the Council informed me of Drenn's death. My friends in the army were merely waiting for me to tell them that Thorn killed his brother in order to take Drenn's place as Crown Prince.

"At least I won't have to listen to your bitching," I kicked the charred body at my feet. "Besides, I have people at the front to visit tonight, and plans to make. Don't wait up; I won't be back here again." I *stepped* away.

* * *

Sherra

I didn't know it, but Linel had breakfast with his Diviners—three of them—every morning. Food was set in front of us in the officers' mess tent as Linel and Armon listened carefully to what they had to say.

"All I see is a blinding light that brings fear—and death screams," Olan, the eldest among them, told Linel. "They say they see the light and experience terrible fear," Olan nodded to the other two Diviners.

Listening carefully while I ate, I watched Linel and Armon closely as Olan delivered his news. Everything he said matched my dream from the night before—except he'd had no words of invitation to go elsewhere. Could I discount that summons, when I realized the warning was a true one?

"I have a question," I said while Linel and Armon considered Olan's words.

"Go ahead," Linel nodded.

"Olan," I turned to Linel's chief Diviner, "Do you have a feeling with your visions—that perhaps this light is so dangerous that the army should flee?"

Olan exchanged glances with the other Diviners before coming back to my question. "Yes," he lowered his eyes and stared at his plate. "In my visions, I have a terrible feeling that the army will die if we do not."

"I dislike the idea of deserting," Linel snapped immediately.

"General Linel," I said, "If the army dies, there is nothing to protect Az-ca. If the light comes, as Olan says, perhaps it is prudent to get out of its way—temporarily."

"I still dislike it," Linel rumbled.

"In our visions, there is nothing that tells us we have any power to fight against this evil from the enemy," Olan whispered. "Please, listen to your Diviners in this—we work hard to give you our best information every time. This fearful light—I think we will not survive it."

Sherra, is there something you're not telling us? Armon sent mindspeak.

I dreamed of what Olan speaks, I replied to Armon's question. *A terrible light, followed by fear, screams and death. This is nothing to discount, Armon, please believe me. Also, Linel is ill, as the King is ill. I felt it when I touched him last night to connect with his power.*

I'll inform the Prince.

Thank you—I didn't want to tell him last night—he had enough worries already.

Agreed. Armon shifted in his chair, making the folding seat creak under his weight. *Do you truly believe the army should evacuate if the light comes?*

I can only relay what I saw and felt in my dream, and it aligns closely with Olan's description.

Is there anything else you saw?

Only that we have to leave before the thing causing the bright light hits the ground, I responded, taking care to leave Pottles and the voice out of my narrative.

Chapter 20

Are you saying that when it hits, the bright light will come?

Yes, I believe that's it, I agreed. *If Olan, the other two Diviners or I see whatever that may be, please take it to heart and order the army to step everyone away.*

Where should we go? Armon asked.

I'd say Secondary Camp, at the very least—if the light is as bright as I imagine it could be. I found the images terrifying.

I suppose it couldn't hurt—we can always come back should the images prove false, Armon replied. *Stepping in and out takes no time at all.*

Then convince the General, I said. *He's balking at the idea.*

I'll take care of it.

* * *

Kerok

You're saying Sherra saw the same in a dream? I mindspoke with Armon after he'd had breakfast with Linel, Sherra and the Diviners.

Yes. She's quite worried about it, too. Suggested that if it arrives, whatever it may be, that we should order the army to step *away to Secondary Camp.*

What about Vale, instead? I suggested, naming the northernmost supply village, roughly ten miles south of the battlefront. *You can move some there, while sending Linel and the rest to Secondary Camp. Perhaps you can tell what the damage is quickly, and send for the others if it isn't as bad as what the Diviners think.*

That's a good idea, Armon concurred. *I'll select some of our best to fall back to Vale, and tell the others to meet at*

Secondary Camp, although we have no idea what will bring on the bright light.

It sounds strange—to be so frightened of a bright light, but I can't deny the accuracy of the Diviners up to now, I said.

Sherra says Linel is ill—like your father is, Armon admitted. *She said she felt it when she connected with him to recognize his power for her shield.*

Damnation, I cursed. *Look, get through this and I'll send Linel home. I think you and a few others can handle the army, with my mindspoken input in important decisions.*

I hoped you'd say that—he isn't looking good.

Make sure he gets away if necessary—even if you have to tie him to Dayl to do it.

I will.

Good.

How are things going there?

Father doesn't want to cremate Drenn, so we're placing him in the catacombs. Barth is going through Drenn's suite, looking for anything that doesn't belong, and the entire palace is waiting for Merrin to pop out of walls, I think.

That sound horrifying.

It is. We're jumping at shadows, now. How's Sherra?

Fine, except for the dream she had. She says the ill-feeling from the enemy is still present, but she's coping so far.

Good. Tell her I'll entertain mindspeak from her at any time.

I'll relay that message, my Prince.

* * *

Sherra

"I've arranged to send hand-picked troops to Vale, here," Armon tapped a map on General Linel's work table. "At Prince

Chapter 20

Thorn's suggestion. Everyone else will go to Secondary Camp and wait for word from me, is that clear?"

I stood in a corner of the General's meeting space, listening as Armon gave the highest-ranking officers an update to carry to their troops.

"When will we know?" someone asked.

"When I give the word," Armon said. "If that word comes, leave immediately. Don't wait. Understood? If we determine it's safe to come back afterward, that word will also come from me."

"Understood, Colonel."

* * *

"Armon, things are getting worse," I said as he and I walked toward Linel's tent for the midday meal.

"Worse?" Armon stopped walking, and Caral stopped beside him. Levi and Misten had joined others in the officers' mess tent to eat, while Armon agreed to sit with the General and discuss updates on the plan. "What things?" Armon asked a follow-up question.

"The—feeling," I floundered for the proper word. "From the enemy, and somehow, it's bleeding into—here," I flung out a hand to include the entire camp. Whatever it was, it contained enough intense anger to burn us to death.

The boom from a warrior's released blast hitting the ground in the center of camp knocked many down, and those who weren't shielded or prepared died a fiery death.

"Get the General," Armon shouted as another blast was launched. "Dayl," he shouted.

Dayl, Linel's messenger, *stepped* to Armon's side. "Take the General out of here. Now," Armon ordered. "I don't care if he doesn't want to go. Do it."

371

The Rose Mark

"As you command," Dayl said as a third blast rocked our portion of the camp. He disappeared as rock, dust and debris rained down on the shields Caral and I had erected.

I had no illusions about this turn of events—they hadn't happened in my dream and weren't taken into account.

Az-ca's army had just gone to war against itself.

Chapter 21

*S*herra
    Shields up, I shouted into every newly-trained rose's mind. *If you see the attackers, get a message to me or Armon quickly.*

On the southwest end of camp, Wend's voice sounded in my mind. *They've gathered there to fire at the rest of us.*

Armon was in contact with Kerok—I could tell by his stillness and unfocused eyes.

"Let's go," I told Caral, indicating that we should *step* Armon to a place where we could fire back at the traitors.

She and I *stepped* him to Wend and Marc's position, a short distance from mid-camp, where the regular mess was located. Marc had been supervising the mess hall as he normally did when the first blast was fired.

The Rose Mark

Not far away, a new blast crater lay, with remnants of tents and burned bodies littering the steep sides.

The first, unexpected blast had killed many, before the remaining escorts nearby could lift shields to protect themselves and their warriors.

"Prepare for us to fire," Kerok appeared beside Armon, shouting his orders to Caral and me.

Had I ever expected that our first real battle experience would come fighting our own?

The short answer was no.

Kerok hadn't expected it either, and I'm sure he had an ultimate culprit in mind, just as I did.

He and Armon launched blasts together, which sailed through Caral's and my shields easily, detonating with ear-damaging and ground-shaking intensity against the shields raised by our attackers' escorts.

Fools, I sent to them. I knew they'd hear me. *Merrin is a liar*, I added.

In the short space of time granted while they considered my words, I heard a strange, droning noise coming from the north.

I turned to look, blinking in the bright, midday sun at the thing that flew toward us.

Unlike a bird, its wings were fixed, and the drone came from whatever kept it aloft and flying toward us.

"Kerok?" I gripped his arm—hard.

The traitors chose that moment to begin firing at us again. Six blasts broke against our shields in rapid succession, drowning out the sound of the approaching machine.

It had to be a machine—it could be nothing else, and I knew as surely as I knew anything that this was what the

Chapter 21

enemy would employ to drop the bringer of death upon Az-ca's army.

Which was doing its best to destroy itself, with no help from the enemy.

Kerok was in danger.

As were Armon, Levi and all the roses I'd trained alongside. The bringer of death was now overhead as more blasts were launched our way.

I had to do something quickly. If the object which was now dropping toward us met with blasts from the traitors, I had no hope that any would survive such a cataclysm.

"Sherra?" Kerok turned toward me in slow motion.

I have this, I sent mindspeak before disengaging from the shield I'd built over our heads and forming another, to capture the falling object and prevent it from hitting more blasts fired in our direction.

"Get it away," Kerok's shout was almost drowned out as more blasts hit our shields.

As you command, I replied.

The answer was a simple one.

So simple.

What did it matter whether I died now or later? At least Kerok could deal with our traitors afterward.

Without interference from the enemy.

Some of my friends could be lying at the bottom of a blast bowl already; I wouldn't know for sure until after this was over—provided anyone survived.

I wanted to make sure of it.

Gauging the power needed, I hardened my shield around the falling object and the machine that brought it, before flinging both toward the enemy camp.

And, to ensure that they reached their destination, I *stepped* to follow them.

* * *

Kerok

I'd turned to fire more blasts toward our traitors, when Sherra disappeared. I wouldn't have known except for Caral's shout.

I learned that day how long it took for an object to sail ten miles toward the enemy before it hit.

It took forever.

It took no time at all.

The earthquake that came minutes later knocked us all to the ground with its duration and intensity. The blast bowl nearby opened wider and attempted to swallow the entire camp.

Step *away*, I shouted in mindspeak. *You know where to go.*

Then, I started screaming Sherra's name aloud and in mindspeak.

There was no answer.

Armon *stepped* me away; if he hadn't, I'd likely have let the ground open beneath my feet and swallow my body.

Ten miles away, too far to see the flash of light that surely came, I imagined the enemy camp was destroyed.

* * *

"Armon?" I asked as I was lowered onto a chair in Vale's Command Center. The earthquake had shaken it, too, but the ground hadn't opened up to swallow tents and bodies.

"I can't get a reply," Armon mumbled. "My Prince, Hunter is asking about your health and continued existence. What shall I tell him?"

"That I am physically whole," I replied.

Chapter 21

As for my soul, that fragile thing was now completely gone.

* * *

Doret

Kyri and I waited at the tiled-rose landing, hoping against hope that things would come right.

"Merrin did this," Kyri hissed as the wait became longer. "Fuck him for being one of *those*."

Those. The *unseeables*. One had to *see* those around them, in order to locate them. He'd raised Az-ca's army against itself, just as the enemy prepared to bomb the hell out of them at the same time.

Sherra.

Merrin's fault, this. If I ever found the bastard, I'd kill him myself. His meddling had resulted in the Crown Prince's death—much too early.

Thorn was needed elsewhere, instead of babysitting paranoid, ass-kissing council members.

"This is taking too long," Kyri dropped her chin and stared at her feet. Her arms went around herself. Sherra was hope to us.

Hope was now gone.

That's when I realized I was crying.

"Pottles?" The voice was barely a whisper.

She was hurt.

"Quickly," Kyri gripped my arm. We barely managed to catch Sherra before she fell.

* * *

Kerok

Two weeks passed. Armon had gone with me shortly after the ground stopped shaking in Vale, and we'd visited the enemy camp.

The Rose Mark

There was no evidence left behind that it had ever been there. Only a very deep hole, the likes of which I'd never seen, was left behind.

Word came from others, too, that to the west, more of the land bridge between Az-ca's border and the enemy lands had fallen into the sea, narrowing that already slender connection.

It was slight compensation for the deaths they'd intended for us.

Merrin was still missing.

Some of the traitorous fools who'd listened to him had surrendered themselves. Others had likely joined him, wherever that was.

We'd lost many in their initial attack; Jae and her warrior were dead, as were several others that Sherra had trained.

Father had taken to his bed not long afterward, and was attempting to abdicate. I told him to wait for a bit, while I mourned my rose.

Hunter had given me a list of names—council members who'd been deep in Drenn's favor and couldn't be trusted.

I had no doubt that were Barth to do his divination, I'd find the ones responsible for alerting Merrin to Drenn's death.

That same story came from the traitors who'd surrendered themselves. They'd been told that I'd murdered my brother.

I took them to see Drenn's body in the catacombs, after having their power burned out of them by Garkus and Kage. Merrin had gifted Drenn with the weapon which brought his demise.

I think they believed me.

Father would pass judgment on them soon; I doubted any would keep their lives after murdering so many of their fellow warriors and escorts.

Chapter 21

With a sigh, I opened a desk drawer and withdrew Sherra's book from it; I'd retrieved it from its hiding place shortly after her death. It was the thing I'm sure she'd touched the most. When I became King, the book would no longer be outlawed; I'd made that promise to myself already.

"That wasn't Sherra's book."

The voice startled me so badly I almost fell from my chair. A shield was already up around me—I wanted no surprises coming from Merrin.

A woman I didn't know stood inside my locked study door; she'd *stepped* inside the room to accost me. Dark hair fell past her shoulders. Dark eyes studied me with an intensity I disliked. "Who are you?" I demanded.

"You know me," she shrugged. "You just haven't seen me before."

"I'll be the judge of that," I snapped while sending mindspeak to Barth and Hunter.

"Your mother told you all about me," she smiled. "I only came to tell you that Sherra is recovering, and should be well enough soon to learn what I have to teach her."

"Stop lying," I whispered as Hunter began to pound on the outside door. He should have been able to *step* inside the door, as my visitor did—my shield didn't extend that far. Something—*she*—prevented that from happening.

"It isn't a lie, and that's not Sherra's book. Her book was buried in a pot outside her village. Doret retrieved it because it was hers, first. The book you hold belonged to your many-times great-grandmother, and was buried with her body in the catacombs. Your brother found it and thought to cause mischief."

"Thorn," Hunter shouted outside the door. "Let me in."

"I won't keep you," the woman's smile turned mischievous. "I have things to accomplish, just as you do. I'll return Sherra to you in a few months—after I've taught her."

"Stop saying lies," I shouted at her.

"I'm not." Her words were calm and a smile still played about her lips. "By the way, if you need anything before Sherra returns, call my name. And, since you can't seem to recall that name, I'll give it to you. Mindspeak Kyri. If it's important, I'll actually answer."

She *stepped* away just as two guards broke down my door to allow a frantic Hunter inside.

Epilogue

*S*herra
    "You look younger." My first words to Pottles were more a croak than plain speech. Her face leaned over mine as if she were studying me, blind as she was.

"Hmmph," she snorted and pulled away. "Not the first time I've played an old woman. Not the first time I've faked my death, either."

"The blindness?" I had to know. At least my voice sounded better this time.

Pottles didn't answer at first, but busied herself pouring a glass of water from a pitcher near my bed.

"You were very close to death, young one," Pottles informed me as she helped me sit up to drink. "We almost didn't save you. I will say this, however. The first time I saw you make fire, I almost laughed aloud. You're the finest student I've ever had, and I never taught you a thing."

The End

Sherra and Kerok's tale will continue in *Rose and Thorn*, Book two of the Black Rose Sorceress series.

Names of Characters and Places Appearing in this Book:

Ana: North Camp Instructor, Second Cohort
Armon: Colonel in Az-ca's army, currently serves as First advisor to Prince Commander. Chosen by Caral
Az-ca: Desert country ruled by King Wulf; always at war with barbarians from Ny-nes
Barth: King's Chief Diviner
Beckley: Warrior, chosen by Reena
Bela: Former washout
The Book of the Rose: A book in the King's library, describing talents and duties of Black Rose escorts
Bray: Barth's secondary Diviner
Bulldog: North Camp Instructor: Sixth Cohort
Caral: Fourth Cohort trainee at North Camp
Colonel Kage: Training Instructor for warrior trainees in the King's City—becomes a King's assassin
Colonel Weren: Training Instructor for warrior trainees in the King's City
Commander Alden: Post Commander for Secondary Camp
Dayl: General Linel's personal messenger
Doret: Former Queen of Az-ca; more than 200 years old
Drenn Wulfson Meris Rex: Crown Prince of Az-ca
East Camp: one of four training camps for black rose trainees
End-War: crippling event that changed and destroyed nearly everything on the planet
Falia: Instructor at North Camp
F'nexscot: AKA the King's City
Gale: Armon's former escort
Garkus: Drill instructor at Secondary Camp—became a King's assassin

Names of Characters and Places Appearing in this Book:

Geb: retired warrior—now works as a traveling instructor for all trainees

General Linel: Chief Commander of the army in the Prince Commander's absence

Grae: Kerok's deceased escort

Hari: escort abandoned by her warrior (Narris)

Harnn: Bela's warrior

Hayla: black rose trainee

Hunter Lattham: King's advisor, Uncle to Merrin, Drenn and Kerok

Jae: black rose trainee—Sixth Cohort, North Camp

Kerok: AKA Thorn Wulfson Kerok Rex, King Wulf's youngest son and Prince Commander of the army

King Wulf Carlson Alexander Rex: King of Az-ca

Kyri: Female Diviner—believed to be a legend or myth

Lera: escort abandoned by her warrior

Levi: Captain, serves as Secondary Advisor to Prince Commander. Chosen by Misten

Lieutenant Marc: Chosen by Wend

Lilya: North Camp Instructor, Fourth Cohort

Merrin: Nephew of Hunter and King Wulf; cousin to Drenn and Kerok (on mother's side)

Merthis: small village where Sherra was born

Miri: North Camp Instructor, Fifth Cohort

Misten: North Camp trainee, Sixth Cohort

Narris: warrior-turned-traitor who left his escort behind (Hari) before deserting army

Neka: North Camp trainee, First Cohort

Nina: North Camp Instructor, First Cohort

North Camp: One of four camps where black rose trainees are taught

Ny-nes: Land of barbarian enemies

Names of Characters and Places Appearing in this Book:

Nyra: Levi's deceased escort

Olan: Chief Diviner for the army

Pottles: Blind pot seller and friend to Sherra (see Doret)

Poul: Assassin for King Wulf

Reena: Former washout

Secondary Camp: Location for final escort training after warriors are chosen

Sherra: Black Rose trainee from Merthis.

Tera: North Camp trainee—Sixth Cohort

The Rose Mark: a forbidden book

Thorn's Book of Advanced Divination Techniques: a forbidden book

Ura: North Camp trainee and one of the Bulldog's pets

Vale: Northernmost supply village for Az-ca's army

Varnon: village elder in Merthis

Veri: North Camp trainee and one of the Bulldog's pets

Welton: Chief Physician, military post

Wend: North Camp Trainee, Sixth Cohort

Wendal: Assassin for King Wulf

Yasa: AKA Bulldog, or *the* Bulldog

Printed in Great Britain
by Amazon